Praise for the suspense novels of
Diana Diamond

The Good Sister

"[A] satisfying and highly unsettling suspense thriller . . . Diamond keeps readers guessing until the very end, and her thrilling story is backed up by taut writing and snappy dialogue."

—*Publishers Weekly*

"Diana Diamond's gripping thriller takes sibling rivalry to a whole new level."

—*Marie Claire*

The Babysitter

"A multifaceted, remarkably suspenseful thriller."

—*Booklist*

"Vivid . . . thoughtful exposition and careful plotting."
—*Publishers Weekly*

More . . .

The Trophy Wife

"A gripping page-turner."
—*People* magazine, A Beach Book of the Week

"[A] flawless gem . . . sharp, brilliant, and strong, the novel is sure to be a girl's best friend—and maybe even a boy's . . . [Diamond's] convincing action scenes are real enough to leave readers breathless . . . a clever and genuinely surprising ending tops off a superb thriller."
—*Booklist* (starred review)

"Diamond alternates laughs with chills in this tale of marriage, kidnapping, and high finance in the Susan Isaacs/Olivia Goldsmith school of social satire . . . a strong climax and satisfying epilogue conclude a smart, suspense-packed novel."
—*Publishers Weekly*

"A must-read for anyone who has ever wished revenge on a duplicitous lover . . . fast-paced . . . climaxes with a shocking denouement."
—*Women's Own*

"Tinged with revenge and intrigue, this thriller twists and turns to an unexpected end."
—*Library Journal*

"It moves, it's imaginative, and it's satisfying. Diana Diamond has spun a tale that grips the reader and doesn't let go."
—Mary Jane Clark, author of *Nobody Knows*

St. Martin's Paperbacks Titles
by Diana Diamond

The Daughter-in-Law

The Good Sister

The Babysitter

The Trophy Wife

The First Wife

Diana Diamond

St. Martin's Paperbacks

THE FIRST WIFE

Copyright © 2004 by Diana Diamond.
Excerpt from *The Stepmother* copyright © 2005 by Diana Diamond.

Cover photograph by Barry Marcus
Photographed at The National Academy of Design

Library of Congress Catalog Card Number: 2004040553

ISBN: 0-312-99333-1
EAN: 9780312-99333-7

Printed in the United States of America

St. Martin's Press hardcover edition / June 2004
St. Martin's Paperbacks edition / May 2005

St. Martin's Paperbacks are published by St. Martin's Press, 175 Fifth Avenue, New York, NY 10010.

10 9 8 7 6 5 4 3 2 1

Thanks for the wonderful folks at Rosedale

Prologue

Eight Years Ago

The snow had been falling on and off all night, dusting the tops of trees and coating the roads that snaked through the mountains. With the moon and stars hidden, there was no light. The only sounds were an occasional stir of wind and the soft thump of snow dropping from a branch.

There was no sunrise, just a gradual glow in the eastern sky that made it possible to see the edges of the tall Adirondack peaks and gave the snow a bluish cast. What breeze there had been faded and vanished. Everything was perfectly still, a winter landscape frozen in time by an artist's brush.

Suddenly, a gunshot. It came as a roar rather than a crisp crack. A shotgun rather than a rifle. As the first sound faded, new blasts came back from the mountains, echoes bouncing off a dozen different mountain faces until they were soaked up by the trees. Then, as quickly as it had been shattered, the silence returned.

High up in one of the craggy peaks lights flashed on to reveal a house, a soft structure of wood and stone designed to blend into the mountains. Then came a scream. A woman shrieked hysterically.

Before long, the pastoral scene came to life. At the base of the mountain, other lights came on. One showed the outline of a rustic inn. Others, some distance away, brought out the silhouette of a small town. A car moved carefully up the mountain slope, invisible except for the headlight beams that traced a road and poked out over bottomless ravines. When it came closer to the house, its engine noise began to vibrate through the silence.

Sometime later the snow stopped and the sun appeared through the overcast as a blotch of light. Then another car started up the mountain. Its headlights were on even though they were probably unnecessary. The blinking red and blue lights on the roof weren't needed, because there were no other cars to warn. But they served to announce an emergency somewhere up ahead.

Sergeant Pete Davis was the only one responding because he was the only law-enforcement officer in the area. The town of Mountain Ridge in the Adirondack Park didn't have much crime other than hunting out of season or fishing without a license. Occasionally a fistfight would break out in one of the area taverns, but all that demanded was that he push the drunken brawlers apart and sit between them for a few minutes. Nothing that he would call a crime.

This was different. The caller had told him that a woman had been killed, blown apart by a shotgun in the hands of an intruder. Her husband had been wounded. Killed! That meant murder, and as far as Pete Davis could recall, no one had ever been murdered around Mountain Ridge. And an intruder? Pete knew almost everyone who lived within fifty miles, most on a first-name basis. All of them felt free to walk on other people's property, but there was no one who would break into a home, much less shoot anyone. He didn't know the people who owned the big chalets on the mountaintops. But they were all big wheels from Boston, Albany, and New York, not the kind of people you would catch breaking and entering. He had called a nearby doctor, who shared his own amazement at the report. "Murdered? You sure it isn't some sort of hunting accident?" But he would get up there as quickly as he could to take a look at the wounded victim. He had treated gunshot wounds before. Hunters were usually more apt to shoot themselves than the deer they were tracking.

The police officer turned into the driveway, noted the tire tracks even though they were nearly buried, and saw the German sedan parked close to the front door. When Sergeant Davis climbed out of the Jeep, a man who seemed perfectly composed opened the front door and stepped out to meet him. They exchanged nods of greeting. Then Pete stepped inside the house and turned into the living room. He stopped abruptly, gagged on the taste of the coffee he had downed before leaving, and turned his head away from the scene. But he had to look back. He was a policeman, and this certainly seemed to be a murder.

At the end of the room, behind the open steps that led to the second floor, the wall was spattered with blood—hundreds of tiny droplets, as if there had been some sort of religious sprinkling. The middle steps were splintered, one even cut in half. At the foot of the stairs was a woman in jeans and a blouse, her arms and legs splayed, her bare feet pointing upward. There was a puddle of blood big enough for her to have drowned in. But what made the policeman sick was that her neck ended in shreds of skin and bone. There was no face, no hair, no head at all. It was her head that was splashed on the steps and on the wall in tiny gobbets of blood and gore.

More blinking lights came, now accompanied by sirens that wailed through the valleys. They were followed by helicopters: two with television news logos circled over the house, pointing cameras into the windows; three in state police colors landed officers and then flew out to search the countryside. Uniformed troopers rushed in and out the front and back doors. First the house and then the surrounding grounds were marked off with yellow tape. A cordon was formed to block all unauthorized entrance.

An ambulance was waved through, and after a few minutes a man was brought out on a gurney. The ambulance pulled away with its siren screaming and lights flashing. Later, a panel truck made its way up the mountain to claim a body bag. It was in no hurry when it left.

At the base of the mountain, outside an inn, men and women wearing press passes were demanding access to the site. If television stations could fly over the crime scene, then all journalists had to be given access, they argued. They howled when the troopers blocking the base of the road ignored them. All they could do was swarm like bees around each official vehicle that came down the mountain. But even then their shouted questions weren't answered.

One reporter jumped up onto the running board of the ambulance and looked through the window. "It's him—Andrews," he shouted back to the others.

"What about Kay Parker?" someone demanded.

Then the panel truck reached the inn. Reporters knocked on the windows, and the driver nodded his response to the question they were all shouting. "It's her!" one of them screamed, and they all rushed back to the inn to file their stories.

Socialite Kay Parker, the darling of New York charities and art foundations, had been brutally murdered. Her husband, communications czar William Andrews, was wounded. Police were searching for an intruder who had broken into their posh mountain getaway.

For days thereafter, the mountain wasn't allowed a moment of peace.

Part One

The Romance

I

She could hear the gate alarm sounding, but she thought she could make it across. The ringing and the flashing came first, warning that a train was coming. Then it usually took several seconds before the striped wooden bar swung down. But this time it dropped instantly, the moment she bumped her SUV onto the tracks. *Damn!* She shifted into reverse just in time to see the other gate drop down behind her. She was trapped on the tracks with a freight train charging toward her.

The clanging bells seemed to get louder, more incessant in their warning. And then there was the light, shining on her from the distance and getting brighter by the second, so bright that she couldn't see the locomotive behind it. She grabbed the handle and threw the door open. Then with all her strength she hurled herself out of the car, tumbled through the air, and landed with a crash. The night table rocked, and the glass of water that she kept by her bedside poured down on her face.

"Damn!" Jane Warren was lying on the floor, looking up at the overturned water tumbler. Her alarm clock was clanging furiously. Bright sunlight was streaking through the blinds, hot on the bed she had just hurled herself from. She sat up abruptly and stared at the clock until she understood that it had been ringing for half an hour. "Damn!" she repeated. Her day had just started and she was already running late.

Coffee! She padded into the kitchen and took a mug down from the shelf. Then she saw another disaster. The pot wasn't squared under the spout of her coffeemaker. Soggy grounds had oozed over the edge and down into the space between the counter and the refrigerator. The coffee that might save her life was spilled down the front of her kitchen drawers and onto the floor. For a few seconds she thought that she was going to cry.

Jane threw bath towels at the puddle of coffee and across the wet carpet in her bedroom, then processed herself through the shower and into her underwear, jeans, and a sweater. She was in her car, turning out of the garage, just fifteen minutes after she had escaped certain death under the wheels of a freight train.

She pulled down the visor, with its vanity mirror, and set to work with her cosmetics. Lipstick went just on her upper lip and was transferred to the lower lip by a grimace, a smile, and then a pout. Blush went on with a dab to each cheek and was blended in with the heel of her hand. She rubbed a finger into the eye shadow, wiped the excess on the bottom of the driver's seat, and then spread it over her eyes, closing them one at a time so that she could see what she was doing and get an occasional glimpse of the road. Then, using her right hand to steer, she aimed a razor-sharp eyebrow pencil into her face with her unsteady left hand. She had one eye finished when she turned onto the parkway, a narrow, twisting two-lane road that had been built in the 1930s. The other eye would have to wait until she reached her office.

But even with one brow off color, so she seemed to be perpetually winking, Jane had achieved a minor miracle. Her fair skin, usually a bland alabaster, had subtle highlights across the cheekbones. A mysterious blue tint over her eyes complemented their deep tone and changed their shape from round to almond. Her lips, usually noticed only when she showed her generous smile, were now dark and suggestive. Her deep brunette hair, worn in a cascade of curls, seemed stylishly casual. In less than half an hour she had gone from plain to foxy, and from downtrodden to down-to-business. She liked what she saw in the mirror even if it was only a disguise for the wet towels and unmade bed that she had left behind.

She tapped the steering wheel impatiently in the stop-and-go traffic while the dashboard clock kept reminding her that she was late. Not that there was a fixed starting time. In the newspaper business the flow of news events set your schedule more than arbitrary work hours. Entertainment editors filed their stories after midnight and slept in. Sports editors worked hardest on the weekends. At her financial desk, the afternoons when the markets were posting their closing prices were generally much busier than the mornings. But still, she had her local business column to write under her J. J. Warren byline. That meant calling brokers, bankers, and business executives, who were generally much harder to reach after lunch. She hated to waste the morning in gridlock. Her day was off to a terrible start.

Suddenly it got worse. When she pulled into the garage beneath her office building, her recently divorced husband was standing in her parking space. Arthur Keene slouched against the wall in a wrinkled black suit coat and baggy trousers, pretending not to notice the Honda CRV that turned into the space and rolled toward him. He didn't even look up until the car had lurched to a stop, with its front bumper touching his knee. Only then did he make eye contact with the woman behind the wheel and favor her with his confident smile.

"Art, I'm late for a meeting," Jane lied as she stepped down from the car. "I haven't got a minute. . . ." She beeped the car locks and started for the elevator.

"I'll ride up with you," he offered, falling in next to her.

"I'd rather you didn't."

"Then talk to me here. I need you to find a couple of my disks."

Jane stopped just short of pushing the elevator button. "You took all your disks."

"No, I'm missing two of them. One has my notes for the Martha's Vineyard play. The other is my latest draft of *Hudson Falls*."

"You took all your disks the day after you moved out. Remember, you came over in the morning and spent the whole day collecting your stuff from the computer."

"Jane, I know what I had then and what I don't have now. There are two of my disks in with all your crap."

She pushed the button. "I'll look. I'll call you if I find something."

"You don't know what you're looking for. Let me look."

"No! You're out of the apartment. Read the agreement."

"You don't even have to be there. All I want to do is let myself in and look for my disks."

The elevator door opened and Jane stepped inside.

"No! I don't want you going through my things."

"Jane," he pleaded. "They're major works. I have to find them."

The door closed across Art's anguished expression.

Major works, she thought, shaking her head in despair. Art had never completed a single play, much less had one produced. They had wasted their six-year marriage waiting by the telephone for his genius to be appreciated. Her career as a journalist had been dismissed as a "temporary accommodation with middle-class values," while his was a "statement on behalf of humanity." The problem had been that her "accommodation" had to pay the bills that his "statement" ran up.

Art had been a dreamer even when she met him. But at that time, fresh out of college, dreams were easily mistaken for ambition. Art was at the head of the class, cocksure that he was destined to have an impact on the world of letters, certain that he would hit social mores like a meteor striking the earth. It had taken her three years to realize that he was waiting for an adoring audience to assemble, and another three years to decide that his work was, at best, mediocre. Art was sure that he was important. Over time, Jane realized that he really wasn't.

And yet the divorce had been his idea. He had sensed that Jane was impatient, tired of putting her life on hold in deference to his fantastic potential. Then she had suggested that he consider a job in the Arts section of her paper. Not permanently, of course. Just something to ease the financial pressure while keeping him in his chosen world of theater. He had found the suggestion insulting, proof that Jane had no idea of the stretch of his ambition. "What do you want?" he had demanded while smashing dinner dishes against the edge of the sink. "Am I supposed to give up everything? Join you in headline hunting and rumormongering?" He had demanded his freedom and rushed through the proceedings as if every second spent with her sucked the creative juices from his flesh. It was only when the court granted his wish that he realized Jane would no longer be obligated to fetch his supper and pay his bills.

For her part, she had been crushed by his demand for a divorce. It seemed an announcement of her failure at the first serious enterprise she had undertaken. If she couldn't make a simple thing like marriage work, how could she hope to survive in the more complex affairs of modern life? But in the sea of legal filings and court deliberations, Jane had seen her boat plow ahead while his foundered and sank. Two decisive promotions had carried her up to a senior editor's position and given her an honest endorsement of her worth. Art had tried to capture his emotions from their split in a new play and had sunk deeper into obscurity, if that was possible for an unproduced playwright. Minutes before the divorce was granted, he had cornered her outside the courtroom and allowed that he was considering the wisdom of giving her one more chance. Jane had answered with her middle finger.

The elevator door opened into the reception foyer of the *Southport Post,* a middling member of a suburban newspaper chain that covered the bedroom communities of southern Connecticut. The lobby was impressive with fabric-covered walls decorated with comments by Pulitzer and Mencken, set in three-dimensional pewter letters. The receptionist was a young woman imported from England, with a public school accent that suggested a higher standard of learning. Even New Englanders felt humbled after cooling their heels in the waiting room.

"Good morning, Grace. Please tell me that there is still some coffee. . . ."

"Perhaps a tad," Grace answered. "Shall I bring it to your office, or will you send somebody?"

"If you could just pour it for me, I'll carry it myself."

Grace responded with an expression of curiosity, her head

tipping to get a more focused look at Jane's face. "Just black, right?"

"Any way at all," Jane answered, wondering if Grace had suddenly found her attractive.

She balanced the paper coffee cup down the carpeted aisle of the business department, which was really the heart of her newspaper. Trapped between *The New York Times* and *The Boston Globe* in an area blanketed by cable and satellite news, the *Southport Post* had little hope of breaking big stories. Its front page was copied from the wire services with a focus on state and local issues. Inside, the editorial content was devoted to soft news from the immediate area—local politics, school-board issues, and meetings of the Rotarians. The business department, on the other hand, was rudely aggressive in selling ad space to the local car dealers, furniture stores, culinary boutiques, and dress shops. It did a great business with advertising inserts for shopping malls and supermarkets. Taken together, the business departments of the eight papers in the New England Suburban Press organization sold more space than the *Times* and *Globe* together and racked up sales figures that matched either one.

The carpet disappeared when Jane reached the editorial offices at the back of the floor. There were two rows of desks flanking the center aisle and fabric-covered cubicles along the walls. The desks were for the classified people who wrote ads of twelve words or less, using abbreviations for every noun and eliminating most of the verbs. Classified took in nearly as much money as display ads, at about a tenth of the cost. The cubicles housed the reporters, giving their telephone conversations a sense of privacy even though their voices carried over the walls. The rear offices, sealed off with glass barriers, were for the senior editors for news, business, sports, and society. Their rewards included windows, carpeting, and side chairs across from their desks.

Jane went straight to her office and sat hunched over her coffee. She barely forced a smile when Jack Dollinger, the news editor, sauntered in and settled into her side chair. "Bad night?" he asked. Dollinger was twice her age, old and foolish enough to think that Jane found him attractive. He masked his romantic heat, stoked by her recent divorce, under a pretence of professional patronage.

"Bad morning," she answered.

"I just read your latest piece on William Andrews. Quite interesting . . ."

She cut him off with a trembling hand gesture. "Give me a minute, Jack. If I can get this coffee down, there's a good chance that I'll regain my hearing and my eyesight." She sipped without raising the cup from her desk.

"A really bad morning." He chuckled.

She lifted the cup and gulped. Then she managed a nod. "As bad as it gets!" She told him about leaping out of bed to escape the onrushing train, the spilled water, and the coffee explosion that had wiped out her kitchen.

"That's your first cup?"

"The very first of the day. It's a wonder I made it here alive. And then who did I find in the parking lot, waiting to greet me, but my ex. I hoped it was all part of the nightmare."

"But it was real?"

"Too real. Art thinks that even though we're divorced, I'm still responsible for his laundry."

"Any luck with his new play?" Jack feigned interest in her husband's work while secretly enjoying Arthur's ineptitude.

"He hasn't finished it. Still rewriting the third act. The wife has a few redeeming qualities that he's trying to get rid of."

He stood up slowly. "Let me take you to lunch. Maybe you can salvage the second half of your day."

She dropped her paper cup into the wastebasket. "Let's see how it goes."

He paused in her doorway, staring at her for a moment. "Something the matter?" she asked.

"No . . . oh, I almost forgot. Roscoe wants to see you."

Jane looked up at the mention of the managing editor, whose summonses usually meant criticism rather than praise. "What did I do now?"

"Something to do with your William Andrews series. At least I heard him mention Andrews several times during a phone call."

She frowned. "I went too far, didn't I?"

"A bit emotional," Dollinger allowed. "But overall, I think you were completely fair."

William Andrews was better suited as a subject for *Fortune* or *Business Week* than for a suburban daily like the *Southport Post*. Beginning in his twenties with a small investment in a cable franchise, he had created a communications and media empire that reached around the world and connected with satellites in space. He controlled broadcast networks on three continents, major newspapers and magazines in a dozen countries, Internet services, and even a film studio. It was difficult for a thinking person to get through a day without making contact with one of Andrews's properties. Jane had made him the subject of several of her business columns because he had begun buying up chains of small-town newspapers, extending his reach even further into society's roots.

"Morning, Jane," Roscoe Taylor said, making a show of checking his watch. "Nice of you to join us."

"Don't bait me, Roscoe. It's been a bad morning and I just had an unscheduled meeting with my former husband. I'm still in a rotten mood." She sat across from him.

He studied her for a moment. "I like it," he decided. "Bold, unconventional, but certainly memorable. It reminds me of an ad campaign for a shirt manufacturer that ran many years ago. A great ad campaign because I still remember the name—Hathaway."

"What in God's name are you talking about?"

"Your new one-eyed look. One brow outlined and the other unadorned. The Hathaway man always wore a black eye patch."

Jane reached to her face as if she hoped to feel the difference in color. "Oh hell! I did it in traffic. I finished only one eye."

"Well, don't tell anyone it's a mistake. Take full credit. It's a bold initiative."

She got up and started for the door. "Excuse me, Roscoe. I feel like such an ass."

He laughed. "You look like you're winking at me. I'm amazed your husband didn't think you were inviting him back."

"Arthur wouldn't notice if I had only one ear. My eyebrows never made it onto his radar. But now I understand why I thought Grace was coming on to me." She had the doorknob in her hand when she remembered what had brought her into the managing editor's office. "Oh, what did you want to talk to me about?"

"Your William Andrews articles."

She winced. "Was I too rough with him?"

Roscoe shrugged innocently. "I hope not. He's our new boss. He just bought the Suburban chain."

Her knees weakened. "He what?"

"Bought the New England Suburban Press. Us included. We're now part of the Andrews Global Network. And you're interviewing him in Manhattan this afternoon."

2

Jane walked in a trance back to her office, retrieved her hand-bag, and headed for the ladies' room to restore her missing eyebrow. She mentally scanned each of the three articles she had written, running through them one paragraph at a time as she tried to remember exactly what she had said about her new boss. *Damn!* She was staring at unemployment.

She had started the series when Andrews Global Network picked up two small television stations in the central part of the state. Her theme was that one company shouldn't have such far-ranging control of communications. News and public opinion shouldn't be filtered through one person's preferences, and advertising opportunities shouldn't be monopolized. Then, with a little digging, she was able to give a national picture of how many editorial sources had effectively been silenced and how many jobs had been lost to the Andrews juggernaut. It was dull economics, but Jane had spiced it up with the image of Andrews as a spoiled kid who simply wanted more toys to play with.

The articles had been picked up by the wire services and then run in regional papers across the country, a genuine coup for the editor of a small suburban paper. One syndicated column had even referred to J. J. Warren as the David bold enough to stand up to Goliath.

Damn, she thought again as she remembered some of her better lines. Citing an ad contract between his new station and a national fertilizer company, she had written, "Andrews already dictates national and state policies and preferences. Now he is reaching into small-town America to help us with our lawn care." When his network had picked up a reality show that featured contestants eating worms and lice, J. J. Warren had accused him of "bringing his own abominable taste to the nation's dinner table."

Now he was her boss, capable of finding her in his vast organization and crushing her like a bug. Which was exactly what he would do if his reputation as a ruthless egomaniac was to be believed. Her only hope, she decided, was that in the global affairs of his enterprise, William Andrews had never taken notice of even a word that she had written. What she needed to do was drop out of sight for a few months, let her J. J. Warren byline die a natural death, and then reemerge as just Plain Jane. It would be suicide for her to walk into his office that afternoon and interview him about his latest acquisition.

She had to get out of the assignment! Roscoe Taylor would certainly understand that confronting William Andrews would be a career-ending move. Why in God's name would he have set up the interview, anyway? Did he think he could cozy up to the predator who had just devoured him?

Oh God! Jane knew the answer as soon as she asked herself the question. Roscoe didn't ask for the interview. William Andrews did! He had seen the J. J. Warren articles and he was summoning her to his castle for a public execution. Suddenly it was perfectly clear. Her words had angered the media king and he had made it a point to find out which of his peasants was responsible. Then he had bought the entire newspaper chain just to bring her under his control. Now he was awaiting the arrival of the offender, while his headsman was sharpening the ax.

She charged back into the managing editor's office. "Roscoe, who set up this interview with Andrews?"

"I did. With his PR people."

She looked at him skeptically. "Why me?"

"It seems appropriate. You're our expert on the man who just took over our company. Who better to tell our readers what this is going to mean to them?"

"Andrews didn't set it up?" Her suspicion was obvious.

"No, although his press guy jumped at the idea."

"Did they ask for me . . . by name?"

Roscoe got the drift of her questioning. "You mean because they want to get even with you for sticking pins in the great man?"

She slipped into the chair across from him. "Yes. Something like that."

He rolled his eyes. "You can't be serious."

"I'm totally serious! I write some articles he doesn't like, so he buys my paper and gets to fire me in front of a gathering of business reporters. Wouldn't that be a convincing way to tell the press to be careful what it says about him?"

Roscoe was even more amazed. "You think that Andrews Global Network bought our chain just so William Andrews could have the pleasure of firing one obscure reporter?"

"I wouldn't put it past him," Jane answered. "I'll bet his ego is more important to him than the pocket change he spent buying us out."

He laughed.

"I'm serious," she insisted, jumping to her feet. "I think I'm going to be the guest of honor at a lynching."

"Jane, get real! Much as I hate to put a dent in *your* ego, they didn't ask for you by name. I set up the interview. And when I told them that J. J. Warren would be our reporter, they said, '*Mr. Warren* should come right up to the penthouse.' They think you're a Jim, not a Jane."

She slumped back into the chair, thoroughly chastised. "Oh . . ." She sounded disappointed that she wasn't worth a public hanging.

"Now, why don't you get into your best boardroom attire and get into the city early. Go shopping so that you're in a better mood. And get there on time to make a good impression. You're the first citizen he's going to meet from his newly conquered country. I'd like him to think that he's getting his money's worth."

She nodded.

"And go back to that one-eyed look. It really was distinctive."

She dragged herself back to her desk, glanced at the phone messages that had come in, and decided that they could all wait. Jack Dollinger stuck his head in. "Lunch?" he asked, reminding her of his earlier offer.

"I'm booked," she answered. "I have a meeting in the city with the great man himself."

"William Andrews?"

"The same."

Dollinger was stunned. "My God! You better read back over your articles and come up with some damn good explanations."

"Roscoe says Andrews doesn't have any idea who I am."

Jack grimaced. "Maybe he doesn't now, but I'll bet there's someone on his staff who's paid to brief him by the time you get there."

She gathered up her laptop, a few floppy disks, and her car keys. There was no point in hanging around. Jack Dollinger wasn't making her feel any better.

She spent the drive home trying to convince herself that Roscoe was right. A man of global affairs who had gone falconing with Saddam Hussein and had danced with Queen Elizabeth probably had no interest in the petty complaints of a suburban reporter. More than likely he had never heard of J. J. Warren and wasn't aware of any of the stories she had written. He probably didn't even know that there was such a newspaper as the *Southport Post*. Odds were that the only thing he had seen was the balance sheet for the suburban chain and that he had bought the earnings rather than the publications.

But while that line of reasoning was comforting, it didn't hold up well against Jack Dollinger's logic. Good public relations executives hired services to find every mention of their employers in every kind of media. Every morning William Andrews was probably handed clippings of every article in which his name was taken in vain. Her hints at megalomania and accusations of bad taste couldn't have gone unnoticed.

But would he make the connection? Even if Andrews had seen the pieces, he probably wouldn't link them with the *Southport Post*. More unlikely was that he would remember the name J. J. Warren. And even in the event that he did, would he connect Plain Jane with the obnoxious J. J. who had offended him?

Art's car was in her parking space. *Damn again!* Wasn't anything going to go right today? Rather than wait for the elevator, she raced up the stairs to her second-floor garden apartment. Typical of her former husband, the door had been left unlocked; equally typical, her home office had been trashed.

He raised his hands defensively as soon as he saw her. "Don't worry! I'll put everything back where it belongs." Then he went on the offense. "Do you have any idea how many unlabeled disks you have? How do you ever keep track of anything?"

"I'm not the one who lost a play," Jane countered. "I have no trouble keeping track of my things."

He went on with his complaints. "I've had to open twenty or thirty disks just to find out what was on them. I've read enough of your dreary stories to make me sick."

"Did you find your disks while you were ransacking my things?"

"Jane, I can't find anything in this chaos. Will you just take a few minutes and help me?"

"I can't. I've got to be in the city this afternoon," she answered as she crossed over the mess he had created. "And I want you out of here before I leave." She went into her bedroom and slammed the door behind her.

"I can't leave without my disks," he called after her.

She opened the door a crack. "Don't bother to pick up. Just leave everything where it is and lock the door behind you." Then she added, "I mean it, Art. I don't have time for this nonsense."

She was in the shower when he skulked into her bedroom. His voice startled her. "You know, we don't have to fight all the time. We can still be friends." He went to the bathroom door and leaned against the jamb.

"What are you doing in here?" Jane screamed. She turned her back to him even though she was scarcely visible through the rippled glass of the shower door.

"I'm asking for a little help. Those disks are important to me."

"Will you get out of here so I can get dressed?" She was boiling slowly into a rage.

"Like I've never seen you with your clothes off," he grumbled. He turned and shuffled out of the room.

He was still there, slouched in a soft chair, when she emerged from her bedroom, now dressed in a pinstripe suit over a plain white blouse. "Please, Art. I have an interview with William Andrews, and I can't be late. I promise I'll look for your damn disks as soon as I get home."

"I don't think they're here," he admitted.

She stood in front of the hall mirror while putting on her stud earrings.

"William Andrews?" he went on. "That's the guy you hammered in some of your stories. . . ."

"The very one! And he's just taken over our whole chain. He's my boss now, so I can't keep him waiting."

Art snickered. "He owns the chain? Boy, are you in deep shit!"

"Not as deep as I'll be if I'm late for the interview."

He eased out of the chair and walked up behind her. She handed him the earring back, a gesture that had become automatic during their years together. He pulled at her earlobe and locked the back onto the pin. "Maybe I should move back in," he contemplated. "You're not much good on your own."

She studied herself in the mirror, pulled down her jacket, and straightened the collar of her blouse. "I'd rather give up wearing earrings," she told him.

They walked out together and rode down the elevator in complete silence. Then they split as each walked to a car. "I'll call you about the disks," he promised.

"Do that," she said, climbing into her car.

When she turned the key, there was nothing more than a click. Her small SUV had decided not to start.

3

Jane reached the receptionist's desk at the stroke of three, exactly the time scheduled for her interview. She tried to hide her anxiety and shortness of breath. "Jane Warren of the *Southport Post*," she said. "I have an interview with Mr. Andrews."

"Have a seat," the woman answered in a tone that fell just short of being a direct order. "Mr. Andrews is running a bit late, but I'll tell his assistant that you're here." The receptionist was wearing a suit very similar to her own, dark with a chalk stripe. Jane felt a bit upstaged. Her first impression wouldn't be nearly as impressive as she had hoped.

Art had come to her rescue. She waved him down as he was backing out and wailed that her car wouldn't start. He listened to three or four repetitions of the dead starter and then lifted the hood with a sense of authority that made it appear as if he knew what he was doing. He looked, touched, and then moved the control connectors back and forth. Over and over he instructed that she "try it now." The clicking sound never varied.

"Screw the car," she snapped. "Just drive me to the train station."

"No. This is simple. I'll have it in a minute." More poking and pulling and then "Try it now." More clicking!

Finally she screamed. If he wanted to play with her engine, she was going to borrow his car. Only then had he given up on his debut as a mechanic and driven her to the commuter line station.

She had to run to catch the train as it was pulling out and had to pay a surcharge for not buying a ticket at the station. She had been on the verge of relaxing when the train ground to a halt just short of Grand Central. And when she finally made it to the street, her taxi got tied up in traffic. Her heart was still pounding when she rode up in the elevator.

She sat on a plush sofa, her laptop open, jotting down the questions she planned to ask. There were two choices. She could be the hard-hitting reporter and skewer William Andrews on tough, serious questions. How had he managed to acquire enough stock for the takeover without filing his intentions with the Securities and Exchange Commission? Since he had recently purchased a television station in the same market, how did he plan on getting around the Federal Communications Commission rules against multiple outlets in the same market? How did he plan on maintaining competition among his various properties? Or she could play the loyal employee and toss up the slow, fat pitches that he could knock out of the ballpark. Won't your vast media sources make the suburban chain papers even more valuable to the readers? Are you going to be offering more upward mobility to employees of the newspapers? How would you describe the importance of locally based media? J. J. Warren, the young business editor who was beginning to attract a following, would take the tough approach and nail the greedy bastard to the wall. But Jane Warren, the recently acquired employee who dressed like his receptionist, decided on the more condescending alternative. If she was meek enough, he probably wouldn't connect her with the paper's irreverent coverage.

She noticed people rushing in and out, heard the receptionist announce calls for Mr. Andrews, and saw two recent arrivals ushered in ahead of her. She checked the global clocks that stretched dramatically across the wall, found the one for New York, and realized she had been waiting for nearly an hour. On her home turf, she would have reminded a receptionist that she had a deadline. Here in the big leagues, she sat quietly and cooled her heels.

"Ms. Warren?" The receptionist summoned her like a teacher calling a pupil. Jane rose slowly and walked to the desk. "Mr. Leavitt will see you."

"Who's Mr. Leavitt?"

The woman seemed annoyed. "Mr. Leavitt is an executive vice president, Mr. Andrews's assistant." Her tone implied that anyone of importance would certainly know who Mr. Leavitt was.

Jane's first emotion was relief that she had been granted a reprieve. The great man was busy, so she was being pushed off onto an assistant. That seemed to indicate that she hadn't been summoned to her own beheading. But her second emotion was anger. She had come a long way at considerable inconvenience, and she was being treated like a nobody.

"Is Mr. Leavitt going to sit in on my interview with Mr. Andrews?"

"I wouldn't know," the young woman answered, taking on the importance of the people whose gate she kept.

"Why don't you ask him," Jane suggested, sounding casual even though she could feel the heat rising in her cheeks.

The receptionist sighed with frustration, keyed her console, and asked, "Mr. Leavitt, is Mr. Andrews going to be able to keep his appointment with Ms. Warren? She seems to be concerned." She listened, frowned, then sighed again. "Please have a seat. Mr. Leavitt will be right with you."

Jane took a small measure of satisfaction in irritating the receptionist. But she went back to her place and resumed her wait. Maybe she should have taken Leavitt when he was offered.

The door opened for a short man in white shirt and tie. His suit coat had apparently been discarded inside during the heat of battle. He paused at the desk, followed the receptionist's glance at Jane, and then approached with an apologetic shake of his head. "I'm so sorry! It's been an impossible day and it seems to be getting worse." His hand was out. "Bob Leavitt. I'm Bill Andrews's assistant. And you seem to be J. J. Warren. . . ."

Her knees felt weak. If she was J.J., then they must have read the articles. "Jane Warren," she answered on the chance that she might still be able to hide her identity.

He gestured for her to sit and then lowered himself onto

the sofa beside her. "Right now Bill is on a conference call with a couple of European managers. And the second it's finished, he's going to come racing through that door with some of our top executives running to keep up. We're on our way to the airport, off to a meeting in Paris."

She tried to look disappointed. "Okay. I suppose we'll have to reschedule. . . ."

"No," Leavitt said with a half smile that suggested he had a better idea. "What I'm going to do is make sure that you're in Mr. Andrews's car. It will take us half an hour to get to the airport . . . probably closer to an hour in rush-hour traffic. You can do your interview on the way, and then I'll have the car take you back to your office." He paused to take in her reaction. Jane was a bit wide-eyed and at a loss for words. "I know it's terribly inconvenient," Leavitt went on, "and a lot to ask. But it will keep you on schedule and give Bill a chance to answer some of the questions you've raised."

She thought for only a second. "That will work," she decided.

Leavitt seemed delighted. "Great! Mr. Andrews will really appreciate it." He stood up quickly. "Now, if you can just wait here one more minute, I promise you I'll be right back. And again, thanks for your patience and understanding. As I said, not much has gone right today."

Her fears vanished as she began to feel the heady warmth of importance. The chairman's car! Not bad for someone from a small suburban chain. And keep the car so that she would stay on schedule! *He must think that my time is valuable.* Oh, of course he was a showman, and probably his concern was simply an act to turn a hostile reporter into an ally. But so what? Obviously, he had kept abreast of her series, and instead of having her drawn and quartered, he was paying the respect due a significant journalist. She was nearly giggling with self-satisfaction.

The door exploded open, and all six feet four inches of William Andrews charged out. He was talking as he entered, carrying on simultaneous conversations with the two secretaries who flanked him, each struggling to jot down the essence of his thoughts. "No, move that to Wednesday!" he snapped to his right, and then turning to his left, "Tell Archie to fly over and meet me at the hotel tomorrow night. I want to see the Houston deal."

"You're in Washington on Wednesday," the woman on his right announced.

"Then Thursday! Find an hour in my schedule."

And then from the secretary on the left, "You're having dinner with the minister tomorrow night."

"I'll see Archie after dinner," Andrews answered as if nothing could be more obvious.

He had reached the elevator when his handlers appeared, three men in dark suits, each marching with a notetaker at his elbow, and a slim woman in slacks and a blouse who was dictating to a younger version of herself. The elevator door opened to admit the executives, then closed in the faces of the secretaries, who were still struggling to jot down final instructions.

Jane watched the parade in awe, then tried to keep track of the women who rushed off in different directions. It had taken only twenty seconds from Andrews's entrance until the waiting room emptied out. She was supposed to be in his car, and somehow she couldn't picture the people who had just flown past waiting around for her arrival. She sprang to her feet and lunged toward the elevator bank. Robert Leavitt came up behind her and beat her to the button. "Don't worry! We'll catch up in the lobby."

He had his jacket on now, and a colorful tie that seemed to explode from between the lapels. Unlike the frenzied faces in Andrews's entourage, Leavitt seemed relaxed. Jane tried to size him up without taking her eyes off the blinking lights that counted down the floors.

He was in his forties, she guessed from the thinning light hair cut painfully short. He had a round face with large blue eyes and a mouth that seemed in a perpetual smile. Not a jock, she guessed from his soft neckline even though he didn't seem overweight. Not as intimidating as the other executives who had rushed by earlier. They had worn their black jackets and dark open-collared shirts like the uniforms of an attack force, a casual look made sinister by their aggressiveness. Leavitt seemed completely comfortable in his suit and tie.

"What do you do for Mr. Andrews?" she ventured.

"A bit of everything. Basically try to smooth out the image of the organization."

"Public relations," she guessed.

He nodded. "Some of that. Also government policy. And then some internal relations. My title is executive vice president, and it seems to cover anything that Mr. Andrews doesn't have time to do himself."

The elevator opened onto the lobby, and Leavitt steered them to a side entrance where two limousines were parked at the curb with their doors open. Jane saw Andrews get into one of the cars and picked up her pace. But then the woman who had crossed the lobby behind him slid in beside him, and then one of the men. As she and Leavitt reached the door, the car pulled away. "Wasn't that my interview?" she asked Mr. Andrews's executive assistant.

He nodded. "Something must have come up."

She sighed in defeat. Just as she was beginning to feel confident and important, she had been brushed off like dandruff.

"No matter," Leavitt said, leading her toward the second car, which the two other men were climbing into. "We'll catch him out at the airport."

Jane stopped in the middle of the sidewalk. "Let's just postpone the interview. He's obviously involved with something else, and I'll reschedule when he has more time."

But Leavitt tugged her toward the car. "He never has more time, and he really is eager to meet you. We'll all be standing around the terminal for an hour, and I'm sure I can get the two of you together."

She let herself be loaded next to the two executives. "This is J. J. Warren," Robert Leavitt said. Then he introduced Gordon Frier and Henry Davis. The men grunted as they squeezed together to make room. He got into the front seat, next to the driver, and then turned back to the passengers.

"J.J. is the journalist Bill mentioned," he said. And then, with mock seriousness, "She's looking to skewer us, so I'd advise you to be on your best behavior."

They favored her with a smile, and Jane laughed nervously. "I wouldn't skewer anyone," she said. But then added that anything she overheard would be on the record. They made small talk all the way to the executive terminal at La Guardia. But she couldn't keep her mind focused on even the most banal comments about the traffic and the weather. *The journalist Bill mentioned,* she kept thinking, wondering just what he might have said.

It might have been dismissive. "This pushy bitch has been sticking her finger in our eye. It's going to be a pleasure to kick her ass out onto the street." Or maybe he had been diplomatic. "I've got to humor her for a few minutes to get her onboard with the program." Or, she could only hope, it might have been complimentary. "This lady is damn good. She's raised some tough questions, and I have to come up with answers." Any of those scenarios would fit with Leavitt's comment that Andrews really wanted the interview. But the important new information was that Andrews knew of her stories and had thought her important enough to tell his staff about her. She was clearly a blip on his radar, and he was well aware that he would be meeting an outspoken critic. So there was no point in trying to hide as Plain Jane. Win or lose, she would have to ask the tough questions and press for answers.

They moved slowly, stop and go, between the lines that backed up at the tollbooths. From the bridge they could see the airport lights, but it still took them an additional half hour to get there. When they pulled up in front of the executive terminal, Frier and Davis bounded out and ran to the doorway. Leavitt helped Jane out, then reached ahead to move the revolving door. They turned away from the shuttle flight gates and went into the art deco waiting room that originally served seaplanes. There was no sign of the Andrews Global Network executives. The room was nearly empty.

Bob Leavitt went to the counter. Jane was right at his heels, so she overheard the clerk say that Andrews and his party had gone into a private office. He turned to Jane. "Give me just a second to find out what this is all about." He disappeared through a door marked PRIVATE before she could repeat her offer to postpone the interview. When he returned, he was smiling optimistically. "More phone calls," he explained. "But I got his eye, and he indicated that he would be right out. It should be only a few minutes."

Jane nodded that she didn't mind the additional wait. "I guess this is what you mean by 'smoothing the rough edges.' Explaining Mr. Andrews to those of us who don't know him has to be a full-time job."

"No, that's half the time. The rest is explaining ordinary human beings to Mr. Andrews. He has no idea what they're like."

She asked about the men in the car. "The way they cut off their conversation, they must have been planning to rob a bank."

Leavitt laughed. "That's about what they're doing, but I think they'd put a different spin on it. Frier finds promising acquisitions, and Davis comes up with the money to buy them. As you can imagine, nearly anything they talk about is highly privileged."

"And the other two? In the first car?" she pressed.

"John Applebaum runs our publishing operations. He's the one you'll be working for once we get your newspapers integrated. Kim Annuzio heads up the broadcast properties." She had heard of Applebaum and Annuzio. They made constant appearances in the business press, generally inspiring fear rather than affection. Leavitt had more to tell her, but his voice was drowned out by the whine of a Gulfstream business jet that was taxiing up to the terminal. He shrugged an apology and looked out at the plane. Then he jumped to his feet and started for the private door. But the door opened before he reached it, and once again William Andrews appeared as if shot from a cannon. Now he was flanked by Frier and Davis, with Applebaum and Annuzio only a step behind. He glanced at Leavitt, exchanged a word, and looked over Leavitt's shoulder at Jane. Then he snapped his head toward the wait-

ing jet in a gesture that said "C' mon, let's go" and continued
his trajectory to the terminal door. Leavitt ran back to Jane.

"We've got to go right now," he shouted, even though he
was right next to her. "Something about a weather hold that
we don't want to get caught in." He took her laptop in one
hand and then steered her into line behind the Andrews executives. "I'll get you a seat next to him. You can have the
whole trip for your interview."

"Aren't you going to Paris?" she yelled.

"That's right!" He was doing his best to keep her moving.

"Where am I supposed to get off? Labrador?" Her eyes
flashed anger. She was being led around like a lap puppy.

"In Paris. We'll put you on a flight back as soon as you're
ready."

"I don't have a thing with me," she snapped. "I haven't
packed—"

"No one has anything. Just buy what you need. They have
great stores in Paris."

Jane planted her feet in the doorway. With the roar of the
engines, any further conversation was impossible. She shook
her head and reached for her computer. But Leavitt continued to tug on her arm. "You'll be back in the morning," he
bellowed.

That's right, she realized. Over tonight and back in the
morning. And what better way to start with her new boss than
join him and his top management team aboard the company
jet. She pursed her lips, nodded, and let herself be steered to
the boarding steps. Within seconds she was strapped into a
seat looking across at Robert Leavitt, who didn't seem in the
least perplexed by the dramatic change of venue.

4

Cocktails were served as they were taxiing out to the runway. There was a quiet moment when the plane accelerated and climbed out over New York City. Then hors d'oeuvres were brought out to accompany the cocktails. Jane munched a miniature quiche and sipped a chilled Chardonnay. Leavitt scooped up cashews to go with his martini.

Across the aisle, seated in a comfortable curved lounge, John Applebaum and Kim Annuzio were in a serious conversation. Kim was in baggy slacks and a loose blouse, far more assured in her casual look than Jane was in her pinstripes. Jane recognized the role reversal. The important people dressed down, and the help dressed up. She would have to remember that if she was ever invited back. The two women made eye contact and raised their glasses in a toast. Kim's expression seemed authentically friendly, but John Applebaum's eyes were narrowed into a scowl. She remembered that he was the one who would soon become her boss.

Behind the forward compartment where they were sitting was a bulkhead that created a conference room. An aisle ran past the conference room to quarters at the rear of the plane. Through a glass partition, Jane could see Frier and Davis at the conference-room table, poring over papers and laptop computers. Then the door to the rear quarters opened and William Andrews, now without his jacket, stepped out. Jane's hopes rose as he started forward, but then he turned into the conference room and joined the two executives. Their heads leaned together over the documents.

Andrews was an imposing figure, tall and lean with broad shoulders and weighty arms, more basketball player than business executive. His face, like his frame, was long and thin with a prominent nose and strong cheekbones. His eyes, behind frameless glasses, seemed to be squinting, so that

Jane had no idea of their color. Andrews wore his hair long, not quite ready for a ponytail but over the back of his shirt collar. He was gray on the sides and dark on top, casually styled with no defined part. His appearance stressed the artistic side of his endeavors rather than the financial, the physical rather than the mental. She might have guessed a campus career if she hadn't studied his career as a tycoon.

"You seem to be quite comfortable rushing around like this," Jane said to Robert Leavitt. "I think the pace would drive me crazy!"

He shrugged. "I suppose I've been with him so long that it seems normal."

"How long? When did you join Andrews Global Network?"

Leavitt chuckled. "Join? I was born here. Bill and I were college roommates. His senior thesis was an application for a community antenna license. That's what a cable system used to be called. We moved out of the frat house and right into a two-room office."

"That was in Pittsburgh," she said, showing that she had done her homework.

He nodded. "For a couple of months. Then we used the license as security and bought another system in Harrisburg. In five years, we had twenty-four cable franchises and linked them together in a network that covered four states. We moved our headquarters sixteen times. It's been quite a ride!"

"Have you enjoyed it?"

He shrugged. "I don't know. It hasn't been dull."

The flight attendant set out place settings and began serving a dinner of poached salmon. He brought plates into the conference room but set them on the far end of the table, away from the conference. William Andrews never seemed to notice the food.

"He doesn't eat?" Jane wondered aloud.

"With customers and backers. For him, dining is a business function. It has nothing to do with nutrition."

Jane leaned back from the table. "But still you like him. He's a social misfit, but nothing he does offends you?"

"I wouldn't go that far," Leavitt answered. "He can be offensive, is always ungrateful and sometimes downright rude. But the work is exciting, and I can't complain about the money."

"Do you have time for a life of your own?" she asked.

"Not much," Leavitt agreed with a smile. "A few hours here and there. Fortunately, I'm not married. Except to the company."

Andrews jumped up from the conference table and backed out into the aisle. When he started forward, Jane thought she was about to get her interview, but he stopped at the end of the aisle. "Bob," he said, "let's go."

Leavitt undid his seat belt. "My master's voice," he said with a look of resignation. He swung out into the aisle and followed Andrews into the conference room. That left Jane looking across at the still scowling John Applebaum and Kim Annuzio, who was now absorbed in her laptop.

Dessert came, an apple tart glazed with raisin sauce. And then cordials, in Jane's case a ruby port. It was close to ten P.M. back in New York, and probably past midnight over the Atlantic when the meal was cleared away. Andrews and his people were still talking vigorously in the conference room. Applebaum had been summoned to join them, and Kim had closed her computer and was looking out her window at the starlit sky.

"Are they going to keep going all night?" Jane asked.

"I'm not sure." She undid her seat belt and slid across to join Jane. "We haven't been introduced," she said, and mentioned her name. "You're J. J. Warren," she added before Jane could introduce herself. "I've read your articles on the company."

"And you'd like to push me out the door," Jane suggested.

"Not at all. I thought you did a good job, as far as it went."

"Where else should it have gone?"

"I was hoping you'd look at the properties we've acquired," Kim answered. "You say we can control editorial opinion. But generally we leave the properties running pretty much as they were. We make them more efficient and more profitable, but we're not trying to promote an ideology or a viewpoint. We're trying to make money."

Jane nodded thoughtfully. "I'll look into that in the next piece. But the potential for propaganda is still there, and I think that's more important than your shareholders getting richer."

Kim shrugged. "That's the dilemma, I suppose." She slid back across to her seat.

Was she being set up? First Leavitt tells her how hard they're all working, and then another executive makes a pitch that she might take a different viewpoint. *What's next?* she wondered. *Maybe Applebaum will stop by and offer me a raise.*

She opened her computer and went back to work on the questions she would ask. They were tough and potentially embarrassing, reflecting the latest change in her opinion of William Andrews. According to Kim, he was all about money. Leavitt had described him as ungrateful and rude. And he was a total bastard in dealing with her. He had agreed to the interview, charged his old college roommate with keeping her at the ready, and then ignored her as if she were an insect too insignificant to swat. Well, screw him! If he managed an interview, she would hold his feet to the fire. And if he didn't, she would tell her readers exactly what kind of a horse's ass he was.

She glanced up. He was pacing around the conference table, jabbing a finger in front of him to emphasize whatever point he was making. His top executives were nodding their approval over their laptops as they raced to capture his every thought. "Screw it!" she told herself in a full voice. She slammed the computer shut and snapped off the overhead light. If he wanted an interview, let him come and ask for it.

When she awoke, the flight attendant was setting a glass of orange juice in front of her. Robert Leavitt had returned and was sitting across from her, absently spooning cold cereal into his mouth while reading a printout of the latest news. He had a linen napkin tucked into his collar and spread across his shirt and tie.

"Damn," Jane said, sitting up straight. "I fell asleep."

Leavitt set down his news report. "You didn't miss anything. When the meeting broke up, they all went to bed." He nodded to the curved lounge where Gordon Frier was sound asleep. "There are bunks aft," he went on, explaining the absence of the others, "and Bill has his own cabin in the tail."

The steward brought her coffee and promised to return with fruit and yogurt.

"Let me ask you something," she said, and went ahead without waiting for permission. "If I were from the *Times,* or *The Wall Street Journal . . .*"

"The same thing would have happened," he said, anticipating the end of her question. "William Andrews is an equal-opportunity ingrate. He's stiffed lots of journalists and left it to me to convey his apologies. So when I apologize on his behalf, you shouldn't feel that you were stiffed just because you're not a big-city editor."

"How does he get away with it?"

"He doesn't," Robert answered. "He gets crucified by the press."

Jane nodded. "He should. I'm going to do a story about what it's like to sit around waiting on his royal pleasure."

Leavitt pushed his cereal bowl aside and leaned closer. "Look, I'll do everything I can to get the two of you together. Once this fire drill is over—"

"Forget it," Jane snapped. "You said you would put me on the first plane back to New York. That's what I want—my return ticket."

He nodded. "Okay, but the first plane going back won't take off until one o'clock. So let me get you settled into a hotel where you can run up a big room-service tab and catch a few hours' sleep. Then I'll have a car take you back to the airport."

She shook her head. "That won't be necessary."

"It's only fair," he reminded her.

After a few seconds' reflection, Jane announced, "You're right. It's the least that the great William Andrews can do for me after dragging me halfway around the world by my nose. I'll run up one hell of a room-service tab."

Her coffee, fruit, and yogurt appeared before her. And

when Leavitt pushed up the window shade, she could see the shape of the French coast bordering the Channel. She watched carefully, until the suburbs of Paris passed underneath, and caught a glimpse of the Seine snaking around Notre Dame on its way to the Eiffel Tower. *Not bad,* she thought again. Maybe she should tell Robert that she needed a rest day before she headed back, and then spend a night on the town. That way she could really run up an enormous bill and pay herself back for the inconvenience. It wouldn't matter how much she spent. Once her article appeared she was going to be fired anyway.

They touched down at Charles de Gaulle and taxied to the executive hangar. William Andrews charged out of his private quarters the instant the door was opened. He was unshaven and unkempt. Apparently he had stretched out in his clothes. And the eyes behind his glasses were bloodshot.

Jane was in his path, standing in the aisle as she smoothed her skirt and picked up her briefcase. They came face-to-face and then nose-to-nose. Andrews swayed forward, his body language telling her to either get out of the way or get moving. She stood her ground.

"Mr. Andrews, I'm J. J. Warren, the editor you were supposed to meet back in New York."

He blinked as if trying to make certain that someone was actually standing in his way. "J. J. Warren?" he asked.

"From the *Southport Post.* I'm the one who said that you had the SEC and FCC in your pocket. I was going to give you the opportunity to tell your side of the story."

He stared at her, his brow wrinkling as he tried to make sense out of her intrusion. Then the pieces fell into place. "Oh, yes. J. J. Warren. We're going to do an interview."

"No, we're not," she contradicted him. "We *were* going to do an interview, but you blew it. What you're going to get now is a feature article that tells my readers just what an insufferable stuffed shirt you actually are."

He still seemed to be groping for information. Robert leaned in close and whispered the relevant facts in his ear.

"Ms. Warren is with the New England Suburban Press organization that we just bought. You wanted to meet her."

There was another flicker of recognition. "Yes . . . of course. How are you, Ms. Warren?"

"Pissed-off, thank you," she answered. "You may be able to treat your flunkies with indifference and bully your critics. But not me! I say what I see. And what I see is an insensitive gorilla used to pushing people around. And what I want you to know is that I don't push easily. So just wait your turn."

She shouldered her laptop and started down the aisle at a graceful pace. William Andrews followed meekly, and then came his wide-eyed, open-mouthed staff. Robert Leavitt filled in at the rear, scarcely able to suppress the laughter that went along with his broad smile.

5

Jane stirred, stretched like a kitten, and enjoyed the luxury of satin caressing her bare skin. She rolled onto her side and gathered the pillows into a soft mound so that she could bury her face. Then she pulled her knees up to her chest, settled into the cozy quiet of the womb, and sighed with content. Wherever she was, she planned on staying for the full term.

Where was she? The question perplexed her for a moment because this certainly wasn't her bed and she generally slept in at least a T-shirt. Now she was naked, rolled up in a ball, and floating in what seemed to be a pond of rosewater. Was it possible that she had died and gone to heaven?

Probably not, because she could hear traffic noises—revving engines, high-pitched horns, and rumbling trucks. All strange sounds, recognizable even though they weren't the sounds she was used to hearing. She blinked an eye open and saw a cream-colored cascade of bedspread, beautiful but certainly not hers. She was in someone else's bed!

She sat bolt upright, her eyes suddenly wide-open. The room was huge, with towering walls that disappeared into the darkness. There was only one streak of light that pushed between the drapes, falling across an intricate pattern of an Oriental rug. It was just enough to illuminate the corner of the footboard so that she could make out the carved fleur-de-lis and the gold detailing on the off-white panel. *Paris,* she remembered. She had fallen asleep in Paris.

Jane bounded out of bed and ran to the window, poking her face into the split of the drapes. Through a huge French door, and over the rail of an iron balcony, she saw a wide boulevard with a center divide. Traffic whizzed in both directions, oblivious of the clusters of pedestrians who risked their lives in timing the space between cars. Across the street was a row of white granite town houses with storefronts at street level. Cartier, Chanel, and Ferragamo were among the discreet signs.

"Paris," she said with a sigh. She teased the drapes open a bit so that she could get a better look. "Damn," she said, suddenly wheeling away from the window. The streets were full. What time was it? What time was her flight? She saw the clock on her night table—9:15. The sun was out, so it must still be morning. And what had Robert Leavitt said about the first flight back to the States being in the afternoon? She caught her breath. She hadn't overslept. But what were the arrangements? Did she have a ticket? Was she being picked up, or was she supposed to make her own way to the airport?

She remembered her parting scene with William Andrews in the aisle of his private jet. Oh, Jesus, what had gotten into her? Why hadn't she just stepped out of his way and kept her mouth shut? What had she called him? She was grateful that she couldn't remember. She knew it was something spiteful and insulting, but it was easier to remember that she had been just a bit intemperate. In the car she had suggested to Robert Leavitt that her days with Andrews Global Network were probably numbered and that the number more than likely was one. Maybe she had already been terminated, in which case there might not be a ticket or a limo to the airport.

But if they had dumped her, they had certainly let her fall into luxury. The room might have been a ballroom with its fabric-covered walls, crown moldings, and intricately worked plaster cornices. The ceiling, visible as soon as she turned on the three-tiered crystal chandelier, was a blue sky with puffy clouds supporting cherubs who flew out of the corners. Two decorated armoires flanked the double doors to the next room.

She eased open the double doors and blinked into the glare of sunlight coming through another set of French doors. The sitting room was sumptuous, a backdrop against which Empress Josephine might have received admirers. The walls were a brocaded fabric framed in gilded moldings. Paintings—a Loire landscape and two portraits of long-dead gentlemen—were hung. A chandelier, like the one in the bedroom but much larger, hung over two French Victorian sofas that faced each other over an inlaid table. There was a mantel at the far end serving as backdrop to an arrangement of Empire chairs. Jane wandered in, her jaw dropping just a bit, and spun around slowly to take it all in. "Not your typical Holiday Inn," she said to herself. "Where in God's name am I?" The answer came instantly: in front of an open window without a stitch of clothing on.

Her clothes, Jane remembered, were in one of the armoires. She slunk back into the privacy of the bedroom, took the clothes off the shelf, and laid them out on the bed, her suit and blouse, panty hose, half-slip, bra, and panties. Then she went into the bathroom, hoping to find enough shampoo and scented soap for a decent shower, and maybe a hot radiator or towel bar that would let her dry her underwear. Otherwise, she wouldn't be able to rinse them out in the sink.

The telephone rang, a symphony of jingles coming from the suite's four telephones, including one hanging next to the bathtub. Jane picked it up and answered in English. The response was also in English, flavored with a French accent. "Mademoiselle, there's a gentleman here with a package for you. Some things for your trip."

My tickets, she thought. "Oh thank, you. Could you have someone bring it up and slide it under the door."

The operator chuckled. "I'm afraid it won't fit under the door, Mademoiselle. There is . . . apparel."

Great, Jane thought. They had bought her some traveling things. She wondered which of the executives had guessed her sizes, and figured it must have been Kim Annuzio. "Just leave it inside the door," Jane answered. "I'm going to be in the shower."

"Very well," the woman's voice said cheerily, and then she clicked off the line.

Jane looked around the bathroom, another room with high ceilings but with walls and floor of white tile. The huge tub, set on lion-paw feet, was ergonomically shaped with the back high and the foot low. It was placed away from the wall with its polished copper pipes completely exposed. A handheld showerhead was clamped to a vertical pole so that it could be slid up and down. There was no curtain. Overflow from the tub drained through a scupper in the center of the floor.

She moved the bottles of soaps and oils close to the tub, climbed in, and began experimenting with the valves and levers. When the water was delightfully hot, she routed it up to the showerhead and held the unit close to minimize the splashing. It felt so refreshing that she closed the drain and settled down so that the tub would fill around her. In just a few minutes she was slouched in water up to her chin, her hair in a lather of scented soap. She would have lingered much longer, but she still had no idea when her flight would be leaving. She stood to rinse under the shower and then stepped out onto wet tiles.

There were ivory white bath sheets hanging on the heated towel rack. Jane picked one of them up, draped it over her shoulders, and began drying her hair as she walked back into the bedroom.

"Ahem!" Someone cleared a throat. The sound had a low, masculine resonance.

She froze, realizing that the towel was bunched around her head and that she was pink and naked from the shoulders down. She lowered the towel until she was peeking over its top edge, out through the double doors, and into the sitting room. William Andrews was sitting in one of the chairs by the mantel, totally absorbed in the painting of one of the gentlemen.

"Mr. Andrews . . ." It was an involuntary gasp.

"Ms. Warren," he answered, still making a point of not looking in her direction.

She wrapped the bath sheet around herself as she backed into the bathroom. Then she remembered that her clothes were out on the bed. Andrews had turned when she left the room, so he was looking right at her when she jumped back in to retrieve her underwear. She snatched up her things, dropped her panty hose, hesitated as to whether she should bend to pick them up, decided against it, and ran for cover, closing the door behind her.

"Damn!" she swore under her breath. He had ignored her and then dismissed her. Now he had come back to humiliate her. She looked at the opaque glass bathroom window and wondered if it opened and if she would fit through it. Plunging out to a swift death in an alley seemed less painful than going back to the sitting room.

There was a gentle knock on the door.

"Don't come in!" she yelled. And when she realized how ridiculous that sounded, she called, "I'll just be a minute," in a much more controlled voice.

"There are a few things here that you might need," Andrews said from behind the door.

Jane turned the handle and eased the door open. A shopping bag slipped in, hanging from his shirtsleeved arm. She snatched it away and closed the door so quickly that she nearly caught his fingers. Then she set the bag on the marble slab that framed the sink and looked in on several small store bags.

There was underwear—panties, bra, and slip, all edged with lace. They were a French brand, frivolously elegant and far more expensive than anything she would have bought for herself. Next she found a pale silk blouse with dressy cuffs and collar, and a pair of soft slacks, pleated and baggy. Farther down in the shopping bag were toothbrush, floss and toothpaste, comb and brush, and a complete assortment of designer cosmetics.

Jane rushed into the new underwear and brushed her teeth while combing her hair. Bad enough that the first time William Andrews had really noticed her she was a full frontal nude with a towel wrapped around her head. But now she had left him cooling his heels. But then she thought better of it. Why should she be so accommodating? The bastard had ignored her for a full day and then barged into her hotel suite without warning. He should be the one writhing with embarrassment for his social barbarism. He should be pacing anxiously as he rehearsed the words of a very appropriate apology. So let him wait. She put the hairbrush down and decided to follow her dentist's detailed instructions for flossing her teeth.

When she was dressed, she spent a minute in front of the full-length mirror, tucking the blouse in just so and making another pass with the hairbrush. She turned for her final pose and was delighted with what she saw. Her permanent wave had survived the steamy shower and had fluffed up nicely. It looked attractive and even a bit risqué. The makeup base was just the right shade, adding a warm tone to her skin, which was usually too white. The eye shadow was subtle and the lipstick was bold. Someone—probably Kim—had noticed her coloring the evening before.

But what she enjoyed most was the look of the outfit, perfectly suited for a business day but equally appropriate for a casual lunch or even an elegant dinner. Generally, she didn't pay a great deal of attention to her clothes. Her casual attire, and indeed most of her office clothes, were practical items taken from the rack at the Gap or Old Navy: tidy, trendy, comfortable, and washable. But these were fashionable, feminine, and even sexy. She was feeling almost confident when she opened the door and crossed into the sitting room. "There!" she announced. "I think this is a bit more appropriate for finally getting to meet you."

"Appropriate, and very lovely," he answered, standing and coming to her with his hand extended. The smile he greeted her with was wide and full of laughter. "I have several apologies to make," he said. "For yesterday, last night, and then of course this morning. Where would you like me to begin?"

"Could we begin with a cup of coffee?" Jane replied. "My brain is used to several cups by this time, and it could shut down at any moment."

"Sure. There's a place down in the lobby." He watched while she slipped into her heels, which made the outfit even more feminine. Then he opened the door and stepped back so that she could pass ahead of him.

The "place down in the lobby" turned out to be a dining room with tables adorned in white linen and glistening silver place settings. The waiter who greeted them might have been a field marshal in a Balkan monarchy. He wore fringed epaulets, brass buttons, and thick stripes of rank on his cuffs and poured claret-colored coffee from a silver pot. *What a difference a day makes,* Jane thought. This time yesterday she had been on her hands and knees wiping up coffee grounds with her T-shirt.

"My first apology," Andrews began as he added hot milk, "has to do with yesterday. I kept thinking that there was only one more thing I had to do before we could sit down for your interview. But events kept cascading until we had to take off immediately if we wanted to beat the weather. And then all the issues that needed to be resolved had to be worked out during the flight. Our people are off right now making presentations that we firmed up in the middle of the night. Had I known we would never get a chance to talk, I wouldn't have kept you waiting."

Jane smiled. "No problem. I understand." It did seem plausible, especially since he was taking the time to meet with her now.

"And then this morning, when we were getting off the plane, I was simply mad at myself. I bumped into you in the aisle and remembered that we were supposed to talk. I was furious that I had forgotten and left you hanging."

Less plausible, she thought, and not very original for a lie that he had all morning to work on. But still, someone in his position didn't even have to try for an apology.

"I was, as you put it, an 'insensitive gorilla.'"

She blew a bubble in her coffee and lifted her eyes over the rim of the cup. He had quoted her accurately, but fortunately he seemed more amused than offended. "That's where I owe you an apology," Jane tried, but he held up a hand to cut her off.

"And then this morning. I knew you had no luggage, so I picked up a few things you might need."

"*You* picked up a few things. . . ." She was smiling skeptically.

"Yes, *I* picked up a few things. I have a reasonable knowledge of women's apparel. I'm not a eunuch, you know."

She knew he had been married, had two children, and had lost his wife tragically. But still she couldn't picture the great William Andrews thumbing his way through a shelf of unmentionables.

"I had the desk clerk call, and when you said she should send them up, I thought I should bring them myself, make my apologies, and perhaps start our interview right then and there. I didn't anticipate that . . ."

"I'd barge out of the shower without bothering with a robe."

"I didn't, but I certainly should have considered it. It's been a long time since I lived . . . intimately. But I want to assure you that I did the gentlemanly thing. Instead of looking, I turned my back and made polite noises."

Not very flattering, Jane decided. She was showing everything she had to offer and all he did was close his eyes and clear his throat. Not that she expected to be attacked, but he might at least have taken in what was there for the taking. She wasn't a movie star or a fashion model, but she was young, firm, and nicely figured. The least he could have done was look!

"So, if you will consider my apologies and if you'll tolerate me even if you can't forgive me, I'd like to make amends. I have from now until a luncheon meeting with a business associate to answer your questions. You can keep your room overnight and then fly back with us tomorrow morning."

Jane was amazed. "That's very generous, but all I'll need is an hour or two at the most. I don't need to stay the whole day."

He assured her that he was free all morning and that she could take all the time she needed. "You might enjoy an afternoon in Paris. Besides, if you fly back late tonight, you'll land in New York in the wee hours of the morning. Believe me, it's better this way."

She tried another excuse about her need to be back on the job. She would have to call Roscoe and, as she explained, "clear it with my boss." Andrews smiled at the obvious. He was her boss, and there was no higher authority whose permission she needed. She finished a second cup of coffee, and then they adjourned to a private conference room.

"How did you buy the New England Suburban Press group without filing your intention with the SEC?" He might have apologized, but this was still going to be a tough J. J. Warren–style interview. Other people had accumulated the stock, he answered. He simply bought them out. There was no proxy fight, no hostile takeover. And how would he handle the Federal Communications Commission? Andrews had stacks of economic data to show that the station and the papers were not in the same market. If he lost a regulatory challenge on one of the papers, he would simply sell it off. Wasn't he becoming the only editorial voice in broad regions of the country? He didn't think so, and he offered the constant criticism of a reporter named J. J. Warren as a prime example. "There are hundreds of editors and pundits on my back every day."

He was affable but always frank and quick to the point. He argued his positions logically, and when they disagreed on an interpretation, he was happy to agree that they disagreed. He was forthcoming even on delicate matters of his private wealth, handing her a personal financial statement as soon as she raised the issue. By noon he had delivered information that it would have taken her weeks to gather from outside sources. At no time had he been evasive, patronizing, or cajoling. No one could have been more respectful of her role as a business reporter.

"Would you like to sit in on my luncheon meeting?" he offered when she was closing her laptop into its case. She said she wouldn't think of intruding. But he argued that if she wanted to see how his business was run, this would be a great opportunity. He wanted an exclusive on a French news service. The news service wanted broad distribution. This, he thought, was the heart and soul of a communications network, and a rare chance for her to cut through the self-serving platitudes that the press and the networks usually issued. "All I ask is that you keep the names and precise agreements off the record." It was, she knew, an opportunity that would be available to only the top echelon of business reporters, and too good to turn down. "If you're sure I won't be in the way," Jane finally agreed.

The restaurant was small and informal, a comedown from the elegance of the hotel. But, as she quickly realized, it had a three-star rating and was the personal kitchen of one of the world's most revered chefs. William introduced her as an associate with one of his newspaper chains, technically true but incomplete. She amplified, stating clearly that she was a reporter and then assuring them that the details of this particular meeting were off the record. The French executive laughed. "You Americans!" he said, more in admiration than derision. "For French reporters everything is on the record, even meetings that they never attended. They make up stories for the record."

The men helped her order, insisted that she try a particular white Burgundy, and included her in all their small talk. The business portion of their meal was squeezed in before the dessert. William mentioned a figure of 6 million euros. The Frenchman, with his napkin to his lips, asked if that was for just the United States. William said it was for all of North America and covered translation rights for Mexico and Central America. The Frenchman waved his hand. No, he had other sources for Spanish-language coverage. News, he said, should be in all languages and should never be translated. Andrews nodded. He had heard that viewpoint before. "All right. Let's say English-language broadcast in the U.S. and Canada."

"For six million?" the Frenchman asked.

"Based on the number of sets, I'd say the figure would be more like four."

A nod, and then, "Four! I suppose that's right."

Then the dessert came, berries in a sugary cream sauce, and the additional coffee she needed to offset the wine.

As they walked to the river, William Andrews explained that he had a few matters to take care of that would keep him busy until perhaps six. They could have cocktails before he had to join his other associates for dinner. He put her into a taxi that would take her back to her hotel.

"I must thank you for being so open and forthright," Jane complimented. "I was worried about this interview . . . for obvious reasons . . . and didn't know exactly how I would handle the usual platitudes and cover-ups. I needn't have worried."

He smiled. "I'm afraid I wasn't completely honest."

"Oh! When was that?"

"When I said I didn't look. I did take a quick peek." He closed the door and waved to the driver.

Why, you dirty old man, she said to herself. What kind of pervert would take advantage of her that way? But she found herself smiling. At least he had looked.

6

She did her own shopping in the afternoon, searching for a little black dress and minimum-size costume jewelry. She overspent on a perfume that she had bought just once in the States, where the price was even more outrageous. And she stopped at a lingerie shop, where she bought more of the French intimates that had been delivered to her door. Then she did a few of the tourist things—a bateau down the Scine, an elevator to the top of the Eiffel Tower. She even rode on the Ferris wheel in the Tuileries Gardens. She still had Notre Dame on her list when she ran out of time and caught a bus that ran along the river to her hotel. She was modeling the dress in front of her mirror when Andrews called from the lobby.

She found him in the lounge with a bottle of champagne that was chilling in a silver bucket. "Okay?" he asked, indicating the champagne, and as soon as she smiled he signaled to the waiter. "I see you did your own shopping. Very nice! Very nice indeed." He toasted her new dress.

"And you?" she asked.

Andrews shifted in his chair. "I have some friends here that I try to visit whenever I get a chance."

"Business friends?"

"No, personal. Actually, it's family, but it's not so much a pleasure as a chore. Usually I'm in and out of Paris. But today I had the time, so I thought I'd bite the bullet." He seemed eager to change the subject. "Did you decide on your story line? Hopefully, I'm not still a 'rapacious monopolist' or an 'insensitive gorilla.'"

She colored just a bit. Her words seemed unnecessarily hurtful when spoken by their target. Now she needed a change of subject. "I have enough business material for a book, let alone an article. But I'd like some personal background. Something beyond your official biography."

"For instance?"

"Well, for instance, how often do you get to see your children? Is there any time in your schedule for family life?"

He thought for a moment and then decided. "Not enough, I guess. My family has been . . . abbreviated. There's just the children . . . young adults, I suppose . . . and they're in school. I see them on vacations and at school events, and I try to have them with me during the summer."

"That's Cassie and Craig," she said, confirming what she knew from her research.

He nodded. "Cassie is fifteen, and Craig thirteen. Difficult ages to get close to. Last summer I chartered a sailboat on the Costa Brava. Just the three of us, mastering the elements together. Ten days of thrills and excitement!"

"It sounds wonderful," Jane said.

"It was hell! After two days I wanted to throw both of them overboard. By the end of the first week I was considering throwing myself over. We made port, left the boat, and coexisted in a hotel, where we could each plan an individual daily agenda. I couldn't wait to get them back to school, and I think they were just as eager to be free of me."

Jane sympathized even though she admitted she had no experience with children. "My husband promised we'd start a family as soon as his first play was produced. At the rate he was going, my biological clock would have stopped ticking." He asked, so she gave him a brief résumé of life with Arthur Keene. She tried not to be too critical. Arthur was rolling his dice in the arts, a risky financial plan at best. He needed someone to mind him so he could concentrate on his plays. "That's not me," she said. "He'll be better off if he hooks up with someone more inspired by his talent."

They had discussed her life outside the office, which gave her an entry to probe into his. Jane knew that he had married Kay Parker, a young socialite who had more than fulfilled all her youthful promise, and that they had been a public monument for ten years. Kay had died violently during a skiing vacation in the Adirondacks. An intruder had broken into their lodge and killed her with a shotgun blast. William had been wounded in the attack.

It had happened eight years ago, before William Andrews had put together his global empire. But even then, he was a successful businessman in a highly visible industry. Kay had become his partner in building and promoting his network, but she still dominated the society pages. The murder had made headlines in the tabloids, and rated two columns on an inside page in the *Times*. There were running references to the tragedy during the following weeks as the police found and then discarded new leads.

"How do you recover from a personal tragedy like the one you suffered?" Jane ventured. And then to give him a lead, she added, "I suppose having business challenges gives you something else to think about. Did it help you refocus?"

His eyes flashed an instant of anger and then went glassy. He suddenly seemed to have trouble swallowing.

"I'm sorry," she said right away. "I thought it might explain, in some way, your . . . drive."

He recovered and forced a smile. "That's okay. It's not my favorite topic, and I hope you won't dwell on it."

"Please, forget I asked. . . ."

"No, it's a fair question. How did I get over such an event? And the answer is that I never have. It's with me all the time, and it's certainly with Cassie and Craig. Trying to distance myself from it is probably what pushes me so relentlessly into my business. I guess that trying to get away from it also makes the kids so . . . selfish."

Jane didn't know how to respond. She fidgeted with her empty champagne glass until the waiter rushed to refill it.

"They're very lonely," he said of his children, curiously, as if he were trying to sift through clues for answers. "They don't have any friends, even at school. It's as if they're afraid to reveal themselves to other kids. Afraid of being hurt again."

"That's understandable," Jane commented.

"Yeah, I suppose so. The fact is that I don't have any close friends, either."

He signaled for the check as a way of showing that he would rather put the subject aside. But Jane didn't want to end their meeting in such gloom. "But you do have friends. Bob Leavitt seems as true a friend as I've ever met. He knows you and respects you but still enjoys pointing out your foibles."

Andrews considered her point and admitted, "You're right. Bob and I go back a long way together. We've always trusted each other . . . always been honest with each other." He smiled and shook his head at some past memory. But just as quickly he became serious. "He was the first one at the lodge that night. He probably saved my life."

"Really?" She wanted him to go on, but the check came and then they were on their feet and walking across the lobby.

"Hey," he said as if the idea had just struck him, "why don't you come to dinner with us. A lot of boring business talk, but it might be better than dining alone. Unless, of course, you've made other arrangements?"

"Oh, sure." Jane laughed. "Three or four guys have offered to buy me dinner." And then, more seriously, "But you might have things to talk about in confidence."

"Okay, we'll agree that it's off the record. Anything you hear is as privileged as your sins in a confessional."

"You're sure the others won't mind? They were all struck dumb when I got into the limo last night."

He led her away from the elevators and out to the front door. "Then we won't talk business. We'll have plenty of time for that on the flight home."

His car was waiting, held at the ready by a white-gloved doorman and a uniformed chauffeur. He gave no instructions. The driver already knew where they were going.

Jane took up her interview even though she knew she was trespassing. "You said Robert saved your life. Figuratively, I imagine."

"Literally! I probably would have bled to death."

She was turned toward him, eager for him to continue.

"Bob was staying a couple of miles from the ski house, at the Bass Inn, where we had just held a business meeting. I called him, along with the police. He was the first one on the scene. I had been shot along with Kay, but I didn't realize it. I mean, obviously I knew I was hit and that I was bleeding, but it didn't seem to register."

"You were probably completely involved with saving your wife."

He winced and then shook his head. "No. I knew she was dead. Nothing could have saved her. I just slumped into a chair and did absolutely nothing. It was probably five minutes before I picked up the phone. And when Bob got there I had bled all over the chair. Apparently one of the pellets had hit an artery. I was bleeding to death and I didn't give a damn. He did the bandaging and got me a doctor. From there they took me to the hospital."

"I never heard that you were so badly wounded. The press reports—"

He interrupted. "That was another thing that Bob handled. He talked about 'minor injuries' in the fourth paragraph of the release. The truth might have panicked our stockholders."

Lights went flashing by as they left the highway along the river and entered the central tunnel. Andrews looked idly out the window.

Jane tried to wrap things up. "I'd like to put a sentence about the . . . tragedy . . . into my piece. I think it helps explain your business success. But I'll run it by you first."

He didn't hear her. Instead of responding, he said, "You know, I've never talked about that night. Not since the investigation finished. I've thought about it, and even visualized the whole thing over again. But I haven't had one single conversation about it. I suppose that everyone thinks the subject is off-limits, probably because I've never brought it up." He turned to her. "You're the first person who asked, and pressed for answers."

She felt chastised. "I'm sorry. I should have guessed . . ."

"No, no! Maybe it's good for me. Maybe I should talk about it." Then he admitted, "It's hard to know what helps and what hurts. The kids won't talk about it. It's as if they never had a mother. I guess it hurts to remember."

They were out of the tunnel, on the Boulevard Haussmann, approaching the opera district. The window displays of fashion and jewelry were dazzling, and the pedestrians vied with automobiles for control of the streets. The restaurant, in the middle of a block, had one of the humbler facades.

The others had assembled—Frier, Davis, and Applebaum, still dark, open-collared, and menacing; Kim Annuzio, wearing a suit coat over her blouse and slacks. Leavitt was the only one in a tie. The waiters made light of setting another place at the large round table and squeezing in another chair. "My interview with J.J. here has been going very well," Andrews said to explain the unexpected addition. "She promised to write nice things about me, and if you play your cards right, she may give you some of the credit for our success." There were nods and smiles all around, but no one seemed terribly pleased at having her join them. Only Leavitt complimented her dress. "She's agreed that while she may remember what she hears tonight, she'll go to her death rather than reveal a word." Still no one seemed reassured.

Andrews waited until they had finished their first two bottles of wine before raising business topics, and by then his executives had loosened up a bit. He sat like a moderator directing the conversation back and forth, getting a range of opinions on each subject raised. The conclusion that came together over dessert was that they had a deal to buy control of a French cable distributor and that the government would take their side before the European antitrust court.

"About all we could have expected," Andrews concluded.

"I'd like to be sure that the local managers will stay on," Kim added. Henry Davis was still unhappy about the interest rate that the French bankers were charging, guessing that they were paying an additional half percent just for political support. It was over brandy when Leavitt put Jane in the spotlight. "Any first impressions, now that you're getting to know us?" he asked. All eyes were on her.

For an instant she considered an empty compliment. But she decided it was better to show them that she took her work seriously, and she began outlining the concerns of the financial community. Growth opportunities were limited by legal restrictions and public resentment. Their debt ratio was too high. Each of her comments elicited a defense, and the conversation began to heat up. Andrews signaled for another round of cognac.

Most dangerous, Jane said, was the perception of a one-man company. While Andrews's reputation for success was a major selling point, it also raised fears that the company might collapse if anything happened to its leader. That thought was instantly sobering. It was well after midnight when the party made its way back to the hotel.

Lying in her queen-size bed beneath the painted blue sky, with cherubs peering down at her, Jane thought about the new life she had been leading for the past twenty-four hours. A private jet across the ocean. A wildly expensive French hotel. Shopping in the best stores with the most fashionable names. The company of one of the most famous businessmen in the world. The grand restaurants and the vintage wines. And most of all, the heady conversation with important people listening to her and taking her seriously. Quite a change from her suburban one-bedroom with coffee sloshed down the front of the cabinets, from delicatessen salads eaten at her desk, and from her small glass-walled editorial office.

It gave her a completely new sense of worth. Only two days ago she had been cutting wire-service reports to fit limited space and trying to make still another shopping plaza sound like an earth-shaking economic event. Her biggest story of the previous week had been a chamber of commerce luncheon—the standard chicken and peas with a house white wine—where the guest speaker was the owner of a car dealership. Today had been haute cuisine with people whose decisions could bring down a bank, an industry, and maybe even a country. It was going to be hard for her to get excited over her beat on the *Southport Post*.

But most memorable of all were the moments when William Andrews, who had told her several times to call him Bill, had taken her measure and seemed to like what he was seeing. He had trusted her with his disappointment in his children, a secret that few parents ever share. He had told her about his wife's death, a subject he claimed he never discussed. For a few moments he let himself be vulnerable, dangerous at all times for a tycoon of his stature and certainly foolish in the presence of a stranger. But he had trusted her as if she weren't a stranger and, for a few moments, even needed her to listen. He had admitted pain, an admission of weakness that most men would never reveal.

She wondered what she would write about him. A man impelled to build an empire big enough to overshadow an enormous loss. Someone who had suffered and now tried to insulate himself from any further pain. Or maybe a person who lived in terrible despair inside an impenetrable shell of financial power. Would he regret the moment he had taken off his armor? Or would he see it as the beginning of his recovery from his wounds? Had she seen the last of William Andrews? Or would her role in the basement of his empire bring them together again? And if they did meet, would they resume the empathic relationship they had developed during the day? Or would they have to begin again as strangers?

7

Jane wore her new slacks and blouse into the office, raising eyebrows as she walked down the aisle to her desk. She dropped her laptop on a chair, set her coffee on the desk, and was just sitting down when Jack Dollinger poked his head in.

"Where have you been? No one could reach you."

"Paris," she answered as she sipped and then winced at the unexpected heat.

"Paris?"

"Paris, France."

He didn't believe her. "We called Andrews's office. The girl said you had been there and left. She had no idea where you had gone. We were worried."

"Just a routine assignment," Jane lied.

Jack Dollinger still wasn't listening. "I even drove by your place, and when I saw your car parked, I rang your bell. Then I phoned. I figured you were home sick."

"No. I'm feeling fine."

"Then where were you? We were all worried."

"I was in Paris," she answered, this time making eye contact. "Andrews had to leave in a hurry for a meeting with French officials. I went along so I could interview him on the plane."

He smiled. "You're serious?"

"Of course. Isn't that the way we do business around here?"

Dollinger laughed out loud. "Roscoe has a fit if we take a taxi. Wait until he hears that you've taken a private jet." He moved her computer onto the floor so he could sit. He obviously was ready for a long and adventure-filled story. Jane gave him just the highlights while she drank her coffee. She omitted the frustrating hours when she was left to cool her heels and played up the daylong private interview. She finished with an account of her holding court over an executive conference.

"You're shitting me," he finally decided.

Now it was her turn to laugh. "It was all so unbelievable," she admitted, dropping her pretense of sophistication. "He acted as if I were with the *Times* or the *Wall Street Journal*."

Roscoe Taylor made a show of checking his watch when she came into his office. "You're five hours late, but that would be a day ago. Now you're twenty-nine hours late. Don't you believe in calling in?"

"I was in Paris, interviewing William Andrews," she said smugly.

"I know! But I had to find out from some guy named Robert Leavitt. My own business editor never bothered to let me know."

She was surprised. "Bob Leavitt called you?"

"Bob? You call him Bob! And I suppose you call William Andrews just plain Bill."

She nodded. "That's what he said I should call him."

Roscoe was into his curmudgeon persona. "So you were traipsing through Paris with Billy and Bobby when you were supposed to be working on a profile of the rapacious bastard who just took us over."

"I was working on a profile," she answered, copying his mournful cadence.

"And may I see it?" Roscoe asked. "Or are you going to send it to Leavitt for approval?"

"It's not finished," she said, avoiding the fact that it wasn't even started. "And I'm not sending it to Robert Leavitt or anyone else on the corporate staff. I'll be showing it to you because I work for you." She paused, and then with much less authority asked, "I still do have a job, don't I?"

"That depends on how I like J. J. Warren's latest attack on William Andrews."

She went back to her office and got to work, sifting through her own research and the mountains of business data that Andrews had given her. Jane was still working when she looked up and realized that she was the only one left in the office.

She pulled the disk out of her computer and put it into her briefcase with all her notes. Then she drove home in the SUV that Art had had fixed and left at her door. She was disappointed when she found Art in her apartment.

"What are you doing here?" She breezed right past him and into the kitchen to find something to pop into the microwave.

"Thank you, Arthur, for getting my car fixed," he said, "and for leaving it in my parking space so that I'd be sure to find it."

She stuck her head out of the kitchen. "I'm sorry. That was very nice of you, and I really appreciate it."

"So invite me to stay for dinner," he called after her.

Jane returned. "I have a frozen dinner, and I have some ice cream. You can have your choice, but then you have to go. I've got enough work to keep me up half the night."

"The frozen dinner," he answered, and followed her back to the refrigerator. "Where were you last night? I called to get your okay for the repair, and all I got was your machine."

She read the directions on the package and put the frozen dinner into the microwave. "I was in Paris."

"Sure," he said. "And I was at the Tony Awards giving an acceptance speech. Where were you?"

"In Paris, interviewing William Andrews. I flew over with him on his private jet."

He could tell she was serious, so he stood at attention and smiled. "And . . ."

"And . . . I have to write the story tonight, so you'll have to eat and run." She took the ice cream out of the freezer. It was rock-hard, and she couldn't make any headway with her ice cream scoop, so she put the whole package into the microwave.

"Well," her ex-husband asked, "what's he like? A ball of fire?"

"No," she said. "Quite human. Soft-spoken, vulnerable, appreciative . . ."

"Oh, so he took you to bed?" Arthur assumed.

"Jesus, Arthur. I can't wait until you make it past the second act. No, he did not try or even suggest anything improper. And if he had . . ." She seemed uncertain as to what she would have done.

"He didn't blast you for all the things you've said about him?" He was smiling in anticipation.

"No! All he asked was that the piece be fair."

Arthur rocked back in his chair: "Oh, please be gentle," he begged, imitating a man who would ask a woman to be fair.

The microwave pinged. She took out the steaming dinner and the soupy ice cream. He looked at the dinner. "What is it?"

Jane studied the dinner and then went to the trash can, where she had tossed the box. "It's a delicious beef fillet with a medley of garden vegetables."

"Wonderful," he said, setting the formed plastic dish on the table. "And the wine?"

"There's a bottle in the refrigerator door."

"No," he said. "That's a white and the entrée demands a red. Then it has to have time to breathe."

She leaned back against the sink with the ice cream container in her hand. "It will have to breathe on your time, Arthur, because I need you out of here in exactly ten minutes." He began picking at the beef fillet.

"Oh, I found those disks I was missing. They were in the glove compartment of my car. Sorry about the confusion."

"There wasn't any confusion," she answered while licking the spoon. "I knew I didn't have them." She dropped the container in the trash and went to her desk. She was busy working when Arthur came out of the kitchen and picked up the pages she had already printed out. He took them to a soft chair, where he slouched with his legs over the arm. He chuckled at one sentence and smirked at another, then re-read the pages.

"This is good stuff. Not as acerbic as the other pieces, but you're not backing down a bit." He stood behind her so that he could look over her shoulder. "Where are you planning on working after he cans you?"

"Good night, Art," she said without looking up from her work. "And I really do appreciate your getting my car fixed."

He picked up his jacket, which he had tossed half on the sofa and half on the floor. "Thanks for dinner," he said on his way to the door. "My only suggestion would be that you put a thin slice of lemon in the finger bowls. And maybe a napkin!"

Jane listened to the door click and then broke out laughing. Arthur could be a lot of fun, and he was generous to a fault. But he needed a mother more than he needed a wife. He was sinking and looking for someone he could hold on to.

Did he really think that the piece she was writing would get her fired? It was scrupulously accurate in the details and neutral in tone. She thought she was correct in telling her readers that her suburban newspaper chain was too small to get Andrews's attention. His subordinates wouldn't challenge its news policies and business practices unless it lost money or incurred the wrath of the FCC. In that case, they would break up the chain and sell off the offensive pieces just as they would change the office furniture if it began to look shabby. But as to the larger picture, she quoted the government's misgivings about media conglomerates that dominated markets. William Andrews, whether he intended it or not, was a dangerous man.

Would he be angry when one of his own properties wasn't spouting the party line? Had he expected that she would get with the program when he took the time to wine and dine her? Would he actually fire her just to still her disturbing clucking at the back of the coop? She would be very disappointed in him if he proved to be so petty.

But she would be equally disappointed if he simply ignored her or judged her work too unimportant to be of concern. She had a quality act, even if it was on a very small stage. She had done her homework, given him his opportunity, and then set down the facts as she saw them. It was good journalism, and William Andrews ought to respect professionalism and recognize quality even when the report was not entirely to his liking.

So what response did she hope for? Maybe a comment passed through Robert Leavitt and Roscoe Taylor that she had done a good job. Or maybe a note from Andrews himself, a routine thank-you written by his secretary and signed by him. Something that might say, "Your profile in the such-and-such edition was well presented. While I cannot agree with many of your conclusions, I can't help but admire the professionalism displayed." A typical example of personalized corporate indifference.

She knew she wouldn't be fired. Roscoe would quit before he would obey an order to give her a pink slip. But there were other ways of punishing her if the great man wasn't pleased with what he read. Andrews could easily merge her paper with another in the chain to bring her under a more compliant editor. He could promote her to a dead-end job in circulation or put her in charge of something inconsequential like community events.

On any scale, the downside risks of her story were heavier than the upside potential. Her implied alliance with the executives in Paris as well as pure self-interest suggested that she should eliminate the sniping and give more weight to the company line. After all, the world wasn't going to stop turning because of anything printed in the *Southport Post*. The only thing clearly at issue was her relationship with the new management and its impact on her career.

But she couldn't do it. She could be dead wrong and still be a journalist. But if she tilted the truth one way or the other, she would stop being a reporter and become a pamphleteer. Public relations executives were paid to paint and polish their company's actions until they were nearly unrecognizable. Journalists were supposed to cut through the camouflage and find the hidden agenda. If she tried to win the favor of Andrews and all the other passengers on his corporate jet, then she might as well join them and get in on the perks. A reporter didn't need the love of the people she covered. What she needed was their respect.

Jane sat across from Roscoe while he read her story, searching his face for his reaction. He chuckled. Did that mean he was pleased, or had he found something ridiculous? He frowned. Was something disturbing or just incomprehensible? She had no idea until he turned over the last page.

"Pretty good!" he allowed, which from Roscoe was heady praise. "I think it's the best one in the series. You're less testy and more scholarly. More newspaper and less tabloid. Overall, I like it."

She smiled appreciatively. "So, any suggestions?"

"Just one. Print it!"

"As is?"

"Is there something you're not sure about?"

You're damn right, Jane thought. *I'm not sure that this won't be a career-limiting event.* But she shook her head. "No. It's all accurate."

"Then print it. That's what we're supposed to do around here."

The day it appeared, Jack Dollinger took her out for a beer and a sandwich in a tavern by the railroad station. "Quite a treat," she told him. They usually ate in a coffee shop across the street. Dollinger raised his glass. "A great job," he toasted. "You took the measure of our new owner and found him lacking."

Jane struggled with her first sip. "Is that the way you read it? That I found him lacking?"

He nodded. "Sure! Not lacking in business skills or corporate avarice. But lacking in responsibility to the community. And that's a hell of an indictment for a man who wants to control all our public communications."

She set her glass down. "Oh, Jesus," she mumbled, and her head fell onto her hand. "An indictment?"

"Isn't that what you intended?"

She shook her head slowly. "No. I have nothing against him. I just wanted to be fair."

"You were fair," he assured her. "The man is heartless, and that's what you said."

"No!" She had raised her voice and she was surprised at

her own vehemence. She finished in a softer tone. "He's far from heartless. He's permanently crippled by guilt over his wife's death."

Dollinger put on a skeptical expression. "You mean that business up in the woods when his wife was shot? Let me tell you, we never heard all the facts about that little affair. The stuff about some outsider breaking in was pure horseshit. It was an inside job. William Andrews knows damn well who shot his wife."

"What are you talking about?" she challenged. "How would you know?"

"I was with the *New York Post* at the time," Jack Dollinger began to explain. "Believe me, when we saw dirt, we dug. And when the dirt was on the rich and famous, we dug even deeper. That whole affair was one big cover-up!"

"Jack, I just spent two days with the man. He's not part of any cover-up."

"Maybe not personally," Dollinger countered, "but the people in his company were. This was a hick town with a one-man police force. Andrews's people had that poor rube of a sheriff so intimidated that he was afraid to talk to his wife, much less to the press."

"The state police were called in?" Jane said, repeating information she had gotten out of newspaper files.

"Sure they were. Hours after the shooting. And after about six inches of snow came down so that they had no chance to track the so-called intruder. Then the governor, who just happened to have the endorsement of the Andrews television stations, pulled them off the case. Did you know that there wasn't even an autopsy? Some local doctor filled out the death certificate. No competent medical examiner ever saw the body."

Jane became argumentative. "I suppose you're going to tell me that Andrews did it himself."

Jack shrugged. "Maybe."

"Well, for your information, Andrews was hit by the same shotgun blast that killed his wife. That would be quite a trick, wouldn't it? Being on both sides of the trigger at the same time."

"We heard that he had been scratched. But even that was impossible to prove. The doctor bandaged him up, and then they whisked him off to a private hospital." Jack paused while the waitress set down their sandwiches. Then he went on. "Didn't Ted Kennedy claim he was injured in Chappaquiddick? Hell, he even had the gall to wear a neck brace at the inquest."

Jane was defensive of Andrews. "He wasn't just bandaged, Jack. He nearly bled to death. He and his wife were together, and they were both shot."

Jack shrugged. "Okay, you may be right. It's just that none of us ever bought that business about the intruder whose tracks were covered by the snow." Then he conceded, "But that's beside the point. I liked the piece and I thought you got it just right." He again lifted his beer glass. "Congratulations!"

Jane tried to enjoy her sandwich, and when they returned to the office, she could only manage to dabble in her work. Jack Dollinger's comments had disturbed her, which only proved how much she had been taken by William Andrews's charm. There was no other reason she should care whether all the facts on an old, unsolved crime had ever been brought out into the open. She wanted William Andrews to be an innocent and suffering victim. If he had covered up evidence or faked his own injuries, then he would be an accomplice to murder.

Bob Leavitt had been first on the scene. Andrews had told her that. But how long was it before the police arrived? Snow had covered up his tire tracks and footprints, so he must have been there for quite a while. It was possible, even likely, that Leavitt had acted in his friend's best interest and done all that he could to sanitize the crime scene. But why would it need to be sanitized? An intruder had shot a man and his wife together in a remote lodge. There probably wasn't anything more that a small-town sheriff could reveal. And what was wrong with a governor using his influence to keep the state police from harassing one of his friends? Andrews had seen his wife shot to pieces and had been seriously wounded himself. Perhaps all the governor was doing was saving the victim further pain. Nothing would be gained by passing around crime-scene photos of his dead wife or dragging him in for questions that he had already answered.

But still, Jack Dollinger was an experienced journalist with a nose trained to detect the faintest hint of deceit. And Jack could still remember even the most insignificant details of events he had covered years ago. If his recollection of the murder of Kay Parker suggested a cover-up, then maybe she should do a little more digging. That night she went online to major city dailies to see what information they might still be holding on a crime that was eight years old.

8

The next morning she bumped into John Applebaum in the lobby of her office. She looked curiously at the two men and two women gathered near the reception counter, and then did a double take when she recognized him from the Paris trip. For an instant she didn't know which way to go. Just get on the elevator and act surprised when he dropped into her office? Or cross the lobby and reintroduce herself? He solved her dilemma by looking up and catching her eye just as the elevator arrived.

"Mr. Applebaum," she said with more delight than she felt, "I thought I recognized you."

He met her halfway. "Good to see you, Jane. We're here to begin looking at our new acquisition. Maybe you can show us around."

She loaded them onto the elevator and took them up to the publisher's office, located in the plusher area at the front of the floor. As soon as Jane introduced the guests, the secretary went to pieces trying to announce them and get their coffee orders at the same time. As soon as the publisher appeared, Jane took her leave, walked calmly to the door to the editorial area, and then ran frantically to Roscoe's office.

"Our new boss is here! John Applebaum! He's got his staffers with him to look us over."

Roscoe wasn't concerned. "Probably a bunch of bean counters here to check the books. They won't be interested in the editorial operation."

"He said he'd be in to see us," Jane warned.

He shrugged. "Oh, he'll look around and make a little speech about Editorial being the heart and soul of a newspaper. But believe me, it's the business department he's interested in. If he spends any time back here, it will be to count the paper clips."

He had barely finished when John Applebaum appeared in his doorway, dark jacket over dark open-collared shirt, which seemed to be the corporate uniform. For a moment Jane fantasized that the outfits might be rented by the week from a career clothes company.

"Roscoe Taylor?" he asked, looking past Jane.

Taylor ambled to his feet. "John Applebaum! Jane was just telling me that you might stop by."

"Stop by?" He seemed offended. "You're the people I want to meet. Editorial is the heart and soul of this business."

Roscoe glanced at Jane. She labored to suppress her smile. Then she excused herself and left the men to their discussion. There was a lot of laughter between them, so she figured that Applebaum hadn't brought dire news. She heard them ending their meeting with Applebaum complimenting Taylor on running a tight ship. Then, when she looked up, the new top gun in the chain was leaning into her office.

"Good to see you again, Jane."

She got up to clear her guest chair.

"No, don't bother," Applebaum told her. "I don't have even a minute. But I did want to tell you what a fine job you did on your interview piece. We all thought you got us just about right. Bill was particularly pleased."

She blushed suitably and mumbled appreciative sounds.

"He had to rush off to Mexico City," he went on, "but he asked me to tell you how impressed he was. He'll call you first chance he gets."

"Oh, that's not necessary," she answered.

Applebaum chuckled. "No, and it probably won't happen. Bill's schedule doesn't give him any 'first chance.' But you should know he thought you did a great job, under difficult circumstances."

"Oh, the trip to Paris wasn't that difficult—"

He cut her off. "I think he was referring to the difficulty of writing an objective, in-your-face article about your boss. He encourages initiative and respects courage." And then, his message delivered, he hurried back down the aisle to the business office.

Roscoe replaced him the doorway. "Did he deliver the mantra?"

"What mantra?" she asked.

"That Bill Andrews 'encourages initiative and respects courage.' We're supposed to recite it five times a day while lying prostrate and facing Wall Street."

"Oh," she said. "I thought it was a personal compliment."

"No," Roscoe answered. "It was a crock!"

She laughed. "You don't like him."

"Oh, I like him. He did his homework. He seems to know every place I ever worked and every story I ever wrote. He said that when they were evaluating the property, they all agreed that I was a key asset."

"That certainly was flattering."

"Flattering indeed," Roscoe admitted. "But then in the next breath he wondered if we really needed to pay for three wire services. He was thinking of cutting the whole chain back to two."

"And you said . . ."

"I said I'd probably stick with three even if the other editors thought they could get by on two. That was when he stopped telling jokes and taught me the corporate mantra."

Jane had to wonder. Was John Applebaum simply on a goodwill mission, bringing words of cheer to the whole organization? Had William Andrews really praised her story, or was that just part of Applebaum's spiel? Roscoe seemed cynical, but all good reporters were cynical. So why did she believe that Andrews had taken the time to read her story? Or that he had promised to call her? Maybe it was all part of John Applebaum's goodwill tour.

Art was waiting for her in the apartment. His washing machine was leaking, and he had stopped by to run a few things through hers. Jane made a mental note to change the locks. If she didn't, she would see more of her ex-husband than she had before he was ex.

"I brought dinner," he said. There were two containers of Chinese on the kitchen counter. "And there's a pretty decent Chablis in your freezer. At least as decent as a four-dollar

Chablis gets to be." She took down plates and spooned out the chicken with pea pods and the shrimp rice. He attacked the wine and was disappointed to find that it had a screw-on cap.

"Art, do you remember the Andrews murder?" she asked, introducing a topic that was worrying her. "He and his wife were shot by a burglar, or something. It must have been seven or eight years ago."

He ran through his memory bank. "Yeah. Some nut broke in to their house and shot up the place. She was a big society lady, and he was the new kid on the block." Then he wondered, "Did they ever get the guy? I forget what happened, but I don't remember there being a trial or anything."

Jane didn't think there had been. The intruder had escaped. The problem was that some people suspected that there had never been an intruder. There had been conjecture of a suicide, or some sort of dark secret that Andrews had covered up. She repeated her conversation with Jack Dollinger, but then added that people like to think the worst about the rich and famous.

She went to her computer and began researching the news coverage of the crime while Art sat on the floor and sorted his laundry. They were separately involved when the phone rang. Jane took off an earring and answered. "Hello."

"J. J. Warren?"

"Yeah . . ." She recognized the voice. "Yes it is."

"This is Bill Andrews. Am I interrupting anything?"

She glanced at Art, who was rolling his socks. "No. Not at all."

"I just wanted to tell you that I liked your story. It was a terrific piece of business reporting, informative and well balanced."

"I appreciate that. Thank you very much." Art glanced up. He could tell by her tone that the call wasn't as casual as she was pretending. He gave her his full attention.

"You made me look a bit power-hungry and very aloof. I don't see myself that way, but you may just be right. I'll have to watch myself more carefully."

"Oh no, certainly not aloof," she insisted. "Just . . . distracted."

There was an awkward pause. From his place on the floor, Art mouthed, "William Andrews," with a wide-eyed look that made it a question. Jane responded with an excited nod while she tried to think of something to say. "I heard you were in Mexico City."

"I am. Just got back to my hotel room with half a dozen financial reports that I have to wade through. But before I got . . . distracted . . . I wanted to let you know that I read your piece and thought it was terrific."

"Well, I appreciate your taking the time to call. It really wasn't necessary."

Art was standing, leaning in to hear the conversation. Jane swiveled in her chair to get away from him and waved him back toward his laundry. There was another break in the conversation. This time Andrews filled the void.

"I think I'm going to try to change my image. I don't like being ruthless and aloof."

"You're not! At least, you weren't. That's just the way you come across."

"That's not the way I want to come across. I'd like to be more laid-back. Someone who has a full life in spite of being a workaholic. And I want you to help me."

She was stunned. "You want me to work for you?"

Art reacted with mock applause.

"No!" Andrews snapped. "I want you to have dinner with me. I'll be back in New York tomorrow. Can we have dinner tomorrow night?"

"Tomorrow? Dinner? Why, yes, of course."

Andrews went on quickly, like a boy who is asking for his first date and is afraid to stop talking for fear he'll never be able to start again. "I'll land in Bridgeport. I'll call you when we're on the ground so you'll know when to expect me."

"Okay," Jane agreed, trying desperately not to sound too eager. "Do you need directions?"

"No, I have your address. I'll get directions off the Internet. And could you wear that black dress you picked up in Paris?"

"Sure. I like that one, too, Mr. Andrews," she said.

"Bill," he told her. "Mr. Andrews sounds too . . . aloof."

"Okay. But then you'll have to call me Jane."

"See you tomorrow, Jane." The line went silent. It was a good five seconds before she hung up.

" 'Call me Jane,' " Art mocked. Then he said in disbelief, "You just asked William Andrews to call you Jane?"

"Yes, but only after he insisted that I call him Bill."

"Wow!" Art applauded. "And all from one interview. You sure you had your clothes on the whole time?"

"Don't be an ass," she said, and then she remembered the details of their very first meeting. But she wouldn't go into that with Art.

He was tossing his underwear into his laundry basket. "Are you meeting him in Manhattan?"

"No, he's picking me up here."

"Here? William Andrews is coming to the Shoreline Apartments? The rental agent will go crazy. She'll want full press coverage."

"Art, I swear, if you breathe a word about this to anyone . . ."

He raised his hands defensively. "No fear! But is it okay if I hang around? I'd like to meet the guy."

"Art!"

"Okay. But I would like the big tycoon to know that I had you first."

9

Jane didn't want to wear the same dress Andrews had seen in Paris, so she took a long lunch hour and went shopping at the mall. It wasn't the same experience as the dress shop in Paris, but there were racks and racks of outfits suited for drinks, dinner, whatever. She found an understated number in deep gray with touches of black lace, tasteful, appropriate, and by no means suggestive.

"Big date tonight?" Jack Dollinger asked when she was back at her desk.

"What . . . how did you know?" She had decided that she wouldn't tell anyone in the office that she was having dinner with the new boss.

Dollinger touched his toe to the box that was lying inside her doorway "Doesn't a new dress at lunch mean a date for dinner?"

She was relieved when she realized that the dress-shop box was in plain sight. Jack had just made a lucky guess. "Dinner, yes. Date, no," she lied. Then she jumped into a business story that had come in over the wire and asked which one of them should cover it. The change of subject worked, and Dollinger went away with no further interest in her evening.

But she began to rethink her decision about not telling anyone. Roscoe Taylor probably had a right to know that one of his staff was having dinner with the man at the top of the pyramid. Roscoe was remarkably secure, but still it would be disconcerting to learn that the boss and a young woman who knew all the newspaper's secrets might by sharing pillow talk. And Roscoe would certainly learn. He was a pig sniffing truffles when it came to the activities of his reporters.

Jane sat down across from him and waited until he looked up from his editing. "I just thought you should know that I'm

having dinner with William Andrews. Probably just an ac-
knowledgment of the article, but I suppose there might be a
few words about our operation."

"Thank you," he said with a half smile.

Her eyes narrowed. "You knew?"

"I knew that he was diverting his flight to Bridgeport, and
I knew that he wasn't having dinner with me. And then you
took a two-hour lunch to buy a dress." He raised his palms in
a gesture that asked, Was there any other conclusion?

"Any seeds you want planted? Any words of wisdom?"
Jane asked.

Roscoe smiled pleasantly. "Just 'bon appétit!' "

There was a message from Arthur waiting for her at home.
He had discovered that another of his disks was missing—the
revisions to the second act of his play about the daughter of a
president taken hostage. Could he come over to look for it?
She called back, got him on the fourth ring, and tried to be
brief. "Not tonight, Art. I'm being picked up and I want the
place presentable. I sure as hell don't want you here when he
arrives."

He sighed. "Okay then, but it has to be tomorrow night because I've got ideas that won't keep." She agreed to the next
night. "Be careful," he warned. "He's probably going to demand a retraction."

She showered and rehearsed her wittiest lines of conversation while the water scalded down her back. She tried three
sets of jewelry with the new dress, picking black imitation
pearls that matched the lace trim. She changed the shoes and
the stockings and then tried still another pair of shoes—anything to take her mind off the after-dinner possibilities.

What should she do if he suggested that she join him for a
nightcap in the city? Easy! "I'm dead tired, and I'd hate to
ruin a lovely evening by falling asleep on you." That was direct—I'm not going home with you. And yet evasive. Was
she afraid of falling asleep in the car and missing the nightcap, or afraid of falling asleep in his arms and missing whatever it was that he had in mind?

But what if he didn't suggest a nightcap in the city?

Should she dismiss him at the door with "Thank you. The lamb was delicious"? That would be perfectly proper among business associates. Or should she invite him up for a drink? Generally, that implied you weren't eager for the evening to end. But with the head of the corporation, did it suggest a willingness to please and a determination to get ahead? The fact was that there wasn't anything she could say that would be perfectly natural. "No" could be taken as hostility. "Yes" might seem ambitious. Given their relative status in the corporation, was there any response that wouldn't seem carefully contrived?

Her buzzer sounded. She expected to hear his voice but instead heard someone with an Indian or Pakistani accent. "Mr. Andrews has just received a telephone call, so he wonders if you would come down to the lobby? Or if you would like me to come up and escort you down to the car?"

"No problem," Jane answered. "I'll be right down." She regretted her decision the instant she hung up. He got a phone call? Big deal! He could have told the caller he was busy and to call back in the morning. If he was taking her out, then he shouldn't be taking phone calls. What was he going to do if his damn phone rang while they tasted the wine? Leave her to drink the whole bottle while he did business in the Far East?

She felt demeaned riding down in the elevator by herself, a silk scarf pulled around her shoulders like one of the ladies going out for their night at the ballet. And she was even more embarrassed when the chauffeur, who had dark Indian features, tipped his cap and offered his arm. It was as if William Andrews expected his women to be delivered.

He was still on the phone when she slipped into the seat beside him. He smiled, made a thumbs-up gesture at her attire, and continued with his conversation. The driver got behind the wheel and started out of the parking lot as if they had stopped to pick up a package. She was fitting unobtrusively into the routine of the great man's business day.

Jane reached over, pulled the phone from his hand, and pressed the END button. His hand remained immobile, stunned by the same shock that widened his eyes. She found the button that powered the side window down. Then, with seeming indifference, she tossed the phone out into the night. She turned back to find him in open-mouthed amazement. "It's nice to see you again," she said to Andrews. "I hope you like my dress. I bought it just for you."

Her own brass amazed her. Had she really interrupted his telephone call? And thrown his phone away? What in hell right had she to assume he would treat her as anything but an employee? Why should he care that she had bought the damn knockoff designer dress for him?

His eyes narrowed and his slack jaw closed. Then his mouth broke out into an uncontrolled smile. "I love your dress," he said. Then he leaned over and kissed her.

"Sorry about the phone," she said when he gave her the opportunity.

"It would have just been in the way," Andrews allowed. He kissed her again.

The limo ride suggested the mood for the dinner. It was to be a romantic encounter with none of the business clichés, a merging of persons rather than of product lines and departments. He guided her past a captain who had mastered the art of walking backwards while bowing obsequiously, to a table in front of a stone fireplace. The restaurant was suburban rustic in its decor but definitely upscale in its table settings. They ordered flavored martinis straight up, and he chose a bottle from the wine list. But the menus were incidental and remained unopened. All his attention was focused on Jane, and she felt paralyzed by the power in his eyes. *Stay calm*, she reminded herself. *This probably isn't really happening*. There was no reason why she would captivate William Andrews, who could probably have any woman in the world as his dinner companion.

He began with her. He had missed her terribly since their day in Paris and had wanted to call her. But he was buried in day-to-day nonsense and then turmoil in a Mexican subsidiary. He might have said hello, but he wouldn't have had the time to take her out. So he had decided to call her from

Mexico and arrange their date before he got back to his office and became embroiled in another crisis.

The waiter interrupted, and they took a minute to order, but Andrews instantly brought the conversation back to her. She was bright. He knew she had mastered his enterprise during the interview, and the article she wrote was the most perceptive of anything on Andrews Global Network that had appeared in the media.

She was courageous. No one had ever dressed him down the way she had in the airplane. He really had been acting like an "insensitive gorilla" and she hadn't been afraid to tell him so. "And then tonight, when you tossed my phone out the window . . ." He shook his head in admiration.

She was beautiful, of course. He had seen her in her most revealing attire, he said, reminding her of the towel that had been wrapped around her head. And then, that night, she was breathtaking in her new black dress.

But most of all, she was real. No pretensions. No false modesty. And with enough self-confidence to be herself in any situation. "People often rehearse how they're going to act with me, or what they're going to say to me," William Andrews told her. "And it comes across that way, like lines from a play. But you do what you want and say what you mean. I can't imagine you practicing what you were going to say to me."

Jane blushed, remembering the dialogues she had run in her shower. She hoped her color passed for embarrassment at being so grandly complimented.

He paused again while the wine was opened and the food set before them, then shifted from compliments to questions. "How did you ever get to be a financial editor on a poky, backwater newspaper?" It didn't sound like an interrogation, just an opportunity for Jane to talk about herself.

She began eagerly, realizing how little he really knew about her, starting with her education at a local college and then working her way back to a typical suburban high school stint. "I never really knew what I wanted to do," she con-

fessed. "Just get by, I suppose." Her story was an ongoing series of personal vignettes, devoid of purpose and with no particular ambition. She realized that it must be a dull tale next
to the biography of his first wife and tried to spice it up
whenever she could. Even then it left a lot to be desired.

"You didn't tell me about your marriage," he reminded her.

"A mistake," she said simply. "The wrong guy for the
wrong reasons at the wrong time. Nobody's fault, but just
something that never should have happened."

"You must have loved him," he said with a tone that suggested jealousy.

"Art and I were in the same English class. We worked together in the library and got very comfortable with each
other. He was planning to be a playwright, and that seemed
very artsy and romantic. He never doubted that he would own
Broadway, and I began to believe it, too. By comparison, my
job—writing local society news items for the paper—seemed
trivial and unimportant. I guess I was taken in by his air of
genius. I felt honored when, out of the blue, he asked me to
marry him."

"But you didn't love him?"

"How could I? We weren't even dating. But I did move in
with him, and I guess I convinced myself I loved him because
why else would I be sleeping with him?" She smiled at her
own foolishness. "So we filed papers and got married."

"And it didn't work out the way you expected?"

"I don't know what I expected, but nothing changed. He
kept talking about the importance of his work, even though
he seemed to do very little of it. Meanwhile, I got a couple of
promotions, made decent money, and paid all the bills. It
took me a couple of years to realize that nothing was ever going to change, so when he decided we should split, I had no
real objections."

"Was it painful?" he asked, pressing for details.

"Not at all. Things went on as normal except he moved
into a room in his brother's house. He moved, but not all this
things! He still had to come over to our apartment to use the
computer. He kept food in my refrigerator."

"Is he any good?"

She was startled. "As a husband?"

"No, as a playwright."

She shrugged. "I won't know until he finishes something."

It was over dessert when William Andrews began to lower the mask he had been hiding behind. His life, he said, had been ripped apart and left with a gaping hole. He had worked furiously and moved quickly so that he wouldn't have to look at his wounds. But Jane had slowed him just enough for him to see all that he was missing. "I've got two choices," he said. "Pick up the pace so that I don't notice. That's what I've been doing for the past eight years. Or!"—he paused dramatically—"do something to heal the wound and find someone to fill the empty space."

The message was clear. He wanted her to become part of his life. But that was too fantastic. The great William Andrews didn't need an editor from one of his newspapers to fill the void left by his world-class society wife. So what was he getting at? A clandestine relationship that he could turn on and off according to his needs? A temporary fling until he could gather his wits and find a new Kay Parker?

"Mr. Andrews, I'm—"

"Bill," he insisted. "No woman should call a man she's kissed by his last name."

She started again. "Bill, I don't think you're at all . . . damaged. But I'll help in any way I can." Then she reconsidered. "Not in *any* way. But if you need a hostess . . . or a companion—"

"I can hire hostesses," he interrupted, "and I have lots of companions. I was hoping that you might be more than that. I'd like to . . . see more of you."

"Me?"

He grinned. "Is there someone else having dinner with us?"

Her guard was up. It sounded like the beginning of an invitation to join him for a nightcap.

"I'd like to get to know you better," he went on, "and give you a chance to learn about me. I've been keeping women at arm's length ever since . . ." His voice trailed off into silence.

Was he serious? Was he suggesting that she should try to
fill the void in his life? Or was this a morbid come-on designed to get her sympathy? It sounded like a line. The
chance to help William Andrews recover from his great loss
would get a lot of women out of their garters.

"The day we spent in Paris," Andrews continued, "was the
happiest day I've had in years. And at dinner, when you were
analyzing my company and dazzling my executives, I suddenly felt very proud of you. It was as if you belonged to me
and I was delighted to have you performing so beautifully. I
was like a parent watching his kid at a school recital."

Jane laughed. "You can't be that old."

"Okay," he said, agreeing that he wasn't old enough to be
her father, "then like a guy whose sister just won the Miss
America contest. I've been asking myself, 'Why is it important to me that Jane Warren be admired and respected?' And
the only answer I can come up with is that I've fallen in love
with her."

Wow! If this was a line, it was the best one she had ever
heard. He seemed sincere, struggling to put his feelings into
words. And honest. He was certainly leaving himself vulnerable. But his story sounded too much like a fairy tale, the
handsome prince falling in love with the lowly girl who
swept up the cinders.

"I'm very flattered," Jane finally managed to say. "And I
would like to see more of you. The truth is that I've been
keeping men at arm's length. My first experience was . . . disappointing. I've become very guarded and probably cynical."

He smiled with great relief. "Wonderful. I was terrified
that you'd think I was looking to lure you back to my apartment. That all this was just another line."

Exactly what I had been thinking, Jane thought. "Oh God,
no! Why would I ever think that?" she answered.

He reached across the table, took her hand, and held it ten-
derly. Then he launched into the second step of his courtship.

"How about next weekend at my country house? I'll get
the kids home from school so that you can meet them. Actu-

ally, so that we both can meet them. I haven't seen them in quite a while."

Jane hesitated. She wasn't good around teenagers. Given a choice, she'd rather be shot from a cannon than spend a weekend with his children.

"I'd like you to see me in a family setting instead of a corporate office. We'll have a relaxing day in the country. What do you say?"

She knew she wasn't ready to meet his kids—or anyone in his family, for that matter. But it seemed important to him. The hole in his life had damaged everyone, and he needed to see that she could fill it for everyone. "Okay," she agreed. "Just call me with the arrangements."

William Andrews practically exploded with joy.

He held her hand on the drive back to her house and then got out to open her door. In the process, he and the Indian chauffeur collided, which broke any tension of their parting. He walked her to her door, said good night, and pecked her on the cheek. "I'll call you," he promised.

She was in a swooning mood when she opened her door, floating a bit as if swept off her feet. She turned on the light and pulled up short. Someone had been in her apartment, undoubtedly Art looking for his damn disk.

He hadn't disturbed the furniture or dumped his laundry on the floor. He probably didn't want her to know that he had been there. But the door that slid over her computer alcove was open, and she had carefully closed it on the chance that William Andrews might step in. The papers to the left of the monitor were in a neat stack instead of their usual disarray. Most telling, some of the disks that she kept in her file drawer were stacked to the right of the monitor.

"Damn!" She went into her bedroom, kicked off her heels, and picked up the telephone. It was after ten, but Art was usually up half the night. And if she did happen to wake him, tough. He had no right letting himself in, particularly when she had told him that they would solve his problem tomorrow.

She started to dial but was stopped by a sound out in the

living room. There was an instant of panic. Someone had broken in. But her courage returned when she realized that it had to be her former husband. Probably he was just finishing his search when she had walked in and interrupted him. She put down the phone and started out of the bedroom, still in her stocking feet. She hadn't yet reached the living room when she heard the front door click.

Again she stopped short and listened. Had someone just come in? No, Jane decided, it was Art letting himself out. The bastard was skulking away so that he could pretend he had never been there.

"Art!" she shouted, and ran to the door. She pulled it open and stuck her head out into the corridor. No one was there. She ran to the elevator and pounded on the button, hoping to catch it before its descent. The door opened immediately on the empty car that was waiting on her floor, exactly where she had left it. Then she heard footsteps on the stairs. Jane raced to the stairwell, but she was too late. By the time she got there, she could hear the front door banging down in the lobby.

She took the first step, knowing that she could still get down to the street before he pulled out in his car, but as soon as she stepped off the carpet, she realized she had left her shoes behind. She went back to the apartment, gathered her heels, and jammed them on. But before she could get to her feet, she heard a car accelerating out of the parking area. She kicked the shoes off and lifted the telephone. But, of course, he had just pulled out of her driveway and wouldn't be home yet. "Art, you bastard!" she yelled at what was once his side of the bed.

She phoned him the instant she woke up and was delighted when he sounded as if she had awakened him. "Good morning, Arthur. I was calling to see if you had a productive evening." Her sarcasm was searing.

After a pause, his scratchy voice asked, "Jane?"

"Yes, your onetime nursemaid. I'm just checking in to make sure you weren't injured during your getaway."

Another pause. "What time is it?" he asked.

"Very early, but I wish it were even earlier. I'd like to know that I was causing you real pain."

He cleared his throat and seemed to sip some water, probably from the bottle he always left at his bedside. "Jane, did you just get home?"

"You know damn well when I got home. You were here!"

"Where?"

"In my apartment, hiding behind a chair. I heard you close the door behind you when you left."

"Last night? I wasn't in your apartment."

"Don't lie, Art. You were at my computer, searching for your damn missing disk. You know, the one where the president's daughter gets kidnapped."

He yawned. "Aren't we going to do that tonight?"

"Not anymore," Jane snapped. "We were, but since you took the liberty to let yourself in and search through my files, we'll just have to let the president's daughter die."

Another pause. "Jane, have you had your coffee yet? Because you're not making any sense at all. I was here all night."

"Art, I saw you!"

"You saw me? In your apartment?"

"I saw that you had been through my files. And I heard you leave."

"Jane, I don't know how to make you believe this, but I wasn't in your apartment and I didn't go through your files." Then he asked, "You're not doing another one of your exposés, are you? Maybe one of our selectmen wants to see what you're going to say about him."

He sounded genuinely confused. Art was a terrible liar, usually contradicting himself in the process. He sounded as if he were telling the truth.

"You weren't here?"

"No. I was never even in your neighborhood."

"Well, who then?" Now Jane was the one genuinely puzzled.

"Maybe your new boyfriend has his own secret service," Art suggested. "Maybe they're checking you out to make sure you're not a spy for some socialist cell. Big-time capital-ists are deathly afraid of socialists."

"Don't be an idiot," Jane fired back, and slammed down the phone. She was positive that wasn't what William Andrews had meant when he said he wanted to know her better.

IO

Jane had no trouble gathering information on Bill Andrews's first wife. Kay Parker was all over the society pages for the years between her coming-out and her tragic death. As Queen of the Cotillion, she was photographed with an honor guard of West Point cadets, their swords drawn to protect her virtue. At Vassar, she chaired committees that fed the hungry and bought cows for African villages. Next came her working career as a junior editor for a women's fashion magazine and then as a features reporter for NBC in New York. She had taken a six-month leave of absence to ride with the U.S. equestrian team and scored a few points in international competitions. All that was before her twenty-fourth birthday.

When she moved actively into society, there was immediate speculation of marriage to any number of eligible bachelors. The candidates included the leading man in a Broadway musical who escorted her to the Tony Awards, the great-grandson of a man who had owned railroads and stashed away the profits, a land baron who was developing a thirty-mile stretch of the New Jersey coast, and the backup quarterback of the New York Giants. A corporate executive, no matter how successful, wouldn't stand a chance. Kay Parker was far beyond anyone who earned his money in trade.

Society was stunned when she turned up in Saint-Tropez on the arm of William Andrews. At the time, he was considered "impolite," a general term that explained his casual attire, frequently unkempt appearance, passion for loud motorcycles and speedboats, and business aggressiveness. He was also a regular on the financial pages, making amounts of money that were blatantly obscene to those who thought no one should have as much money as they did. His betters smirked when he used the wrong fork and shook their heads when he dozed at the opera. The thought of their princess be-

ing manhandled by someone who bought his clothes off a
plain pipe rack sent shivers through the ladies and raised har-
rumphs among the men.

The supermarket tabloids claimed, in sequence, that they
were already married, that he was impotent, and that she was
pregnant and abandoned. When they were guests of an aging
French film actress, a grainy photo of the three of them ran
under the headline MÉNAGE À TROIS. One day William and
Kay were suffering a heartbreaking separation, the next they
were into kinky sex, and a day later they were both prisoners
of a drug habit. New York social doyens held their noses as if
the young couple had been wallowing in a barrel of fish.

But then they married in a small church on Sardinia and
honeymooned across the Continent. They were houseguests
of the reigning Rothschild, lunched with the queen of Den-
mark, and had an audience with the pope. They returned to an
apartment that took up the top two floors of a building with a
view of Central Park, and bought a weekend place in western
New Jersey with thirty rooms and paddocks for twenty
horses. The tabloids lost interest, but the society pages began
to see the young couple in a more favorable light. When the
Prince of Wales borrowed their house for his attendants and
his polo ponies, they rocketed back to status.

Kay proved to be thoroughly domesticated. She took her
position in the proper charities and lavished money on the
arts. When her children came, she expanded her interests into
children' hospitals and headed committees to send doctors
and medical supplies abroad. She immersed herself in youth
activities, bringing 4-H to midtown Manhattan and sponsor-
ing Scout troops that regularly hiked in the park.

Jane found her picture everywhere. She was in jodhpurs
next to a champion jumper, in a full-length gown of pearls for
the Philharmonic, on skis with her children at Aspen, in a
stylish suit on the podium at a political convention, in camping attire at a Girl Scout jamboree. Then there was her in-
volvement in the Andrews business affairs. She was by her
husband's side at a satellite launching in French Guiana, ded-
icating an up-link at the palace in Bahrain, hosting a panel of

journalists in Jerusalem, and frolicking with the casts of television sitcoms. She was even photographed in a Red Sox uniform when Andrews Global Network won the rights to broadcast the team's games in Latin America. It seemed that in a typical week Kay Parker had spent more time in front of a camera than Jane generally spent at her desk.

Despite their variety, all the photos were flattering. Kay had high, well-defined cheekbones that made her eyes seem sultry and her smile mysterious. Either she was an expert in cosmetics or she had a makeup artist living with her, because her complexion was flawless. Her hair seemed shimmering ebony that simply grew into a stylist's creation. Her clothes, even those she wore for camping, were on the cutting edge—the latest fashions before they became commonplace. Her figure was perfectly shaped—a model but with a real butt and high breasts. She had somehow remained thin even during her pregnancies.

As she plowed through her research and read the countless articles, Jane began to feel clammy. It was a symptom of the fear that was growing within her, changing her suspicions of inadequacy to stark terror. William Andrews had suggested that there was a hole in his life, but it was actually more like a canyon. Parker had painted his life's canvas with a wide brush. When she had fallen, she had gone right through the painting, tearing away everything but the flimsy frame.

Was that what Bill meant when he said he wanted to know her better? Was he measuring her for a new painting? Good God, it would take a fair-size harem to fill Kay Parker's shoes. An ordinary woman would be doomed to failure.

As she scanned back through the electronic clippings, Jane couldn't find one role that she could fill. The skills of a makeup artist? In the mornings she looked as if she had just gotten out of bed, and in the evenings as if she was ready to go back. Her fashion flair? Her closet was full of quality clothes that would be out of style long before they wore out. Dinner with the Prince of Wales? She probably wouldn't know how to attack the place setting. Polo ponies? She got sick on the merry-go-round. And skiing in Aspen? They could save time by setting her leg before she got on the lift.

Jane was particularly shaken by the shots of Kay smiling out through the flap of a tent with half a dozen Girl Scouts behind her. Even when she was a teenager Jane had thought that young women were vain and spiteful, and the thought of spending a week in a tent full of blossoming adolescents was absolutely terrifying. How had Kay managed to make it look like one of life's joys?

She still had her printouts scattered around her and the photo of the happy campers up on the screen when William Andrews's phone call came through. "It's all set," he announced with genuine enthusiasm. "The house out in White Marsh is open, and the kids are coming for the weekend. You can make it, can't you?" She hesitated a bit too long. "Jane! Is something wrong?"

"No, no. Everything is perfect. I've been looking forward to it."

"Great! Can you cut out early on Friday? I can pick you up in a helicopter at Westchester or Sikorsky. The trip is only an hour."

"I'll have to ask my boss. He doesn't like his people starting the weekend early."

"Jane, I *am* the boss!"

"No," she answered. "Unless you want me to act like one of your staff."

"Oh God, no. I don't want you to act like anything."

Not even like Kay Parker, she thought. "I'll talk to Roscoe. But I won't use your name. It wouldn't be fair."

"Right," he agreed. "It looks like I'd better start sucking up to Roscoe."

II

The helicopter lifted from the Sikorsky field in Bridgeport as the sun was setting in the west. She and Andrews sat side by side in the narrow cabin, each looking through a different window. He had made sure that she had the southern view looking down toward the Manhattan skyline, now a contrast of crimson sunlight and deepening shadows. Lights were coming on in the windows, giving the gritty streets an aura of fantasy that left her speechless.

"Incredible," Bill said. Her only answer was a nod and a smile.

They passed the eastern end of the George Washington Bridge and broke out over the Hudson River, putting all of Manhattan into a panorama. She could see the shadow of her helicopter against the buildings until it was well out over the water, and then the Statue of Liberty came into view. The New Jersey waterfront passed beneath them, then an industrial band of smokestacks and refinery towers. Seconds later the harbor was behind them and they were passing over clusters of suburbs in the process of turning on their lights. Ahead, the sun was touching the tops of mountains in Pennsylvania.

They flew over open country, a picturesque landscape of forests, fields, and pastures beginning to show their fall colors, and then over horse country with tidy paddocks marked out by white fences. Gradually the rotor noise changed and they began a turning descent.

"We're home," Andrews said, and pointed across to a hilltop mansion surrounded by neatly defined fields.

"It's beautiful," Jane said, although she really wanted to shout, "Wow!" The estate got bigger and bigger as the chopper lowered.

They landed softly on a paved square. She noticed the wind sock hanging limp in the stillness and saw the house a few hundred yards away. Even at that distance it looked huge, a white-sided two-story structure that sprawled in several directions under a variety of roof shapes and angles. It seemed the perfect setting for a country squire, a role that seemed completely at odds with the hard-charging executive running away from his past.

Andrews introduced the estate manager, who climbed down from a Land Rover that would have looked more at home on the Serengeti. He was a hands-on type, middle-aged, and well suited to the jeans and sweater he wore. He referred to them as "Mr. Andrews" and "Ms. Warren." William Andrews called him Burt.

The house had a country-farm look that suited its location perfectly. Many of the surrounding estates, built with instant Wall Street fortunes, fancied themselves English manors or Rhine castles and looked ridiculously out of place. Andrews had built with white clapboard, open porches, and trellises to support colorful flowers. The chimneys—there were four of them—were whitewashed stone. The pathways were gravel. Instead of dressing up for maximum attention, the house dressed down so as not to distract from the land. It promised comfort rather than luxury.

The interior, Jane saw as soon as she stepped through the foyer, delivered on the promise. Soft chairs clustered around woven rugs encouraged conversation and intimacy. The living-room fireplace was huge, suggesting a great outpouring of warmth. Kitchen counters were broad, hung with copper pots and pans to support genuine cooking and baking. She fell in love with it instantly.

"It's beautiful," she said. "So comfortable and friendly."

"Kay did most of this with a couple of architects and God knows how many decorators," Andrews commented idly.

"But you do like it?"

"Yeah, sure," he said, but in a tone that made his answer inconsequential. He apparently didn't waste much effort on the decor of his surroundings.

Andrews introduced the housekeeper, Agnes, a businesslike woman with a tall, straight physique. "She's Burt's

better half, and she keeps both Burt and the house running."
She was solicitous of Jane and promised to have dinner on
the table in just a few minutes. "I hope you like duck," she
said, turning back to her stove.

"Where are the kids?" he asked.

Agnes hesitated. "In their rooms. I think they're planning
on eating upstairs."

William's jaw tightened. "No, they'll be eating with us."
He started for the stairs.

"Bill," Jane called after him, and went to the bottom step,
where he had paused. "Meeting me is probably very awkward for them. Maybe they should pick the time and place."

"Don't be silly! They're dying to meet you. They probably
don't know that we've arrived."

She looked after him as he ran up the stairs, wondering
how his children could have missed the arrival of a helicopter. In truth, she was the one feeling awkward. The thought of
making conversation with two unknown teenagers throughout dinner made her ill.

As she predicted, the dinner went badly. Cassie and Craig
presented themselves with all the propriety and dignity that
boarding schools can instill. But their demeanor was bored
and their responses surly.

"Delicious, isn't it?" Jane said at her first taste of the dinner, giving them an opportunity to comment on something of
little importance.

"It's a duck," Craig deadpanned.

She tried Cassie. "What lovely pearls," she complimented,
looking at the string that hung around the young woman's
neck.

"They're fake," Cassie said. And then she added for her
father's benefit that "all the kids at school can tell they're not
real."

William tried to ride to the rescue. "How's the baseball
team shaping up?" he asked his son.

"I don't play baseball," Craig answered in a bored tone.

Andrews grimaced. "I thought you were hoping to play
shortstop?"

Craig tried to pile his string beans like a cord of wood. "That was last year," he mumbled.

Craig and Cassie went at each other when the dessert was served. Cassie demanded a calorie count before she would even taste the custard. "You know I'm trying to lose weight," she scolded Agnes. Craig commented that she'd have to try harder because she had the figure of a pear. Cassie responded with the charge that Craig was still bald below the belt, and the family bonding went downhill from there.

After the children left the table, Andrews sat staring into his coffee. Jane stayed at the table, directly across from him but trying desperately to make herself invisible. Agnes removed the dishes without making a sound. The silence was deafening.

"That wasn't the meeting that I had in mind," he finally said without looking up.

"They're . . . at a tough age," she answered, trying to assure him that he wasn't entirely to blame for their behavior. "I have nieces and nephews who—"

"They need a mother," he interrupted.

Not me, buddy boy, Jane thought. But she said, "They've suffered a terrible shock."

She assented when he asked if she would like to take a walk out to the barn to see the horses. Anything would have been an improvement over the grim mood inside the house. "They're equestrian mounts," he said as they walked across an open pasture. "Kay loved the animals, and she was very involved in competitive riding."

"When did you get into it?" she asked, not remembering anything in her research that would put William Andrews in the saddle.

"Me? I'm not into horses. I'm a city kid." He laughed. "Horses were something you bet on when I was growing up." But then he went on to explain that Kay had had grooms and pasturing arrangements and stud deals. He had kept everything in place, counting on the integrity of Kay's agents and simply paying the bills. "I go riding once in a while," he admitted. "I figure an hour in the saddle costs me about a million dollars."

Jane had not been prepared for the beauty of the horses, or the effect they had on her. They went to her immediately and nuzzled her hand to get the sugar that William had provided. They seemed to look directly into her eyes as if taking her measure. And they apparently decided that she was no threat.

"Would you like to go riding in the morning? We ride out to the Delaware River. Burt drives out ahead so that we have breakfast waiting."

"I don't ride," she said more definitively than she intended.

"Not at all?"

"Oh, I've been on horses. But just old cart horses that hardly lifted their feet. Nothing as spirited as these."

"We're in no hurry," he assured her. "If you want, Burt can set up breakfast at the corner of the property and we can take all morning getting there."

She tipped her head toward the animals that were licking her hands in the hunt for more treats. "Won't they mind? Won't they know that I'm no horsewoman?"

"Jane, don't be silly. They don't even know that they're horses. And I'll keep you between me and Cassie so that if the mount tries to get frisky, we'll be able to quiet him down."

She weighed her alternatives. Refuse outright and she might break the budding relationship. Agree to ride a horse and she might break her neck. "Sure," she said. "Maybe it's something you remember, like riding a bicycle."

It wasn't. In the morning the horse kept shifting and turning as she tried to mount it. She made three false tries at the stirrup and then let Bill cup his hands to boost her aboard. Once she was up she sat as gingerly as if she were astride a bomb.

It didn't help that Cassie and Craig kept exchanging jokes behind the back of their hands. She thought it was her attire—jeans, hiking boots, and a light sweater—topped by a helmet that tipped down over her eyes. But then she decided that it was her posture. She was slouched forward, ready to wrap her arms around the animal's neck at the first sign of trouble.

Bill slid open the barn door. Craig nudged his horse out, guiding it easily. Cassie seemed only to flex her knees, and her horse stepped out as if it had a written set of instructions. Jane clicked her tongue and dug in her heels. Her horse ignored her completely. Andrews took the bridle and led her out along with his horse. Then he mounted.

"Under the big oak," he said to his children.

"That's all," Craig pouted. "I can get there in two minutes. Then what am I supposed to do?"

"We'll just walk over," William answered. "Jane hasn't been on a horse in years, and she isn't up for a race."

Jane laughed. "Sorry," she told Craig. "I'm just hoping that this horse won't bounce too much. Galloping, or bounding over fences, is out of the question."

"My mother won ribbons," Cassie said, ensuring that Jane knew exactly what they expected in a replacement.

"I may need them as bandages," she answered. "Did she win anything I could use as a tourniquet?"

Cassie sneered. "Let's go," she said to her brother. They both jerked forward and spurred their mounts. They were at a gallop within two strides.

"We'll just take our time," Andrews said, noticing the death grip that she had on the reins.

"Lots of time. I have no plans for beating your kids to breakfast."

She was amazed at how pleasant it was. They rode side by side, the horses perfectly content with the slow pace. Andrews struck a few cowboy poses, looking over his land with a sense of mastery, as if he could make the soil sprout. He pointed out trees and rock outcroppings that defined the borders of his land.

"You like this, don't you?" she said, surprised to see his pastoral side.

"Now and then," he answered. "It's a nice break from business. But I sure as hell couldn't do this every day."

They chatted easily. He had no difficulty in recounting

how Kay had found the land and fenced the pastures. He pointed out the corral where the training jumps were still in place. "She was out here every chance she got, usually with her riding friends. But she had a lot of constituencies that kept her traveling. There were yachting friends and partying friends, South American friends and European friends. She didn't have as much time out here as she would have liked. But she trained most of the horses she rode."

The children, he went on, loved to ride with her. "Of course, they weren't into their hormones yet. They were still pleasant and polite. They loved it when she showed them how to take the low jumps. I think it would have helped if she had had more time with them. I've tried every now and then to get them into activities where I might be able to show them something. I'm a fair skier and a damn good sailor. But they've never been interested."

Jane tried to be consoling. Their interests were bound to change. "They'll meet friends who are into skiing, and then you'll be the family hero. The first time some stud asks Cassie to go sailing, you'll be the father she's always adored." He seemed to be in a better mood when they reached the campsite, where Agnes was cooking eggs.

They weren't roughing it. There was a safari table with folding chairs, a brick-walled grill, a plastic jug of water, a Thermos of steaming coffee, plastic plates and tableware. The pickup truck that had carried all the gear out to the campsite, and would take everything back to the house, was parked discreetly behind a stand of trees.

Cassie and Craig had already finished their breakfast and were arguing about their race from the house. As soon as Jane and their father appeared, they pushed back from the table.

"About time," Cassie said. "We'd have starved to death if we waited for you."

"I'll race you back," Craig challenged.

"Sit down!" Andrews barked.

The children seemed stunned that someone should give them a direct order. "We're finished," Cassie snapped back.

"You're not finished until I'm finished," he said in a no-nonsense tone. "And I haven't even started."

"So we're just supposed to sit here and watch you eat," Craig complained.

William forced a smile. "No, we're supposed to chat over breakfast. I have a whole weekend and I'd like for us to make some plans." He held a chair for Jane and then settled in beside her. "Why don't you start, Cassie? What would you like to do today?"

Defeated, the young lady slumped into the chair she had just abandoned. "Jesus . . ." she mumbled under her breath.

Jane found the next twenty minutes actually painful. William Andrews nearly contorted himself trying to nurture a bit of conversation with his children. Cassie and Craig contributed only mumbles and an occasional "that sucks" or "big deal" in response to a specific suggestion. There was a momentary flash of light in Craig's eye when Jane suggested that they might try the whitewater rafting in the Delaware River. But Cassie squelched the idea with "The Delaware isn't even a puddle compared with the Colorado. It dries up in the summer."

"Well," Jane persisted, "it's a lot closer! And I'm new at this. It may be all the river I can handle."

"Are you better at rafting than you are at riding?" Craig asked.

"No. I haven't done either in a long time."

"You'd probably drown," he decided.

"I suppose," Jane concluded, and went back to her eggs.

Craig slouched with his chin in his hands. Cassie drummed her fingers. Andrews ate in silence.

"We're all riding back together," he announced when the children finally bounded from the table and started for their horses.

Craig wailed in protest, "It will take forever." Cassie just rolled her eyes. They went over to the fallen tree where all the horses were tethered.

"I'm sorry," Andrews said to Jane without looking at her. "This wasn't a very good idea." Then he hastened to correct himself. "I don't mean bringing you. I'm thrilled that you're here. I mean trying to create a family moment. I guess I'm not used to dealing with people that I can't fire."

"I'm the problem," she insisted. "Any woman you bring here is a threat to their memory of their mother. They don't like to think of you with anyone but her." She stopped there even though her analysis wasn't nearly finished. She wanted to add that a few years in a public school might do wonders for their humility. They would be amazed to learn that not all their classmates owned horses and that some of them had never been rafting on the Colorado River. At some future moment, she might even suggest that he cut their allowances.

She did a better job of mounting this time and tried to sit with the casual demeanor of the children. She relaxed her grip on the reins and opened her legs a bit to keep from crushing her horse between her knees. Then she did her best imitation of Bill's gaze at the far-off reaches of his spread. They moved off slowly, with Jane and Andrews side by side and the sulking children a short distance behind.

"Maybe you should let them ride ahead," Jane said. "I hate to be the one slowing them down."

He nodded. "In a minute. I'd like to hear at least one civil, polite word from either of them."

Jane's horse suddenly reared up. She had to lean forward and wrap an arm around its neck to keep from falling backwards. Then it bucked, bouncing her into the air so that her feet flew out of the stirrups. She landed hard on the saddle as the animal broke into a gallop. She was moving with frightening speed, struggling to stay on so the thundering hooves wouldn't slaughter her.

12

As the horse raced across the field, Jane could see the house straight ahead. But she knew she would never make it. She was still in the saddle, leaning forward on the horse's neck like a jockey in the homestretch. Her fingers had found the harness, so she had something to hold on to. But her feet were nowhere near the stirrups, and her legs had no grip on the animal's flanks. She was tossing about furiously from side to side, threatening to bounce off at any moment. She felt herself slipping to one side. With each stride there was a new jolt, and with each jolt she was bouncing farther to her right. She was no longer atop the saddle but more to one side. Only the grip she had around the neck and a foot hooked under the edge of the saddle were keeping her on the horse.

Her shifting weight meant that she was tugging harder and harder on one side of the harness. As the horse snapped its head back to the front, the leather strap nearly pulled free. Jane knew that if she lost that grip, she would roll around to the horse's belly and then under the pounding hooves. Somehow she had to throw herself clear, but that seemed equally dangerous. If she just pushed off, she might still get kicked. And even if she cleared the horse's legs, she would be left flying through the air toward a headfirst landing.

Could she stop the horse? She had lost the reins, but she still had a grip on the harness. If she pulled it back, she might also pull back the bit. Wouldn't that make the horse stop? Or would it just make the animal madder? She didn't know, but she had to try something. Another few strides and she would fall.

A hand flashed by her eyes and snatched the harness. She turned her head for an instant and saw that another horse was racing beside her. Another glance identified Craig, who was leaning out of his saddle and holding on to her horse's harness. Just as important, he was pressing against her, keeping her from sliding any farther.

"Whoa!" a voice screamed from the other side. Across the flying mane she saw Bill alongside, reaching over to take the other side of the harness. Then she was pinched in from both sides. Strong hands were pulling back on the reins. The three horses came to a dead stop.

Jane slid directly forward, right over the top of the horse's head. She held on to the harness with a death grip while her feet flew up over her head. She looped through the air, her feet coming around to take the impact of her fall. But her upper body kept traveling until she saw the ground rushing up toward her. She got her hands up in the fraction of a second it took to complete her flip and skidded on her knees and elbows. She was still fully conscious when she came to a stop. Andrews dove down next to her.

"Don't move! Don't try to move anything."

Jane couldn't answer. Her breath had been knocked out and she was sucking desperately for air.

He took her hand. "Can you feel my hand?" She still had no air to form words, but she did manage a jerky nod. "How about here?" He was holding her ankle. Again she answered with a nod.

He stared into her eyes. "You're focused," he told her. Then he added, "That's great. Everything seems to be all right." Then he wheeled to his daughter, who was still on horseback. "Ride back to the camp and get Burt here with the truck."

Jane tried to pull her knees and elbows under her. "Don't move," Andrews snapped. "Lie perfectly still."

"I'm okay," she told him.

"We'll get you to a doctor," he responded.

Jane pushed herself up on all fours. "I'm all right. Just a bit shaken up. Let me try to walk it off."

His expression was skeptical as he helped her to her feet. She stood unsteadily in his embrace. Over his shoulder, she caught sight of Craig, who was holding the three horses. "Thanks," she said. "I couldn't have held on for another second."

"You did okay," he allowed. He involved himself with the mounts so that he wouldn't have to elaborate. Then the pickup came bouncing out into the field.

Andrews helped her into the master bedroom and began filling the Jacuzzi. He left her with Agnes while he went for a scotch, and knocked politely before entering with her drink. She was in the tub with the water bubbling up around her, seeming none the worse for her ordeal.

"This should help," he said, holding the drink at arm's length so that he wasn't looking down at her.

"It's still morning," Jane reminded him. "Maybe a couple of aspirin would be better."

"Yes, yes, of course." He rushed out the door, leaving the drink on the bathroom sink. Seconds later he was back with a handful of pills and a glass of water. He polished off the scotch while she downed the pills.

The damage was slight. Her knees and elbows were skinned and there was a dull ache across her shoulders. She was able to dress by herself and emerge from her room in time for lunch. She heard William and his children at the table before she entered the room.

"We didn't do anything," Cassie was insisting.

"She just doesn't know how to ride a horse," Craig added.

Andrews's voice was soft but still stern. "That horse has never bolted before. There was nothing out there to spook him."

"Maybe it was something she did," Cassie suggested. "She must have kicked him or something."

Bill growled, "She certainly didn't put that burr under his saddle. Someone else had to have done that."

"Maybe she brushed against a sticker bush," Craig said.

"We were out in the open when the horse bolted," his father answered.

"It could have been caught in the saddle from a long time ago," Cassie tried.

"Then how come the horse didn't act up as soon as he was saddled?"

Jane wanted to hear how the investigation played out, but

she didn't want to be caught eavesdropping. The conversation stopped when she entered the room.

Bill stood to hold her chair. "How are you feeling? Everything okay?"

"I feel fine," Jane answered, even though she ached as if a truck had hit her. "Just a couple of bruises."

"See," Craig said, "she didn't even get hurt." Jane nodded pleasantly even though she felt an urge to throw a punch. There was genuine joy in the thought of seeing him with his nose broken. The children used Jane's arrival as their cue to leave. She was relieved that Bill didn't insist they stay at the table.

"Did I hear you say that there was something under my saddle?" Jane asked as if the question had no particular significance.

"A burr," he said. "One of those stickers that grows on bushes. That's what made your horse jump. He's a very gentle animal, not very exciting to ride but steady and predictable. I couldn't understand why he would have tried to throw you like that."

"How did it get there?" she asked politely as she added dressing to her salad.

He shrugged and explained that there were any number of possibilities. The groom might have missed it after the horse's last outing. It could have caught on the saddle when someone laid the saddle on the ground. Or the horse might have brushed against a bush while he was tied up during their breakfast. Jane accepted all the possibilities even though she knew he didn't believe any of them. He thought one of his children had put it under her saddle, and he had confronted them with his suspicions. Naturally, they denied it.

Jane had no desire to wring confessions out of Cassie and Craig. But she wanted Bill to face the implications of what he suspected. His children were determined to drive her off.

"I want to apologize for their behavior today," Bill said. "But I hope you don't think that it is all their fault. I'm just as guilty. I haven't been a very good father."

"It may not have anything to do with you," Jane answered. "I think it's me. They don't want me around."

"That's not true. They don't even know you yet," he said.

"Bill, it's nothing personal. They don't hate me. They just don't like anyone who might, in some way, try to take their mother's place." She let the idea sink in and then said, "Maybe I ought to leave."

He seemed horrified. "No, please. I'm sorry about what happened today. It will get better."

"I might not make it through the night," she told him. "Your kids don't take prisoners." Then she threw up her hands hopelessly. "They don't want me, Bill. They don't want anyone playing the role of your wife."

"I want you," he said. He was dumbstruck by the admission he had just made. Jane looked at him wide-eyed, as amazed as he seemed to be.

"I need you," he added.

"Why?" she whispered. "You have everything."

He shook his head slowly. "I have nothing. Please! Give it another day."

She couldn't believe that she was suddenly feeling sorry for a billionaire, the most important man in global communications. But that wasn't who was sitting across the table from her. This William Andrews seemed hollow, a frail shell about to collapse under its own weight. The global dynamo was out of energy.

They sat looking at each other, William weary and Jane confused. "Okay," she agreed with a quick smile. "But no more horses."

He nodded. "No more horses."

They were by themselves for the rest of the day. He made no effort to involve her with the children, and even when they crossed paths with one of them, he kept his attention fixed on her. He didn't seem to care where Cassie and Craig decided to eat or even if they ate at all. Instead, the two of them took over the kitchen and cut vegetables for an elaborate salad. Jane experimented with the dressing, and he made a great show of selecting the wine. Then they carried their food out to a deck with a market-umbrella-shaded glass-top table and canvas porch chairs. The sun began to set while they enjoyed their dinner, and they were both stunned by the color it cast across the lawns and the hayfields.

"Is this where you plan to live when you retire?" she asked.

"Retire?" Andrews had to smile. He hardly ever used the word.

Jane caught his meaning. "Well, after you own everything on earth and there's nothing left to buy."

"Actually, I'm thinking of selling the place. I had it on the market two years ago, but the kids wailed and carried on so much that I changed my mind."

"Why?" She gestured out to the pastoral splendor that was taking on more color with each passing second.

"I'm not a farmer and, as I said earlier, I'm not into horses." His lips pursed for a second, and he added, "Besides, not all the memories are happy ones."

She could understand. This was Kay's house. It had been her architect and her decorators. She had trained some of the horses. It must have been impossible for him to look around without seeing Kay everywhere. And that had to tear at his heart. If anyone was going to take her place, she would be better off living far away from Kay's many ghosts.

She decided on bed early, using her morning ordeal as an implicit excuse. Her back ached and her arms felt like lead. He was properly concerned and suggested that he take her to a hospital, but Jane insisted that a couple of painkillers and a good night's sleep would do the trick. She left him in the living room opening another bottle of wine.

Jane woke up early in the morning, truly uncomfortable from the cuts and bruises on her knees and elbows, and with a genuine backache. She dressed quietly and slipped down to the kitchen, where she made a pot of coffee. Then she carried a steaming mug outside so that she could watch the sunrise. She was surprised to find Cassie, still in her pajamas, sitting on the steps to one of the porches, said "Good morning" and got a "hi" in response. That was all the encouragement she needed to sit down next to the girl.

They watched silently as the eastern horizon colored to a

blue gray. "Ahh," Jane allowed when the sun, like a cherry, popped into view. A minute later she asked, "Don't you wonder why it's so big and bright at sunset, and so frail in the morning?"

"Are you sleeping with my father?" Cassie asked, cutting to a question that was more important to her.

"Of course not!" Jane said instantly, trying to sound indignant.

Cassie showed no reaction. She kept looking at the sunrise, squinting into what was becoming a golden glow. Jane quickly regretted her outraged tone. It was a fair question from a young woman Cassie's age. Maybe she even had a right to know.

"Are you going to?" That was a tougher question.

"Your father and I have known each other only a few days, Cassie. We haven't talked about it." That was true, as it stood, but then she went further. "I haven't even thought about it." That wasn't true at all. But she hadn't thought about it with any relish. It was more in terms of how she was going to handle the situation when it came up.

"You shouldn't," Cassie said in a tone that offered advice rather giving an order.

"I'd never do anything to hurt you and your brother," Jane said, thinking that was the point the girl was trying to make. "I'd never try to take your mother's place."

"Is that what my father wants you to do?"

"Of course not! Your father loved your mother. He still loves her. He talks about her all the time. No one will ever take her place."

The girl sneered and turned her head to one side. "Then why wasn't he ever with her? Why were they always fighting?"

"That's not true," Jane insisted. Then she realized that she had no way of knowing whether it was true or not. "They were both very busy people," she tried less positively. "There were demands on their time that kept them apart. And even people who love each other sometimes have differences. But that's not fighting."

Cassie shrugged and stared down at her bare toes. Her expression said that the conversation was over. Finally she stood, turned, and started up the steps past Jane. Jane reached up and caught her hand. "Cassie, please put your mind at ease. I'm not trying to take anyone's place."

Cassie looked down at her. "I hope not," she said.

13

They helicoptered to New York on Sunday afternoon, setting down at La Guardia, where the company jet was waiting to whisk William off to Europe. Jane transferred to a limo and was driven back to her apartment in Connecticut. The long drive gave her plenty of time to rerun the highlights of her weekend.

Andrews had displayed a romantic interest in her but also a very practical one. She inferred the romantic interest from the flattering things he said to her and the way he took her hand when they were alone. The practical one was much less subtle. He needed someone to take Kay Parker's place, oversee his household, and raise his children. She reran her trip back home in the helicopter, trying to decide which was more important to him.

He began as they lifted off by thanking her for enduring the disappointing weekend. He had hoped that a happy family setting might show another side of him. Now he hoped that the disaster with his children didn't make him look like an overindulgent fool. "They're usually better than you saw," he said. "By no means angels! They can be difficult and self-centered, like all adolescents. But they were absolutely awful this weekend. You saw them at their very worst."

He went on to explain some of the fun things they did together. He and Cassie often worked side by side in the kitchen, putting together gourmet meals. And he frequently was able to accompany her to the horse shows she competed in. He and his son had assembled a fantastic radio-controlled airplane that they were going to fly together, and he had usually been one of the better-behaved parents at Little League games.

But as he elaborated, he startled himself with the realization of how infrequently he had joined his children. There had been only one occasion when he and Cassie had cooked together, and that was nearly a year ago. Worse, she had given up competitive riding two years ago. Craig had been out of Little League for the past two seasons, and the plane was still awaiting the new engine that he had promised to bring home. In the end, all he could say in his own defense was how quickly the time had passed. "I can do better," he promised himself. "I have to do better."

She had cut him some slack, repeating that his children's conduct was due to the arrival of another woman on their mother's turf. She believed he intended to make a greater effort and was certain that he was a wonderful father.

Then he had talked about her. She was easy to talk to, he said, and fun to be with. He laughed over their foibles in the kitchen when they had tried to prepare dinner. On a more serious note, he admired the way she had downplayed her fall from the horse. Jane decided that he had clearly been more emotional when talking about the needs of his family and that his primary interest in her was as a patch for the gaping hole Kay's death had left in his life.

That kind of relationship, Jane knew, just wouldn't work. First of all, there was no way she could ever replace his first wife. She didn't want to, his kids didn't want her to, and even if everyone had loved the idea, she simply wasn't up to the task. Kay had been sensational. Jane was about average. Second, she had just come out of similar relationship in which she had sacrificed her independence to someone else's agenda. Art had succeeded at nothing, yet he still managed to make her feel insignificant. How much more lost would she be in Bill's giant shadow?

He had expressed his affection and admiration. But he had never mentioned that he loved her. Nor did the word come instantly to her. She admired William Andrews, liked his style, and basked in his attention. But she hadn't even asked herself if she loved him, probably because she was afraid of the answer.

She decided that she should break off the relationship. She could argue truthfully that she just wasn't ready to get serious

with anyone. She was still too close to a relationship in which
her commitment had been ridiculed. Or she could engage in a
bit of a fib and claim that she was still in love with Art. There
had to be some way of putting it without adding to the pain of
loss that he already felt. Or maybe the relationship would die
a natural death. If she made herself less available and stalled
for time, Andrews might well get caught up in some global
takeover that fulfilled all his emotional needs. By the time he
got back to thinking about his personal life, someone else
might be on the scene.

Moments later she decided that she should probably stay
involved with him. She didn't like the idea of someone else
on the scene. The lineup of women—socialites, business tycoons, actresses, models—who would gladly throw themselves at William Andrews probably reached halfway to the
moon. Why should she be so damn honest with her feelings?
He was honest, gentlemanly, and lavishly attentive. She
might well learn to love him.

Back and forth she went as the car plodded up the Merritt
Parkway in Connecticut. At Greenwich she decided to see
just where his interest would take them. By Stamford she had
decided on an unambiguous no. In Fairfield she thought it
best to let time take its course. But when she stepped out of
the limo at the door of her apartment building, she was back
to saying yes. As she unpacked, Jane realized that she was no
closer to deciding how she should react to his attentions than
she was before the weekend.

But she was certain of one thing. Kay Parker's murder was
the fulcrum of Bill's life. If she ever hoped to understand
him, she would have to understand exactly what had happened that so badly afflicted him. She would get on the Internet and connect with all the newspapers that would have
covered the violent death of Kay Parker. And their stories
would give her leads into police investigations, coroner's reports, and all the official records that would accompany a
murder. She was going to learn about Andrews before and after, assess the damage, and then decide if there was any
chance of recovery.

The next morning she sought out Jack Dollinger. He was flattered that she was tapping on the door of his cubicle, rather than he looking in on her, and bounded to his feet in the hope of being helpful. "What can I do for you?" he began.

She sat slowly in his side chair, her manner indicating that she needed his confidence. He settled behind his desk. "Something wrong?" he whispered.

"No, I don't think so. There's just something you said the other day that I'd like to clarify."

"Sure . . ." He was eager to get into a discussion of something that he had said.

Jane leaned closer to his desk. "We were talking about William Andrews and the death of his first wife. You said something about unanswered questions, and I just want to hear what was unanswered."

"Well, the biggest unanswered question was 'who done it?' The police never charged anyone. Hell, they never found anyone they could even think of charging."

"You were with the *Post* at the time?"

He nodded. "Assistant news editor. Really news editor because my boss was never there." He raised his hand to his mouth and mimicked a man tossing down a shot of hard liquor.

"What do you remember about it? I suppose it was very sensational."

"At the *Post*?" He laughed. "The other papers thought we were committing murders just so that we could be first on the scene. If it wasn't a sensation, we certainly would have made it into one."

"So what can you tell me about it?"

"Oh God! Eight years ago. Let me think." He pulled open a drawer to use as a footrest and then leaned back in his swivel chair. "Well, first of all, it was Kay Parker's story. Andrews was a very visible person, starting to build his fortune in radio and television networks and wireless telephones. But he hadn't reached star quality yet. Kay, on the other hand, was America's dream girl. You didn't have to caption her photos. Everyone knew who she was. Sort of like Grace Kelly."

Jane frowned. "Grace Kelly?"

He laughed. "My God, how young are you that you don't remember Grace Kelly? She was in the movies. Blond, beautiful, and very cultured. Sort of an ice maiden in her public life. Everyone in America was wondering which of the leading men she was going to marry, when all of a sudden she announced her engagement to the prince of Monaco. An honest-to-God prince, soon to be king of a country. Yet all of America was up in arms. The nerve of that oily European to deflower America's virgin queen. She became the queen of the country, but no one thought of her as Rainier's wife. The poor bastard never was thought of as a king. He was always that Italian earl or whatever that Grace Kelly married."

Jane smiled. "Like Jackie Kennedy."

He nodded eagerly. "Right. Onassis was a billionaire and an international celebrity, but in the United States he became the damn Greek who seduced Jackie Kennedy."

"So she was the story," Jane said to get him back on track.

"Yeah, we dredged up all the old photos of her. Queen of the Cotillion, benefactor of hungry children, patron of the arts. We had shots that showed cleavage, thigh, and midsection that we always ran next to the photo of her covered body being loaded into a hearse. We really milked it! Circulation was up twenty-five percent all week."

"But there was no killer," Jane reminded him. "How did you keep the story current?"

"Rumors," Dollinger said. Then he chuckled. "We were shameless. We found a new suspect every afternoon over lunch, just in time for the evening edition. First she had a lover, a mystery man who had vowed that if he couldn't have Kay, no one would have her. Then Andrews had a lover, a producer for his New York television station. That gave us two days' headlines. First he had killed his wife so that he could enjoy the assets of his mistress. Then the next day, the mistress had shot Kay Parker so that she could marry William Andrews."

"What about the intruder who shot both of them?" Jane asked.

"Intruders didn't sell newspapers. W
angles until we couldn't find any lover
back on the intruder, the police had
We moved seamlessly from the carna
the pageantry of the funeral. The shots
with his two kids looking over the flower-draped
front page. Half our readers were torn with sympathy, and the
other half thought that he was the killer."

Jane interrupted with a question. "There were people who
thought that he had murdered his own wife?"

"Sure, except no one could find the supposed mistress. I
remember that private citizens were actually following him,
hoping that he would lead them to the other woman. It was
sort of comical, even at the time."

"What did you think?" Jane asked.

Jack Dollinger shrugged. "I guess I decided that it might
just as well have been an intruder. No one else turned up, and
there was no other woman Andrews took up with."

"And the police? Did they have any ideas?"

He shook his head, remembering the irony that surrounded
the question. "There was only one police officer, a sergeant
who also ran a gas station or something. All he knew was what
Andrews had told him. When the state troopers got involved,
the sergeant sort of vanished. And then the troopers couldn't
find anything. In the end, everyone was looking for an intruder.
But his footprints were buried under a couple of feet of snow."

Jane stood up. "If you had to do another story about it,
where would you start?"

"I wouldn't! Now that I work for William Andrews, digging up the dirt of his wife's murder could put me out on the
street." Then he let his feet fall to the floor. "Why? Did
Roscoe ask you to do some digging?"

"No, just curious. I've met the man and I thought I'd like
to know more about him."

John thought. "Well, there was a paper up in Albany that
really took the lead. The *Union*, I think it was. But I don'
know whether it's still in business."

"Thanks!" She repeated the name. "The *Albany Unio*

dialed into its morgue and began entering keywords
ates. It took only a few minutes for her to come up with
. PARKER SHOT TO DEATH.

> Prominent socialite Kay Parker was killed today by an
> intruder who entered her ski chalet in the Adirondacks
> in an apparent attempted robbery. Her husband, com-
> munications executive William Andrews, was also shot
> and was flown to Plattsburg Medical Center, where he
> is listed in stable condition.
>
> A family spokesman, Robert Leavitt, said that the
> murder occurred early this morning. Kay Parker left
> the second-floor bedroom and was confronted by an
> intruder in the kitchen on the first floor. William An-
> drews rushed down the stairs to his wife's aid. Leavitt
> could not say whether Mr. Andrews had been shot
> separately, or had been hit by the same shotgun blast
> that killed his wife. Andrews was unable to provide
> any description of the shooter.
>
> Sergeant Peter Davis of Mountain Ridge said Mr.
> Leavitt, who was staying at an inn near the town, sum-
> moned him to the scene. Apparently Andrews, despite
> his wounds, was able to telephone Leavitt. Leavitt,
> who is a vice president of the communications com-
> pany owned by Andrews, went to the house and then
> phoned the sheriff. Davis said that he had organized a
> search party to cover the countryside surrounding the
> crime scene. Poor visibility and falling snow are ham-
> pering the search, he said, and there are no leads yet.

That was the substance to the first account of the crime.
The story continued with a profile of Kay's life in New York
society that ran another two columns. There was also a two-
paragraph biography on William, naming the communica-
ions companies and stations that he had acquired in the
evious six months. The paper's late edition carried a stock
to of Kay at a charity ball, as well as a brief sidebar indi-

cating that William Andrews was now listed as being in satis-
factory condition.

Jane went to the next morning's New York papers. The
Times carried the intro in the lower left corner of the front
page, and then the full story on page six of its news section.
There was a map of the Adirondacks with a blowup of the
Mountain Ridge area and a locator for the chalet. Pictures
showed the chalet, smiling portraits of Kay and William, and
a photo of two of the posse members in snow-encrusted ski
clothing, sipping coffee. The article described Mountain
Ridge as a crossroads town with a population of less than
fifty that existed as a general store for the surrounding sea-
sonal homes. Sergeant Davis, it mentioned, also owned the
gasoline station.

"The town is ill-equipped to investigate the killing or to
manage the interests of such a high-profile crime," the reporter allowed, quoting several leading citizens. "State police
have taken over the investigation."

The *Daily News* ran the headline SOCIALITE SNUFFED. The
story added nothing to the details of the crime but gave lavish
coverage to Kay Parker's life in the limelight. William Andrews may have been the intended victim, the reporter speculated. His aggressive business style had made him many
enemies.

The *Post,* where Jack Dollinger was working at the time,
had highlighted the lurid. Under a subtitle VICTIM DECAPI-
TATED, it informed its readers that Kay Parker had been hit in
the face at point-blank range by a shotgun blast that carried
away her head. It also hinted that the notion of an intruder
was "highly suspect" and wondered why William Andrews
called a business associate instead of calling either the police
or a doctor.

Jane backed away from the images on her monitor. Even
after all these years, the details of Kay's death were tough to
take. It was easy to appreciate why William's initial actions
were frantic and lacked judgment. Impossible to appreciate
was the impact that such gory details must have had on the

children. No wonder they seemed hostile. She wandered off to get herself a cup of coffee and ran into Roscoe Taylor at the vending machine.

"How was your weekend?" he asked.

"Very nice," she said, but then she guessed that he already knew many of the details. So she added, "I was out at Andrews's horse farm in New Jersey. It's a lovely place, but I could do without the horses."

He stirred sugar into his paper cup. "You and our new boss seem to be hitting it off rather well."

"His kids were there," she rushed to point out, "along with his groundskeeper and house manager. They had planned a very full schedule with a lot of it on horseback. So I'll be standing up most of the time during the next few days."

"Jack said you were interested in the murder of his first wife. Are you planning on writing a book?"

"Just curious," she said, dismissing the topic lightly. She decided not to share any more confidences with Jack Dollinger. When she got back to her desk, she escaped from the old newspaper files and clicked onto the financial markets. It was time for J. J. Warren to get back to work.

Art was waiting in front of her apartment when she got home at the end of the day, supposedly to reassure her that he hadn't been at her computer going through her records. "I swear, Jane, it wasn't me," he told her in the elevator with puppy-dog sincerity. "And anyway, I never would have hidden and sneaked out when you weren't looking."

"Well, someone was here," she said as she opened the apartment door. "Someone who knew I was out for the evening."

He shrugged. "Not me! Honest to God!"

But his real reason for being there became immediately obvious. "So how was the weekend?" His leer told her that he was hoping for salacious details.

"I fell off one of his damn horses." She busied herself with dinner, taking down a big pot to cook the spaghetti. Art began setting the table for two. Jane let him continue.

"Actually, the horse bolted. I'm lucky I didn't break my neck."

"Got any wine?" He was nosing around in the cabinet where they used to keep their liquor.

"Next shelf. In the back," Jane answered.

He pulled out a jug. "This?" he asked disdainfully. "This stuff has been aged in the truck. Didn't I teach you anything about wine?"

"Only that we couldn't afford it," she said. She lit the gas under the water. Art set two glasses on the counter and poured from the jug into each. He tasted his own and reacted with horror but settled into a kitchen chair and took another sip.

"So you fell off a horse. Did Big Bill gather you in his arms and carry you to his bedroom?"

"As a matter of fact, he did."

His eyes widened. "To bed?"

"Even better! To his Jacuzzi."

"No shit? You and the television mogul were together in his hot tub?"

The phone rang. She lifted the handset from the wall mount, said hello, and then smiled pleasantly. "Give me just a second," she said. "I want to get to a different phone." She covered the mouthpiece and snarled at her former husband. "I want to hear you hang this up as soon as I'm on the other phone."

"It's him, isn't it? Your bathing partner?"

"Just hang it up and make sure the water doesn't boil over." She set down the phone and went to her bedroom. The instant she was back on the line, she heard Art curse and the handset rattle to the floor. Only after another indecipherable mumble did the kitchen phone click off.

"Who was that?" Andrews said, making no effort to hide his alarm.

"My ex," Jane said. "He's probably looking for something that he left behind. Sounds as if he can't find it."

He was in Vienna, just back from a dinner meeting. He had been thinking about her all the way across the Atlantic and throughout his day in Europe, and there was something that he had discovered. Something, he said, that he hadn't mentioned before. "I love you very much."

Her heart misfired. There was an awkward pause when she knew she was supposed to say that she loved him, too. But she let the moment pass.

"So I'm cutting my meetings short. There's something I have to do in Paris first thing in the morning, and after that I'll be heading back. Can we get together for a drink or something?"

"You'll be exhausted," she warned.

"I'll catch a nap on the plane." Then he added, "Please. I really miss you."

She agreed and he promised to pick her up at her apartment.

"It was an accident," Art said as soon as she stepped back into the kitchen. "I reached for the phone and burned my hand on the damn stove. When I jumped, I knocked the phone onto the floor. Look!" He thrust his burned hand in front of her eyes. "You can see the mark."

Jane didn't look closely. "Better put some butter on it," she advised. She began breaking the pasta into the boiling water.

Art crept up next to her. "You're not mad?" he asked.

"Why would I be mad? It wasn't my hand."

He stepped around her so that they were face-to-face. "What happened?"

"Bill Andrews just told me that he loved me."

Art kept prodding all through their dinner, but Jane seemed to have gone off to another world. No matter how indiscreet the questions, she refused to be rattled. Yes, she had met his children. No, they weren't particularly friendly. Yes, it was quite an estate, but no, she hadn't an inkling as to how many acres. Yes, she had been in his hot tub. No, he hadn't been in with her. They were putting the dishes into the washer when he asked the question that she knew was coming. "So, did you have sex with him?"

"Don't you think that's a bit personal?"

"It's a fair question. You spent the weekend with the guy and then he tells you he loves you. You must have done something to pique his interest."

"I'd rather not discuss it," she said.

"Then you did get laid!"

"You can think whatever you want."

"I think you gave him the time of his life. I always said you were great in bed."

"Well, you're wrong."

"Wrong? Hey, I remember you between the sheets. I bet he never had it so good."

"You're wrong about us having sex. He was a perfect gentleman."

Art didn't listen. "You know, just thinking about it gets me jealous. That was the one thing you were great at, and I don't like the idea of him getting what I'm not getting. . . ."

"Art! Read my lips. Bill and I didn't sleep together. The only reason I was in his Jacuzzi was that I was sore from the fall. He didn't even stay in the room."

He screwed the cap back onto the jug and put it into the cabinet. "Do you ever think about our getting back together?"

"Who?"

"You and me!"

"Never! Not once."

"I was happy living here with you," he admitted.

"You're still living here," Jane said. "I don't think I'm ever going to be rid of you. But I don't want you here tomorrow. He's picking me up for a drink, and I don't want you here either before or after."

Art smiled. "So, tomorrow is going to be the big night!"

"Whatever it is, I'm hoping you won't be part of it. Even if you think you might have lost a disk or a notebook or left your pen on my coffee table. Understood?"

"Sure! Of course!" Then, as if the thought had just occurred to him, "I wonder if he has any interest in the theater."

"Art, don't you dare."

"Don't dare what? I was just wondering. Lots of business tycoons get into the arts just to show their human side. He might really enjoy getting into Broadway. . . ."

Jane's fists clenched. "I swear, if you bring your plays over for him to read . . ."

"For God's sake, Jane, give me some credit. I just thought that if he was looking to get involved, producing a Broadway play or even off-Broadway . . ."

"No! Don't even think about it."

He raised his hands in a gesture of innocence. "Okay, okay. But if he should happen to mention it . . ."

"He won't," Jane promised, and led her former husband to the front door.

Then she remembered Bill's telephone call. He loved her. He was cutting short his business trip so that he could be with her. That changed everything. He was tall, handsome, dynamic, considerate, filthy rich, and he loved her. So maybe she should be answering the question of whether she loved him. Or at least whether she thought she might fall in love with him. Because tomorrow just might be the biggest night of her life, and she ought to be ready with the answers to all the important questions.

14

Robert Leavitt phoned her office to say that Andrews had called in from over the Atlantic. He was touching down at three and hoped to see her at seven-thirty. If there was any problem, would she please call his office. There was no problem. Seven-thirty was fine. All she had to work out was how she was going to handle a marriage proposal.

"Bill, you're in another world. You're important, financial, and global. I'm nine-to-five. You're a public figure. I cherish my privacy. Basically, I like my life the way it is. Let me stay where I'm comfortable. I'll always enjoy seeing you and spending time with you. But I'm not sure I'd ever be happy living your life." That was one possible answer. Honest, flattering, definite. Surely he would see how unsuited they were for each other.

Or "Bill, I'm not the person you need. You should have someone like Kay, competent at managing your affairs, comfortable among world leaders and business tycoons, at home in high society. I'm a reporter for a suburban paper. I'm comfortable with the local Rotarians, and I'm at home eating pizza in my pajamas." All true, even if it did downplay her abilities and ambition. Jane could learn to handle Kay's multiple roles, and with the right patron she could certainly move up to a major-city daily. But it was a considerate refusal in that it placed the blame on her inadequacies.

Or "As you know, I've just come out of a relationship where neither of us met the other's needs. What you can't know is just how shattering the divorce was to my confidence. I'm not ready to try again. Couldn't we just be friends for a while?" She didn't like this line, because she thought she had met every one of Art's needs, from praising his plays to picking up his socks. But it was easy on Andrews because it put all the blame on her and yet left open the possibility of her future rehabilitation.

Jane wore the basic black she had picked up in Paris but dressed it up with different jewelry. She spent most of her time on her makeup and hairdo, and then began wondering why she was so concerned about her appearance if she intended to say no. Better she should costume herself as an old hag. That way, he might not even ask the question.

Her buzzer sounded at exactly seven-thirty, and she lifted the intercom expecting to talk with the driver. She was stunned when she heard William's voice. "Hi! I had to drive like a maniac, but I'm here. Can you spare a drink for a weary traveler before we head out to dinner?"

"Sure!" She pushed the button, then looked around at an apartment that wasn't ready for company. She ran to close her bedroom door, pausing at the bathroom for the few seconds it took to put her toothpaste into the medicine cabinet and hang a fresh towel on the towel bar. She went back through the kitchen and fired her breakfast dishes into the dishwasher. Then into the living room, where she reassembled the morning paper and straightened the sofa cushions. She was about to clean up the mess around the computer when the doorbell rang. "Time's up!" she said to herself. She stood to her full height, straightened her dress, and made for the door. She opened it onto a large bouquet of roses with William Andrews peering through the petals.

"I already threw away my cell phone," he announced. "I thought these might be a better way to present myself." He handed her the flowers and followed her into the kitchen, where she found a tall vase.

"They're beautiful," she said over and over again. While arranging them, she asked how he had found time to buy flowers. William reddened a bit and explained that his firm had an account with a chain of florists. He hadn't actually picked them out himself.

They went to the living room, and she placed the vase on her coffee table. Then she remembered he had asked about a drink. "I don't think I have your favorite," Jane apologized, thinking of his fondness for single malts. She remembered the jug she had shared with Art and added, "I'm sure I don't have a wine that you would like."

"Any kind of scotch," he said, and she went scurrying off to her liquor cabinet to see what "any kind" would be. She filled two glasses with ice and poured in the bargain blend, just a touch for herself and a double for him. She set the glasses on a tray, added cocktail napkins, and carried the drinks back to the living room. William was standing over her computer, studying the screen.

"You're not using my browser," he said in mock horror, pointing to the icon of a competing service.

"I'll have to change right away," she began. Jane started to laugh, but her voice caught in her throat. Right beside the computer, in full view, was the printout from her research into the murder of Kay Parker.

She pushed the tray under his nose and led him away to the sofa. He sat next to her, toasted "To us!" and took a healthy swallow. "Not bad," he decided. "What kind is it?"

"It's well aged," she answered. "I think I've had that bottle for over a year."

Andrews smiled, tasted again, and then gave her the rundown on his trip. He'd signed on another buyer for one of his services and found a new source for Eastern European programming. A brief stop at his Paris office . . .

She listened, nodded, and even managed a few smiles. But her mind was on the papers lying next to her screen. What was showing? A headline blaring his wife's name? How could he miss it? Or worse, one of Kay's society photographs that had run with a story?

His attitude hadn't changed. He was still pleasant, casual, and chatty. If he had seen Kay's picture, wouldn't he have been stunned? Or if he had seen one of the old headlines, wouldn't he at least be curious? So maybe he hadn't noticed the printout from her research. Maybe the top page was just the second or third column of a story, with no subheads or photos to attract his interest.

". . . as soon as we were out of Paris, I had them take me

up to Amsterdam," he was saying. "That was the important part of my trip."

If he knew, how could he keep rambling on about his business trip? It would be entirely fair of him to ask why she was digging into his first wife's murder. Or he could have taken a page with him to the sofa to continue reading the piece. He must not have noticed what was there. Thank God it was the offensive icon that had caught his attention. Unless he was as good at pretending to talk as she was at pretending to listen. Maybe he was babbling details of his trip while his mind was wondering what she was up to. It could be that he was trying to decide whether he should confront her or let the issue pass. If he did confront her, what would she say?

". . . traffic in Amsterdam is a mess. Cars, buses, and bicycles all fighting for space. And pedestrians stepping off the curb, hoping that the next car will screech to a stop." He shook his head in dismay and took another sip.

She would have to tell him the truth. Maybe she could say, "It's so important to understanding you, a defining moment in your life. I had to know about it." Or was it better to lie? "Just things that came up while I was researching your story. Of course, I left them out."

"The Diamond District is just a few blocks, but you have to park outside and walk in because the diamond merchants do all their bargaining out in the street. But for what I wanted, that's where I had to go. And this wasn't something that anyone could do for me."

He took a small box of polished leather out of his jacket pocket. "This was something that I had to pick out myself." He opened the box and held it out to her. It was the biggest diamond she had ever seen.

"I know you're going to say that we hardly know each other. And my answer is that I already know enough to want to know more. Much more."

Jane was speechless. Her hand was shaking as she reached out for the box, but he took her hand, set the box down, and then removed the ring. "I'm fatally stricken by you, J. J. Warren, and I'm begging you to marry me." He slipped the ring onto her finger. The fit was perfect. The stone blazed an icy white even in the poor light of her apartment. Her mind raced through all the answers she had considered, and her lips began to move with well-rehearsed words.

"Yes" was all that she could get out.

"Yes, meaning that you'll marry me?"

Her mind was beginning to recover. "Yes, if you're very sure that this is right for you. If you've thought of all the . . . consequences. . . ."

"You never know all the consequences," he said. "The people who try to think through everything miss all the important deals. I think I just know when something is right, and I know this will be right for both of us. Assuming you're not planning any more articles about my shady business practices."

Jane laughed out loud and leaned into his arms. They melted into a long kiss. When they parted, she teased, "Is that your real motive? Are you marrying me just to quiet the voice of a free press?"

"It was that, or hire a hit man," he said. "I couldn't put up with the criticism." He pulled her in for another embrace.

"Let's eat," he said just as she was beginning to think that they were never going to leave the apartment. "What this moment needs is a good French champagne." He stacked their glasses on the tray. "And maybe a long romantic night. How long would it take you to throw together an overnight bag?"

He was looking directly at her. It wasn't a gag line. He was asking her to spend the night with him.

"I'm already packed," Jane lied.

He seemed to relax with her answer. "God, you're wonderful."

"Give me a minute," she said, and went off into her bedroom.

She found her overnight bag in the back of the closet and coughed at the dust she stirred when she dragged it out. *Has it been that long?* she thought. It had been. Her last romantic rendezvous had been with Art, before they were married. She tossed in her toiletries, her mascara, and her lipstick. She found her diaphragm but put it back under the sink. She was still faithful to the Pill, which she had started taking when she met Art.

My God, did she still own a nightgown? It had been pajamas during the last two years of her marriage, and a T-shirt ever since. Did she own anything that would provoke a middle-aged man? Jane went through her dresser drawers and found a nearly invisible set of black briefs and a thigh-length dressing gown that had patch pockets to provide a hint of modesty for her breasts. She remembered that she had bought it when Art had complained that she was no longer sensual. He had fallen asleep while she was cutting the price tags off her backside.

A change of clothes for tomorrow? Jane started back to the closet but pulled up abruptly. She wasn't packing a steamer trunk. This was a romantic escapade. She was supposed to be naked, not packed for four seasons. She zipped up the overnight bag, checked her lipstick in the bathroom mirror, and stepped out into the living room.

Andrews appeared from the kitchen. "Glasses are done and everything is in the dishwasher," he announced. "Unfortunately, I don't know how to turn the damn thing on."

He turned his back and stepped toward the door. Jane used the moment to steal a glance at her desk. The article on top of the pile next to her computer carried the headline STATE POLICE UNCERTAIN ABOUT PARKER INTRUDER. He had to have seen it!

15

The car was an expensive sedan that blinked its lights and opened its door locks when Andrews touched his key at the top of the steps. "No driver?" Jane asked.

"Just me," William said. "I was amazed that I remembered how to drive." He tossed her bag into the trunk, ran around to hold open her door, and then raced around again to take his place behind the wheel. They drove to the Merritt Parkway and then headed west through Westport and Stamford. He took the last Greenwich exit, drove through winding streets, and made abrupt turns at dark intersections. Finally, they headed up a tree-lined path to an inn near the New York border and parked in the empty lot. Andrews lifted her overnighter and his own attaché case out of the trunk.

"Is this place open?" Jane wondered.

"It is for us. I've reserved the entire inn. I thought that on such an important night you might like to be alone."

The innkeeper was waiting at the top of the steps to relieve Andrews of the bags. "They'll be sent up," he said in a tone that assured him they really would be. "The dining room is this way. Your table is ready."

They were alone in the dining room at a table in front of the fireplace. The captain seated them, and there were two waiters standing by.

"You've been here before," Jane commented with a wry smile.

"Actually, I haven't. But I selected it myself and I made all the arrangements. It's the perfect place to consummate an engagement. I even took the liberty of ordering for you. Oysters and clams, a duck in cherry sauce, and a few cheeses for dessert. A blanc with the appetizers, a Chablis with the main course, and maybe a port at the end. And, of course, coffee whenever."

"They kept the kitchen open just for us?" Jane wondered.

"Just for you," William answered. "All night and into the morning, just in case you want anything."

They were both in a sexual mood even before the oysters arrived. He was leaning in toward her, ignoring the wine steward, who was being obsequious about opening the French white. She was reaching out to touch his fingertips under the table.

"Would the gentleman care to examine the cork?" the steward asked.

"Sure! But in the meantime, pour the wine," Andrews responded.

They leaned in over the center of the table while they fed each other clams and oysters. Jane swallowed them whole, tasting them at the back of her throat. He smiled as each one went down. She dipped a clam in the cocktail sauce and held it out to him. Andrews contorted to get under the morsel and sucked it down like a pelican. Then he lifted an oyster, still in its shell, and tipped it over her lower lip. Jane was already feeling aroused when the duck made its entrance.

They stared at each other while the captain went through the rituals of flaming the duck, cutting it from the bone, and heaping on the cherries. When he put their plates in front of them, neither lifted a fork. An instant later, when he brought the Chablis, William waved away the ceremony of tasting. He simply lifted his glass and held it out to Jane.

The ducks survived, scarcely damaged by the two diners, who couldn't take their eyes from each other long enough to break the meat from the bone. "Delicious," Jane said after tasting the flimsiest morsel.

"Marvelous," he added, even though his portion was untouched.

They decided to do without dessert. "Maybe just coffee," he suggested, his eyes wild at the thought of taking her into his bed.

"Coffee to go," Jane emended his order. They could have it in their room.

The room tried to mimic an inn along the Colonial stagecoach route. The ceiling was low and supported by hand-hewn beams. The walls were rough, whitewashed unevenly, and stenciled with patterns of birds. The wide-board floor was fastened with pegs and polished to a near-blinding luster. Taking up most of the space was an enormous four-poster with a mattress that was nearly chest-high. It was made up with lace-trimmed pillows and a feathery quilt. The other furnishings were sparse: a straight wooden rocking chair; a washstand with a basin, pitcher, and shaving mirror; a monk's table with an elaborate oil lamp that had been fitted out with an electric bulb; and a giant armoire that cleverly disguised a closet, dresser drawers, and a television set.

The bathroom brought modern convenience to an eighteenth-century setting. The tub was copper, set into an oak base. But there were subtle whirlpool jets and a hook arrangement for hanging the shower hose. The sink was a freestanding basin with a pump handle for a faucet, and the toilet had an overhead water tank operated by a pull chain. It would be easy to believe that George Washington had slept here.

But Jane and Bill couldn't have cared less. As soon as they closed the heavy wooden door, they were in each other's arms. Within seconds they had undressed each other, scattering their clothes in a straight line from the door to the bed. He pulled back the comforter so that she could climb in, and then he joined her in a frantic, tumbling embrace. They ended with him on top, supporting his weight on his elbows, while she locked her legs around the small of his back.

She was fully receptive, but her delight wasn't yet physical. She was enjoying his obvious pleasure, his nearly violent thrusting, his set jaw, the rush of his labored breathing. There he was, one of the most important men in the world, and he was as powerless as a hound filled with the scent of a bitch in heat. William Andrews, enjoying her so much that he was nearly crying out for joy.

When he settled next to her, she rolled on top, sat astride him, and leaned forward so that her breasts were in his face. Then she felt her own swelling of pleasure, and suddenly it was she who had to muffle her gasps.

Then they were side by side and face-to-face, their lips
brushing.

"My God, but you're wonderful," he managed between
breaths.

"Shh . . ." Jane held her fingertips to his lips. She was enjoying the touch of his body, well-muscled through the shoulders, firm buns, and rock-hard legs. He felt as if he should be
an important person, an Olympic athlete or maybe a warrier
king, and she had thrilled him to the point of paralysis. Like
Judith, she could have his head without his uttering a word of
protest. In a few minutes he was sound asleep in her arms.

They made love again in the morning, this time more
slowly and patiently. But when the sun began to rise in the
small glass panels of the Colonial windows, the economic ti-
tan returned. He was up and into the bathroom, showering in
the copper tub. Seconds later he was dressed, sitting in the
rocker with papers across his lap and a cell phone to his ear.
He smiled at her when she climbed down from the bed
wrapped in a sheet, picked up her unopened overnight bag,
and disappeared into the bath.

"I have a car waiting to take you back to your apartment,"
he said when she came into the bedroom. "I have to get to the
airport for a Chicago flight." He was stuffing his papers back
into his briefcase. She stepped into her black dress and
checked what was left of her makeup in the shaving mirror.
"I'll call you tonight. There's a lot that we have to discuss.
Like wedding plans, where we're going to live and—"

She closed his mouth with a kiss. "Last night was the best
night of my life," she said. "I'm looking forward to many
more just like it."

He seemed taken back by the change of subject. Then he
smiled. "What the hell is the matter with me?" he asked.

"Nothing I can't fix," she answered. She kissed him again.

Part Two

The Wedding

16

Art was standing near her door when the limo dropped her off. She decided to ignore him and walk right past, but he cut her off and held out a paper bag. "Coffee," he said. "Black and still hot."

She considered his proposition. "Okay, but just coffee. Don't say anything! Not one damn word!"

He carried his treasure into the kitchen while she went to the phone. "Margaret," she said to Roscoe's secretary. "It's Jane. Will you tell Roscoe that I might not make it in today. Either I caught the flu or I've been poisoned. But after getting up and getting completely dressed, I've decided to go back to bed." A long pause, and then she continued, "Sure, he can call me if anything comes up. And if I'm feeling better, I might even come in this afternoon." There was a quick exchange of sympathy and regret, and then Jane hung up. When she looked up, Art was standing next to her, holding a cup of coffee.

"Big night?" he asked.

She took the cup and sat down by the coffee table. "The biggest."

"Is that a ring?" he demanded, sitting across from her. "Or are you wearing diamond-studded brass knuckles?"

Jane examined the ring and then held out her hand so that Art could see the stone in all its grandeur. "Bill asked me to marry him," she explained unnecessarily.

"The man knows how to ask! Which monarch in Europe is missing the diamond at the top of the crown?"

"I told him that I would . . . marry him."

"I'll bet you did. He wouldn't have given you this for saying no." He whistled softly and shook his head. "William Andrews and Plain Jane! It's hard to believe. Did you kiss a frog, or something?"

"You know, when I was getting dressed last night I kept rehearsing polite ways of saying no. I really didn't think I wanted to be married again. I liked my life the way it is—predictable . . . manageable . . ."

"Boring," he suggested.

"Yes, even boring at times. But when he asked me, I forgot all my reasons and all my rehearsed speeches. I was amazed to hear myself saying that I would marry him."

"Did you see the ring first?"

"No, I didn't," she snapped. But then she admitted, "Well, maybe I did. They all came together. The ring . . . the proposal . . ."

Art nodded. Then he asked, "I don't suppose you had a chance to see if he was interested in theater?"

"Oh sure, right after we finished our discussion on cubism. Are you crazy? It was the first night of our engagement."

"Well, now that you're engaged, it might be something you could talk about."

She sighed in frustration. "Art, I'm not going to ask William Andrews to back one of your plays. At least not until after our tenth anniversary."

"Maybe you could just introduce us?"

Jane stood, picked up the paper coffee cups, and carried them to the trash can. Art rose and stretched lazily.

"Don't get comfortable," she cautioned. "I'm going to soak in a hot tub and then try to get a few hours of sleep. I'd like to be alone."

She followed her plan to the letter. As soon as her former husband left, Jane bolted the door and started her bath. She was hunched down in chin-deep water when she remembered the news articles still lying next to the computer. She remembered Andrews standing only inches away from them and realizing that he must have seen them. The thought made her sit up straight.

He had to have known that it was her research, and it must have been obvious that she was digging into the unsolved murder of his first wife. So why hadn't he mentioned it? He could easily have asked why she was interested. Or he could have told her that she was delving into painful memories and asked her to stop. Maybe he simply didn't want to ruin the evening he was planning by having his past intrude on his future. Or perhaps he couldn't admit that he had been glancing through her papers. But whatever the reason, the subject was certain to come up sometime. She climbed out of the tub, put on her bathrobe, and left wet footprints as she went to her computer to put all her research out of sight. When she picked up the papers, she knew immediately that someone had been going through them.

Jane remembered glancing at her desk to see what Andrews could have seen when he stood at her computer. She could clearly visualize the page that had been lying on top. Now another page with photos of Kay and William was at the top of the stack. The page she remembered was near the middle.

She tried to change her recollection. This had to be the printout that she saw. When she and Andrews left the apartment, she heard the click of the lock behind her. And this morning she had needed her key to get in. Things had to be exactly as she had left them. But they weren't. Jane was sure of what she had seen. Someone had been in the apartment, going through her papers. Who? Probably not Art, who had been waiting outside. And why? What stories was she working on that would cause someone to break in for a look at her notes?

It has to be about the Kay Parker murder, she decided. Nothing in her business coverage would warrant breaking and entering. She sat in her bathrobe and re-read everything she had found from the first two days after the murder.

When she was finished she pulled up to the keyboard and connected to the electronic morgues of the New York papers for the following few days. The story was no longer front page in the tabloids, which had found new tragedies to exploit. But it was still up-front news with a picture of the hearse that had been sent by a prominent New York funeral home to bring Kay Parker back to the city. Search teams, now managed by the state police, were still combing the rugged terrain for clues to the intruder. A lieutenant was quoted to the effect that the snowfall had buried any tracks that the man might have made and had kept neighbors in their homes, so there were no witnesses.

Robert Leavitt, again acting as the family spokesman, said that Andrews would accompany his wife's body back to New York. Andrews was seeking a waiver of the usual autopsy of murder victims. "The cause of death is brutally obvious," Leavitt was quoted, "and the family would like to spare Kay's body any further violence." The coroner must have agreed because no autopsy was performed.

There seemed to be universal agreement that the motive for the crime was burglary. Several ski houses in the area had been broken into over the past few seasons during weekdays, when they were vacant. The speculation was that Kay had caught the intruder in the act and screamed for her husband. When Andrews rushed to the scene, the man had panicked and fired. But the same lieutenant said that police had not yet established how the man had gotten in.

The *Times* went a bit further, reporting that there was no evidence of a break-in. It added an interview with the police sergeant, who had turned his investigation over to the troopers. He raised questions about the intruder's escape, pointing out that there was only one road from the town to the area where the Andrewses' chalet was located. "If he had called me first," he said, reminding the reporter that Andrews's first call had been to Robert Leavitt, "I might've run into the guy coming down the road." Then he added another slap on the wrist for Andrews. "Heck, chances are his friend passed the killer on his way up to the house."

Jane dug into the next few days and found the story back on the front page. There were photos of mourners leaving the funeral parlor after Kay's cremation. The focus was on the loss of an important contributor to New York society, with quotations from the mayor's eulogy. Kay Parker, he promised, was looking down on her beloved city, and her guiding hand would shape New York cultural life for generations to come.

There was also a short interview with the city's chief medical examiner criticizing the omission of an autopsy and the rush to cremation. "You can't know what an autopsy might reveal until you conduct one," he said impatiently. "If the crime had occurred in my jurisdiction, there would have been an autopsy."

She stayed at her computer for the rest of the morning, unable to satisfy her curiosity about the death of William's first wife. Only when she was overtaken by exhaustion did she finally stretch out on her bed, but even then the newspaper stories churned in her mind. She understood why William had phoned Leavitt first. Leavitt was his constant companion and right hand in business. He was there in the mountains precisely to respond immediately to any of William's needs. But why wasn't he staying at the house? If he was there to be on hand, why was he half an hour away in a commercial inn?

Why avoid an autopsy? It was standard in homicide cases even when the cause of death was as obvious as a knife sticking out of the victim's back or a bullet hole through the forehead. The explanation of saving his wife's body further damage didn't ring true for someone as thorough as Andrews. So what was he trying to hide? Was Kay a drug user? Had she been high or drunk when she was killed? Did she have a disease that might be threatening to her children? Jane tossed and turned for half an hour before she finally dropped off to sleep.

The telephone awakened her. She felt around the night table, pushed the button on her alarm clock, and then knocked the handset onto the floor. She was on all fours when she finally got the phone to her ear.

"Am I interrupting something?" William Andrews asked.

"I was asleep. I had a very busy night." She gave a delicious yawn.

He laughed heartily. "I almost fell asleep at my Chicago meeting," he admitted.

Jane leaned her back against the side of her bed. She liked talking to him, she was beginning to discover.

Andrews moved through his topics as if he were checking

them off with a pencil. First was their living arrangements. He wanted her to move into his apartment. She should come over in the next few days when he would be away in Washington at an FCC hearing. "Stay there and go through the place. Anything you don't like we'll get rid of. And if you want to move in any of your things, that's fine. I'm going to tell Eileen to expect a call from you and to make sure you're comfortable."

"Who's Eileen?" she demanded suspiciously.

"Eileen? Eileen McCarty!"

"Okay. Now, who's Eileen McCarty?"

"My housekeeper. She keeps the cupboard stocked and the dust on the run."

"And does she wear a French maid's costume?"

Again he laughed heartily. "That would be a sight you wouldn't want to see. Eileen is old enough to be your mother and probably just as proper. I call her my housekeeper, but she really manages the place. Makes sure I always have food and water."

"She lives in?"

"No, she lives on the West Side. But she gets there early and leaves late."

"I hate her already."

Another laugh. "Don't. At least not until you meet her. And if you don't like her, we can pension her off and get someone else."

His next subject was the wedding. He thought they could get married at the federal court building by one of the judges. "Just us and the kids," he suggested. "And we can have a reception for a few close friends at the apartment. We'll keep it small and private. The quicker we go through with it, the less chance we'll be raided by the press."

"Sounds good," she said, realizing that he was already managing the details of her life.

"Now, your job," he went on. "I know how much you like it, but I don't think you'll want to become a reverse commuter. I think you should give notice right away."

She took a deep breath. "Let's talk about that, Bill. The people at the paper are all my friends. . . ."

"Sure. Whatever you want. But I was hoping you'd be with me on some of my trips, and I'd hate to have you sacked for absenteeism."

He moved immediately to his next concern. He hoped to bring his children home from their boarding schools and move them into the Manhattan apartment. "Not right away," he assured her, "but in time for the fall school openings. So perhaps you could keep that in mind when you're going through the place."

Jane had instant recall of her fall from the horse and of overhearing Bill's suspicion that one of his children put the burr under her saddle. She could imagine Craig pushing her off the penthouse balcony.

"Now, here's my schedule," Andrews continued, rattling off a list of the countries he would be in for the next two weeks. Then he gave his final instructions. He could always be reached through his secretary, Ann Packard, who really ran his office. Ann could always get in touch with Robert Leavitt, and Leavitt always knew where to find Andrews.

"I guess that's about it," he concluded.

"No, it isn't," Jane snapped.

"It isn't? What have I missed?"

"Telling me that you love me. That I'm the most important part of your life."

He stammered for an instant. "Oh God, I didn't say that, did I?"

"If you did, I must have missed it."

"Jane, please bear with me. I haven't loved anyone in so long that I've probably forgotten how."

"I love you, Bill," she told him.

"And I love you. I really do."

She held the phone dangling from her fingertips for a full minute after he hung up. It had been one of the least romantic conversations she had ever had with a man, and only a few hours after they had been rolling in bed together. He had

shown no recollection of their physical love. It was as if he
had pulled into a gas station, filled up, and was now back in
the fast lane. Was he marrying her or simply adding her to his
busy schedule? Art had assumed that her life would become
an appendage to his own, which never made sense because
Art had no life of his own. But it made perfect sense that a tycoon like William Andrews would never break stride to meet
a wife's needs. Could she really expect him to sit still, truly
listen to her, and honestly try to understand her?

The telephone began screeching its off-the-hook alarm,
jarring her out of her melancholy moment. *Let's see what hap-
pens next,* she thought. *I'm not married yet.* She would take at
least the next step and introduce herself to the other two
women in William's life, his housekeeper and his secretary.

She didn't wear her ring into the office the next day, nor did
she mention to anyone that she was engaged. Jack Dollinger
was very solicitous of her health and of the illness that had
kept her at home. "Check with your doctor," he advised.
"There's a lot of pneumonia going around." Roscoe Taylor
was more suspicious. "What did you have, a hangover?" As
always, he seemed to know more than he was letting on. He
asked about her research into Kay Parker's violent death. She
denied that it was research. "Just morbid curiosity. It seems
to have been a terrible tragedy."

"A mystery," he corrected. "Who did in the fabulous Kay
Parker? And why?"

"You don't believe it was an intruder?"

He shrugged. "If it was, it had to be one of the neighbors.
Someone who could have made his escape without going
back down the road and through the village. And all the
neighbors checked out. No motives and great alibis."

Her eyes narrowed. "You've been digging into this, haven't
you?"

Roscoe smiled. "Not digging! I just happened to be talking to an old friend who did a lot of work on the story. He remembers rumors that there was another woman in William

Andrews's life. A traveling companion. But nothing that could be proved. And he remembers a lot of political pressure to get the whole affair over with quickly and quietly. The publisher told his editor that he would be held personally responsible for anything printed, and the editor moved my friend onto another assignment."

Jane felt herself bristling. "What are you saying, Roscoe? That there was a cover-up that included the press?"

"No! You know me better than that. What I'm telling you is that Kay Parker's death was certainly a tragedy, but it remains a mystery. It pops up from time to time in true-crime tabloids, and the suggestions are not always flattering to Andrews. So if you're getting involved with the guy, you can expect to be spattered in occasional rounds of mudslinging."

She sat back. "I am involved, Roscoe. He asked me to marry him."

Taylor smiled. "My best wishes. Once again William Andrews has demonstrated an uncanny eye for value."

"Do you think I'm getting in over my head?" Jane asked sincerely.

"Not in the least. You can play in any game that he does. Personally, I think he's unworthy of you. But you are stepping out into the limelight. It will be a very different life for you."

17

Eileen McCarty turned out to be a smallish woman, probably in her fifties, with a hint of an Irish brogue. She was welcoming and pleasant but decidedly nervous to be meeting with a new "woman of the house."

She had been waiting in the foyer, dressed in a tasteful pantsuit, when Jane stepped off the private elevator that had carried her up twenty-five floors to the penthouse. She offered her hand and announced, "I have coffee in the breakfast room."

Even at a quick glance, Andrews's penthouse was unbelievable. There were two archways from the foyer, and the one they entered opened to the central rooms. First was a reception area with a leather sofa, armchairs, and a coffee table. The walls were done in panels of brocade beneath crown moldings. There was an Oriental carpet on the floor. The area was as big as her living room, Jane noticed, and this was just an appetizer to the rooms behind. Next came a formal dining room with a long table and seating for sixteen. There were sideboards and serving carts and a glass breakfront that displayed a department store window's worth of china and crystal. Two chandeliers with Tiffany glass lamps hung from the ceiling. The door to one side, she would later learn, connected to the kitchen. The door on the other side led to the climate-controlled wine cellar.

She was dazzled the instant she stepped into the living room. It was two stories high. The far wall was a single sheet of glass looking out over a patio railing at the expanse of Central Park. To one side was a piano, set up as a cocktail bar amid a gathering of soft chairs. Ahead, commanding the view of the park, was a grouping of light, elegant Danish pieces. A long sofa, a trio of straight yet soft conversational chairs, and a giant coffee table. She guessed that a dozen people could gather around the table without feeling in the least bit crowded. To the left were two other sofas facing each other over a glass table, with complementary side chairs. The room could handle a hundred people with a third of them sitting. What she realized when she was well into the space was that there had not been any attempt at an overall decorating scheme. The room simply provided the space in which each of the various furniture groupings was free to make its own statement.

Above, to either side, were balconies that Jane guessed connected the bedrooms. On the left wing she caught a glimpse of ceiling-high bookshelves in what she assumed was a library.

Eileen McCarty led her to the far left edge of the room, where a breakfast area reached in just far enough to share the glass facade. It was served by another door leading to the kitchen. They sat in leather-strapped dining chairs at a marble-top table. A silver coffee urn, cups, saucers, plates, and silverware were waiting. Eileen poured two cups and uncovered a plate of miniature Danish.

"My God," Jane observed breathlessly, "my whole apartment would fit in the living room."

"With room left over for mine," the housekeeper said. "And the crime of it is that it goes empty most of the time. I understand that Mrs. Andrews did a great deal of entertaining, with often more than a hundred people. But that was before I was here. Now there's hardly ever more than two in any room at any time."

She had been hired six years ago, she said, after the penthouse had gone unused for a while. "Mr. Andrews couldn't stand to come back to the place. He had everything redecorated before he opened it up again. Except their room. That's the way she left it."

Eileen knew nothing about Kay Parker except what she had read about the fabulous socialite in the papers. Like everyone else, she had been heartbroken by the girl's terrible death. But she didn't know anyone in the family and had never worked for them. She had just answered an ad in the paper for a household manager.

"I had no idea who it was. Even when I was given the name Andrews, I never put it together with Kay Parker. And it wasn't Mr. Andrews who interviewed me but rather Mr. Leavitt. When I heard who it was, I thought, *Well, you'll never get this job, Eileen*. You could have knocked me over with a feather when they called me back."

It took her a while to figure out why they had picked her, Mrs. McCarty said as she poured more coffee. "Then I realized that they didn't want anyone around who could understand all the grand things that Mr. Andrews and the other gentlemen talk about. It's hardly likely I could compromise something that I couldn't make sense of."

She launched into the prelude to her guided tour. "The apartment was built by Mr. Andrews fifteen years ago as a gift to his wife. It occupies the top two floors and half the roof of the building. Mr. Andrews bought it while the building was under construction, so the initial design was to his specifications. Mrs. Andrews redecorated it each year. It has nine thousand square feet, with twenty-six rooms, eleven baths, and a pool and cabana on the roof. It is served by two of the building elevators and has its own internal elevator."

"It sounds more like a cruise ship," Jane joked.

The penthouse had its own emergency generator in case the building or the city lost power, an independent water supply, and a security system linked directly to the nearest police station. Jane nodded politely as she took in all the information. But she could taste the fear at the back of her throat. What in God's name was she getting herself into?

Eileen waited until Jane had finished her coffee and then led her off on the tour. They had taken one archway out of the elevator foyer. The other led to what Mrs. McCarty referred to as "the service area." This included a stainless-steel-and-tile kitchen that would have been the envy of most four-star restaurants, with doors leading to the dining room, breakfast room, and the service corridor. Also off the corridor were three suites, each a bedroom, sitting room, and bath, intended for a housekeeper, chef, and butler. None had been in regular use since Mr. Andrews reopened the penthouse. She used the housekeeper's room if he needed her to stay very late. A cook or a caterer might stay over when Mr. Andrews was giving a dinner party, but that didn't happen very often.

"How often is that?" Jane asked.

"Oh, maybe half a dozen times," Eileen told her.

"That's all? Half a dozen times a year?"

"Oh, heavens no," Eileen answered. "I mean since I've been here."

They went up the stairs that led from the living room to the second level, open steps without a handrail, which matched the minimalism of the Danish furniture grouping. On the second floor, Jane toured four guest bedrooms, each with its own bath; a billiard room with a bar and card table; Andrews's home office, which had an enormous desk, computer center with two PCs, and a communications console with six screens that could be switched to any broadcast on any of the Andrews networks; and the library, which in addition to three thousand volumes had its own computer for Internet access to any library in the world. She walked from room to room with her head swinging in wide-eyed awe. When he had told her to make any changes she wanted, Jane had imagined that she would be changing a few sets of drapes. In this apartment, changes in decor would be like changing the look of the lobby at the Metropolitan Opera. The scale was beyond her experience.

They entered the master suite, a feminine room with floral wallpaper, satin recliners, and an enormous canopied bed. The furnishings were white, tooled in colors that picked up the floral tones. The white carpeting was ankle-deep. Eileen pushed open the door to the walk-in closet and Jane saw row upon row of dresses, evening gowns, and smartly tailored suits. There were stacks of thin drawers designed to hold lingerie, hosiery, and other silks and satins. A floor-to-ceiling rack displayed at least a hundred pairs of shoes.

"Mrs. Andrews's things," Eileen commented. "This is the only room that wasn't redecorated."

"Where are his things?" Jane asked.

"He generally uses the first guest bedroom. The few things he keeps here in the penthouse are in the guest closet."

"What about the children?"

"Oh, they're hardly ever here. At school most of the year, and out at the farmhouse during the summer. Except, of course, when they're traveling abroad."

"But where are their things?"

"In New Jersey, I suppose." Then she added, "I'm not at all involved in the farmhouse."

They went up another flight of stairs and Jane found herself in the rooftop cabana. There were several small changing rooms, a kitchen, still another bar, and two baths. Outside the sliding glass doors was a wooden deck with a built-in swimming pool. Jane asked about the tall wooden cabinets, like folded grandstands, that stood at one end of the pool.

"A dance floor," Eileen McCarty answered. "I'm told it folds out over the pool and leaves a band shell behind, but I've never seen it down. I heard that Mrs. Andrews gave many rooftop parties. Mr. Andrews likes to swim, but he has never used the dance floor. I'm not sure it still works."

They wandered back to the living room, where Eileen gestured Jane onto the central sofa. "That's about it," she said. "Do you have any questions?"

"Not yet. I'm still a bit breathless. It must be quite a responsibility staying on top of all this. . . ." She gestured expansively to indicate the incredible scope of William Andrews's in-town apartment.

"It would be if people were living here," the woman answered. "But really all I have to do is cook a few meals and make a bed or two. Mr. Andrews and his business friends aren't really here that much. Oh, I do some shopping, mostly by telephone, and I keep an eye out for anything that needs fixing or painting. The cleaning service does the rest."

"Well, I won't add much to your workload," Jane said. "I may even be able to pitch in and help. I think we'll get along very nicely."

"And I do, too," Mrs. McCarty said. "I don't mind telling you that when I heard the future Mrs. Andrews was coming for a visit, I thought I might be done for. I was afraid that you'd be one of those ladies who want the help to sound

British and to speak French for the children. But you seem like the real thing."

Jane didn't mention that she too had been dreading their meeting. Housekeepers, she knew, often took their social position from the people they served. A woman used to waiting on economic royalty might have been insulted at the thought of serving a commoner.

She retraced the tour, now taking her time to work through the first level of detail. She immediately decided that there would be no changes in the kitchen, because she wouldn't be doing much cooking. There were machines in there that she had never seen before and some that actually frightened her. Her haunt would be the breakfast room. In fact, she would probably use a laptop to work there. The table was as big as any desk and there was already a phone line. The unobstructed view of the park made it a perfect place for writing. She could use any small space to set up her computer and files.

The living room was beyond her. Any project would be massive and time-consuming. She wouldn't even change the artwork, even though the modernists had never been her favorites. The dining room was also intimidating, but she thought she could brighten it up a bit with some silk flowers.

On the second floor she peeked into Kay Parker's bedroom and decided to leave it for last. The other rooms would be much easier. There would be no changes to his office. She wouldn't dare. Nor to the billiard room. She didn't play the game, so she had to assume that the dark furniture, forest green accents, and needlessly elaborate table lighting were things that pool players treasured. The workout room had weights that she couldn't lift, but there was a treadmill she thought she could learn to love. The guest rooms were okay but darker than she liked. Maybe new window treatments to let in sunlight, and brighter bedspreads. The two front rooms would be for Bill's children, and she decided that she would let them design their own spaces. Paint, paper, whatever they wanted, and stereos with enormous speakers. This would be her best opportunity to get off to a good start with Cassie and Craig.

The library was going to be a problem. It was stocked with books that everyone would like to think they had read. She wanted more contemporary writers, art books, and travel guides. She also thought she should have a few shelves that would appeal to teenagers. But that she could do over time. There was no need to make the library a priority.

And then there was the grand boudoir, the monument to Kay Parker. The room described Andrews's first wife better than any news clippings could. Feminine, in the floral prints and colors. Tasteful, in the grand design of the space. Aristocratic, with the formality of the environment. Willful, with a floor-to-ceiling closet of shoes. Sexy, with drawer upon drawer of lingerie. Social, as demonstrated by the variety of suits, dresses, and ensembles. Wealthy, in the obvious disregard of cost. It would be hard to imagine a room that screamed out any louder the long list of Jane Warren's inadequacies.

Her own apartment was painted in an off-white, furnished with pieces from her first apartment, from Art's apartment, and from the annual sale at a national furniture chain. The decor was as unoriginal as the standard floor plan. Her shoes were scattered on the closet floor, two pairs of heels, two pairs of comfortable flats, and two pairs of sneakers. Her lingerie was basically a collection of oversize T-shirts, three pairs of pajamas, and one truly sexy black garter belt outfit that Art liked her to wear when he had had too much to drink. The final insult was that everything had been bought on sale.

Okay, Jane thought, *I'm not in this lady's league. But you know what? I don't want to be. I wouldn't want to live with all this fanfare. This is pretentious, and for exactly that reason, the most unromantic room I've ever seen.*

This is where she had to begin. If she were to make a home for Bill, herself, and the children, the shrine had to be shut down. She would pack Kay's clothes and move them out. Kay wouldn't be wearing them again, so maybe she would donate them anonymously to one of those outfits that provided clothes for poor women entering the workforce. Wouldn't that be a gas! Kay Parker's designer suit out on a job interview. Then she would split the closet, half for Bill's clothes and half for hers. She'd have to go on a shopping spree just to fill her half. The floral wallpaper had to come down, maybe in favor of a layer-painted wall that would be gender-neutral. And the delicate furniture would have to be replaced with something heavier and more masculine.

The bed was going to require a bit of thinking. Kay's bed was a woman's place of rest, a soft refuge from the cares of the day. It was a sanctuary that a man would beg to enter. Jane wanted something earthier, a bed that cried out for bouncing, tumbling lovemaking. She wanted Bill to know that it was his and that the woman in it wanted very much to be his. But what? Not something with hearts and cupids, and certainly not with mirrored headboard and ceiling. She had no idea what was needed, but maybe that's what interior decorators were for.

She found her overnight bag at the foot of the stairs. "It was down at the concierge's desk," Mrs. McCarty explained. "I had it brought up."

Jane had forgotten completely about it and hadn't even thought about where she would sleep. The housekeeper suggested the master bedroom, but Jane had no desire to sleep in Kay Parker's shrine. Nor did she want to move into the guest room that Bill was using. That, she thought, would be presumptuous. She decided on one of the other guest rooms, which Eileen assured her was ready and would be "no trouble at all." Then she decided to eat out so that Mrs. McCarty wouldn't have to worry about her dinner.

She ate quickly and inexpensively and got back to the apartment at nine. She sat for a while in the living room, looking across the park at the glorious skyline, wondering how she was supposed to make a home in a place that baffled all her life's experience. She was completely aware that the train from Connecticut and the private elevator had carried her into another world.

Jane was lying awake in one of the guest rooms when she heard a telephone ring. She tried to answer it and realized that the apartment was equipped with a key system in which each room had a direct-dial extension. She reached for the blinking button.

"Where are you?" Bill's voice asked.

"In your apartment, of course."

He laughed. "I know that, but which room?"

"I don't know, but the bed is like a rock."

"Well, try another bed. There are lots of them."

"Sure! I'll be like Goldilocks. I'll keep changing beds until one is just right."

"What about the master bedroom?" he asked.

She drew a deep breath. "Not until I make some changes."

"Oh!" He was surprised. "You don't like it?"

"It's beautiful, but it's not me, and it's certainly not you. Besides, there's no room in the closet. Did you know that it's still filled with your first wife's things?"

"Yes," he answered. "I suppose I did. That's the one room I haven't changed. . . ."

Another deep breath. "Bill, I don't want to take anyone's place."

"Of course, of course. You're absolutely right. I want you to redo the rooms exactly the way you want them."

"The way *we* want them," Jane corrected.

Andrews laughed. "I guess I'm going to have to learn a new language." Then he added, in a more serious tone, "You're just going to have to bear with me for a while. I've been on my own too long!"

She was gaining ground, Jane thought, so she might just as well keep pushing. "And, Bill, I think I'd like to open up the pool and dance floor on the roof. It would be a perfect place for that reception you mentioned."

"Great idea," he answered. "It sounds as if you're already putting your heart into the place."

They spoke affectionately for a few minutes until Andrews announced that he had to rush off to a meeting.

"I love you," Jane managed to get in before he hung up.

"And I love you. I already told you that, didn't I?"

"Yes, you did," she answered, even though she knew he hadn't. As he said, she was going to have to bear with him for a while.

Her hand stayed on the phone long after she had hung up.

All their conversations seemed ambivalent—moments of tenderness interrupted by the urgency of business. Was that the way her life was going to be?

Another of the telephone station lights went on, and Jane stared at it curiously for a moment. Someone was making a call. There was someone else in the apartment. But there couldn't be. Mrs. McCarty was gone for the night. The elevator was down in the lobby, locked to anyone who didn't have a key. She lifted the handset and pushed the lit key. There was a beeping sound. She was locked out of the other line. It didn't seem possible, but she knew there was someone else inside the penthouse.

18

Jane slowly lifted herself out of the bed, slipped into her jeans, and tucked in the T-shirt she was wearing as a night-gown. She left her shoes behind as she eased open the bed-room door. The apartment was well lit by the skyline glare coming in through the glass living-room wall. Jane could see the furniture settings in the living room below, the piano bar on one side, and even the breakfast room near the kitchen. Nothing seemed unusual or out of place. Nothing was mov-ing. She listened and heard the silence of the apartment over the soft street noises from outside. Not a sound other than a motor hum from below, probably the heating system or maybe a kitchen freezer.

Yet she had seen the light go on. Someone had to have lifted a telephone somewhere in the apartment. Jane looked back through the open door of her room at the phone on the desk. The light had gone out.

Was it a problem with the phone? A light that went on and off accidentally, or a handset that was off the hook? She was certain that the light came on long after she had hung up her own phone. The fact that she couldn't access the extension seemed to confirm that the line was in use.

She slid along the outside of the balcony, panning her eyes down over the railing into the corners of the space below. But she stopped when she reached the top of the stairs. Why should she go down? If there was a burglar in the rooms be-low, the last thing she should do was confront him. God, but it was eerily like Kay Parker, going down the stairs of the mountain chalet and confronting an intruder.

But what if he was up there on the bedroom floor, lurking in one of the other guest rooms? Maybe in the room that Bill used. Or maybe in Kay's room. Then she should go down and get out of the apartment as fast as she could. But that was dangerous, too. She would have to go back to her room to get her elevator key. And then the elevator would take time coming up from the ground floor, time during which she would be trapped helplessly in the foyer.

She remembered the building staff down in the lobby. A night doorman. A concierge. Call down and tell them that someone had broken in. They could call the police and then come up in the elevator. She turned back to her bedroom, now more desperate to get to the door and close it behind her than she was to keep an eye on the living room. She went straight to her desk without turning on the light and found the telephone. But before she could pick up the handset, another light flashed on. She tried a different line. More rapid beeping! All the phone lines were tied up. She was trapped in the huge apartment with no communications and no elevator, a prisoner of whoever had broken in. The wonderful new world atop the New York skyline had turned into a death trap.

Something crashed downstairs—a dish, a lamp, maybe even a bottle from the liquor cabinet. Jane froze and listened to the silence that followed. There was nothing, not even the motor hum she had heard before. Then there was a creak, soft, muffled, and distant. It was a footstep at the bottom of the stairs. Whoever was down there was coming up. She went to the door and pressed her ear against it. Another sound, like the first. *Another step,* she thought. She found the doorknob and turned the lock. But that wouldn't help much. It was only a flimsy privacy lock. One good kick and the door would fly open.

Should she scream? Would that startle the intruder and make him aware that someone was home? Or would it drive him into action and send him rushing to silence the screamer? It might not matter at all. No one would hear her. She was two levels away from the closest building resident, and twenty-five floors above the street.

Her cell phone chirped somewhere behind her. The cell phone! She ran back around the bed and dug into the pockets of the clothes she had carelessly discarded. Another chirp. Her hand followed the sound until she found the glowing data screen. "Yes," she said in a horse whisper, and heard Bill's voice. "Hi, I tried to call you back—"

"Bill, someone's in the apartment. The phones are knocked out. He's coming up the stairs."

"What?"

She nearly shouted. "Someone is coming after me."

"Hang up! Dial nine-one-one! I'll call the lobby!" He clicked off. Jane ended the call and pressed 911.

"Police emergency," a woman's voice answered.

"Help me. Someone has broken in to my apartment."

"What's the address?"

"It's a penthouse. Fifth Avenue, across from the park."

"What's the address?"

What in hell was the address? Bill had given it to her. She had written it down. She had read it off a piece of paper when she stood in front of the building. What was it? *Six-something,* she thought. She knew there was a six in it.

"Ma'am, I'm not showing a caller ID number. Are you on a cell phone?"

"Yes!"

"Then you'll have to tell me the address."

She blurted out a number. That was it. It sounded right.

"Okay, help is on the way," the woman's voice said. "Stay on the line. Keep talking to me. Can you see the intruder?"

"I'm locked in my bedroom," Jane said. But not really, she knew. The lock wouldn't keep anyone out. She groped for the chair and carried it toward the door. But then she heard another footstep, this one right outside her door. Someone tried to turn the doorknob. The lock jiggled. "He's right outside my door!" Jane screamed into her phone.

A telephone rang in the lobby, startling the night man who was dozing behind his desk. He dropped his feet from the desktop and reached out with one hand. "Front desk, Joseph speaking." With his other hand he tried to wipe the sleep from his eyes. A second later he was bolt upright. "Yes, Mr. Andrews."

The distant voice was shouting, talking too quickly to be distinct. "Where? . . . Your penthouse?" Joseph listened. "Who's there?" The call didn't make any sense. The penthouse elevator hadn't moved since he came on duty. And the penthouse was empty. Mrs. McCarty had gone home. Mr. Andrews was logged out.

It took steely discipline for Andrews to start over again, this time more slowly. A young woman who was using his apartment was in great danger. There was an intruder in the penthouse, and the telephones had been disabled.

"I'll call the police," Joseph decided.

"Get someone up there now!" Andrews shouted.

Joseph screamed at the night porter, who was asleep in a soft chair. "Get up to the penthouse. Find out what's going on!"

"What's happening?" the woman was shouting over Jane's phone. "Are you all right?" Jane wasn't able to answer. She had all her weight against the door and was trying to drag the desk chair under the knob. The door was still rattling softly as someone turned it from the other side.

"I've called the police!" Jane shouted through the door. "They're on the way!" The door stopped rattling. Quick footsteps faded toward the stairs. The front doorbell rang, followed in a few seconds by loud knocking. She heard the warble of a siren, growing louder in the street below.

19

The porter opened the door for the police, who flooded into the apartment with guns drawn. Lights were turned on in every room, and the officers poked through every closet. One of them went outside and flashed a light into the corners of the patio and the overhang of the roof. Another went upstairs to the roof and searched the cabana rooms and the space behind the planters. The burglar, it seemed, had vanished.

"You ever see anything like this?" one policeman asked another as they looked behind the racks in the wine cellar.

The response was a head shaken in awe. "Did you see the beach club up on the roof? Where do people get this kind of money?"

"No wonder they hear footsteps and see ghosts."

Robert Leavitt came through the open door while the search was still in progress, and Jane rushed into his arms. "Thank God you're here," she said, holding on to his arm. "These people think I'm crazy."

He sat her down on one of the living-room sofas and brought her a snifter of brandy. "The alarm system calls me if there's an emergency here," Leavitt explained. "I didn't know you were in the apartment until Bill called me and said you were in trouble."

"Make them believe that," she said, gesturing to the prowling policemen. "They keep asking me what drugs I've been taking."

A plainclothes detective sat down across from them, found out how Leavitt fit in to the picture, and began his interview. Jane took him step-by-step through the events of the evening since her fiancé first called her. She went over the light that had appeared on her telephone, disappeared, and then come back on—proof that someone had been in the house. When she had tried to call out, all the lines were blocked. She told him about the crash somewhere in the living room, a lamp or vase that had been knocked over. Then the footsteps on the stairs, and finally the hand turning her bedroom doorknob. She had forgotten about her cell phone until it rang—her fiancé, who had forgotten to tell her something but found the telephones dead when he tried to call back. She had followed his instructions.

The officer listened patiently, jotting down an occasional note. Then he told Jane and Robert the results of the search. The elevator hadn't gone up to the penthouse all evening, so he was having trouble understanding how a burglar could have gotten in. Someone could have walked up the fire stairs or taken an elevator to a high floor and then gone up the fire stairs. But the fire doors were locked from the inside, and there was an alarm down in the lobby whenever one opened. Then there was the penthouse security system. Anyone coming through the front door or the service door would set off an alarm unless he punched in the right code within twenty seconds.

"Someone was in here," Jane interrupted.

The detective nodded but continued with his report. The police had checked the phone system as soon as they arrived. They had gotten a dial tone on every line. He had just spoken with the telephone company, and there had been no service interruption detected by the computers.

"You can disable this phone system just by pulling one electronic card in the control box," Leavitt said in Jane's defense.

"You could," the officer answered, "but you'd have to use a key to open the box. There are no scratches, and the lock wasn't jimmied."

Then he raised the issue of the crash that Jane had heard. "A vase or a lamp?" he asked her.

"Or a dish, a glass, a bottle," she answered sharply. "I heard something break down here."

But there was nothing broken, the detective told them. They hadn't found a broken lamp or a shattered dish. If an intruder knocked something over, there would be broken pieces on the floor. Unless he had paused to clean up his mess, which wasn't the general m.o. of second-story men.

"You think I dreamed this whole thing?" Jane challenged.

The detective raised his palms in a helpless gesture.

Leavitt showed a momentary flash of anger that he instantly brought back under control. "Ms. Warren isn't a hysterical woman," he said. "She's a competent journalist who checks things out very thoroughly."

"I'm not criticizing the lady," the detective responded evenly. "What I'm saying is that there is absolutely no evidence of a break-in, nor anything to suggest that an outsider was in the apartment. The fingerprints on the outside of the bedroom doorknob are the same as the ones on the inside— Ms. Warren's. Nothing was disturbed, nothing stolen. So I can file a report, we can keep an eye on the building, and we can call back every couple of days to see if anything new has turned up or turned up missing."

Order slowly returned. The police left, stationing one man in the hallway as protection against someone returning. The porter came back up twice to see if there was anything he could do for his prize residents. One by one, Robert Leavitt turned off the lights.

At three in the morning he started to leave, but Jane prevailed upon him to stay for another brandy. He agreed and poured one for her as well, and decided that if Jane didn't mind, he would crash in one of the guest rooms. She was delighted that he would be able to stay.

"Does all this strike you as eerily familiar?" she asked when they were both seated at the piano bar.

"No, not really. We've never had a problem here. I guess we've just assumed that the security is foolproof."

"Not here," she said. Then she asked, "Weren't you the first one on the scene when Bill's first wife was killed?"

Leavitt nodded, still not sure of her point.

"Bill's wife was killed by an intruder the police were never able to identify. Officials began to doubt that there had been an intruder. Now, when I'm going to marry Bill and become the second Mrs. Andrews, another vanished intruder appears, tries to break in to my bedroom, and then disappears without a trace."

"I suppose it is spooky when you look at it that way," Robert conceded.

"It's a lot more than spooky when I may be in line for the same fate."

He smiled, dismissing her concerns. "Jane, this was most likely just a common burglar. Vacant penthouses are probably irresistible to them. And it may not have been even that. Couldn't the telephone problem have gotten you on edge? You're not used to the sounds in the city, and maybe your imagination was playing—"

"You think I made all this up?"

"No, of course not," Leavitt assured her. "I think it was all very real to you. And calling the police was exactly the right thing to do. I just don't believe that whatever happened tonight has any connection with . . . eight years ago."

They sat quietly for a moment. Jane saw no point in arguing her case. She had to admit that to the police, and probably to Robert, a break-in at her lofty perch was unlikely, and there was absolutely no evidence of an intruder. But then she remembered there were a few facts on her side that nobody had yet considered. "Would it change your mind any to know that someone has been snooping in my apartment?"

His calm expression tensed. "When? Tell me about it."

"Last week. Twice, when I was out with Bill." She explained the first occasion when the person was still in the apartment and she had heard him let himself out. Leavitt was concerned, not just about the intrusion but about her walking in on the guy. His escape out the door was fortunate, he thought. If Jane had confronted him, she could have been killed. Then she told him of finding her notes reordered. She had particularly noted which page was on top just before she left with Bill, and that page had been moved when she returned.

"What were the notes about?" he asked, joining her in trying to figure out a motive.

She hesitated, and then told him, "I've been looking into Kay Parker's murder. Just to try to understand Bill's grief. The printout was on my desk, and I checked to be sure there was nothing showing that might be hurtful to him."

"And that's what the person was looking at?"

"Yes," she said. "At least, it seems that way."

Leavitt sat thoughtfully, then raised his hands in surrender. "I don't get it. Why would anyone care? That was eight years ago, and it was a dead end even then." He offered another interpretation. "Is it possible that you found Kay's death disturbing . . . frightening? Could you be carrying that image around with you, maybe putting yourself in her place?"

Her anger showed. "Look, I didn't imagine that someone got into my apartment. Someone was there—twice! And I didn't dream up tonight. There was someone in the house, and he came up the stairs looking for me." But even as she said it, she had a moment of doubt. Was it possible she was imagining that Kay's gruesome ending might also be hers?

20

The wedding plan changed. Instead of "just family" at the federal court building, they decided on family and close friends in the roof garden with an appeals court judge presiding. Craig would stand up for his father, even though Robert Leavitt would sign as the legal witness. Jane planned to have Cassie as her maid of honor. She had no close relatives, so her guest list would be mainly her friends from the office. She couldn't invite Art. It would be tacky to invite an ex-husband, even though Art was the closest thing she had to a child.

The reception, too, was to be kept modest—cocktails and heavy hors d'oeuvres in the roof garden. William's guest list was limited to a few company executives and their significant others and no more than a dozen business associates. Jane decided on Roscoe Taylor, Jack Dollinger, Marie Lyons—the secretary she and Jack shared—and their spouses. She added a young friend from her health club, Diane Trotta, to demonstrate that she had friends her own age. She was embarrassed to realize how few close friends she actually had. Craig invited a classmate from school, and Cassie asked a boy she had met at an equestrian event. A trio of strings would provide the music.

Simple as it sounded, Jane ran into problems immediately. First was the date of the affair. William's secretary, Ann Packard, proved to be domineering and defensive. "There is no available weekend for the foreseeable future," she said curtly, as if that was the final word on the wedding. There was only one weekend in the next two months when Mr. Andrews could be in New York, and two of the executives he would certainly invite would be away then.

"He'll have to cancel something," Jane suggested, certain

that Bill would regard their wedding as more important than one of his business meetings.

"Fine," Ann answered, clearly indignant that her decision was being challenged. "Who would you suggest we disappoint? The prime minister of Canada or a prince of the royal family of Saudi Arabia?"

"Whichever one is a month from Saturday," Jane said, trying to be every bit as imperious.

"Neither Mr. Applebaum nor Ms. Annuzio will be available," the secretary snapped, playing her trump card.

"Oh, that's too bad. Mr. Andrews will be terribly disappointed."

It took a few seconds for Ann to come to grips with the reality of a regime change. She made a desperate move to maintain her exclusive right to budget William Andrews's time. "I'll have to discuss this with Mr. Leavitt."

Eileen McCarty wasn't very helpful. Her mind was a complete blank on the names of suitable caterers. "Mr. Andrews hasn't had many parties since I've been here. The cook and I handled his small business dinners."

Then Craig proved balky when she got him on the telephone. "A what?" he demanded when she suggested that a dark suit would be appropriate for his role before the judge. And then, "Are you trying to tell me what to wear?"

By the end of her first day of preparations, Jane felt thoroughly defeated. There was a school of pilot fish permanently attached to the great shark she was about to marry, and none of them took to the idea that the meal ticket might let himself be distracted. The secretary wasn't about to give up control of William Andrews's date book. Jane sensed that she would have to tear it out of her cold, dead hands. The housekeeper wasn't up to the task. And the children bristled at any sign of discipline in their selfish little lives. Art had eventually given her a major role in planning her first wedding because there wasn't much that he could handle by himself. It seemed that William might not have any role to give her, because he had already parceled out his needs to retainers.

"How's it going?" Bill asked when he called her the next morning.

"Wonderful," she said, unable to conceal her sarcasm. "Why don't you and I run off to a justice of the peace and never come back."

"I'd love it," he said. But then he immediately added, "Seriously, is everything under control?"

"Depends on whether you want to offend a prime minister or a prince, whether you mind if I serve hot dogs, or if you care what your son wears to our wedding. Right now I think he's planning on cargo pants and sneakers."

She went through her list of problems and was pleased that he exuded sympathy. "I've been in such a rut that the people around me have turned into stone. They're all terrified of change." But he didn't offer to solve her problems. "Just be patient," he said. "They'll come around and learn to love you as much as I do."

She agreed but then added that someone had to set the wedding date. "You'd better plan on shutting down Andrews Global Network for a Saturday. Otherwise, you and your guests will all be out of town."

He promised that he would set a date and that if it wasn't the Saturday she had suggested, it would certainly be within the next month. She asked him if he had any ideas on caterers. He mentioned the address file he thought Kay had kept on the computer. Or failing that, there might be something in the phone book in his desk drawer.

Jane went to the office, sat at the computer, and began reviewing the list of files. Kay's personal records, she soon discovered, were behind a firewall that required a password. There was no way she could get through. She would have to connect one of the young computerniks from her office to Kay's directories and let an expert try his magic.

She went to William's desk and found the drawers locked. The locks were fragile, a simple toggle turned by a key. She could probably open it with a nail file, but she didn't want to risk telltale scratches. She went back to the computer desk and found a small key among the rubber bands and paper clips. The key opened the drawers of Bill's desk.

She found an address book and looked under "C" for caterers. There were none. Maybe "P" for parties. Again there was no listing. Patiently, she went through the address book, trying every conceivable entry. Nothing suggested caterers.

She saw a checkbook, a large leather-bound volume with three checks to a page and a whole journal for recording the payments. Maybe there was a check to a caterer. She laid the book on the desk and opened the cover. A year's worth of monthly checks had been torn from the pages. Each had the same entry in the journal: "$100,000 to Selina Royce." The last check had been entered just a few weeks ago. The first journal entry was eight years earlier. William was paying someone a hundred thousand a month and had been doing so for the past eight years. Just who in hell was Selina Royce?

Jane's imagination went wild. A blackmailer, she decided. Selina Royce knew William Andrews's darkest secret, and she was charging him a hundred thousand a month to keep quiet—$1.2 million a year! It must be quite a secret. She thought about the timing. The first check had gone out just a few months after Kay Parker's untimely death. So if it was blackmail, it stood to reason that it had something to do with the murder.

But why would Bill be paying off someone in connection with the murder? Unless he was involved in some way. It was unthinkable, but suppose he had killed his first wife, as some of the reporters at the time seemed to suspect. Could Selina Royce, whoever she was, have known? Was that why he was sending her monthly checks?

Jane went back to the address book and looked under "R." And there was the entry, Selina Royce, 24 Boulevard Haussmann, Paris. Her husband-to-be was sending over a million dollars a year to a woman who lived in the fashionable center of Paris.

She slammed the books closed and stuffed them back into the desk. She sat silently, trying to take in the information she had just uncovered. Blackmail? If that's what it was, then Bill was probably involved somehow in his wife's death. But maybe it wasn't blackmail. Andrews was a young, virile man living without the wife he adored. Certainly he would be interested in women, and just as certainly he could easily afford to keep a mistress. That could be the answer, and it was easier to imagine than her fiancé's being a murderer.

But even then the information was unsettling. Probably Selina Royce was the reason for William's frequent trips to Paris. She remembered that at their first meeting, when he had introduced himself to her and taken her on a tour of the city, he had broken away for the afternoon in order to attend to a business affair. Could that have been a liaison with his mistress?

Jane was suddenly frightened to the point that her hands were shaking. She had spent the day trying to make arrangements for her wedding to a man she was growing to love. A man who, at worst, may have killed his first wife and, at best, was keeping a mistress whom he had continued to finance even while he was proposing to her. A man who was resented, maybe even hated, by his children and who had created a safe space by surrounding himself with a staff of loyal sycophants. My God, what did she really know about William Andrews? She knew about his public life, which was undoubtedly the creation of his PR department. She was well aware of his financial assets. She had met his children, who were spoiled, and a few of his employees and underlings, who clearly resented her intrusion.

There were a few other things she knew. When called out of his world of endless competition, he could be soft, sympathetic, and caring. He was a considerate and romantic lover. In some way that she didn't fully understand, he seemed to need her. But who or what was he? What secrets would unravel as they spent more time together? What role would she play in his life?

She would go on with the wedding arrangements. She had agreed to marry the man, and he seemed aware of the problems she faced in competing with the memory of Kay Parker.

But she would leave no stone unturned to find the answers to the questions he posed. In particular, she would find out exactly who Selina Royce was and what hold she had on Bill that made her worth more than a million a year.

Jane got back to business. She started with the caterers listed in the phone book, looking for the ones with high-rent addresses. Then she introduced herself to each one by saying, "I'm calling for William Andrews, the late Kay Parker's husband." Some of the caterers didn't make the connection. But there were two who nearly jumped through the phone at the mention of Kay's name. A bit of grilling showed which of the two had handled most of Kay's parties and remembered the details. That was the one she invited for an interview.

She also browsed the shops of interior decorators, looking for hints of masculine taste and democratic restraint. She found one she liked, and the man who owned the business seemed to understand her problem in dealing with Kay's carefully preserved bedroom. "Best to bite the bullet," he said. "Half measures never please anyone." Jane invited him up to see the apartment. Then she caught a train out of Grand Central and headed back to Southport to see what Roscoe knew about a woman named Selina Royce.

He shook his head at the mention of the name. "No one I can remember," he said. "But I'll ask. There are still a few of us around who reported on the fantasy life of Kay Parker." He scribbled a reminder on his desk pad and then asked without looking up, "Is everything going well? Are you okay?"

Jane settled into a chair. "I'm an outsider," she announced. "I'm going where I'm not wanted."

"The groom's ardor is cooling?"

"That might be impossible. The groom is already frozen."

Roscoe folded his hands behind his head and tipped back his chair. "Maybe you're moving too quickly? You might take a little more time to get to know each other."

"Roscoe, he's surrounded by gatekeepers who won't let anyone get through. They portion out his time in thirty-second increments. They cover up his past as if he had an earlier career as the Boston Strangler. Bill lets them get away with it. He tells me to be patient, that they'll come around."

Jane stood and eased the office door closed. Then she took her boss through her research into Kay Parker's death—the doubts about the existence of an intruder, the time delay in summoning the police, the previous night's business meeting at the inn that seemed never to have taken place. "The investigation was a travesty," she concluded.

"Powerful people don't like ordinary folks looking into their affairs," Roscoe said, not at all surprised that Jane's investigation had confirmed his own suspicions.

Jane moved to the edge of his desk, nearly in his lap, when she whispered her findings about Selina Royce. "William Andrews has been sending a hundred thousand a month to a woman named Selina Royce in Paris."

That news widened Roscoe Taylor's eyes. Everything Jane had been telling him was old news. Her sense of alarm could easily be written off as paranoia coupled with prewedding jitters. But a hundred thousand a month from his private account smelled of blackmail. And the existence of blackmail indicated a secret that William Andrews didn't want revealed, no matter what the cost. "How hard do you want me to press on this stuff?" he asked. "Not knowing might be a lot easier for you to live with than what we might dig up."

Jane paused. "I guess I really want to know," she concluded.

"You want to know enough so that I should try to find the lady in Paris and put a stringer on finding this Royce woman's family? Because Andrews Global Network could easily find out that I'm snooping."

Jane thought for a moment and then decided. "If you can do the fieldwork, I'll stick with the newspaper morgues."

21

Jane smiled when she let herself into her own apartment. It was little more than a closet after a week in William Andrews's penthouse, and the furnishings were bland. But it was hers. She had felt the heat of the spotlight and now she savored the delights of her anonymity. She kicked off her shoes, changed into jeans, and then scanned a week's worth of mail while she waited for her coffee to perk. Then she sat down at her computer, logged on to the *Times'* morgue, and began searching for Selina Royce.

It didn't take her long. She started with the name and the year of Kay Parker's death. When that came up blank, she went a year earlier. Two entries popped up. The first was an article on her move to the Andrews Cable News network from a cable service in San Antonio, Texas. Andrews had acquired the property, installed a new manager, and then brought Selina to New York. The second was a photograph taken at a cable news awards dinner. She recognized Andrews, a bit younger and leaner, and Robert Leavitt, whose hair was longer and parted in the middle. She also picked out Gordon Frier, one of the executives she had met on her trip to Paris. There were three women in the photo, one flashing Kay Parker's society smile. Jane had to check the caption to identify Kim Annuzio, who, with her hair styled and wearing an off-the-shoulder dress, didn't at all resemble the executive in slacks and blouse. Then, seated between Andrews and Leavitt, was Selina Royce, terribly serious and very attractive.

Her look was evening-news grave rather than morning-news giddy. She wore her dark hair long and close to her face. Her chin was held high, displaying a long neck that blended into perfect shoulders. Even in the computer reproduction of a grainy news photo, she seemed a happy marriage of brains and body, not at all unlike Kay Parker.

There was William, sitting comfortably between Kay and Selina, touching neither one of them and totally involved with the camera. It was a scene of harmony at a moment of victory, with the two women as alike as a pair of queens flanking the king. Yet within a few months Kay would be dead and William would be paying a monthly stipend to keep Selina in Paris. It seemed impossible. Jane couldn't imagine what must have happened that morning at the ski lodge.

She went back through all her printouts. Over and over again was the mention of an intruder, a figure who seemed to have arrived from nowhere and disappeared without a trace. Someone Robert Leavitt would have had to pass on the road as he drove up from the inn to William's aid. She found the newspaper report on the neighbors who had been questioned. What struck her was that none of them knew the others except by name and for a passing nod. They were all successful families who came up to the mountains on weekends precisely to be alone. They were escaping the business and social ties of the city and had no interest in making new friends in the woods. They all said that they knew who Andrews was but had never met him. There was no reason why any of them would be involved in either his business or personal life.

So who was the intruder? Jane asked herself. Someone who arrived and left on foot. A hunter who happened on an expensive house that he thought was empty, broke in, and then panicked when he was caught? Or perhaps a professional sent by someone from either Kay's or William's past? Social leaders and business dynamos left a wake of drowning enemies yearning to be avenged. But they generally weren't people who would go to a hit man.

Jane reacquainted herself with the speed of the inquiry. Kay's body had been shipped, mourned, and cremated in just a few days, without ever being scrutinized by a medical examiner. The local sheriff had never secured the crime scene but had, instead, sent a posse out to search the vast wilderness of the Adirondacks. The state police had been polite and deferential in questioning William Andrews and had been careful that their investigation wouldn't track mud across his carpet. They simply accepted his version of the tragedy and tried their best not to inconvenience him.

He had testified only once, at the coroner's inquest, and without any cross-examination. The officials had kept apologizing for asking him to repeat the painful events and seemed more relieved than he was when the ordeal was over. The report specified Kay's death as a homicide, caused by a massive trauma to the head. It noted that death would have been instantaneous, ending any discussion about whether Andrews should have called a doctor before he called his business associate.

Jane re-read Robert Leavitt's interview. He had traveled up to the Adirondacks with Andrews and his wife for a business meeting that was part of William's holiday. Other executives from the company had arrived separately and left that night. Leavitt had been preparing to leave himself when the call came in.

He immediately got into his car and drove the long climb up the twisting mountain road. When he arrived at the lodge, he found William slumped on a sofa, with Kay's body behind him at the foot of the stairs. Kay, he said, had been gruesomely decapitated. William was wounded in the arm and chest. There was blood all over the steps leading up to the second floor.

Leavitt phoned the police. Had he considered calling a doctor first? No, he said. There was no question that she was dead. No, he hadn't touched the body. There was no need to. He could tell at a glance that she was gone. But he saw that William needed medical attention right away. He called the doctor down in town. The doctor had already been informed by the police and was on his way.

Why didn't William Andrews call the police? He was wounded and hardly coherent. Why didn't Leavitt call the police first, before he started up to the chalet? Because William Andrews seemed vague and confused. Leavitt didn't know what to make of the call until he reached the lodge. What did Andrews say on the telephone? Just that there had been a tragedy and that Kay was dead. He asked Leavitt to come immediately. Didn't the fact that Mr. Andrews said his wife was dead suggest that Leavitt should have notified the police? It should have, but it was all so unbelievable. He had been with her just the night before. It seemed more as if something had happened to William. Finally, had he seen anyone coming down the road as he was heading up? Not that he remembered, Robert testified. But he couldn't be sure. He was fixated on getting to the Andrewses' house and probably wouldn't have taken notice of a car going down the hill.

Pretty straightforward, Jane concluded. If it wasn't an intruder, then the only other suspect was William Andrews. But according to the coroner, Andrews had been sprayed with the blood and gore of his wife's shattered skull. So he had to have been behind her when she was shot in the face. Who else could have done it? One of the business associates who had been at the meeting? Perhaps someone had intended to threaten William but had been attacked by Kay. Jane could visualize a scene where a wife would jump between her husband and his attacker. But William would have recognized someone from the meeting. And besides, Leavitt probably would have noticed a colleague passing by even if he wouldn't have been aware of a stranger.

Absent from any of the reports was mention of Selina Royce. She wasn't involved. She wasn't a witness. So what could she know that would end her promising career as a television personality and drive her into European exile? What hold did she have on William Andrews that could possibly be worth over a million a year?

Jane re-examined everything, finally focusing on the only still-open questions. What was the meeting about, and who was at the meeting? Answers to those questions might suggest a motive and might produce additional suspects.

In the morning she phoned Roscoe and told him about Selina's connection to San Antonio. That might be the best place to start his inquiries. Then she added the information about the business meeting the night before the killing. Could that be relevant? The police had never explored it. Then she returned to the city to meet with her caterer and decorator.

There was a message waiting from Ann Packard that set the wedding date for the Saturday four weeks away. Mr. Andrews had freed up his calendar, and she was quite sure that the others would be able to rearrange their commitments.

So it was the Saudi prince who would be inconvenienced, Jane told herself as she called back with a quick thank-you. She oozed that it must have been difficult rearranging so many busy schedules, trying to win her husband's secretary as an ally.

Eileen McCarty told her that the swimming pool people were up on the roof, checking the dance floor that automatically closed over the pool. "Wonderful!" Jane gushed. All of a sudden things were falling into place. She wanted the dance floor down for the wedding and reception.

The caterer's meeting also went smoothly. Peter Tipper arrived with an assistant and presented a menu of heavy hors d'oeuvres that included the cuisine of the entire civilized world, as well as dishes from regions still suspected of cannibalism. A taste of each would be more food than a five-course feast. The bar was Dom Pérignon champagne, Macallan twenty-year-old scotch, and Hennessy cognac. The liquor was top-shelf—even the tequila had been aged—and the beer represented eight different countries. *Hardly a simple wedding reception for a few close friends,* Jane thought. This was her first opportunity to cut the ties to Kay Parker's extravagance.

While Tipper looked on in horror, Jane began cutting the menu, starting first with the foods she couldn't pronounce. She reduced the assortment of hot hors d'oeuvres to six and cut the champagne supply in half. Tipper groaned. Then Jane added a beer to the list, a local brew in a tacky green bottle that she had heard Roscoe order a number of times. Eileen took Peter and his aide up to the roof garden to measure for their tent and kitchen setup. The construction estimate, Jane noticed, was more than the annual rent on her apartment.

The decorator, Arnold Kallen, was impressed the moment he stepped off the elevator. As he went from room to room, he rattled off the names of colors, materials, and furnishings, his voice growing higher with each new name that caught his eye. Only once did his glance seem disapproving. He stood near the piano, pursed his lips, and then decided that it should be rotated about twenty degrees to improve the view of those sitting at the piano bar. He pronounced the first floor "glorious" and said he "wouldn't dream of changing it."

The second floor was a different story. He suggested exactly what Jane wanted to hear. The guest rooms needed to be brightened, the children's rooms should be youthful and frivolous, and the office could be modernized. Kallen took copious notes and measurements. He stopped dead when he reached the doorway to the master bedroom, seemingly undecided whether to laugh or genuflect. Then his hands gestured wildly. "Is . . . Mr. Andrews . . . comfortable with this?"

"He sleeps across the atrium," Jane said.

The decorator nodded and tried to be diplomatic with his next question. "Who does . . . sleep here?"

"No one has for several years. It was Mr. Andrews's first wife's room."

"And both you . . . and Mr. Andrews . . . plan on . . ."

"We plan on sleeping together and sharing the master suite," Jane said to ease the man's embarrassment. "I want a very big bed, romantic lighting, and a shower big enough for two."

"I understand." The smile on his lips said that he really did.

"I think we also need a Jacuzzi—"

"For two?" he interrupted.

"Why not?" Jane said. Then she added, "And a television that pops up out of something for nights when I'm home alone."

Arnold Kallen began writing and measuring. "And the things in the closet?" he asked.

She wanted to be glib and suggest a tag sale, but Kay's closet might be a problem. She couldn't gauge Bill's sentimental attachment to her things, or which outfits Cassie might hope to wear. "I'll have the closet empty before you start," she promised, wondering if she could get any response from Bill on short notice.

Kallen returned on Saturday to meet with the Andrews children, who were visiting for the weekend. Jane explained that their father hoped they would be spending more time at home, and she wanted to redo their rooms to fit their preferences. Neither Cassie nor Craig showed much interest.

"Who wants to live here?" Cassie demanded. "I like being at school and at the farm."

Craig mentioned a wall-size screen for his video games so he'd have something to do in the city. "I won't be here much," he decided.

Jane knew that Bill would be disappointed, but she wasn't unhappy that the children would rather be elsewhere. If they were with her, she would probably cause a ruckus by sending them out to find summer jobs. The kids went up to the roof to swim in the pool. Kallen left with instructions to "just make their rooms light and airy."

She moved her things out of Bill's room even though she wanted nothing more than to fold up into his embrace. So far, her engagement to Andrews had been a series of trials and disappointments. She wanted to enjoy some of the rewards. But the children shouldn't see their father bedding down with a girlfriend, so it was important for them to say their good nights from separate doors. Maybe, after the kids were sound asleep . . .

William arrived late that night and went straight to his own room. A few minutes later he knocked on her door. "I hoped we could spend a few minutes together," he said when she answered. But it wasn't the few minutes she was hoping for. He was still in his shirt and tie.

He suggested a nightcap and they went down to the piano bar, where he poured each of them a brandy. Robert Leavitt was on his way over, bringing some papers from the office. His week had not gone smoothly, and he gave her a quick summary of the details. The Federal Communications Commission had rejected his request for an exception, and a cable system he was courting had gone to another bidder. He and Leavitt needed to decide on a counterattack. Then he asked about her week.

She painted it as brightly as possible. The wedding date was set, the guests had been invited, and the caterer had been hired. The children were home and eager to see him. The swimming pool was open, and the dance floor had been fixed. Then she eased into the negatives. He would have to make a decision about the clothes in Kay's closet. He nodded gravely but didn't commit himself to doing anything right away. She gave him a quick rundown of the changes she was planning for Kay's suite. He seemed pained.

"You do want me to change it into *our* room, don't you?"

"Yes, yes. Of course." But he showed no enthusiasm. He could just as well have been agreeing to a dental procedure.

Then she told him about his children and their lack of enthusiasm for personalizing their rooms.

He said he would talk to them. "They've been through a lot. Try not to be too hard on them."

Hard on them? She was offering to redo their rooms. In a sense, promising to re-establish the household that had been blown away by the blast that killed their mother. But now wasn't the time to plead her case about raising his children. He had been away on a failed mission and seemed discouraged. "You know what? Why don't we take our drinks up to the pool and go skinny-dipping?"

He smiled as if the idea was outrageous. "This isn't the tallest building in the neighborhood," he said.

"Good! We'll give the neighbors something to talk about."

"You go," he said. "I have to wait up for Leavitt."

Jane felt a twinge of anger. This wasn't the homecoming she had been expecting. He had taken her report as if he were presiding over a business meeting and seemed disappointed in the message and the messenger. Being married to William Andrews was going to be thorns as well as roses. "Okay, I will," she said in a demonstration of independence. It wasn't so much that she wanted to go swimming but rather to show that she, too, could have her own agenda.

She regretted her choice as soon as she stepped out of the cabana. She was wearing a terry robe over her swimsuit, but she still felt the early-fall breeze blowing across the rooftops. She dipped a toe and found the water delightfully warm. But still, she knew how cold the night air would feel when she got out. "Big mouth," Jane chastised herself as she took off the robe. She went down the steps and slipped into the water, where it was warm and comfortable.

Wonderful! She was in total silence, high above the traffic noise, looking up at stars and out over the lit skyscrapers of New York. Kay Parker certainly knew how to live! Jane could imagine her floating weightlessly there, in her orbit over the earth. But she wondered if Kay and Bill had ever gone skinny-dipping together. That didn't strike her as likely. Kay wasn't the type, and he wouldn't have had the time. Then there were the possibilities introduced by her recent discovery of Selina Royce. Maybe the Andrews-Parker marriage wasn't quite the paradise that the society writers had constantly reported.

She was beginning to guess at their relationship. Kay was a public persona, a celebrity in her own right, in some ways her husband's rival for public adulation. In her private life, she was a genuine American princess, playing dress-up with the other ladies at court. And Bill was totally absorbed in his empire, a king who needed a queen for the sake of the peasants. Did they love each other as much as they loved themselves? Did they ever laugh at the ridiculous luck that brought them such privileged lives?

There was a sound, a precisely engineered click followed by a droning hum—a motor starting close to the deep end, where she was swimming. Then a rattling sound as a machine went into action. She looked around. Nothing had changed, but the rumbling left no doubt that something was moving. She stared into the darkness beyond the lit edge of the pool.

It came at her quickly, breaking into the light as it reached the water. A large wooden beam was rolling over the pool, coming straight toward her head. Jane righted herself and reached for the bottom with her foot, trying to run. But at the deep end, she couldn't touch bottom. The beam was closing quickly. She thought of ducking down and letting it roll over her head. But then she understood precisely what was happening. The dance floor was closing over the swimming pool. The beam coming toward her was the edge of the first panel, followed by others that would seal her under the water.

22

The floor panels were stacked in a machine that rolled them out one after another. As each panel slid out, it locked into the edge of the panel ahead and then pushed out over the pool, dragging the next one behind it, like the slats of a bamboo window blind.

She kicked off and swam furiously toward the shallow end. But her stroke was panicked and ineffective. She was thrashing rather than swimming. She felt the closing edge with her foot as she kicked. The door of the trap was sliding over her. She wasn't going to make it.

Jane screamed, her voice louder than the rumble of the mechanism. But her cry seemed useless. No one could get to her in time. She planted a foot on the moving edge and pushed off. For a second she was in the open, reaching out to the steps at the end of the pool. She grabbed the ladder and raised herself up out of the water. But there wasn't time. She would never make it out before the floor reached her, and if she was halfway out, the heavy wooden edge would cut across her like the blade of a guillotine. She had only seconds to save herself, and only one choice to make. Jane let go of the ladder, took a breath, and dropped under the water. She held her breath as the floor closed over her.

Her world went silent, as if she had suddenly gone deaf. She was in an eerie space of water brightly illuminated by the pool lights, sealed in on all sides. Every detail of the pool was clearly visible. She could see the tiles, the water-circulation inlets, and the steps. Over her head she could see the steel bars that reinforced each of the dance-floor panels. She took hold of the ladder and pulled up until she broke the surface. The water was at eye level when her head touched the bottom of the dance floor. Jane tilted her head back until her face was out of the water. She gulped for air and found that she could breathe—but just! The surface was still oscillating so that tiny swells were washing across her mouth and nose. If she wasn't careful, she could easily swallow water. If she lay perfectly still, she could breathe. But her feet sank and her shoulders rolled. Even the slightest movement created waves, and the waves rolled back over her face. Jane clutched at one of the steel braces. For a few moments she was able to hold herself still. Breathing was easier, but the tension in her shoulders shot pain across her back. She couldn't last long without letting go.

It would be easier, she decided, to sit on a lower step of the ladder and steady herself with her head bent back and her face in the clear. She tried one step, but it left her at the water level, gurgling with each breath. The next step was too high. Her face was pressed painfully against the wooden plank above. There was no position that would let her relax and breathe calmly.

She tried another scream that sounded deep and resonant in the small space above the water. It didn't seem loud enough to get anyone's attention. She banged her fist against the panel. The short stroke she was able to take produced nothing more than a knock. Once again she felt herself sinking, the water licking over her face. Jane knew that she couldn't hold herself still in the narrow air space for very long. She began to understand that her life was in danger.

There was only a three-inch gap between the water and the wooden ceiling that held her prisoner. She couldn't hold herself still for more than a few seconds, so she had to time her breaths very carefully. Come up slowly, break the surface, and breathe deeply. Then let herself settle back with just her eyes above the water. Wait patiently until she needed another breath, then tip her head back until her mouth and nose were clear. It was a routine that she knew she could keep up for a while. But for how long? It was the middle of the night. She might not be missed until William woke up in the morning, seven or eight hours from now. Could she stay awake and hold her concentration for that long?

The lights snapped off, a change every bit as dazzling as if

The First Wife 179

they had suddenly flashed on in the darkness. In the glow of the pool lights she had been able to analyze her predicament. Now she was in total blackness, as if lost at the bottom of the sea. She came up too quickly, banged her head, and swallowed water. She was suddenly choking, gasping for air and breathing in more water instead.

Don't panic, she told herself, but panic was already setting in. She was disoriented, unsure whether her face was in the narrow opening or still underwater. She was short of breath but terrified of taking in more water.

Don't panic! She felt for the ladder, sweeping her arms under the water. Her hand hit the metal pipe and then she was able to feel the steps. She let the ladder guide her as she rose, her arm raised to feel the rough bottom of the dance floor. Then she brought her face up slowly. She sputtered and threw up the water that had been locked in her throat. She drew a deep breath, taking in air but also more water, and the cycle of choking started all over again.

Stay calm! She rolled on her side so that half her face was pressed against the dance floor and she was able to spit up more water. But she couldn't control the gasp for air that drew still more water into her lungs. And that set her thrashing again.

There was plenty of air lying in a layer across the top of the water, and more seeping in from the outside. If she could just develop a rhythm—press her face against the wooden ceiling, breathe, and then let herself relax. Even if she sank a bit, she would still be safe as long as she could rise up gently for the next breath. But the choking and gasping were exhausting, and with the fatigue came even greater disorientation. Jane couldn't make her body work the way she knew it had to.

She began bobbing slowly, trying not to disturb the water surface and make waves. She got into a rhythm that seemed to work: surface to draw a breath, let herself sink a bit, and then surface for the next breath. She began counting the seconds to keep her mind occupied so that she wouldn't panic. But the process became hypnotic. She felt herself choking and realized that she had drawn a breath underwater. Later she felt herself sinking, exhaling a trail of bubbles. How long had she been trapped in the swimming pool? It seemed like hours, but it was probably no more than fifteen minutes. How much longer could she hold on?

The lights flashed on, snapping her back to her senses. She had not heard footsteps or the click of the switch that had turned the pool lights back on. But someone must be there. Jane took a deep breath and screamed at the tiny opening where a connection between two floor panels rested on the edge of the pool. She listened carefully. Nothing! She called again. No one was there.

"Christ, help me!" she yelled. There was another terrifying moment of silence. Then a click and the whir of a motor. And then a rumble as the panel above her face began moving back toward the deep end of the pool. As soon as the floor slid past her. Jane exploded out of the water. In two rapid strokes she was holding on to the edge at the shallow end. Then she began to cry hysterically.

Bill Andrews reached down to her. She caught his hands and then threw her arm around his neck. For an instant, he tottered, fighting to avoid being dragged in. Then he pulled back and got his hands under her arms. He hauled her up until her torso was lying on the deck, her legs still dangling in the water.

"You're okay!" he shouted at her. "It's all right!" He pulled her up into his arms and dragged her knees up onto the edge. Then he lifted her until she was standing, her weight leaning against him. "You're okay," he repeated. He led her toward the cabana, and she walked with faltering steps.

"Thank God you came up," she said when he eased her down onto a deck chair.

"Leavitt just left. I thought I'd come up and dry you off," he explained. "When I saw the pool covered, I thought you must have finished your swim. I damn near went back down to find you."

"Jesus, I was drowning. The pool cover closed over my head."

He draped a towel over her shoulders and found another one so that he could begin drying her hair. "You're freezing," he warned her. "Can you walk to the steps? You should get downstairs and into something dry."

He led her straight to his bedroom and slipped into the bed next to her so that he could warm her in his arms.

When she came down in the morning, Bill was at the breakfast table with Cassie and Craig. He rose and seated her. "Feeling better?" he asked.

"Much better!"

Craig stopped chewing long enough to ask, "Did you really get caught under the pool cover last night?" Then he turned to Cassie with a conspiratorial grin.

Jane nodded and then smiled, determined not to be overly dramatic. "I did get myself trapped," she answered.

"That's not supposed to happen," Craig said. "There are electric eyes and stuff to keep it from closing if anyone is in the pool."

Jane answered, "They must have burned out." But then she asked how the motor could have started. "Who could possibly have thrown the switch?"

"A mechanical failure," William said. "No one could have thrown the switch. It's right next to the pool. You'd have seen anyone who came up."

"But it worked for you," Jane remembered. "You pushed the button and everything worked normally. So nothing was broken. Somebody must have pushed the switch."

Cassie and Craig ignored the discussion as they finished their pancakes. But Bill persisted in his view that it was some sort of mechanical failure. "There's no way to get on the roof except through the apartment. And no one let anyone in. Everyone was asleep until Robert got here."

"Look," Jane said with a hint of temper. "The pool and deck were serviced yesterday. Everything was in working order. So why would it suddenly decide to close . . . ." Her voice drifted off as she realized the import of what she was saying. If there was no way to get to the pool except through the apartment, then whoever pushed the button must have been in the apartment. If it wasn't a mechanical failure, then someone in the family had tried to kill her. "I guess we'll have to talk to the service people," she mumbled, seeming to concede the point.

Mrs. McCarty stepped into the breakfast room with another plate of eggs. "What happened?" she asked, looking from face to face. William responded, explaining the previous night's accident. "She had a close call," he concluded.

Eileen helped herself to the coffee and eggs. "I'll call the company," she promised. "There must be something that needs to be fixed. Machines don't turn themselves on, and no one would want to hurt you."

Jane could think of people who might want to hurt her. Cassie or Craig could have decided that they didn't want their father to have a new wife. Bill's secretary and his office staff might resent a new figure in the chain of command. And someone very close to Bill, such as someone who was at that unusual business meeting eight years ago, might want to stop her snooping into the death of Kay Parker.

Maybe no one wanted to kill her. Maybe it was to frighten her and warn her not to insert herself into the affairs of the family or dig into its secrets. Was it possible that she was the problem Andrews had to discuss with Leavitt?

Or was it possible that she was becoming paranoid? Maybe it was just the damn switch or a short circuit. But still, she shouldn't let her guard down until she found out.

Jane made sure she was on the roof when the serviceman came. With Mrs. McCarty looking over her shoulder, she explained exactly how she had turned on the light and then slipped into the pool. She had never been near the switch for the cover; in fact, she hadn't known where it was located. She had swum a few laps, but she wasn't absorbed in exercise. If someone had come out onto the deck and stopped next to the dance floor housing, she most likely would have noticed.

The switch was working perfectly, the repairman decided, and he demonstrated the internal sequence of its operation. She didn't completely follow his explanation, but he was plainly convinced.

"How else could the motor have started?" she wondered.

He thought. "Well, if you ran the power line to the motor and bypassed the switch . . ."

That didn't seem likely unless there was a fledgling electrician in the household.

"Or if you killed the power and flipped the switch," the man speculated. "Then it would close when you turned your circuit breaker back on."

That didn't seem very likely, either. But it was possible. She wondered if Bill could remember whether he found the switch turned on or off. If it had been set on CLOSED, then someone would have had to set it before she reached the pool. She was certain that she had been nowhere near the switch.

As she was going down the stairs, Robert Leavitt was letting himself into the apartment, carrying a thick briefcase. He peeled off his jacket and went into the breakfast room, where he poured himself a cup of coffee. Jane slipped into a chair across from him.

"I'm glad last night's meeting broke up early," she said.

He seemed puzzled.

"Didn't you hear what happened to me?"

He put down his cup and gave his full attention to her shortened version of her struggle in the swimming pool. "If Bill had been five minutes longer, I wouldn't have made it," she concluded, "so I'm lucky your conversation didn't drag on a bit longer."

Then she got into the problem of the switch and the fact that nobody had touched it. She explained the serviceman's theory that if the switch had been set in advance, the pool cover could have been closed by switching the circuit breaker back on. Was that really possible?

He laughed. "I'm not your man. Switches and relays and cutoffs . . . they're all a mystery to me. Changing a lightbulb is my scientific highlight."

She reminded him of the break-in that had occurred her first night in the apartment. Didn't it seem likely that there might be a connection between the two events? Someone had come into the apartment and left without leaving a trace. And now someone turns on the pool cover without ever being near the switch. He answered that he didn't see how there could be any connection other than the apparent failure of electrical systems in both cases.

Then she asked if he knew of anyone who might want to keep William Andrews from marrying her. "Someone trying to give me second thoughts or scare me off?"

"Jane," he answered, "Bill has a lot of enemies. And there are any number of people who would love to control him. Why don't you ask me something easy?"

"Okay," Jane dared. "Who is Selina Royce?"

23

Robert Leavitt had never heard of Selina Royce, or at least that was the way he played it. He posed with his hand on his chin, as if digging deep into his memory bank, and then shook his head slowly. "No, I don't remember anyone by that name. Where would I have known her?"

Jane was beyond playing games. She reminded him of the Texas cable network that Andrews Global Network had bought and the date when Selina had been transferred to New York. Then she told Robert the date of the awards banquet at which he had been sitting next to her, apparently as her escort.

"Well, then, I must have known her at the time. I just can't remember her," he decided. "But give me a few days and I'll see if I can find her in the personnel records." Then he asked casually, as if it were of no concern, "Why are you interested in her?"

"Just that she turns up in stories and morgue shots covering the early years of the company," Jane lied, trying to sound convincing. "She seems suddenly important to Andrews Global Network, and then she just vanishes."

He shrugged. "No one comes to mind, but I'll find out what I can."

Lying bastard, Jane thought. *He's protecting Andrews, both the man and the company. Let's see what he comes back with after he's pretended to check his records.*

The next morning, on the train back to Connecticut, she thought about her fiancé and his college roommate. Was Bob's accounting of Kay's tragic end the truth, or had he been constructing his friend's alibi? Did he know about the monthly payments to Selina, or was that a secret Andrews had kept from him? She felt sure that Bob liked her, thought she was right for Bill, and would defend her from the company guardians who would like to be rid of her. But when push came to shove, Bob was Bill's friend and confidant. She had to expect that he would check with Bill before he shared any secrets with her.

Jane reached home and was delighted to find that Art was not camped out on her doorstep. She wanted some time to herself to dig even deeper into the murder of Bill's first wife. She also wanted to get to her office and give the address of Kay's computer to the newspaper's information systems specialist. She knew that given time, he would find his way through Kay's firewall and into her hidden secrets. But her message lamp was blinking, and when she listened it was Art's voice. "I've got some news that will blow your panties off," he said. "Maybe now you'll show me just a bit of respect."

She thought he must have mastered the intricacies of his washing machine or figured out which end of the vacuum cleaner connected to the hose. But when she called his number, he insisted on coming right over. He had an angel, and one of his plays was going to be produced. She couldn't deny him his moment of "I told you so." Art had never hurt her. Just exhausted her. She told him to come over. The she went out to buy a bottle of champagne.

"Billy Rifkin," he said, mentioning a New York impresario as soon as he was through the door. His intentions were like hers. He was carrying a bottle of cheap champagne with a plastic cork.

"Which play?" Jane asked as she set the glasses on the coffee table.

"The one about the president's daughter," he said proudly. "His secretary called and said he had heard about the play and wanted to read it. I sent it, and two days later I had Rifkin on the telephone."

"He called you?" Jane asked, exaggerating her excitement.

"Called to congratulate me. He said it was 'genius.' He also mentioned 'thrilling, exciting, memorable, and surefire hit.' "

"Wow!" she allowed as Art popped the cork. She remembered the first act of the play, written while they were still married. *Lucky if it makes television,* she had thought to herself. But Billy Rifkin was known for his insight into audiences. He didn't back losers. So there must be something that she had missed completely.

"To wonderful reviews," she said, raising her glass.

"To a great box office," he added as the second toast.

Art began talking, and there was no turning him off. He took her through the plot of his play and then the more dramatic individual scenes. He ran through a gallery of actors whom he might consider for leading roles and wondered whether he should open first on Broadway, or if it might be best to bring the play over from London. It was the Art who had dazzled her as an undergraduate, assuming that he was already an important world figure. Now she found him childish and presumptuous. But still, she listened attentively. It was an important moment for him.

When he had told his story twice and speculated on all the implications of his success, he asked about Jane's new life. He was no longer in awe of William Andrews or openmouthed at Jane's incredibly good fortune. The phone call from Billy Rifkin had raised him into the heaven of superstars where he was now Andrews's equal in stature and in a far more prestigious field.

Her response was positive but tepid. A wedding date had been set, and plans were generally on track. She wasn't sure that their bedroom would be ready on time, and she still hadn't convinced the best man that a football jersey wouldn't be appropriate attire. But she supposed that, in the end, everything would work out.

"You sound like you're organizing a blood drive," Art said. "Shouldn't you be a bit more excited?"

"I will be," Jane said, trying to crank up a bit of enthusiasm. "Right now I'm weighed down in details."

She was a bit giddy from the champagne, but as soon as Art made a triumphant departure, she dressed for the office. She was still working for the paper, even though she had filed only one column in the past week.

She found Sam Simon, her company's information systems guru, in his office. Sam was in a T-shirt emblazoned with a beer-company logo. A ponytail, streaked with gray, hung down his back. The office looked like a garage workshop with clusters of monitors and racks of circuit boards all interconnected with fiber-optic cable. She gave him the phone number and machine number of Kay's computer and told him about her problems with the firewall.

"A dial-up link?" he asked in horror.

"It's an old setup," she said. "It probably hasn't been used in years."

He sighed in exasperation. "It will take a lot of time. But on the other hand, the firewalls they used back then were child's play." He pinned the information to one of his several keyboards and promised he would look into it, "first chance."

She found Roscoe at his desk. "Any news?" she asked.

"Aren't you supposed to be telling *me* if there's any news?"

Jane blushed, then apologized. "I haven't been covering my beat, have I?"

"There's only so much you can do from a telephone booth in Manhattan. The stories we cover are up here in Connecticut."

She begged his indulgence until after her honeymoon, promising that she would keep her apartment and be in the office "three or four days a week, at least." But then she went back to the question she had meant to ask. Had his promised investigation into Selina Royce turned up anything?

There were no problems in Paris, Roscoe told her. A French reporter had found her at the address Jane had provided. Her name was over the mailbox, so she didn't seem to be in hiding. The reporter had identified her and would keep an eye on her to see who came calling. San Antonio was another matter. They couldn't find any relatives in the area. And there was no Selina Royce in the records of the cable service that Andrews Global Network had bought. As far as her station was concerned, she never existed.

"I've seen her picture, Roscoe. I read the news report about her transfer to New York."

He held up a hand against Jane's protest. "I know she's a

real person. All I'm saying is that you're never going to find
her in San Antonio. And I'll bet you won't find her anywhere
in Andrews Global Network's records, either. The connection
between the lady in Paris and the one who vanished from
New York has been pretty much erased."

"Maybe the paper trail is gone," Jane said. "But people
must remember her. The top executives in the company must
have known who she is. William Andrews's ever-faithful secretary must have talked to her. Or at least forwarded messages to her."

"Any of them apt to talk about her?" Taylor wondered
aloud.

"None of them ever tell me anything," she said bitterly. "I
can't even find out where he's having lunch."

"Maybe if you had a bit more time . . ."

She knew exactly what Roscoe meant. If she weren't rushing into a wedding, she might, over time, find some answers.
But she probably wasn't going to learn anything in the next
three weeks. And the things she learned after the wedding
probably weren't going to do her any good.

She phoned Robert Leavitt and asked if she could meet
him for lunch the next day. He wouldn't be available the next
day, his secretary announced. Would Jane care to tell her exactly why she wanted a full hour of Mr. Leavitt's time?

"Oh, it's silly," Jane lied. "I need some ideas about
William's wedding gift. Mr. Leavitt has known him for so
long, I thought he could . . ."

"Isn't that sweet," the secretary gushed. "Let me see . . .
tomorrow is out. Would Wednesday be all right?"

24

The restaurant was small and intimate, delightfully French, and from what Jane could gather, frightfully expensive. Bob arrived only seconds after she did, a bit winded and slightly red in the face. They let themselves be led to a small table, and Bob immediately began chatting about gifts that his friend would enjoy. He suggested a powerful telescope that could be set up on the roof. "My God, is he a voyeur?" she teased, and then learned that Andrews had a great interest in astronomy. He also suggested opera recordings, indicating that her fiancé loved fine music, or perhaps an antique chess set. "I didn't know he played chess," she said, realizing that she knew almost nothing about the man she was going to marry.

But when the entrées were served, Jane got to the information about William Andrews that she really wanted. "Bob, there's another reason I had to see you. I asked you about a woman named Selina Royce. I have to know what you found out."

He used a sudden cough and a raised napkin to cover his moment of confusion. Then, much too casually, he told her that he had asked his secretary to check into it. The personnel records didn't go back that far.

"But you must remember her," Jane insisted. "She was one of your rising stars."

He had regained his composure. "There are lots of rising stars on television," he said. "Most of them fizzle when they get fat or pregnant."

"Did Selina Royce get pregnant?" Jane suddenly saw a new possibility for why Andrews might be sending her an annual retainer.

"I don't know. I don't remember her at all."

Jane tried for a kill. "Bob, for God's sake, you sat right

next to her at an industry awards affair. I think you might
have been her escort."

He smiled to cover his mounting anger, which made him
seem even angrier. "There are a dozen industry dinners a
month. I don't remember who I was sitting with a month ago,
much less back—what was it?—eight years ago."

He resumed eating in a way that said the conversation
was over. Gradually he worked his way back to the wedding
gift. Had she thought of a western saddle for his trips to the
horse farm?

She couldn't push any harder. She knew that he was lying,
and she guessed that he suspected she knew he was lying.
Even when confronted with irrefutable evidence, he would
stonewall. There was nothing Leavitt wouldn't do to protect
his longtime friend.

What were her choices? The only obvious recourse was to
confront Bill directly. *Who is Selina Royce, and why are you
sending her a hundred thousand dollars every month?* Some
answers would be acceptable, even if hard to swallow. If he
was raising a love child, fine. That would be honorable and
responsible, even though his failure to have mentioned a
child would be cowardly. Or if he had ruined her career or did
great damage to her personal life, he might feel forever responsible. But if she was his mistress, Jane would walk away.
Maybe after many years a wife could tolerate her husband's
infidelities, but no woman would enter a marriage knowing
that she was sharing her husband with another woman. And
if it was blackmail, then Jane would have to believe that the
woman knew Andrews's darkest secret. And that could only
be that he had killed Kay Parker.

But how to confront him? Wouldn't she be challenging his
character? And suppose—like Robert Leavitt—he simply
denied any knowledge. Should she call him a liar and tell him
that she had been snooping through his checkbook? That
probably wouldn't bring out the truth. To be honest with herself, she really didn't want to lose William Andrews, a man
who seemed to love her and was a romantic catch beyond her
most unlikely dreams. But should she make a lifelong com-

mitment to him while an important part of his life remained a dark secret?

She remained suspended between her choices, like an object caught between two magnetic poles. Whenever she tried to move toward one choice, she was pushed back toward the other. It was easier to busy herself with the mindless details of the wedding, ordering flowers while telling herself she hadn't yet made up her mind and sending out invitations to a wedding she wasn't convinced would really take place. The evenings when Bill was home were tense and uncomfortable for her. She kept looking for an opportunity to raise an issue that she didn't have the courage to address, and then regretting when she let a chance slip away. At the newspaper she was continually distracted. Nothing in the local business community was as important as the decision she was afraid to make.

A week after her luncheon with Robert Leavitt, Roscoe Taylor waved her into his office. "News from Paris," he said in a soft voice that wouldn't carry past his open door. "Miss Royce had a visitor a few days ago. It took my friend a couple of days to find out who he was. He had to follow him to his hotel and then wait until someone he knew was on duty at the desk. That's how he got a look at the hotel records."

"Who?" Jane asked, hardly able to breathe. She was terrified that Roscoe was going to name William Andrews.

"Robert Leavitt," he answered.

"Robert Leavitt!" She was stunned for an instant. And then it made sense. Bill's closest friend and dedicated protector. The man who tried to smooth out the rough edges of the Andrews corporate empire. He would certainly be the one to do her fiancé's dirty work. Like paying off blackmailers and lying to his future wife.

25

The apartment filled with light as the sun climbed over the East River and crossed into Manhattan. There were flowers everywhere—bouquets on the tables, a spray across the piano, and garlands leading up the banisters to the second floor. Until that morning, plans for the wedding ceremony had been on hold. If it was raining, or threatening to, the ceremony would take place in the living room, in front of the vast two-story window with its expansive view of Central Park. Even in the rain, Central Park would be beautifully romantic. But if it was sunny, then the wedding would be held in the roof garden, which had already been tented and decorated. The bright sun and the early fall weather made the decision obvious.

"D-day," Jane mumbled to herself when the light from the window hit her face. "And I'm going to look like hell. The bride from the crypt." She sat up so she could see herself in the vanity mirror. "Oh God!" There were dark circles under her eyes, her new hairdo was a mess, and her mouth seemed to have disappeared. She flopped down on her pillow, sat up abruptly and punched the pillow into a new shape, and then set her head down again.

She had tossed and turned all night, involved in a debate about the rest of her life. The romantic sentiments, William Andrews's professed love for her, and the sheer momentum of the wedding plans that she had set in motion argued for going through with the ceremony. *You love him and he loves you,* she had assured herself over and over. The honeymoon was planned, the clothes bought, and the bags packed. The decorators were ready to move in the instant the newlyweds departed, to transform Kay's boudoir into a real husband-and-wife bedroom. It was a promising launch into a life that she could never have dreamed of or even imagined. Besides, what woman wouldn't kill for the chance to be married to the dashing prince of the media world? Of course she would go through with the wedding.

But cold logic argued the other side of the debate. First, she knew almost nothing about the man she would be committing to spend the rest of her life with. Sure, she had read all the press flak and official biographies that painted him as a business genius and philanthropist. He was on every list of the world's ten most desirable bachelors. But he was also a workaholic already married to his global business affairs. True, he had committed to a weeklong honeymoon on a sailboat when they would be out of contact with the world. But she was already hearing such phrases as "keep me informed" and "in an emergency" and was already imagining an endless line of seaplanes setting down in the water next to them. Maybe he was the ideal mate for a woman who wanted wealth and stature but didn't particularly care for men. But Jane had already gotten tired of living alone in his huge apartment. Satellite phone calls from places she had never heard of were no substitute for the touch of a husband.

He was damaged goods. The shotgun blast that had destroyed his wife had also ripped through his soul, leaving him crippled in matters of the heart. He seemed to feel no intimacy even when they were in bed together, no real joy even when he was smiling. He was always on the move, as if terrified of ever coming to rest. All people, she knew, had episodes when past agonies rose up to torment them. But Bill seemed a prisoner of his past agonies.

He was secretive, perhaps even deceiving. His account of Kay's murder was incomplete and implausible. Once the notion of a mysterious intruder was dismissed, it seemed certain that he must know who the killer was. How could he live with that knowledge? More to the point, how could she? Even more damning, he had never even mentioned the name of Selina Royce. The prenuptial agreement, which she gladly signed, outlined his assets and liabilities in great detail. Nowhere was there a hint of any obligation to a woman in Paris who was receiving more than she would get in the event that she and William divorced.

And Selina Royce was real. Roscoe's Paris agent had described her as late thirties/early forties, attractive, and very fashionable. It was all the information Jane needed to hate her. But the report had added that she seemed to be very private, with few friends and basically no social life. She took long walks and spent a lot of time sitting in cafés, always in a hat and sunglasses. "A bit weird for a Parisian courtesan," the man added, and Roscoe had assured her that his friend knew about such things. Had Andrews visited her? Jane asked. "Not while my guy was following her," Roscoe had answered. "Do you want me to keep on this to see if he shows up?" Jane had decided that she didn't want to catch Bill in the act. Sooner or later, she hoped, "he'll tell me all about her."

Finally, there were the bodyguards—the loyal retainers who kept watch over all the Andrews secrets. She couldn't forget the look on Robert Leavitt's face when she had suddenly asked him, "Who is Selina Royce?" She remembered his coughing spell when she asked the same question at the restaurant.

There were other gatekeepers. His secretary claimed never to know how to reach him. Yet Bill had commented on the dozens of calls he received from his office when he was overseas. His top executives were never available. Her invitations to them had been funneled through Ann Packard. Jane had little hope of knocking down the barriers and having a running dialogue with the man she was going to marry.

She had been in turmoil all week and had been awake all night, but still she hadn't made a decision. She would probably go ahead with the wedding. It was too late to call it off, wasn't it? But she couldn't decide whether it was the right thing to do. She didn't know a great deal about William Andrews, and some of what she did know was frightening. But then again, how well did most brides know the man they were marrying? Didn't the true persona present itself after the wedding? Sometimes for better, as when she learned how much Art enjoyed painting her toenails. And sometimes for worse, as when he had turned out to be permanently unemployed and incapable of keeping track of his own socks.

She stepped into her bathroom and began repairing the

damage of a sleepless night. First a shower, cold as she could stand it. Then some foundation to bring a bit of healthy color to her face. Then makeup to brighten her eyes and reestablish her lost mouth. She decided to leave her hair for the stylist, who was due to arrive with the photographers.

Jane slipped on a robe and wandered down to the breakfast room, where Mrs. McCarty offered her a full menu of breakfast choices. "Just coffee," Jane said. She hunched over the cup, scarcely cheered by the morning light playing on the contours of Central Park. Only when she had sipped a bit did she begin to take in the view.

Cassie appeared, her hairdo wrapped in tissue paper. She reached the table and then pulled up short. "What happened to your hair?"

"I slept on it."

"You're not supposed to do that. It's all messed up." She seemed annoyed that Jane had desecrated her coiffure.

"I'll work on it," Jane promised.

Craig sauntered in, still in the jeans and T-shirt he had worn to bed. "You look crazy," he said to his sister. "Why is your head wrapped in toilet paper?"

Cassie bristled. Jane giggled bubbles into her coffee.

"Is that what you're going to wear to the wedding?" Cassie demanded.

"There ain't going to be no wedding," Craig pronounced, sliding into the table.

Jane's head shot up. Cassie gasped. Craig grabbed a slice of toast and began to butter it.

"What do you mean, no wedding?" Cassie demanded. Jane turned to Craig for his answer.

"Can't have a wedding without the groom, and Dad left on business early this morning."

Cassie's face fell. Jane reached over and took Craig's hand to interrupt his buttering. "Your father left this morning? What time?"

The boy pulled his hand free. "Couple of hours ago." Then he stuffed the toast into his mouth.

No wedding, Jane thought, and was surprised to find that

she felt relieved. She would have her postponement without having to ask. But what was she going to do with the judge and the thirty privileged guests from Andrews Global Network? She thought of disabling the elevator. When they couldn't get up, they would eventually go home. But she knew nothing about the mechanics of elevators. And besides, Bill's loyal retainers would climb up the side of the building rather than risk being a no-show.

Maybe coffee in the dining room! Let the guests arrive, have someone explain that he had been called away on an emergency, apologize for the inconvenience, and send them on their way.

"So what are you going to do?" Cassie demanded.

"You'll have to greet our guests and tell them that your father has been detained," Jane tried.

"Me? No way! I'm not going to look like a fool!"

Jane smiled. "Think how much more foolish I'll feel making the announcement. I'm the bride who's been left at the altar."

Cassie's face hardened. "You know, this wasn't such a great idea to begin with. I'm not going to bail you out." She stormed off, tearing the tissue paper from her head as she raced up the stairs.

Jane turned to Craig. "Did he say where he was going?"

Craig shook his head. "He didn't say anything. Mr. Leavitt came, and they left together. Like they always do." She was thoughtful for a moment until she suddenly remembered the caterer.

"Oh my God, the caterers!"

"What about them?" Craig asked.

"They're probably already in their trucks circling the block."

"So what?"

"So how would you like a hundred chicken livers wrapped in bacon for your lunch?"

She carried her coffee up to her room. Even though she was relieved at what would probably be a lengthy postponement, Jane was hurt and angry. What could Bill have possibly found more important than their wedding? What was so urgent that he would humiliate her in front of his children and friends? Why would he leave without even telling her where he was going? Had he even thought of her on their wedding day?

Her phone extension rang. *Bill,* she thought, and rushed to pick up. But the voice was Mrs. McCarty's. "The caterers are here. Perhaps you ought to come down and meet them."

"I'm dressing," she lied. "Would you get them started?"

"Started where? The living room or the roof garden?"

"The roof garden," Jane decided. If things kept going the way they were, she would probably want to jump off.

The phone rang and again she was disappointed to hear Mrs. McCarty's voice. "The hairdresser is here."

Jane couldn't force the truth through her lips. "Send him up," she said cheerily. Immediately she heard footsteps on the stairs, cracked her door, and called, "In here!"

The man wore an open shirt, showing the chains and medallions that hung around his neck. He stopped abruptly in the doorway, snapped off his sunglasses, gasped, and asked, "What did you do to it?"

"I slept on it," she answered.

He backed up a step. "You did what?" His shocked expression gave way to rage.

"Look, I've been through this already. Can you fix it?"

"It's . . . totaled . . ."

"Do what you can," she said.

"What I should do is tow it to the junkyard," he said, but he stepped into the room and began looking through his carrying case. "You'd be better off if I were a magician instead of a stylist." He sat Jane at the vanity and stood behind her, examining the mussed hairdo in the mirror. "Oh well, into the breach!" He started combing it out.

When her phone rang again, Jane decided to ignore it. The stylist might resent being interrupted and she was at his mercy, even if all she had to dress for was to tell her guests that the party had been canceled.

Watching him work, she decided that the man *was* a magician. Her hair took on a contour and seemed to fall naturally along the sides of her face. He tied selected strands into ridiculous curls, but when he combed them out, they added body. He took her head in his fingertips, moved it one way or another, sighed, and then plunged back into action.

First came the cleanser, which he used to remove the base she had painted on in the morning. Then a new liquid that he mixed in a petri dish and kept comparing with her cheekbones. And then brushes and colors that he mixed on a palette. In less than an hour he changed her from a scullery maid to a princess. "Cinderella!" she announced.

"You're not planning on taking a nap?" he asked suspiciously. "At least not before the photographers get here."

She had been planning to wear something very simple when she met her guests with the bad news. But with her newfound beauty, she decided on something more elaborate—maybe even the coffee-colored flared sheath she had bought as her bridal dress. But then she would need still another dress if they rescheduled the wedding with the same guests. "The hell with it," she announced as she took the dress off its hanger.

Jane checked the clock. It was after one P.M. She still had an hour before the guests would arrive for the three o'clock ceremony. She decided to visit the roof garden to see what they would all be missing.

She was stunned. The casual garden that surrounded the pool had been as completely transformed as she had. A chain of flowers hanging from antique streetlamps marked off the area, and stands of fall flowers were planted at the corners. The seating was down both sides of the pool, which was dotted with floating flowers. A Gothic arch of flowers marked the place where the judge would preside, lending just a hint of religious significance.

The strings had already taken their places in the band shell: a violinist in formal wear, a harpist and cellist both in full-length gowns. They continued their tuning and practicing after favoring Jane with a smile. And there, on one of the several white-cloth tables, was an enormous silver ice bucket, bristling with the necks of champagne bottles. The caterer, dressed in tails, rushed to greet her.

"I hope you're pleased, Mrs. Andrews," he said.

"Not yet," Jane answered, and then saw from his horrified expression that she should clarify. "I'm not yet Mrs. Andrews, but more than pleased with what you've done. It's . . . glorious."

He bowed as if accepting applause. "And you will be Mrs. Andrews before you know it," he promised.

Oh God, she thought, *should I tell him now and get it over with?* Instead, she asked if she might have a glass of champagne. He snapped to like a soldier on a parade ground, pulled a bottle out of the ice, and opened it expertly. He gave Jane a flute and poured it half full. She thanked him, then as an afterthought reached out and took the bottle.

Two glasses later, she saw that it was time to go down to the foyer and face her guests. She wobbled a bit as she stood. Champagne wasn't her normal lunch, and she thought she could feel the bubbles in her brain. She set down her glass, smiled at the caterer, who was hovering to receive her next command, and then made a determined effort to walk a straight line to the stairs. She squinted at a figure rising before her, focused, and was amazed to see William Andrews, in white tie, coming toward her.

"Bill?"

"You look lovely," he answered. "Is it bad luck for me to be seeing you before the wedding?"

He was smiling. The bastard was smiling as if he were enjoying a private joke. "I'll show you some bad luck," Jane snarled. She lunged forward and aimed a roundhouse right fist at his smile. But the champagne had dulled her coordination and she missed badly, stumbling into his arms. "You insensitive gorilla. Do you know how worried I've been? Left standing at the altar so you could run off and make another million!"

"Didn't Bob call you?"

"No, he didn't. And even if he had, I'm not supposed to be marrying Robert Leavitt. Why didn't you call?" Her anger had given way to confusion, and there were hints that she might be about to cry.

"I did! Right before I got on the helicopter. I rang your room, but you didn't answer."

She vaguely remembered the phone call she had ignored while the stylist was working miracles on her appearance. "That was you?"

"It must have been," Andrews agreed. "And Bob promised to call you again after I took off."

"Took off from where?"

"From the farm. There were a few things that needed to be taken care of before I disappear for a week."

Her anger flared again. "You had to be with your horses on our wedding day?"

He laughed and drew her close. "Not my horses—a few legal matters. I was just clearing the decks for our honeymoon."

Relief flooded through her, and Jane suddenly felt like laughing. She hadn't been abandoned at the altar, and she didn't have to go down and face the wedding guests. Her misgivings about William Andrews vanished as he rescued her from disgrace, and she suddenly found herself holding on to him for dear life.

"Are you laughing or crying?" he asked.

She wasn't sure, but she knew that she was going to catch hell from the stylist if her mascara ran.

William took her down to her room and ordered up a cup of coffee. He went to his children's rooms and ordered them into their wedding garments. Then he dashed down to the foyer as his first guest, the judge, arrived with his feathered and bejeweled wife.

Mrs. McCarty brought up the coffee, apologizing that she had been delayed several times en route. "Some of these people would forget their heads," she complained, and then hoped that the coffee was still hot. Jane downed the cup and felt the caffeine snap her like a whip. She heard more guests arrive, bellowing congratulations to William. Then the party moved up to the roof garden, where the strings began playing. Seconds later the caterer arrived at her door and announced that they were ready for her entrance. He led her up the stairs and posed her at the foot of a white runner that circled the guests on the bride's side and ended up at the flowered arch, where Bill and the judge were waiting.

A bow tapped on violin strings and after a pause, the opening strains of Pachelbel's Canon whispered over the rooftop. Cassie took her place in front of the bride. Jane noted with sadistic pleasure that one side of the girl's hairdo had fallen. Craig raced forward to join his father, fanning furiously at the cigarette smoke he was still exhaling. Cassie began to proceed down the aisle in measured steps, smiling wherever cameras were raised. Jane stepped out and began her march toward a fate unknown. The dark suits in front of the Gothic arch sparked the thought that she might be on her way to a trial before the Inquisition.

Her white aisle began to curve, and the rooftop started to spin slowly. As it turned to the left, Jane stepped with great determination to the right, trying to keep her course in a world that was suddenly disorienting. She looked out at the New York skyline and found it tipped precariously. She looked at the neat rows of guests and saw them disappearing into the edge of the pool. Jane tried to steady herself. But it was impossible. To the strains of Pachelbel's Canon, the rooftop garden circled in one direction while the New York skyline rotated in the other. She knew she was in trouble and tried to find a friendly face in the congregation. All the faces were turned toward her with broad grins and wide eyes, like circus clowns or television puppets. They were all looking and laughing, wild with delight, while she was spinning, trying to reach out for help.

Jane tried to focus on the Gothic arch where she knew Bill was standing. But the arch had collapsed, and the three men—Bill, his son, and the judge—were elongated cartoons, their legs bent at the knees and then stretching out to the left to connect wildly distorted bodies. All three of them were smiling insanely.

Then she was pirouetting, spinning to her right on one foot, the other held delicately in the air. It was a triumph. She was dancing weightlessly while all her guests were grinning with delight. From the corner of her eye, she could see the skyline, rotating to the right like the figures on a carousel, moving faster and faster. And then the carousel stood on its end so that the buildings were rotating up and down like the cars on a Ferris wheel. Jane felt herself falling, her weight off her feet, her body tumbling weightlessly into the vortex of the spinning buildings. She landed with a jar that shook the air out of her body. And then the entire celebration turned to midnight black. For a moment she could hear the strains of the strings and the gentle murmur of her guests. But an instant later everything went absolutely silent.

26

He was standing over her in the white tie formal he had been wearing. "Are you awake?"

Jane squinted, unable to believe what she was seeing. "No. I'm still asleep and dreaming."

"How are you feeling?"

Feeling? Was she sick? She looked around her bedroom and saw her wedding dress draped over the back of a chair. Her shoes were neatly paired beneath it. She should be wearing them. She was about to be married. Jane sat up abruptly. Too abruptly, because the background headache she was feeling was suddenly in the forefront. "What happened?" she asked.

"You fainted," Bill said. "Just as you were starting down the aisle." He leaned forward and kissed her cheek, then said with mock displeasure, "I've taken quite a ribbing about your drinking yourself unconscious to get out of marrying me."

"Drinking?" Jane was mystified. "All I had was a little champagne, and that was . . . when was it . . . this morning?" She looked at the clock. "Oh my God . . ."

"Don't worry," he told her. "The guests have left for the evening. Most of them will be back tomorrow if you still want to get married."

She lowered herself back down in the bed. "Bill, something knocked me out cold."

He agreed with her and supplied her with any number of plausible excuses. The wedding preparations had been too rushed. She was trying to do too much, taking over his household while traveling to her job in Connecticut. His absence in the morning had put her under a great strain. Anyone might have fainted.

"Bill, it wasn't the tension and it wasn't the champagne. It was a drug, like the injection you get from a dentist. You start counting backwards and the next thing you know, you're waking up."

"We'll screen our guests tomorrow to make sure there aren't any dentists," he said with a laugh, then kissed her cheek again.

"Tomorrow?" She was suddenly shocked by the idea. "Will I be okay by tomorrow?"

"Well, maybe a slight hangover, but the doctor says you're in great shape."

"The doctor?" She had no recollection of any doctor.

"I couldn't just leave you there, lying in the aisle. We brought you downstairs and called the doctor. His expert opinion was that we should let you sleep it off."

Jane thought of what the moment must have been like. Her collapsing in the aisle, the turmoil among the guests, the men carrying her down the stairs. Her first opportunity to shine as William Andrews's new hostess and she had turned it into a fiasco. And then the doctor's verdict, that she was drunk! At that moment she would have welcomed a diagnosis of stroke or brain disease.

"Bill, I'm so sorry," she said. But she knew she hadn't been drunk. Yes, she had taken a few flutes of champagne. It may have been on her breath to provide a ready diagnosis. But wine couldn't have hit her like that. She had been fine until she drank the cup of coffee just before going up to the ceremony.

She sat bolt upright. "The coffee. There must have been something in the coffee."

"Don't worry about it." He tried to ease her back down onto the pillow.

She looked around quickly. "Where's the cup? There was some left in the cup."

"I don't see any cup," Bill answered. "It's probably in the dishwasher or on the caterer's truck. But it doesn't matter. The important thing is that you're all right."

She started out of the bed. "It matters to me." His hand restrained her. "Bill, I wasn't drunk and I'm not hungover. Mrs. McCarty told he that she had been distracted when she was bringing up the coffee. She had to handle other things. She probably put the cup down."

"And you think someone put something into it. Jane, that would be a terribly sick joke."

"It isn't a joke. Someone doesn't want us married. Someone rigged that damn dance floor to close over my head, and someone put something into my coffee. Don't you see . . ."

He was losing patience. He had been terribly frightened when his bride collapsed in front of his eyes, then mortally embarrassed by the verdict that she had fallen into a drunken stupor. Now she was raving about plots to prevent their marriage. "Jane, I want you to get a good night's sleep. Put all this aside and we'll talk about it in the morning." He stood up abruptly and left her room.

Jane was the first one down in the morning, and she sat in the breakfast room even as the sunrise was beginning to paint color onto the skyline. Mrs. McCarty brought her coffee and then sat across from her. "How are you feeling, dear? You have to take better care of yourself." She was truly concerned.

"You remember the coffee you brought up to me yesterday, just before the . . . ceremony began?" She couldn't say "wedding." There had been no wedding.

The housekeeper nodded. "Yes, of course."

"You said you were delayed. Did you ever put the cup down on a table or something?"

"On the piano bar," she answered. "One of the women needed a safety pin. And also on the library table. His Honor forgot to bring a Bible. That's what took me so long. If I didn't know you were waiting, I'd have gone back to the kitchen for a hot cup."

Jane allowed herself a moment of satisfaction. The drink she had taken only minutes before her collapse had been available to anyone in the apartment. To Cassie and Craig, who had probably put the burr under her saddle. To the imperious Ann Packard, who was holding on to control of Bill's affairs with all her might. To the executives who wanted

William Andrews's talents all to themselves. To Kim Annuzio, who might have both professional and romantic designs on Bill. To Robert Leavitt, who probably resented her delving into the mysteries surrounding Kay Parker's death. There were lots of suspects who would hate to see her have any more control over the man who sustained them all.

Bill sat across from her. "You look great," he began.

"I feel fine."

"Fine enough for a wedding? Because if you're not, I can have the guests called. We can put this off to a future date."

Jane thought of all the people who might want to keep her and Bill apart. "I think I'm up to it," she said with an enthusiastic smile.

"We'll keep it short and simple, in the living room, and with whatever food the caterer can come up with on short notice."

"I'll have to wear the same dress," she said.

"No one will notice," Andrews answered. "They only saw it for a second."

27

The flowered arch had been moved in front of the window, with the New York skyline as a backdrop. All the flowers that had decorated the alternate site for the wedding were still in place, still in full bloom under the soft afternoon lighting. There were a dozen guests, all people who had been on his side of the aisle. The judge was waiting.

Cassie went up the stairs in her bridesmaid dress, this time with her hair perfectly styled. "I'm supposed to walk down ahead of you, whenever you're ready," she announced. *Good,* Jane thought. *That way I can keep an eye on you.*

Cassie turned and posed at the top step. Below, the piano began pounding out the strains of the "Wedding March." Cassie started down, one careful step at a time. Jane waited until she was halfway down and then, for the second time in two days, began her walk down the aisle.

Bob Leavitt and Craig were waiting with Bill near the arch. Cassie took a position to the other side of the judge and looked back at Jane. Her expression was one of complete joy. Jane had to give her credit. The kid could really act.

Bill stepped forward and took her arm, then led her forward until they were standing in front of the judge, who was wearing a dark business suit with a light tie.

"Dearly beloved, children, relatives, and friends," His Honor began. Jane listened to the traditional wording as if she were a guest at someone else's wedding. She didn't focus on the true meaning of the ceremony until Bill, asked if he would love, honor, and protect her, said that he would. And then it was her turn. She listened carefully to the promises being asked of her and thought that she really should ask for time to consider. Instead, she heard herself say, "I do." Then Bill was kissing her, the judge was shaking her hand and pecking at her cheek, and the small gathering of guests was applauding happily.

"Mrs. Andrews," Bill said as he turned her and led her toward the dining room. He seated her at the center of a table set for a light supper and took the place next to her. The caterer, who had bounced back from yesterday's disaster, poured champagne, and Robert Leavitt rose with a toast that hoped for their long life, continuing love, and, who knows, maybe even another son and heir. Hens were served in cognac sauce.

"Are you happy?" Bill asked, leaning toward her.

"Happy and amazed," Jane answered. "How did you do this so quickly?"

The conversation over dinner was spirited, with tales of her husband's foibles dominating. Jane learned that he had bathed in the Fountain of Trevi, fallen down the side of a pyramid at Luxor, and insulted the archbishop of Canterbury by calling him "Your Holiness." He had testified before the wrong committee of Congress, met with the president with his fly open, and congratulated the governor of New York for the economic miracle of New Jersey. Bill laughed harder than anyone, seeming most human when he was down off his pedestal. But Jane noticed that not one of the many stories concerned his travels with Kay, or even came from the years when she was alive. Even in the most lighthearted moments, Kay was off-limits.

She looked around at the happy faces, wondering which one of them might be furious that the marriage had taken place. The corporate guests—Robert Leavitt, Kim Annuzio, Gordon Frier, Henry Davis, and John Applebaum—were completely involved in roasting their chief executive and seemed to be enjoying every moment of it. The children were angelic. She couldn't help wondering which one of them had spiked her coffee. They were all pictures of innocence. She began to doubt her earlier certainty. Maybe it was the stress of the previous weeks, mingled with a bit of wine. Perhaps the sinister plot to keep her and Bill apart really was all in her mind.

They adjourned to the piano bar, and the judge formally signed the marriage license. "You're legal," he told William Andrews. "In fact, this may be the only legal thing you've ever done." Bill served as bartender, pouring round after round to the off-key singers. Network executives took off their jackets and loosened their ties. Henry Davis, the financial vice president, began to doze in one of the soft chairs. Kim Annuzio kicked off her shoes and gyrated to a rock beat.

Jane was delighted as character after character stepped out of his corporate role and became recklessly human. The automatons surrounding William Andrews seemed to be human after all, which made Bill less of a mysterious icon. Even Cassie and Craig, on the sidelines of the party, looked like normal young adults. "This is going to work," Jane told herself, delighted that the marriage she had just entered might even turn out to be joyous. She laughed out loud when Bill pulled her out into the center of the room to join Kim in her spastic dance steps. She was still dancing when the skyline behind the picture window turned red with the sunset.

"It's time to go," Bill suddenly announced.

"Go where? Isn't this where we live?"

"On our honeymoon. I hope your bags are still packed."

"Now?"

"Isn't this when you usually have a honeymoon? After the wedding?"

The party moved to the foyer, where John Applebaum, head of the publishing division, loaded their duffel bags onto the elevator. Then Jane and William Andrews were pushed in by their waving guests. Someone even managed to throw a handful of rice before the elevator doors closed. A limo whisked them to the heliport, where the helicopter was waiting for the short flight to the Westchester County airport.

The pilot pushed their bags into the small luggage space. Then he helped them climb into the cabin. They found a bottle of champagne chilling in a bucket of ice. William poured while the pilot climbed aboard and started the turbine engines. Jane left the wine in her glass.

"This is a different chopper," Andrews noticed for the pilot.

The man nodded. "Yes, sir. We sucked in some debris yesterday when we landed at that mountain house. So we've got it in the shop, checking out the engine. Just a precaution." The whine grew into a howl, and the helicopter lifted off.

Mountain house? Jane remembered Bill saying that he had flown out to the house in New Jersey, which was in rolling horse country, definitely not on a mountain. There was only one house that fit with his claim of winding up a private legal matter. That was the ski chalet upstate that was built on the top of a mountain, accessible by only one road. The house where Kay Parker had been murdered.

Andrews raised his glass in a toast. "Here's to one whole week without a single interruption." She clicked her glass against his but sipped very slowly, now concerned about thinking clearly. What had she just learned?

That her husband, on the day of their wedding, had gone to the site where his first marriage had ended in a blast of gunfire. Why? Was he selling the place to put an end to the past? Did he want to be sure that Kay, and the agony of her death, would never intrude on his new marriage? That was a comforting thought. Or had he gone back to a shrine? Maybe to tell his first wife that no matter what, he would always love her? Or perhaps to ask her permission to get on with his new life? That was something Jane didn't want to consider.

The momentary elation of the wedding party vanished. The image of her husband, happily entertaining his friends, faded. His romantic rush to have her to himself seemed fabricated. Once again, William Andrews became the secretive, ghost-ridden figure she had come to fear.

Was she making too much of it? Maybe he was simply authorizing necessary maintenance on the house or meeting with an architect about renovations. Or perhaps some legal matter concerning the property had to be settled in a local court. There were countless possible explanations that had nothing to do with his first marriage.

But one thing was certain. He had lied to her. Whatever he was hiding was more important than an honest beginning with his new wife. She realized that she couldn't trust him, that he saw her as a danger to the secrets he was protecting and would never let her share the truth of his past. And now she was going to be alone with him in a sailboat far offshore, out of touch with the rest of the world. Jane set down the champagne glass and turned her face to the window.

28

They were in Tortola aboard a forty-foot sloop, rocking easily on the ebbing tide. Jane was grilling fresh snapper over a hibachi that projected out over the lifeline. Bill was up and down from the cabin, setting a table that fit across the cockpit and bringing up the wine they would have with dinner. He blinked into the light of the sun that was setting over St. John.

The jet from Westchester had taken over four hours to St. Thomas. Another hour was needed for the transfer to a small floatplane that flew over the sugary white beaches of St. John and put down in Soper's Hole at Tortola's western end. And then came the launch ride out to their charter, a new boat with clean lines that tugged gently on its mooring.

She had napped while Bill received their provisions from a tender. He had stocked steaks, fish, and lobster in the ice chest and had filled the cupboards with fresh island vegetables. Beer and soda had gone into the ice with the meat, and the rum and gin were put into a liquor cabinet that was designed to keep them safe no matter what the weather. She had come back up in a bathing suit and followed him around the deck as he checked out the rigging, the sail locker, the anchor, and the mooring lines. She went over the side for a quick swim around the boat while he tested the batteries and electrical circuits and measured the fuel and water. It was midafternoon when he appeared on deck in his shorts and dove over the side to join her.

They swam together, embraced at every opportunity, and kissed passionately at the foot of the ladder. Then they climbed aboard, showered together in the head forward of the master cabin, and fell still damp into the queen-size bunk. They made love slowly, drawing out each touch, each sense of intimate pleasure, for as long as they could. They climaxed together in a steely embrace that nearly crushed her. When he fell away, Jane smiled broadly. There had been nothing aloof about his lovemaking. In her arms, he was all that she had ever hoped for.

She dressed in shorts and a T-shirt, dug into the ice chest, and found a snapper cleaned, skinned, and perfectly boned. She sliced up a squash and cut a potato into small chunks. She mixed fruit juice into a marinade and poured it over the fish. Clad only in shorts, Bill staggered from the forward cabin, paused to slip his hands under her T-shirt and kiss her neck, and went topside to start the grill.

Now they sat over the dinner, nibbling at the edges. He moaned with exaggerated pleasure. "Delicious!" he pronounced.

Jane laughed. "You weren't that loud in bed. It is true! Men would rather eat than get laid."

"Not true," he protested. "We're equally interested in food and sex."

They finished dinner and were sipping their wine, watching the sunset turn the water crimson, when a telephone buzzed in the cabin below. Jane turned a suspicious eye toward her husband, who was making a point of ignoring the phone.

"What's that?" she asked.

"A satellite phone. It comes with the yacht." He still made no move to answer it.

"There's a telephone on board. You promised we'd be incommunicado."

"It's hurricane season. We need to have communications."

"How do you suppose someone found out the number?"

He shrugged. "Beats me. Do you want me to answer it, to see who it is?"

"If you touch that phone, I'll throw it overboard just like I did your cell phone on our first date."

William smiled at the recollection. "You know something? That was the moment when I knew I loved you. When you plucked the phone out of my hand and threw it out the window, I thought, 'Now, that's a woman.'"

She laughed. "I don't know what got into me. There I was, with the most important man on the planet, throwing away his link with his empire. It's a wonder you didn't throw me after it."

"It's getting late," he said with a forced yawn. "Time for bed."

"What about the dishes?"

"The seagulls will take care of them."

Jane lay awake well into the night, her new husband sleeping easily with one arm thrown across her. It was just the two of them, she realized. Andrews Global Network was on another planet, lightyears away. Cassie and Craig's torments couldn't reach them. It was just she and a man who seemed to love her madly. She couldn't remember ever feeling so content. She still didn't understand why he loved her, but maybe all newlyweds were conscious of their incredible luck. Nor did she know what secrets he was hiding. But didn't it take years for married couples to reveal themselves fully to each other? She couldn't understand his past any more than she could predict their future. But what she did understand was the moment. She seemed to be as happy as any human being was ever likely to be.

She awoke to the sound of lines running through blocks, and the snap of a sail as it first found the breeze. There was golden light easing through the portholes, and it moved up the bulkhead as the boat gently heeled. Jane kicked out of bed, retrieved the panties and T-shirt her husband had dropped beside the bunk, and climbed up until she could see into the cockpit.

"Are we moving?"

"Under way," he corrected. "Take a look."

She went to the top step. They were moving easily, splitting the channel between two small islands of thick green foliage, headed straight toward St. John, a huge mountain that rose abruptly out of the sea. The sails were ballooned out over the side in an easy reach.

"I'll make some coffee," she suggested.

"Better hurry. It's going to get choppy in a few minutes and you won't want to be down below."

He was right. Just as she poured two steaming mugs, the boat heeled steeply. She saw white water rushing past the porthole. "What happened?" she asked once she had climbed cautiously back to the cockpit.

"We're into the wind," he answered. They had turned into the teeth of the prevailing southeasterly. The sails were pulled taught. "We'll be tacking into the breeze for the next hour or so, until we're well out in the channel. I'm going to need your help." He gave her a brief explanation of how they would move the jib from one side of the boat to the other each time they changed heading. Then he had her practice with the winch so she got used to the force she would be working with. They were nearly on the beach at St. John when he threw the wheel over. She cast off one sheet and began cranking in on the other. She felt the boat die as it came across the wind, then leap back to life when she took in the other sheet. "Whoa!" she cried out in delight.

"Nicely done, matey." They charged away from St. John on a northeasterly heading toward the Tortola coast.

For the next two hours they beat a course to the east, back and forth across the wind. They were working as a team, William steering ever closer to the wind and trimming the mainsail while Jane dashed from side to side to tend the jib. Their mugs of coffee, now cold, sat untouched in the cup holders.

"Ready about," he called for the dozenth time.

"Aye, aye, Captain," she teased.

"Hard alee," and he spun the wheel. She tossed one sheet off its winch and carried the winch handle to the other side, where she pulled the line tight and began cranking. The sail that had gone limp filled and tightened until she could barely pull in more line.

"Bend your back to it," he ordered. And then they both burst out laughing. The boat heeled over and steadied on its new heading. The coast of St. John fell away to the south, and they were out into the more open waters of the Drake Channel.

"Next tack, we'll stay with a southerly course," he decided. "It will be more relaxing."

"No way," she answered, "this is too much fun. I feel like I'm really pulling my weight."

"And I feel that I've finally found a partner."

He couldn't have pleased her more. Not found "a new partner" or "another partner," but he seemed to mean the partner he had always been looking for. Was he saying that the fabulous Kay Parker had never filled the role? That would be hoping for too much. But she felt sure that, at least for the moment, he had forgotten about Kay. She was the one who was trimming his sails.

They came about, and settled on a bow reach toward Norman Island, famous for the secure anchorage inside its bight, and the watery caves on its western shore. Jane went below and made crab-salad sandwiches. She brought them up with fresh cups of hot coffee. They were locked onto the breeze, heeling slightly, and making good speed through the water. She slid in next to him, behind the helm, and fed him from her plate so that he could keep his hands on the wheel. A small island passed by to port as they drew near the entrance to Norman Island's harbor.

Half an hour later they were riding at anchor between two other sailboats that were on cruising vacations. Bill lowered the inflatable dinghy and tested its small outboard. They climbed aboard and headed into shore, where they stretched out on a patch of sun-baked sand.

Was this the time? Was this her chance to get answers to all the questions about Kay Parker that were swirling in her mind? And maybe get a sensible explanation of the payments he was making to the woman in Paris. She had given him any number of opportunities to volunteer the information, but he had always retreated. At times it seemed as if he were determined to hide the truth not just from her but even from himself.

Jane rolled onto her stomach and propped up on her elbows so that she was nearly face-to-face with him. "Bill," she said. He opened his eyes, saw her, and smiled. "Tell me about your first wife."

There was no reaction. He simply let his eyes close sleepily. "I'd rather talk about my new wife," he said pleasantly.

"I should know something about her," Jane persisted.

"Why?" he responded, a smile beginning to play on his lips. "Do you think I'm still in love with her?"

"I think she's the most important person in your life. I don't think I'll ever really know you until I understand what she was like."

His eyes opened and his expression turned serious. "You must have researched her when you were looking into me," he answered. "God knows, she generated enough press coverage."

Jane thought of the clippings that he had seen next to her computer. He was telling her that he knew she had been digging into his past. "That's all about her public life, not her private life," she countered. "I guess I want to know more about what she meant to you. About the two of you together. Like, how did you meet? Was it love at first sight?"

Bill raised up on an elbow. "We met at a fund-raiser," he said. "We were introduced by a director of the Metropolitan Museum."

"And?"

"And what? We bumped into each other at different events. I escorted her to a few charity balls, and the newspapers started referring to us as an item. So . . . we became an item."

"You fell in love," Jane suggested.

He weighed the question. "Yes, we did. But not 'love' in the way you mean. More like a recognition that we were right for each other. I think that Kay and I were more in love with ourselves. We probably saw each other as fitting additions to our already glittering lives."

Jane was shocked. "That sounds too calculating. Like a marriage to form an alliance between countries."

Bill corrected her. "That's the way I see it now, looking back from a distance. At the time, it didn't seem calculating. Society said we were in love, and I suppose we thought it must be true. We were both ambitious, public people. How would we have known anything about love?"

"Did she move in with you?"

He burst out laughing. "Kay wasn't the type to move in with anyone."

"Oh," Jane said with mock indignation. "Not a tramp like me who would climb into any old bed!"

"No, not a woman who would risk giving anyone even a momentary advantage over her. She was always guarded, unfailingly discreet."

"And you liked that?" she wondered.

"I admired it. Kay kept to her priorities. She knew what it took to be the belle of the ball."

Jane felt chastised. Not that she was particularly interested in being admired, but that her shortcomings next to the first Mrs. Andrews were so obvious. She rolled away, onto her back. Maybe the things he could tell her about his first wife would be too humbling for her. Was that why he didn't talk about her more freely? And who knows how badly she might fail in comparison with Selina Royce? Perhaps that was a question better not asked.

Back on the boat, he cooked dinner on the grill while she set the table and struggled with the wine cork. They ate ravenously, stimulated by the sea air. When darkness fell, he stripped off her clothes and threw her over the side. Then he jumped in naked after her, found her by the ladder, and made love to her while they bobbed up to their chins.

"I've never done that before," Jane breathed with delight.

"Me neither," he claimed. "It just seemed like a good idea."

She was on deck the next morning when they pulled the anchor and raised the sails. They ghosted out of the bight, turned the corner at Treasure Point, and found an anchorage off the caves. They boarded the inflatable dinghy, raised the motor, and paddled through the first opening into a series of underground ponds that were connected by shallow streams. In the light carried into the caves by the crystal-clear water, they saw crabs and lobsters clinging to rocks and watching them cautiously. Schools of tiny fish scattered each time they dipped an oar. Jane shivered when a snake slithered down from a ledge and slid into the water, and then laughed at the comedy of two snails racing across a water-polished stone.

When they finally paddled out and hauled themselves aboard their boat, she cooked a breakfast of bacon and eggs, which William assured her was the best he had ever tasted.

"Are you trying to charm your way back into my bed?" she challenged.

"The thought never crossed my mind."

"It didn't? Some honeymoon this is going to be!"

They dove over the side, frolicked around the boat, and then came back aboard to take the sun. Jane stretched out on the cabin roof, her head near the hatch and her feet under the boom. William was on the deck next to her. She was just about asleep when he announced that he was going down for a beer. "Want one?" he offered.

She shook her head sleepily and let the warmth lull her back to her dreams.

She heard the phone ring, really nothing more than a short, soft beep. Was it the phone? Or just one of the navigation instruments announcing that it was still on the job? Then she heard her husband's voice, a muffled whisper behind a cupped hand. He had been next to the phone when it sounded and had picked it up instantly.

"Yeah . . . it's okay . . . what's up?"

So he had given someone the number. Probably Robert Leavitt, and obviously with instructions to call only if it was absolutely necessary. Otherwise, the damn phone would have been ringing constantly.

"Who?" A pause. "Why would Taylor care?"

Taylor? Roscoe Taylor? Was that who they were talking about?

"I'm sure you're right," her husband whispered. "But why?" He was quiet for several seconds and then said, "No, I don't think she put him up to it." Another long pause, then, "She has no trouble asking her own questions."

She? Is he talking about me? What had she put Roscoe Taylor up to? Had Leavitt learned that he was looking into the brief career of Selina Royce, the woman he pretended never to have met? She suddenly felt chilly, as if a breeze had come up.

"Okay, tell him about the spot we're opening for an editorial director of the whole chain. He probably already knows that there's no great demand for old newspapermen." He listened, then concluded with "No, whatever you decide. Don't call me, I'll be home on Sunday." She heard no click. He must have eased the phone back into its cradle.

She kept her eyes closed when he came back up.

"Are you asleep?" he asked.

She groaned. "Almost."

"I'm sorry about that. I left orders that I wasn't to be called."

"Was that the telephone?" she asked, her eyes still closed as if she were too intoxicated by the sun to care.

"I grabbed it quickly so it wouldn't disturb you. And I got rid of him quickly."

"Who?" Jane asked conversationally. She didn't want it to sound like an interrogation.

He drank from the beer bottle. "Bob Leavitt. I asked him not to call back again. Anything he has can wait until Sunday."

Again, she was careful not to sound too interested. "What did he want?"

"Well, actually it was something you'll be happy to hear. We're promoting your friend Roscoe Taylor to editorial director for all the papers in the chain. It means more prestige and more money for him, and we think a better editorial product for the company."

She smiled, still keeping her eyes closed. "That's wonderful. I hope he won't think that the boss's wife had anything to do with it, because he's a great journalist. We need more like him."

He drank again. "Better get in out of the sun," he said. "You're starting to turn pink."

She showered in the forward head, wincing at the cold water and then slowly coming to enjoy it. But she couldn't shake the half of the telephone conversation she had overheard. Without a doubt, the "Taylor who was digging" was Roscoe. And if it involved something that she might have put him up to, then it had to be the inquiries about Selina Royce that he had been making in San Antonio. Then the rest of Bill's side of the conversation made sense. They were offering him a fat promotion, probably with the unwritten understanding that he stop looking into matters that didn't concern him. And if he didn't get the message, then he would indeed find that there wasn't much demand for old newspapermen. What her husband had decided on was a power play, pure and simple. Team players were rewarded. Those who wouldn't join the team were crushed. It was Roscoe's choice.

29

Jane dressed in the head so that she wouldn't be offering her husband any suggestion of intimacy. Right now, she didn't feel like being in his arms. The easy, loving husband she was just learning to love had deserted her. The secretive, paranoid power broker she feared was back in business.

There was an uneasy silence over their lunch. His mood had obviously changed with the telephone call, probably because he now suspected that his wife was searching into the dark corners of his past. He kept up the pretense of good humor, complimenting the food and cheerfully recalling the morning's visit to the caves. But his enthusiasm was hollow and difficult to sustain. Clearly his mind was elsewhere. For her part, Jane felt as if she had been thrown back to the periphery of his life. She was outside his protective wall, and he was perfectly willing to lie to keep her there. Kay Parker and her untimely death were at the core of his being, and he would go to any length to keep them from being disturbed.

They set sail again, back on the easterly heading that required them to tack across the wind every few minutes. Andrews again became the enthusiastic captain, lavishing praise on even her most routine accomplishments. She was still excited in her role as partner in keeping the boat alive in the face of headwinds. The sheet handling, the crackling of the sails, and the occasional bath in salty spray took her mind off the betrayal she had suffered. It even brought her husband back from the edge of gloom that he had been tottering on.

They found a mooring off the beach at Cooper Island and went ashore to a small resort that was built just out of sight behind the first row of trees. Bill promised her the best rum punch in the islands and made good at a small bar that stood at the water's edge. They ordered a second, carrying their drinks with them to the resort dining room, where they feasted on lobster. They were both more relaxed when they motored back to their boat and made love passionately while stretched out in the dinghy. Then they skinny-dipped from the inflatable to the swim platform and fell into their bed.

Andrews fell asleep right away, but Jane found herself tossing. Despite his reassurances and the pleasure she found in his company, she was beginning to doubt that she truly loved him. She had felt love in the strength of his embrace and in the moments when they were handling their boat with skill and vigor. But there was no abiding love that she could count on to see her through the difficult moments. How could there be when she couldn't trust him? It seemed that the most she could hope for was to be his occasional wife. As he had said of Kay Parker, he wasn't going to give anyone even a temporary advantage over him.

She decided to confront him. A straight question! *Are you offering Roscoe a promotion to stop his inquiries about Selina Royce?* Or perhaps more direct. *Who is this woman, and why are you paying her a fortune every month?* Or even, *Exactly how did your first wife die?*

He would be startled and defensive, but the issue would be on the table without any ambiguity. He would have to decide to tell her and take her into his confidence, or lie and shut her out forever. And then, maybe, with the truth as a backdrop, they could begin building a real, full-time marriage.

But in the morning, her courage deserted her. He seemed eager to please her and enthused over their next port, called The Baths, a crystal-clear pool surrounded by gigantic boulders on the island of Virgin Gorda. The gloomy introspection she had noticed the day before seemed to be gone. And, in truth, she was afraid. Afraid that her questions would widen the chasm that had cracked open between them, or even bring on the kind of power play she had heard him use as a threat to Roscoe. She could be a team player and reap the bountiful rewards. Or she could be obstinate and find herself out in the cold. Or maybe even dead, like William Andrews's first wife. That thought made the boat seem isolated and dangerous.

He took another phone call. Or maybe he had placed the

call. Jane couldn't know for sure. He swam back from the beach supposedly to start their dinner, leaving her to explore the pools that were formed under the boulders. He was going to return in the dinghy to pick her up, but Jane decided to swim back. When she reached the ladder, she heard him talking inside the cabin. He hung up as soon as she climbed into the cockpit.

"Another emergency?" she asked sarcastically.

He seemed annoyed that she had caught him. "It was just something I thought of. A question that I wanted to get settled. I picked a time when you wouldn't be bothered by it."

"What was the question?" She wondered how much further he would carry his lie.

"A technical issue. Nothing interesting." He wasn't going to explain himself. Instead, he began preparations for getting under way.

"I thought we were going to eat here," Jane reminded him.

"I know another spot just a bit up the coast," he said. "I think you'll like it better."

They set sail, this time with the wind coming from the starboard quarter. They were heeling only a bit and making good time over calm seas. He had fallen quiet, despite her attempts to make conversation. She could tell he was distracted, deep in thoughts that he had no intention of sharing. Jane went below and fixed them each a drink, rum painkillers, sweet but potent. They sipped while the sun made another fiery exit.

The wind picked up, driving them even faster. The flat sea came alive with rollers that picked up the stern of the boat and pushed it like a surfboard. "This is exciting," Jane said, not sure whether she was just excited or maybe a bit apprehensive. "We're making good time," he answered, but still didn't open up to conversation.

Jane stood to go below into the cabin, thinking that finger snacks would help her cope with the drink. At that instant the boat jolted to leeward, sending her staggering into the lifeline. She turned just as the boom jibed and came flying toward her head. She put up her arms, protecting her head as the boom drove into her. She felt the lifeline sliding down her back. Then she was falling over backwards into the white wake that was rushing by. She plunged into the cold darkness.

She was fully alert when she came to the surface. There was still enough light in the sky for her to make out the boat racing away from her. She could hear Bill screaming at her, but she couldn't understand what he was saying. He threw something—the life ring that was fixed to the rear of the cockpit. She saw it land halfway between her and the boat. But it disappeared behind the swells that had been pushing them. She gulped in air and began swimming in the direction of where the ring had hit the water. But she was afraid that each new swell was pushing it farther away from her. Maybe it was better to save her energy so she could keep herself afloat.

The boat was still moving away, turning across the wind as if coming back to her. Bill seemed to be standing at the foot of the mast, working on the lines. But Jane was bobbing up and down in the waves and lost sight of the boat each time she was down. It was rapidly growing dark. In another few minutes she wouldn't be able to see the boat at all.

She was down between swells, alone and suddenly frightened. When she rose up, she caught sight of the boat, its sails lowered, pitching broadside over the waves. The sea and the wind were pushing it farther away. It seemed powerless to turn back to her. She couldn't see the life ring. It had to be within twenty yards of her, probably just on the far side of the next sea swell. But then she was falling down behind a wave, dropping into a trough where there was just water and sky.

30

Jane fought against panic. How could she drown when she was within twenty yards of a life ring? When the boat was no more than a hundred yards away? But when she came up on the next peak, the boat was still rocking broadside. The life ring was nowhere in sight. Could it have broken when it hit the water? Had it already sunk? She caught a glimpse of the shoreline, now dark and vacant. How far away was it? They had been sailing only a few hundred yards off the island's volcanic edges, a distance she should be able to swim. But the sea would be in her face.

Fear began to take over. Was Bill coming back for her? Had he swung the wheel, causing the boat to turn and the sail to jibe? Jesus, had he planned to put her overboard? She thought of his telephone call and the gloomy, nonresponsive mood it had caused. What had he learned? Why wasn't he coming back for her?

There were running lights on the boat, red and green at the waterline and white high up on the mast. Was the boat coming at her, or had it turned away? It seemed no nearer, and the light on the mast was still swinging widely. The boat hadn't steadied in any direction. The life ring was no longer an issue. It could be floating just a few yards from her and she would never find it in the darkness. The boat disappeared as she slipped behind another wave.

How long could she stay afloat? And hour? Maybe two? Sometime during the night her strength would falter, her breathing would become less rhythmical. There would be no chance of rescue until daylight. Her best chance was to strike out for the shore.

When she rode up the next crest, the boat came into view, now closer and steadier in the water. It was on its way back to her, kicking up a gray bow wake on the black surface. She screamed with all the air she could muster and waved frantically until she dropped down into the next trough. Could he see her? Probably not. She took another breath and screamed again.

There was a bright light on the boat when she saw it next. Bill was panning a searchlight over the waves, trying to locate the voice. Jane waved frantically, but the beam of light was well short of her. She heard the boat's engine, a low rumble from the small diesel. Then she heard the sound of the bow slicing through the water. "Over here!" she called. The light swung to her and hit her face with a blinding glare.

Bill's voice came. "I've got you! I'm coming to you!" The engine noise lowered and then went silent.

The boat went past her. She could see Bill at the helm, turning the boat behind her so that it was between her and the open sea. He was out of the cockpit and back on the swim ladder, reaching down to her. She caught his hand and swung her feet to the ladder. He lifted her aboard.

His arms were around her. He kissed the top of her head and hugged her as if he were trying to wring the seawater out of her clothes. "Thank God, thank God," he said over and over. Then Jane began to cry hysterically.

She went below to get into dry clothes and heard the engine start while she was changing. She was still sobbing and gasping for breath when she went back up to the cockpit and sat across the wheel from her husband. "I don't know what happened," Andrews said. "I was worried about jibing and turned even farther toward the wind. One of the waves must have caught us square. All of a sudden we were swinging and before I could stop it, the boom came over."

Jane nodded, not sure of what he was telling her. "I got my arms up just in time," she remembered.

Bill was lost in his own recollection. "I threw the ring, but the light never came on. There's a lamp that's supposed to turn on when the ring hits the water. I threw the damn thing at you, but then I couldn't find it."

"I saw it hit the water . . ." Jane started.

"I got the sails down pretty fast. I turned into the wind and freed the halyards. But then the engine wouldn't start. It must have taken thirty seconds for it to catch. . . ."

"More like thirty minutes," Jane said. "I thought you weren't going to make it back."

"I would have come back in the dinghy," Bill assured her. And then he was back to the beginning. "I can't believe that I let the mainsail jibe! It must have been a wave!"

They motored into the bight on the northern end of the island and saw several boats bobbing in a protected cove. He wanted Jane to stay in the cockpit, but she insisted on going forward to catch their mooring. He shut off the engine and welcomed her into his arms. They sat quietly out in the open until Jane fell asleep.

They left the boat in Soper's Hole and climbed aboard the single-engine floatplane that he had chartered. The plane took off to the east and then turned back over the sprawling harbor with its flotilla of yachts so they could have one last look at their honeymoon vessel. As soon as they boarded the jet on St. Thomas, Andrews picked up the telephone and got back to work.

She watched aghast at how easily he made the transition. He talked with Gordon Frier, evaluating the worth of a cable company in the Canadian Maritimes. "I know it has coverage," he said as if he had been studying it for the past week, "but nobody lives up there! We'd have to run it as a social service. I mean, who in hell wants to advertise to a bunch of fishermen?" He hung up and then instantly dialed Henry Davis, who had the week's financial consolidation waiting for him. "Will we make our numbers?" he growled. After listening for a minute, he cut in with "C'mon, Henry, it's a simple question. Will we make them or not?" He didn't seem pleased with the answer. And then it was John Applebaum, who headed up the newspapers and was Roscoe's immediate boss. "How about that promotion for Taylor?" he asked. "Good," he said when he heard the answer.

He spared Jane a moment. "Roscoe has accepted the promotion," he told her with a smile. She had to wonder whether the smile was congratulating her on her friend's good fortune or was a cynical announcement that her most important ally had sold out.

When he started another call, Jane snatched the phone from his hand. "Is there a window around here that I can open?"

He shook his head. "Not unless you want to kill us all." He reached for the phone, and she surrendered it without a struggle.

"Technically, we're still on our honeymoon until we land," she reminded him.

He studied her, nodded, and turned off the phone.

She wasn't overjoyed when they returned to their apartment. She had expected her renovations to be finished, but the master bedroom was still raw plaster, and nothing had been done to the children's rooms. Cassie and Craig were still at home and had little to say by way of greeting. "We're being picked up tomorrow," Craig said, referring to the limo service that would return him and his sister to their schools. Cassie had her earphones on and couldn't be disturbed.

Then Andrews disappeared into his office and closed the door behind him. He had a full week's work to catch up on and no time to console his new wife. "Could you make me a sandwich," he wondered, "and maybe fix a pot of coffee?" Her dreams of belonging came crashing down. She pretended to be asleep when Bill looked in and decided not to disturb her.

But she wasn't even drowsy. Her mind was whirling through the events of her courtship and marriage, looking for a pattern and at the same time hoping not to find one. In her entire life, there had been only a few moments of danger, but since she had gotten close to William Andrews, threatening "accidents" were coming fast and furious. Was the runaway horse a sinister scheme or just a childish prank? Had someone pushed the button to close the dance floor on top of her, or was it an unexplained mechanical failure? Did she really pass out from a few sips of champagne, or had she been drugged into unconsciousness? Had she been knocked overboard by a sudden wave, or had her husband intentionally turned into a dangerous jibe? She could easily link all these events to attempts to keep her from marrying William Andrews and to end her snooping into the death of Kay Parker. But just as logically, she could argue them all away as odd coincidences.

Any number of people were legitimate suspects, even the man she had married. True, he had twice rescued her in life-and-death situations. But on the boat, her accident had come after a mood-altering phone call. Wasn't it possible that he decided to kill her and then, when she was drowning in front of him, couldn't go through with it? Jane was determined to find some answers.

In the morning she led the swimming pool engineer up to the roof. "Now take me through this step-by-step. I want to know all the ways that this thing can be made to open and close." They went to the toggle switch that was behind the band shell. It was a simple snap switch with one position marked OPEN and the other CLOSED. Logic argued that she would have seen anyone who came out on the roof to throw the switch.

"Another way," the engineer told her, "is to use the circuit breaker. You could turn the power off on this line and then set the switch to whichever position you wanted. Then, when you turned the power back on, the floor would move to whatever the switch was set on."

"You can kill the power to just this line?" Jane asked.

"Sure. It's a single circuit with its own breaker. All you have to do is open and close the breaker."

"Where's the breaker?"

"Downstairs in the line-entry box. That's where the breakers are for every circuit in the house."

"Where downstairs?" she asked suspiciously.

"In the foyer, right outside the service door."

So that's how they did it, she thought. *That's how they were able to close the dance floor on top of me without coming up to the roof.* She felt an instant of triumph until she realized that "they" could have been anyone. One of the kids, certainly. Or Bob Leavitt, who was visiting the apartment

that night. Or any of the corporation's executives. They all
had keys to the private elevator and were in and out of the
apartment for their constant meetings with Andrews. Even
Bill himself, if he was of a mind to put an end to her snooping, a possibility reinforced by her accident on the sailboat.
Learning about the circuit breaker didn't do much to narrow
her list of suspects.

Still, knowing how it was done was important. It put to
rest the notion that the pool cover just happened to malfunc-
tion. It warned her again that whoever had decided she was
an intolerable danger had no qualms about keeping her out of
the family.

Bob Leavitt called to tell her that her husband would be
leaving for Chicago within the hour. He expected to be back
by the next afternoon.

"Is he there?" she asked.

"Yes, but on a conference call."

"Would you tell him I'd like to speak with him!" She
didn't care if she sounded bitchy. That was the way she suddenly felt. She waited the full hour until his scheduled departure for Chicago. When he hadn't called, she packed an
overnight case and headed downtown to the station, where
she got on a train for Connecticut.

There was a light in the window of her apartment, which
would have disturbed her except that Art's car was parked in
her space. She paid the taxi, went up the stairs, and let herself
in. He was sitting at her computer, her research into Selina
Royce up on the screen. He shut down as soon as he realized
she was standing behind him.

"What are you doing here?" Jane demanded.

"You mean here, in your apartment? I just came over to do
some work on my play. It's noisy at my brother's house."

"That wasn't your play. That was my research," she
charged.

"Oh, that. Yeah, I just happened to come across it. What's
so important about that girl? What's she got to do with
William Andrews?"

Jane wouldn't let herself be distracted. "You let yourself

into my apartment and were going through my things. Do you know I could call the police?"

He sneered. "Get off it! I was working on my play and I happened to see what you were looking into. I was curious—"

"You didn't *happen* to see anything. You brought up my files and were reading them." Her voice was getting louder.

"Big deal. It's all public record stuff. It's not as if you're working for the CIA." Art grabbed his jacket and stormed out of the apartment.

"Don't forget your play," Jane called after him, reminding her former husband that he hadn't brought the play he said he was working on.

31

Twenty minutes later she was knocking on the door of Roscoe Taylor's town house. He was smiling when he opened it but was suddenly concerned when he saw who was there. "Jane . . . my goodness, Jane . . . come in, come in." He backed away and followed her into the living room, where a baseball game was on television. "Damn Red Sox," he said as he snapped it off.

"Don't let me interrupt," Jane started, but he cut her off.

"This is a surprise. What brings you here?"

"You don't want to know. Let's just say that I'm caught between two husbands. One is spying on me, and the other one nearly drowned me. I need a friend."

"Of course, of course. But first a drink and then something to eat. I've got some fish—frozen, I'm sorry to say. But if you have a couple of cocktails before, it isn't half bad."

She slumped into a soft chair and accepted the martini he brought her with loving care. Then he returned with his own.

"To your recent promotion," Jane said, raising her glass.

He blushed. "I'm glad you already know. It saves me the embarrassment of telling you about it."

"What embarrassment? You've earned it, Roscoe."

He sat down, his fingertip tracing the rim of his glass "I may have earned it, but that's not why I got it. I got it for dropping our investigation into that news anchor in San Antonio. Pure and simple, I took the money and ran. What's embarrassing is the way they pulled it off," he said. "There's nothing subtle about the William Andrews team. John Applebaum called me at three o'clock and told me they were creating a new position. 'To improve editorial quality right through the organization.' And I had the experience and the integrity that they were looking for. He said they appreciated that at this stage of my career I might not want to take on new responsibilities. So he told me to sleep on it, and if I wanted to 'join the team,' to give him a call in the morning." He shook his head. " 'Join the team.' I didn't like the sound of joining anyone's team, and that was even before I knew what they meant.

"At five o'clock, your husband's gunslinger, Robert Leavitt, called. He said he had heard the news and hoped I would be joining the team. Then he told me, 'There's just one little matter I should call to your attention.' Selina Royce, he said, was a very difficult episode for the company. 'It's not something that we're eager to go through again.' It was pretty clear. Team members join in the cover-up."

Jane sighed. "That's from a guy who couldn't remember whether there had ever been a Selina Royce."

"I should have told him to go fuck himself," Roscoe lamented. He lifted his drink and downed nearly half of it.

"No, you did the right thing," Jane insisted. "Whatever you learned probably couldn't have been all that important. And you deserve the job and the recognition."

"Thank you," he said softly, as if his sins had just been forgiven. He finished his drink and then asked Jane, "Another?"

"Not if I'm ever going to stand up and walk."

When he returned with his refill, Roscoe began talking before he reached his chair. "I will tell you what I did find out. That is, if you want to hear some sly innuendo about your husband."

She sighed. "I suppose I asked for this. . . ."

"There's no need to know. I can take it with me to my new job in the clouds."

"I'd go crazy wondering what it was," Jane decided.

Roscoe leaned back into his storytelling posture. "William Andrews must have seen her on her San Antonio station, or met her at some sort of cable event. Whatever, he approached Selina Royce and offered her a position with the Andrews network. She accepted. Who in hell wouldn't want to move from San Antonio to New York? Trouble was that she had an ironclad contract with the station. She couldn't leave for another two years. When Andrews heard about it, he tried to buy out her contract. According to my sources, he offered two million for a contract that was paying her less than one hundred thousand."

Jane gasped. "What kind of ratings did she have? The whole audience?"

"I don't know," Roscoe answered impatiently. "But whatever she had, her station owner turned Andrews down cold. Selina was his property, and no matter how much William Andrews was worth, he couldn't have her."

"So he bought the whole cable system," Jane surmised.

"You've got it!" Roscoe said. "The whole company. He attached it to one of his Southwest properties, fired the owner, and brought Selina to headquarters. He paid five million just to get an evening news anchor from San Antonio."

"He was in love with her," Jane said.

Roscoe shook his head. "It doesn't make sense. I mean, William Andrews could have had any woman on the planet."

"So what happened?" Jane asked.

"She disappeared," Roscoe answered. "Do you know she never did a network news show?"

They sat thoughtfully, staring at each other. Jane finally ventured, "If he was keeping her as a mistress, Kay might have found out. And from what I've learned about the first Mrs. Andrews, she wouldn't have put up with it for a minute. So, suppose she told Andrews to get rid of her. And suppose Selina learned that she was on the way out?"

"Yeah, then Selina might have reason to kill Kay Parker," Roscoe agreed. "Or maybe Kay came after Selina, and Selina beat her to the draw."

Jane found herself nodding at the logic. "Either way, Selina would be Kay Parker's killer. But why in hell is Bill paying her a hundred thousand a month?"

Roscoe pursed his lips. "Well, if he was in love with her . . ."

"He'd be paying to keep her out of the hands of the police," Jane said, finishing the thought.

"Or," Roscoe continued, "suppose William Andrews had someone else kill his wife. Then Selina would have him by the short hairs."

"No," Jane insisted. "If he had Kay Parker killed in order to have Selina, then why wouldn't he still have her?"

Roscoe looked at her sadly. "Maybe he does."

Jane pulled back as if he had aimed a blow at her.

"I don't know anything like that," Roscoe hastened to assure her. "We're just speculating here, and we could be miles off the mark."

"But what you're suggesting is that Selina is still his mistress, and he keeps her in Paris so that there won't be any second thoughts about Kay's death." Jane sighed. "But if that's true, then where do I fit in? I mean, if he's having a happy affair with the woman of his dreams, then why would he bother to marry me? I don't bring one damn thing to the party!"

Roscoe asked, "Isn't it possible that he's fallen out of love with Selina, and into love with you?"

Jane snickered. "He's still spending a lot more on her than he is on me."

"Maybe he has to in order to keep her from stirring up a fuss. Isn't it possible that he has to pay her so that he's free to love you?"

She shook her head. "Thanks for the compliment, Roscoe. But it isn't very likely. He was paying her long before he ever met me."

Again they sat in quiet thought. Roscoe broke in with "None of this really makes any sense. There has to be a simpler explanation."

"But if there is," Jane pointed out, "why wouldn't he tell me about it?"

The implications of Roscoe Taylor's report tormented her during the train ride back to the city. How could her husband still be in love with Selina? She had just spent a week alone with him, and his every gesture told her that he loved her deeply. He had rushed to marry her when he had every opportunity to postpone the wedding. Was it possible for a man to be in love with two women at once?

Why was he paying Selina Royce? If she killed Kay, why

would he have gone to such lengths to protect her? Perhaps he felt guilty that he had brought her into his life. Maybe he felt that he had a ·hand in the deadly confrontation. That might explain his covering up for her and helping her escape. But all that money over all those years? Wouldn't she have a life of her own by now?

Then, that night, Bill told her he had to leave for Paris. "Something just came up . . . ," he started to explain.

"Take me with you. I love Paris!"

"Oh, I don't think so. It's just a quick trip. All business."

"It's business to you," Jane countered, "but it's a joy to me. I won't be in the way. I'll go to the Picasso, or maybe the Orsay. I'll sit in a sidewalk café and see if I can get picked up by a Frenchman."

He laughed. "You'll have no trouble doing that. I'll take you if you promise to stay in the museums."

"It's a deal."

"I'll send a car," he said. "We landed at La Guardia, but I think they may have moved the plane up to Westchester for maintenance."

"See you on the plane," Jane bubbled.

Museums like hell, she thought as soon as she hung up. This was her chance to find out exactly what her husband's relationship was with the woman who had probably once been his mistress.

Part Three

The Murder

32

She fell asleep with her head resting on her husband's chest and didn't wake up when he slid out of the small bed and went up to the plane's conference room. Gordon Frier and Robert Leavitt were both aboard, and they joined Andrews for an all-nighter. They were all red-eyed when the plane landed in Paris.

They checked into the Hôtel George V, where Bill had caught her coming out of the shower, and were escorted to a penthouse suite that seemed to be his regular quarters. They slept for a few hours and then had a breakfast of cheese and ham brought to their room. At nine-thirty, Bill donned his suit, picked up his briefcase, and kissed her good-bye like a commuter going off to the train station. Jane slipped into jeans and a sweater, applied a little makeup, and put on her most comfortable walking shoes. She stopped at a shop in the lobby and bought a pair of oversize sunglasses.

She walked several blocks away from the hotel, down to the Seine and the Place de l'Alma. She got into a taxi at the foot of the bridge and asked for the Place de l'Opéra. Then she walked west on Boulevard Haussmann until she reached Selina Royce's address.

There was a fashionable shop on the street level, with exquisite lingerie and beautiful dresses in the window. At another time the shop would have been irresistible, but she was on a very different mission. There was an insignificant doorway to one side, serving the four residential floors above. Each French window led to an iron-railing balcony. Shutters were closed over most of the windows to ensure privacy from the identically styled buildings across the wide street.

She pushed the door open and stepped into a hallway that led to a large and elegant lobby behind the shops. At the end of the lobby were doors opening out onto a garden with a central fountain. To the left were two brass-cage elevators. A uniformed concierge, seated at a desk near the elevators, rose to greet her.

He glanced at her hand, found the wedding ring, and asked "Madame?" His bow indicated that he was waiting to be helpful.

Jane answered in English. "I seem to be lost. Does Arthur Keene live here?"

"Monsieur Keene?" He looked puzzled. If he had known Art, he probably would have broken out in laughter. "No, I don't think so," he said politely in heavily accented English. "Perhaps you have the wrong address."

She showed him the paper she had written the address on. He squinted at it, shrugged, and announced that this was indeed the address she was looking for. "But, unfortunately, no Monsieur Keene."

"Sorry," she said. "I must have copied it wrong." On her way out she stole a glance at the brass postal boxes. Just as Roscoe had told her, Selina Royce's name filled one of the slots. She went down the hallway and back onto the street. It was a luxury building, apparently catering to those with more money than they needed. Selina would fit that description. She looked around and spotted a café across the street, just a few storefronts down. Jane crossed over, took a seat by the sidewalk, pulled her sweater tight against the fall chill, and settled down for what might be a long wait. If she had guessed correctly, Andrews would be stopping by for a visit. She hoped she was wrong, but the fact that she was watching the doorway meant that she thought she was right.

She ordered a small baguette sandwich and a bottle of water, then sat back to watch. The busy thoroughfare, with its glamorous pedestrian traffic, presented constant distractions, and it wasn't easy to keep her attention focused. An hour passed. Maybe he wasn't coming. Maybe the rendezvous was all in her imagination. She ordered coffee and sipped it slowly; then when the waiter seemed to hover, she added a pastry. It was past midday, and there had been no sign of her husband. People had gone in and come out of the doorway, a middle-aged man and two women who were too old to fit a profile of Selina.

Jane began to feel conspicuous. She was starting her third hour at the café and was the only one using the outdoor tables. She paid her bill, got up, and found a store window directly across the boulevard from the doorway. For another hour she pretended to window-shop, always keeping the entrance in sight. A woman came out, this one more in keeping with Selina's age and general description. The woman began walking toward the opera house. Jane was tempted to follow her. Maybe it was Selina, on her way to a meeting with Bill. Very possible! Why had she assumed that he would visit her apartment? But on closer inspection, the girl seemed wrong. Tall and skinny rather than statuesque, and probably too young to have been a news anchor eight years ago. Jane gambled, and stayed put. She had lost confidence that her husband would be coming to the apartment. What had seemed to be a perfect plan now seemed ridiculous.

Maybe she should go back to the lobby and simply ask for Selina Royce. "Whom shall I say is calling?" the concierge would certainly ask. And then tell him, "Mrs. William Andrews." But then what would the other woman do? Invite her up for coffee? That didn't seem likely. What was more probable was that she would send word that she was not at home and then call Bill to warn him off. She wandered back to the café and sat in the chair she had abandoned. The waiter probably recognized her, but he gave no sign of it as he took her order for a glass of wine.

She began another vigil, sipping the wine and nibbling on a dish of peanuts. The young woman she had almost followed returned, far too quickly to have been at a midafternoon liaison.

A taxi maneuvered to the curb a few doors away from her, attracting her attention because of the horn blasts from the cars it cut off. She had almost turned away when William Andrews stepped out. He leaned into the window to pay his fare and, without looking either left or right, bounded into the doorway of Selina Royce's building. She swallowed hard. Her worst fears were playing out in front of her.

What now? Jane hadn't planned that far. He was inside with his mistress. Should she charge across the street, push past the guard, and then confront them together? She had a delicious moment thinking of catching the two of them together, but then she realized how ridiculous she would look, standing in the doorway and screaming, "J'accuse!" Especially if he was simply dropping off a check. She decided to wait and ordered another glass of wine.

Now the waiting became unbearable. Half an hour was more than enough time for him to pay hush money. As her wait drifted toward an hour, she did battle with the images of what might be going on in the apartment. She couldn't believe that her husband could be making love to another woman. Why would he keep a mistress a continent away? But, of course, he flew to Europe several times a month. With his resources, Paris was just the next town.

She fantasized about other cities. Was this the only one, or did he keep women in other places that he frequented? She stopped just short of entertaining the notion that he might be an international philanderer. But it wasn't easy to sit watching the doorway he had entered, realizing that nearly two hours had passed with no sign of his return.

She felt a lump in her throat when he appeared at the doorway, glanced around furtively, and then rushed off toward the opera house. He could find a taxi to take him back to the critical meeting that had been his excuse for flying across the Atlantic. Or he might just go back to the hotel and await her return from her museum jaunt.

She realized she was crying.

33

The tears oozed out from under her sunglasses and were running down her cheeks. Damn it, she loved him! She had fallen in love when he first began paying attention to her, consummating her feelings on their honeymoon. But he didn't love her, at least not in the same way. Now it seemed completely plausible that he would go to any length to keep her from stumbling onto his secret.

The door opened again, this time to a stylish young woman wearing a scarf over her head that touched the rims of her sunglasses. She seemed to be the right age and height. She was tall, well proportioned, and spirited. She stepped into the street and walked in the opposite direction, away from the Place de l'Opéra. There was a sensual sway to her hips that turned a few heads moving in the opposite direction.

Jane threw money on the table and jumped up to follow. She kept the woman in sight from the other side of the street and crossed at her first opportunity. Then she walked, no more than thirty yards behind, watching as Selina negotiated the frantic pedestrian traffic. She couldn't help but notice her regal stride, tall and erect, head held high, as if she were the only one on the boulevard. Jane felt as if she were chasing breathlessly, an athlete in walking shoes after royalty in high heels. For a second she wished she were Selina Royce, fresh out of bed with her lover and strolling down the most fashionable street in Paris.

The woman turned into a bank office, and Jane followed as far as the lobby. Selina strode past the tellers' windows with supreme confidence, up to one of the officers' desks. While she waited for the man to come around and position her chair, she looked up and seemed to come eye-to-eye with Jane. For a second each was reflected in the other's sunglasses. But then Selina turned back to her banker. He seemed delighted to see her, an old friend who made large deposits.

Jane found that she couldn't take it anymore. She had seen all she could stand of her husband's other life. It was time to go back to the hotel and confront him. But how? What would she say to the man she truly loved?

"I know where you were this afternoon," and then watch him squirm to find an appropriate explanation? Or maybe something more specific: "How did you enjoy making love to Selina Royce? I'll bet she's a real tiger in bed!" But she hesitated. Confronting him would be a declaration that she was leaving him. If she had any pride left at all, she couldn't go on living with him once his affair was out in the open. She still hoped against all odds that there was some other explanation.

He was seated at the bar when she entered the hotel, and she sat down beside him. "Busy day?" he asked as he signaled to the waiter.

"It was," she answered. "Lots of walking."

She ordered an iced tea. She was still feeling the wine she had at the sidewalk café. "How about you? Did your meetings go well?"

He shrugged. "Okay, I suppose. You never get everything you want."

"I thought you always got everything you wanted," Jane said. Her tone wasn't teasing. She was making an accusation.

Andrews shook his head.

"Oh, by the way," Jane went on, as if the thought had just struck her, "were you over near the opera house today?"

His eyes widened. "No, why?" he asked, and then busied himself with his drink.

"I thought I saw you," she said cheerily. "I was walking on Boulevard Haussmann toward the opera, and I thought I saw you getting out of a taxi. I tried to catch up with you, but I lost you in the crowd."

He recovered from his shock. "Good thing you didn't catch up. You would have bagged the wrong man. I was at the ministry all day, near the Trocadéro."

You lying bastard, she thought. But she managed a credible smile. "Well, I must be thinking about you all the time if strangers are starting to look like you."

He touched her hand as if he was pleased by her comment. But his look was back to business almost immediately. "What were you doing near the opera?"

Now she began lying. "Well, I started the day at the Picasso, and then I remembered that they give tours of the opera house. So I had a bite at a café and walked over for the tour."

"How was it?"

"How was what?"

"The tour."

"Great," she said with feigned enthusiasm. "The backstage is enormous. And you should see some of the chandeliers."

"Do they still take you down into the sewers where the phantom used to live?" The question was innocent enough, but she sensed a trap.

"No, they didn't," she said. "Come to think of it, they never even mentioned it."

He nodded, and sipped at his drink. Jane wondered whether she had given herself away.

He was quiet during dinner, letting her do most of the talking. She filled the void by babbling about the wonders of the city and how she might like to live there someday. "Maybe when you own all the cable in the world, we could have an apartment here." He nodded as if it might be a good idea, giving no indication that he already had one. Over dessert, he delivered his news. "I'm going to have to stay here for another day or two."

"Something wrong?" she wondered.

"Like I said, today's dealings didn't go all that well."

"I'll stay with you," she offered.

He shook his head. "No need to. I can get you a flight back in the morning."

"Back to what?" she asked. "The apartment smells of paint and plaster. I'd just as soon stay here. There's lots more that I have to see. I can spend the whole day on the Left Bank."

When they returned to their suite, he surprised her by suddenly becoming romantic. He climbed into their bed naked and watched while she took a nightgown from her drawer. "I'd hate to see that get all wrinkled," he teased.

She took the nightgown with her to the bathroom. "Don't you have a busy day tomorrow?" she said over her shoulder.

"You know what?" he said before she could close the door. "I'd like to see you just the way you were when we first met. Remember? The only thing you were wearing was a towel wrapped around your head."

Jane couldn't believe what she was hearing. He had just spent the afternoon with another woman. Now he was coming on to her as if they were still on their honeymoon. *The bastard has chutzpah,* she thought, *not to mention boundless energy.* She thought of locking herself in the bathroom, but the invitation was too exciting to resist. She undressed, hung the gown on the back of the door, and carefully wrapped a towel around her head.

When she awoke, he was sitting on the edge of the bed, fully dressed and ready to leave. "Just wanted to say good-bye," he said, and he pushed her hair back from her face and kissed her cheek.

"Was I that uninspiring?" she asked. "It looks as if you can't wait to get out of here."

"I'll be back for lunch," he promised, "maybe even sooner."

"I'll wait for you. I'll go down to the spa for a massage. We can go over to the Left Bank together."

She showered slowly and dressed casually, then went down to the dining room for juice and coffee. At the spa, she spent half an hour in the gym running on a treadmill, then stretched out on a table and put herself in the hands of a masseuse. Her mind wandered back over the events of the day before.

Her husband loved her. Either that or he was a brilliant actor. His tenderness in their lovemaking had taken her back to the sailboat and moments of bliss in his arms. His affection was real and his need for her obvious. She never for a moment felt that she was being used.

Yet he was involved with another woman and had been for many years. Selina Royce was exquisite, and though Jane had no doubt that she, too, was attractive in her own way, she knew she wasn't an international beauty. Bill would be much more interesting to the paparazzi with the woman she had followed yesterday on his arm. Maybe, after all these years, he still needed her. Probably he still loved her. But then why hadn't he married her? There was nothing to stop him. As far as the public was concerned, all he would have to do was rediscover an old associate and ease Selina into his public life. There was no reason he would have to go on loving her from a distance.

It was more likely that he was buying her loyalty. She knew things about Kay Parker's final moments that he had to keep secret. Jane had assumed that was the reason for the monthly payments, but maybe the blackmail involved more. Maybe Selina also needed to believe that she was important in his life. She might never have mentioned the damage she could do to him and spelled out the price of her silence. It could be that he kept her as an intimate part of his life to ensure her loyalty, and the money was just to maintain her in a style befitting their relationship.

But either way, he was a liar. He was lying to her and maybe lying to Selina as well. There had been many opportunities for him to explain. He could have told her when Leavitt first revealed that she was asking about Selina Royce. He could have told her on the boat when he found out that Roscoe Taylor was digging around. The truth was that he *should* have told her when he asked her to marry him.

What should she do? Try to ignore it and accept the part of his life he shared with her? Be content to be queen of the castle even though he made regular trips to the harem? And just hope that sometime in the future he would be able to break free from the other woman, maybe even tell her what Selina's hold on him had been?

Or confront him? Tell him exactly what she knew and explain that they couldn't go on together until he filled in all the blanks she didn't know? Would he tell her the truth in order to keep her? Or was his secret so dark that he would give her up rather than reveal it?

If only Roscoe had stayed on the case! Given more time, he probably would have uncovered the story, and then she would know what she was dealing with. Had he killed his wife? Did his mistress kill her? Or was there actually an intruder who killed Kay? What part had Robert Leavitt played in the whole affair? Clearly, he had helped cover it up, but had he also participated in the crime?

The masseuse draped a bath sheet over her shoulders and helped Jane climb down from the table. She went to the shower and washed off the lotion. Then she wrapped the towel around herself and walked into the sauna. The rush of dry heat nearly drove her back out through the door. But she forged ahead and stretched out on the lower bench. Within a few seconds, she adjusted to the temperature and felt herself fall into a deeper level of relaxation.

She rewound the events of the past few days and played them back again, searching for the clue she was missing. The evidence kept directing her back to the day eight years ago when Kay Parker died. The unanswered question was, who could have been there? Kay, Robert Leavitt, and William Andrews were certain. Selina was a possibility. And then there was the business meeting the previous night. Who had attended? Who else was up in the mountains who might have had a strong business or personal tie to her husband and his society wife? Bill knew, as did Leavitt. Probably some of the secretaries as well. It had been a long time ago, but people probably remembered the events surrounding Kay's murder the same way they remembered where they were and who they were talking with when President Kennedy was shot. Who could she talk to? Who might give her a clue as to what happened up on the mountain in the ski lodge?

She took the corner of the towel and wiped the perspiration from her forehead. The towel was hot, as if it had been steamed. So was her skin. She felt as if she were in an oven being slowly roasted. Jane glanced up at the thermometer, wiped the beads of sweat from her eyelashes, and found the arrow pointing to 180 degrees. She sat up, leaned near the coal scuttle, and poured a dipper of water onto the rocks. The water hissed into a cloud of steam. She lay back on her towel. *Another few minutes,* she told herself. She enjoyed the near pain of the intense heat, although she wondered about plunging directly into a cold shower. *The shock,* she thought, *might be deadly. Maybe a warm shower gradually turning to cold.* But after hesitating momentarily, the needle resumed its climb. She wrapped the towel around her and stepped to the door in order to get out. The door wouldn't budge.

34

She pushed again and then slammed her hip against the wooden wainscoting. Nothing moved. The door was jammed shut. *Damn!* She was angry at being inconvenienced, not to mention that she'd be the color of a lobster if she didn't get out soon. The glass window was fogged from the burst of steam she had created by dropping water onto the hot stones. She wiped it clean and looked out. The glass was hot enough to burn her forehead.

She rapped on the window with her knuckles and heard a dead sound. If it was glass, it was a special heat-resistant glass. It had none of the resonance she would expect from knocking on a window. *Damn!* They would probably have to get the hotel engineer to free her. She didn't like the idea of being rescued wearing nothing but a towel.

She checked the thermometer. It read 185 degrees. *How hot do they want to make this place?* She went to the heating unit to turn down the temperature, but she couldn't find a dial. There were white-hot stones being scorched by a gas flame. The flame seemed to be dangerously high.

She ladled more water from the bucket and saw that there wasn't more than half an inch of water left. She poured it all out onto the rocks, creating a new cloud of drenching steam. The flame flickered but reignited instantly. The temperature gauge dipped down to 180 degrees. But within seconds it was climbing again.

It was at that moment Jane realized she was in terrible danger. She had no way of cutting back on the temperature, which would continue to rise. She couldn't force the door open. And her pounding and shouting were deadened by the insulation in the walls. If someone didn't stumble across her plight, she would be cooked like a rib roast.

She wiped the window again and looked out. She could

see the opposite wall, all white tile, like the showers. Some-one had to come past. *Just wait a second. When another woman walked by, pound on the glass and throw your hip against the door.* She'd have to hear the noise, see Jane in the window, and realize that she was locked in. She waited, wip-ing her skin with the towel and then wrapping it around Jane as protection against the heat. She was beginning to feel dizzy and unsteady. *My God, am I already being cooked?*

She rapped on the glass again and then used her knee to pound against the door. She waited. No one came. What if there was no one? What if the spa had no more customers and was closed for lunch? By the time they came back and real-ized she was missing, the heat would have roasted her.

A shadow flashed past on the white tile wall. Two women, wrapped in bath sheets, suddenly came into view, walking side by side and chatting happily. Jane screamed at the top of her lungs. They kept walking. She pounded on the glass and crashed her knee against the door. The women never broke stride. Apparently, they never heard a thing. "Jesus," she prayed, "I'm going to die in here."

All she had as tools were the long-handled ladle and the water bucket. She took the ladle, held it like a baseball bat, and struck the window. The glass held firm. The ladle broke, the deep cup splitting away from the long, thin handle. Jane took the bucket, swung it around behind her, and fired it into the window. The glass cracked, a single jagged line that ran from one corner to another. But it never threatened to shatter and fall out of its frame. She used the bucket again and again, but all she could do was add another crack that ran from the original break to another corner. It was some kind of safety glass that could crack or even shatter but would never fall out. And it was a double pane. There was another, just as stub-born, on the other side.

She was exhausted. Just lifting and swinging the bucket was more than she could handle in the intense, energy-draining heat. Jane slumped back onto the towel, putting her weight on the edge of the bench. The heat burned at her mouth and ears and seemed to suck the moisture out of her

body. Reason told her to relax, stay perfectly still, and conserve whatever energy she had left. Her survival instinct had
other ideas. If she yielded, it would take only a few seconds
for the intense heat to burn away her consciousness and leave
her to die. If she was going to survive, she had to break out
now, with the little bit of energy that was left to her.

She lifted the water bucket by its handle and swung it with
all her might. The glass she had cracked now burst into a star,
but it held firm in the window. Jane swung at it again. It took
still another blow to send shards flying. She tried to pull the
remaining pieces out of the window opening, but the glass
was too hot to touch. She retrieved her towel from the bench,
wrapped it around her fist, and punched out the remaining
glass. But there was another pane on the other side of the
thick door, and when she swung the bucket, it crashed harm-
lessly against the inside window frame.

She wiped the second window and caught a glimpse of the
tile wall leading into the showers. Now when she knocked,
anyone passing by the door was bound to hear her. But how
long would that be? The thermometer was passing 210 degrees. The air burned her lungs as she breathed. The empty
bucket seemed to have gotten too heavy to lift.

She punched her towel-covered hand against the outside
glass. It made a dull thud, but the glass remained intact. Then
her arm began to bleed, slashed by the bits of glass still
imbedded in the inside frame. She held the towel against her
arm and looked around frantically. What else did she have to
work with?

A shadow flashed by the steamy window. Jane reached in
with a bloody arm and knocked her knuckles against the
glass. But the shadow had already passed. Whoever had
walked by was already too far away to hear her feeble
knocking.

She looked at the fire, its flames licking the rocks that
were giving off the intense heat. There was no way she could
lower it. Then she thought of the rocks. If she could lift one
of them, it would easily smash through the window. She
folded the towel to double its thickness and then folded it

again. But even with the towel, she couldn't get her hand down into the furnace. Her skin seared instantly.

She felt dizzy. She needed to sit down on the bench. But she knew that if she did, she would never get up again. She would die, pounding feebly against her oven door.

The handle! She saw the handle that had broken off the ladle. Maybe she could knock one of the stones out of the fire. She picked it up and stuck its narrower end down between the rocks. She pried one of them up from the grate and was able to push it on top of the other rocks. She moved another and then another, slowly building a pile until the highest stone was even with the rim of the furnace. She knocked it off and it fell to the wooden floor, which began to smolder and blacken.

Jane reached for the stone with the folded towel and for an instant had a grip on it. But then the towel smoldered and her fingers began to burn. She had to pull her hand away. How long before she would be able to touch it? Too long! The rock could hold heat for an hour. She looked at the thermometer—220 degrees. All she had left were seconds. She took the handle, thrust it into the window opening, and began to poke at the outside glass. It rattled but held firm. Jane backed up, raised the handle like a spear, and hurled it against the glass. A crack appeared across the center of the pane.

She jammed the rod back into the opening and struck again and again. Other cracks appeared, and then the window starred. But it was too late! By now the wooden handle seemed as heavy as a railroad tie. Her blows were becoming more and more feeble. Jane knew she couldn't stop. She had to keep striking! But the air was too hot to breathe. And her arms were too tired to lift. She felt herself slumping, beginning her death slide down the inside of the door.

35

The two women finished their shower and stood talking in the shower room while they toweled off. It had been a relaxing morning for them. An aerobics class and then a session with a yoga instructor who wore an Indian loincloth and a turban. They had taken an aromatic massage, showered luxuriously, and were hungry for the lunch that awaited them at a fine restaurant. They were in no hurry. Lunch would be leisurely, and they were planning an afternoon of shopping. There was nothing to hurry for.

They chatted as they wrapped themselves in towels and walked carefully across the wet tiles. Then they stepped out onto the hardwood floor that led to the dressing rooms.

Suddenly one howled in pain, started to dance on one foot, and screamed again. She steadied herself by leaning on her friend, lifted a foot, and saw that she was bleeding. She screamed again, this time in outrage. There were small pieces of glass scattered across the floor. He friend backed away to keep from cutting her own feet. Then she joined in the screaming, as the two women loudly demanded the manager.

An attendant, dressed in gym clothes, came running and listened to the shouted complaints about the broken glass. She began apologizing profusely, used a towel to cover the glass, and helped the women step across. It was an afterthought that made her glance around for the source of the problem, and by luck she saw the cracked window in the sauna door. Only then did she notice that the night lock, used to secure the room after hours, was in the locked position.

She sorted through her key ring, found the key, and opened the lock, struggling against the pressure from inside the door. When it was free, the door swung open. The three women gasped as a bloodied naked body toppled out across the threshold. The attendant ran for help. One of the women knelt next to Jane and felt for a pulse. She looked at the other and nodded sadly.

The emergency medical team arrived within minutes, used an electrical device to shock her heart back to a steady rhythm, bandaged her cut arm sufficiently to stop the bleeding, and wheeled her away on a gurney. Jane never stirred as she was bounced across the sidewalk and lifted into a waiting ambulance. Not even the high-pitch warble of the siren was able to wake her.

When the light came, it came slowly, a faint flicker that grew into a pewter-colored glow. There were sounds, voices that seemed to be playing at too slow a speed. Then someone was calling her name. Jane tried to answer, but she couldn't. There was something covering her face.

She opened her eyes and saw shadows moving around her, all faceless and with bodies that rippled like reflections in a pond. They were speaking to one another, but in a strange language she couldn't understand. And there was one form, leaning close to her face, that kept calling her name, but she didn't remember how to answer. Besides, her head ached as if it might explode. It was easier to close her eyes and drift back off to sleep.

The next time she was conscious, the light seemed to have more color and the voices had a natural pace. She recognized the strange language she had heard. The people around her were speaking French. Of course! She remembered that she had been visiting France. She saw faces staring down at her, a man and a woman. "Jane," the woman said. The man smiled. She tried to answer, but the mask was pressed over her face. She moved her eyes and noticed the clear plastic piece that covered her nose. The best she could do was smile back.

There was a flurry of activity, with people running in and out. Her bed was raised up a bit, and the mask was replaced with a small plastic tube that rested over her lip. She noticed that her right arm was connected to a medical drip and that there were electrodes attached to her body. She was in a hospital, she understood, and the people racing in and out of the room were trying to save her.

Jane began to remember, but with no great clarity. She could envision the sauna with the jammed door, and she remembered pounding on it and trying to force it open. There was something about glass, but she wasn't sure what. And the heat! She remembered breathing hot air and feeling that her skin was about to burst into flames. But then what? Had she forced the door open? Had she walked out? She couldn't remember.

Bill was standing at the foot of the bed. But how did he get there? Jane was positive that he hadn't been there a second ago. He was smiling at her. He came around to the side of the bed and took her hand. She liked the way he felt.

"You're going to be just fine," he said. "Everything is going to be all right." She wasn't sure what he was talking about. What was going to be all right? But it didn't seem all that important. The important thing was that she was dead tired. She closed her eyes and hoped that the voices would go away.

When she next woke up, things made sense right away. She was in the hospital. She had been rescued from the hellish room and brought here. Now she was recovering. But recovering from what? What had the heat done to her that the doctors were working so hard to fix? She sat awake for an hour, examining the monitors that were on the wall over her head. Several different traces were running across two different screens. One of them was beeping at regular intervals. Every few minutes a cuff tightened around her arm and numbers scrolled on another display. A nurse came into the room, stuck a thermometer in her ear, and held her wrist. "What's wrong with me?" Jane asked. The nurse answered in French, which told her nothing at all.

Her memory was coming back. She remembered how she had cut her arm by pushing it through the shattered window. The burns on her hands reminded her of her efforts to use one of the fiery rocks to break the glass. She remembered throwing herself against the door and pounding on it with her fists. But she had no recollection of how she had gotten out. Did she finally succeed in breaking free, or had she attracted the attention of someone outside? And how did she get to the hospital? She didn't remember being in a car.

Bill came in, rushed to her bedside, and kissed her cheeks. She fell easily into his embrace and then found that she was crying. He eased her back onto the pillow and told her that she needed to conserve her strength.

"What's wrong with me?" she asked again.

"Nothing," he answered. "You're absolutely perfect."

Jane looked at the wires linking her to the monitors and then glanced back at her husband. "What happened to me?"

"Dehydration . . . heat stroke . . . burns. You scared the hell out of us."

"And now?" she asked.

"You're breathing oxygen and taking medication. You need fluids and bed rest. They're monitoring your heart even though it's behaving perfectly. And, oh yeah, you have a couple of stitches in your arm."

"How did I get out?"

He told her about the two women who had cut their feet on the glass.

"Why wouldn't the door open?" she wanted to know.

"It was locked. There's a deadbolt lock. Only the attendant has a key, but somehow the damn thing locked. Probably when you slammed the door."

"I didn't slam the door," she said thoughtfully. "At least, I don't think I did."

"Whatever," he answered. "I have people looking into it. They'll come up with the answer."

She remembered the other thing that was troubling her. "Why did it get so hot? The temperature just kept climbing. . . ."

"You set it pretty high," he told her.

"I set it?"

"Don't worry about it," he cautioned. "It's all over now."

But she pressed on with the question. "How did I set it?"

"There's a control right outside the door. You probably pushed it up when you went in."

"Bill," she started to argue. But then she stopped herself. She had no idea where the control was or what it looked like, so she was sure she had never touched it. That meant someone else had pushed it up to a very high setting. Carelessness, maybe. But that, coupled with a door that had somehow locked itself, was too much to believe. Like with the dance floor over the swimming pool, someone had caused this accident.

She tried to stay awake after he left. This was the second attempt on her life in the past couple of weeks, and she didn't feel safe even under the protection of the hospital staff. But the fatigue was overwhelming—probably something they were dripping into her arm to keep her relaxed. She felt herself falling asleep and didn't have the strength to fight it.

When she stirred again, a nurse was at her side, checking her monitors. The woman said something in French and smiled broadly. Apparently, she was delighted with the progress Jane was making. This time she was able to fight through her drowsiness and keep herself awake. There were a thousand thoughts floating through her head, and somehow she had to link them together.

There had been two attempts to kill her and a couple of accidents that had put her in jeopardy. Maybe they were intended as threats to scare her off, but any one of them might have been lethal. And there were several people who could have been involved in any of them.

Now, in Paris, there was still another suspect. She had followed Selina Royce through the streets and into a bank lobby. Was it possible that Selina had recognized her from one of the stock photos in the newspapers? Her husband could have told her about his new wife and maybe even showed her a picture. He might have told her that their affair had to end. Would that be reason enough for his mistress to try to get rid of her?

There was another good reason for suspecting Selina. Jane had been locked in the sauna at a women's spa, which made it more likely that her attacker had been a woman. A man would have had a difficult time getting past the fashionable receptionist at the front desk. Certainly he would be noticed looking through the salon rooms or moving through the halls and locker rooms filled with undressed women. On the other hand, Selina could have walked right in, taken a locker for her clothes, and stepped out, wrapped in a towel. That would have given her complete freedom to roam the facility, find her victim, and see Jane when she stepped into the sauna.

The nurse returned, pleasantly surprised to find Jane awake. She carried a vase of fresh flowers and brought them over for Jane's inspection, talking happily in French and oohing and aahing over the flowers. She searched through the leaves, found a card, and handed it to her patient with a broad, knowing smile. They were from Bill, with a short note vowing his love. She watched as the woman set the flowers on the dresser, then listened politely to her exit line and remembered to say *merci*.

Jane looked at the flowers, thought of her husband, and remembered the fact that had been haunting all her suspicions. William Andrews was the only one who had been present during all her accidents. He had been on the horse next to hers, in the apartment when she was struggling in the swimming pool, at the wedding when she was drugged, and at the helm when she was knocked overboard. Now he was with her in Paris, where she had nearly been steamed to death. So if all these instances of violence were connected, her husband was the most logical connection.

It didn't make sense, she had tried to convince herself. He had no need to marry her or any pressing reason to take her into his life. He could have sent her away at any time before the wedding and, even more awful to consider, could have turned away and left her in the ocean. But still, he knew that she was trying to learn the facts of his first wife's death, a secret he was determined to keep. Her getting close to information that could ruin him would be motive enough to scare her off or, failing that, get rid of her.

36

Bill visited the hospital the next evening, explaining that he had been called away to England on business. "We were called before a Crown commission," he said. "Strictly a formality, but a command performance. Some of these people think they're descended from the Tudors, so I can't very well send a branch manager."

"Have they figured out how the sauna happened to get locked?" she asked.

"Not yet," he said without any sign of disappointment. "But we're still digging. The hotel has a detective on it, and I've hired one of my own. Even the police are investigating. We'll find out, and then heaven help whoever turns out to be at fault."

Jane took a deep breath. "It shouldn't be that much of a problem. Someone must know who had the key."

"The matron swears it never left her hands. And there's nothing in her background to suggest that she could have been careless with it. She has no ties to anyone shady who might have borrowed it. The police are checking out everyone who works in the place and all the women who were there that day. Remarkably uneventful lives, particularly the customers."

"Is that it? Background checks?"

He shrugged. "That's the way the police work. The hotel, on the other hand, is investigating the lock. They brought in the manufacturer and they've taken it apart half a dozen times. It seems that no matter how hard they slam the door, they can't get it to lock by itself."

"What about a duplicate key?"

"There's one kept in the attendant's desk, but it's still there."

"Couldn't someone have taken it?"

"Sure," he admitted. "If they knew it was there. But then why would they have bothered to put it back? Most people don't even notice that there's a lock on the door, and the attendant admits that she very often doesn't bother to lock it at night. So that keeps bringing us back to the lock itself and how it might have been set accidentally."

But he didn't want her worrying. He would take care of the investigation. Her job was to get better so they could go back home. "Believe it or not, I'm even trying to clear a few days for us to get away together. Not right away, because when I get back I'll have a lot of catching up to do. But in the next few months . . ."

They speculated on where they might go. He thought in terms of another sailing vacation, maybe down in New Zealand, where it would soon be spring. He enthused over the long stretches of wind-swept ocean among the islands and helped her visualize the wonders of the Great Barrier Reef.

Jane couldn't tell him why she wasn't excited by the prospect of lonely voyages over empty seas. It was ridiculous for many reasons, not the least being that he seemed so obviously in love with her. And yet he was the one person who had been around for all her "accidents." Until there were some concrete explanations for pool motors that started themselves and dead-bolt locks that mysteriously closed, Jane would prefer places with lots of company.

She asked about her recovery. Everyone seemed pleased, but since she couldn't talk to anyone in English, she had no information on her prognosis. "You could go home tomorrow," he said cheerfully. "They just want to watch you for another few days."

"Let's go home tomorrow," she said. "I don't like being watched." He argued a bit, but then agreed that he would take her home after one more day. He stayed late, kissing her lovingly before he left. Jane fell asleep as his footsteps were still echoing in the hall.

When she stirred again, it was the middle of the night. The room was dark except for the streak of light from the open door and the green glow that came from the monitors over her head. There was a nurse in her room, a tall woman standing near the dresser, assembling some sort of medical equipment. Jane decided that she didn't want to exchange pleasantries in a language she didn't understand. She closed her eyes and pretended to be asleep.

She heard soft footsteps as the nurse moved around the room. Then she heard her door click shut. Jane opened her eyes, assuming that the nurse had left and closed the door behind her, but she was still there, now crossing the foot of the bed as she went to the window. When she tipped the blinds, the last bit of ambient light vanished from the room. Now, even with her eyes open, Jane could follow only the woman's footsteps.

She seemed to go back to the dresser and pause there. Jane heard a tinkle of glass that sounded like something being stirred. She raised her head from the pillow. "What now?" she asked.

The soft voice responded in French, but with just a few words instead of the usual happy banter. Then, in English, the nurse said, "It's just your medication."

She speaks English, Jane thought. *They finally found one I can understand.* She pushed herself up onto her elbows. "You're new!"

"No, just back from my holiday."

"Great! Will you be staying here from now on?"

"I don't think so," said the voice from the darkness. She was directly at the foot of the bed, and Jane could now make out her silhouette in the glow of the monitors. She saw something glisten in the nurse's hand.

"What's that for?" she asked. As the nurse stepped closer, she could see a hypodermic needle.

"An anticoagulant. To stop blood clots."

The monitors illuminated the woman's chest. Jane saw the lapels of a jacket and the flash of jewelry around her neck. "I haven't been getting any shots. Are you sure this is for me?"

The nurse took Jane's hand and lifted her arm. Jane noticed the long, painted fingernails. She looked up as half the woman's face came into the green glow. There was a flash of recognition. She knew this woman. She had seen her before, not here in the hospital but somewhere else. Then she caught a glimpse of the needle, aimed at her bare shoulder.

The woman in the bank, she remembered. Jane couldn't see her eyes, but mentally she could fill in the dark sunglasses that had masked the top of the woman's face and the scarf that hid her hair. *Selina! Selina Royce!*

37

She jerked away just as the needle pricked her skin, and with her free hand, she slapped at the woman's arms. The needle came free, spraying a quick jet of colorless liquid. She pulled back her arm and rolled away, but the woman's hand clutched her shoulder. As Jane rolled back, she let her fist fly. She felt the stick of the hypodermic just as her punch found the side of the woman's head. Her attacker fell back into the darkness, leaving the needle dangling from the flesh of Jane's shoulder. She pulled it free and hurled into the darkness. Then she screamed with all her energy.

She heard the woman stumbling in the darkness. Her door suddenly opened, letting in light from the hall. The woman's figure blocked the door and turned into the corridor. Jane saw a flash of her profile and got a glimpse of the figure she had followed along the street only a couple of days ago. She swung her legs out to pursue her but was tethered by the wires connected to the monitors. She screamed again as she hunted for the call button to the nurse's station. When she pressed a button, the television set on the far wall came to life.

Damn! She poked at all the other buttons on the handset, hit one that turned on the light over her head. Now she found the call button and squeezed it. Just to make sure, she screamed again.

She heard footsteps. A young nurse, scarcely out of her teens, rushed in, stringing together French words as she rushed to the bed. She took Jane's legs and began to wrestle her back into the bed.

"Get her!" Jane ordered. "Don't let her get away!"

The nurse shouted back angrily, nearly throwing herself across her patient. And then another nurse, this one a man, ran into the room. He came around the bed, took Jane's shoulders in a strong grip, and forced her back onto the pillow.

"She tried to kill me. Go after her!" Jane broke away from the man and fell across the young nurse. Together, they wrestled her back into bed. Still another nurse rushed in. While the first two held her, the new arrival prepared a hypodermic.

"Don't kill me . . . please don't kill me!"

The new needle slipped easily into her arm. Jane continued to struggle for another few seconds, but then dropped off into a black state of unconsciousness.

When she came to abruptly, after what seemed like seconds, the sun was pouring in through the window. William Andrews was standing beside her, flanked by two men in business suits. Her doctors and nurses were in an uneven line across her open doorway.

She explained to her husband and the two men, who turned out to be hospital administrators, exactly what had happened the night before. She had awakened to find a nurse, or a woman dressed as a nurse, in her room. The woman had tried to inject her, and Jane had fought her off. Then the woman had rushed from the room. Jane looked to the medical staff. "You must have passed her in the corridor. She ran out just a few seconds before you came in." They listened as the administrator translated and then answered with shrugs and grunts. He announced that no one had seen this mysterious woman.

"Did you recognize her?" the other administrator asked. "Have you ever seen her before?"

Jane started to answer, but then cut herself off. "No," she finally decided. "I don't think so." She wasn't about to discuss with a room full of strangers the circumstances under which she had first seen Selina Royce. Nor was she exactly sure how she would explain the encounter to her husband when they were alone. She looked to Andrews, who seemed to have no doubt that she was telling the truth.

"Were you injected?" a doctor asked.

"Yes, here on the shoulder. Look! There's a bruise."

The medical staff exchanged glances. Then the nurse who had arrived with the second hypodermic said something to the administrators. They exchanged a few words in French, nodding in agreement. One of them told Andrews, "Your wife was struggling last night when the nurse was trying to give her a sedative. She says she might have bruised the patient. The conditions for giving a shot weren't ideal."

"Dammit!" Jane snapped. "The woman stuck me, half a minute before your nurse did. This is where the woman left her needle." She pointed to a bruise on her shoulder.

"Left the needle?" The administrator almost smiled.

His colleague asked, "Left the needle in your arm?"

"Yes, hanging out of my shoulder! I pulled it out and threw it across the room. Over there!" Jane pointed in the direction where the hypodermic had disappeared into the darkness.

"Over here," one of the administrators said as he turned and began examining the floor. The other directed a question to the medical staff. Once again, the answer came in nods and grunts. "I don't see anything," the administrator said from across the room.

"The staff didn't find anything," the other one announced.

Andrews flashed anger. "My wife says that there was a woman in here last night who tried to inject her. Why don't you take that as a fact and start from there."

One of the men cleared his throat in preparation for introducing a delicate subject. "Perhaps she had a terrible dream. The recent stress, her medicines, and the . . . inevitable indignities of medical care . . . might well have planted the suggestion of an assault. Then, while drowsy from sedatives—"

"You think I imagined all this? That I imagined these bruises and needle marks, and tried to run after a woman who wasn't even there?"

"I'm only suggesting—"

She cut him off. "Bill, can you take me out of here today? Right now?"

He looked at the hospital staff, hoping for an answer. "I'm not sure. Would it be all right . . ."

"I don't want their medical opinion," Jane snapped. "I want to get out of this place before I get as crazy as they think I am."

Bill glanced at the administrators. "I suppose so," he considered. They both nodded in agreement. The sooner the better, they seemed to be telling him.

They were in the jet's private quarters, 32,000 feet over the Atlantic. Jane was sitting up in bed, resting against pillows. Bill was in a chair, leaning in to be close to her. She was going back over her harrowing moments in the hospital, reporting every detail of the nurse's attack. Except the one fact that could easily have confirmed her story—the name of the woman who had attacked her.

"There was a needle!" Jane snapped angrily.

Bill took her hand. "I believe you. All I'm saying is that the last thing the hospital wants to admit is that outsiders, dressed as nurses, can get at their patients. They picked up the needle before they called the meeting in your room. And those guys in the suits probably ordered their doctors to act as dumb as they looked."

He had passed on any number of opportunities to tell her about Selina. "I know what this is all about. There's a woman here in Paris that I'm very close to. She hates the idea that I've fallen in love with someone else." Instead, he had avoided the issue, confident that his secret was still safe. In the hospital he had been locked in discussions with the administrators while she was dressed, discharged, and wheeled down to the waiting limo. In the car he had counseled her to rest and not trouble herself with her two near-fatal episodes. "That's all behind us," he said. Then on the plane he had sent her into his cabin to rest.

But Jane couldn't rest. She wanted to talk. She needed to get to the bottom of what she regarded as a string of attempts to murder her. Her husband, she knew, had the answers she was seeking. But he wasn't forthcoming. He valued his secret more than he did his marriage.

"Bill, who could it have been? There must be someone in Paris who hates me for being your wife. An old business rival? A woman you jilted?"

He pretended to be searching his memory. "It's possible, I

suppose. But there's no one I can think of. And besides, how could someone in Paris have tried to drown you in the swimming pool?"

She was on the verge of confronting him with the facts. "Bill, I know about Selina Royce," she could say, perhaps squeezing his hand to signal that she still loved him. "I know you've been paying her every month, and I know that you visited her the day I saw you near the opera house. Is it possible that she's the one who wants me dead?" That would give him the chance to unfold the truth at his own pace. He could explain who she was and why he was obligated to her. The only thing she feared was that he would end up saying that he was still hopelessly in love with the woman.

Or she could hit much harder. "I got a glimpse of the woman with the needle. It was the same woman you visited on Boulevard Haussmann, the one you've been sending money." That would give him only one avenue of escape—to deny that there was any such woman. Then she would know that her marriage was over.

Did all women try to avoid the truth about their husbands and lovers? Did kept mistresses really believe that the man was going to leave his wife, and did wives really believe that the smell of perfume must have come from someone on the elevator? Were they all lying to themselves, trying to pretend that their dream world really did exist? The simple truth was that her husband had bought a company just to acquire rights to Selina Royce, that he had saved her from prosecution when she murdered his wife, and that he had kept her all these years, even while taking a new wife. So why was she denying it and putting her life at risk?

"Try to rest," Bill said again. "We'll talk about this when we have more information from the police, and when you have your strength back." He eased out of the cabin and shut the door quietly.

I have my strength back, Jane thought. *And I don't need any more evidence from the police. All I need is for you to tell me the truth.*

A car met them at the airport and delivered them to the

apartment. Bill settled her in the living room with its wide-screen view of Central Park and instructed Mrs. McCarty to look in on her. Then he was gone to his office, where a week's worth of work awaited. She sat by herself, listening to the workmen finishing the renovations in the new master suite. The decor was inviting, a visible blend of masculine appliances and feminine touches, exactly what she had hoped to achieve. The closet had matching his-and-her sides, and the new bathroom was both practical and sensuous. All that was missing was the husband she hoped to share it with.

She browsed through magazines, turning the pages impatiently and then tossing them aside. When she looked up, she noticed the open library on the bedroom level and went to find a book, something she should have read but had never gotten around to. None of the titles appealed to her. She went down to the breakfast room and began sorting through a week's worth of mail.

Everything was for William Andrews. Circulars, flyers, letters from law firms, and two notices from the building association. Then there were a few items forwarded from her office. One of the letters was in lopsided print, apparently from a child. She was surprised that it was from Sam Simon, the computer guru from the newspaper.

The letter, written in sloping lines, indicated a sloppiness that seemed to go hand in hand with Sam's intuitive genius. He took the long way round in explaining how she could get into Kay's personal records.

She climbed the stairs and went into the office. Kay's computer was off to one corner, shut down with the keyboard drawer closed, exactly as she had left it when she searched for Kay's favorite caterers. She booted it up and went to the listing of Kay's documents and looked at them one at a time until she found one that required a password. She took Sam Simon's letter and followed the steps he had outlined. A second later she was inside a folder labeled PRIVATE CORRESPONDENCE.

Jane was excited when she began, but she quickly settled into boredom. The letters were routine, dwelling on mundane subjects—complaints to her dressmaker, notes to a symphony orchestra committee about an approaching fundraiser, excuses declining invitations. She began to pity Kay for the excruciatingly dull life that hid behind her public glamour.

She broke from her snooping to have lunch in the breakfast room, unsure whether she would bother going back to Kay Parker's trivia. But, she conceded, there might still be something among the collection of congratulations, thankyou notes, acceptances, rejections with regrets. She had been browsing for another half an hour when one of the headings caught her eye: ARNOLD GRAFF INVESTIGATIONS. She opened the file and found a formal letter authorizing "services as discussed" and agreeing to a rate of six hundred dollars an hour plus expenses. If Arnold Graff was what he seemed to be, then he must have a very wealthy clientele. At six hundred dollars an hour, he had to be the very soul of discretion.

She looked at titles of other folders that were locked behind Kay Parker's password and found GRAFF DETECTIVES. She was right. Kay had been dealing with a private detective. She opened up individual files, dated in the months and days immediately before Kay's murder. Each was a report, sent computer to computer so there would be no paper trail between Kay and her investigator. Each detailed the visible elements of William Andrews's life with "the woman in question."

"They got into a limousine together and were driven to an airport, where they boarded the company plane along with other company executives," one report stated. "They were together in the Andrews Global Network conference room for approximately two hours after other meeting attendees had departed," another read. Graff reported that Mr. Andrews had visited her town house at 7:20 P.M. and did not leave until after midnight. Kay had added a memo to that entry, noting that W.A. claimed to be at a critical meeting at a major network's headquarters.

Graff Investigations was meticulous in documenting every minute that it billed and every expense that it incurred—even quarters plugged into parking meters while its operative waited outside the woman's apartment. It had documented that Andrews was spending an inordinate amount of time with his new anchor from San Antonio and that she seemed to be included in his entourage for every trip out of town.

But Graff detectives didn't peek through bedroom windows or hide in hotel-room closets. The detectives' reports stopped at the front door or the office door or the moment the plane took off. On one of Andrews's California trips, Graff had hired an associate to "acquire W.A. when his plane parked at the executive terminal and log his subsequent activities." The report followed a limo to a downtown hotel, where W.A. and the woman associate checked in to adjoining rooms. It noted that two breakfasts were delivered to W.A.'s room the next morning. But there was no suggestion that the two had bedded down together, no innuendo, and certainly no photographs.

Jane read several more of the reports, which built a mountain of evidence that William Andrews was cheating on Kay Parker. More disturbing was that Kay was on to him and was building a court case that would take him to the cleaners. It seemed to Jane that Bill and his mistress had every reason to wish for some terrible accident to befall Kay. So there was a compelling motive to go along with the opportunity presented when Andrews and Kay Parker were alone in their mountain chalet. She had no choice but to conclude that her husband was a murderer. And the fact that he had killed once before moved him up on the list of candidates who might be responsible for her recent spate of "accidents."

She signed off and closed the computer. Then she went downstairs to the living room and watched the sun setting over the towers on the West Side. Bill would be home soon, and they would share a quiet supper, probably in front of the window. She would be sure not to ask any more questions about her near-death encounters, nor would she confront him with the name of Selina Royce. She had a foreboding sense of danger.

He left early in the morning, mentioning that he would

probably fly up to Ottawa that night for a meeting the next morning with Canadian government officials. As soon as he was gone, she dressed and headed for the elevator.

"Where are you going?" It was Mrs. McCarty right at her heels. "Mr. Andrews asked me to stay close to you. What will I tell him when he calls?"

"That I've gone for a walk in the park," Jane answered as the elevator door closed.

She *was* headed down to the park, or at least the park side of Fifth Avenue, but not to take a walk. She needed to make a phone call, and she couldn't risk anyone's listening in. She dialed Roscoe Taylor's number on her cell phone, got his mailbox, and asked him to call back. Then she found a bench just inside the park wall. A few minutes later her phone beeped.

They exchanged pleasantries but didn't get specific about either his new job or her trip to Paris. His decision to join the Andrews "team" had created an awkwardness between them. But finally she pushed the issue. "Roscoe, I need your help. I have to find out if Selina Royce was at the business meeting in the Adirondacks. I'm beginning to think that she was there with Andrews and that Kay Parker walked in on them."

"What happened?" he asked.

"What happened is that I was nearly killed in Paris. Twice, as a matter of fact, and one of the times it was Selina who tried to kill me." She heard him suck in air and then reply, "Jesus."

Jane told him everything, from their arrival in Paris to the flight home. She recounted how she visited the address he had given her for Selina Royce and spent half the day waiting outside. "About one in the afternoon—maybe a bit later— Andrews showed up. He went into the building and stayed until almost three." She told him how she waited, spotted a woman who fit Selina's description come out of the building, and then followed her. "She looked right at me in the bank. At first I thought it was just two strangers making eye contact. But she must have recognized me, maybe from pictures in the paper."

She told him how her husband had denied ever being there and about the incident in the spa. "No one seemed particularly interested in how the door got locked," she said. "It was as if it was 'just one of those things' that no one can explain." Then she went into the incident at the hospital and the official denial that anyone had gone into her room with a hypodermic needle. "They called it a dream, probably induced by stress and medicine."

All through her narration, Roscoe had remained deathly quiet. He made no comments and asked no questions. She continued with the events since she had returned home. In particular, she went into the detective reports she had found in Kay Parker's computer. "There was an affair," she said, "and Kay knew about it. She had it documented by date, time, and place. It seemed as if she was building an airtight case against her husband."

There was a lengthy silence, finally broken by Roscoe, who said in a very soft voice, "You know what you're saying."

Another pause before Jane answered, "That Bill had a motive to kill his wife."

"Have you thought of the implications? Do you have any idea of the consequences of William Andrews being found guilty of murder?"

Jane weighed the question. "That he might well do it again . . ."

He was suddenly angry. "Jane, for Christ's sake, stop thinking of him as your husband. William Andrews is the single biggest figure in world communications. News, entertainment, business networks, everything. He has an empire bulging at the seams with kingdoms he's conquered. There are hundreds of entrepreneurs who'd love to break free, and he has billions of dollars in investment capital counting on him to hold the whole thing together. Do you have any idea what you're up against?"

"I hadn't thought—" she began, but he cut her off.

"You'd better think, and think hard. You're poking around, trying to find out if your husband loves you. And you're thinking that someone else who loves him may be trying to scare you away. What you're really doing is looking for evidence that could send William Andrews to prison. And that would cost networks, cable companies, broadcasters, and God knows how many manufacturers a lot of money. Not just millions, but billions. There are probably a hundred companies out there that would kill you in a second if they thought you were a danger to Andrews Global Network."

"Roscoe, that seems like such a stretch—"

He cut in again. "Let me tell you about my new job. Do you know what I do?" She might have ventured a guess, but he kept talking. "Nothing! I sit here all day reading our papers and sending letters to their editors and managing editors, commenting on their coverage. Letters that I'm sure they ignore, just as I would have ignored them in my old job. And for this they're paying me twice as much as I used to make and giving me company stock. You know why?" Again, he didn't give her time to guess. "Because I was asking questions about William Andrews's former lover and might just have discovered that he had something to do with his wife's death. So they're paying me not to dig and not to ask any more questions."

"Roscoe, I think they need someone in your position. You were promoted because—"

"I was promoted to keep me on the sidelines. What does it cost them? An extra thirty thousand a year. Jesus, that's pocket change next to what they're protecting."

"My God," Jane snapped, "are you saying that Bill married me to keep me on the sidelines?"

"What I'm saying is that if you get too close to the truth, even William Andrews won't be able to save you. There are important men who have bet serious money on his company. Do you think they give a rat's ass about whether you have a happy marriage?"

She sat speechless, listening to her mentor breathing on the other end of the conversation. She concluded, "I guess I have to clear out, don't I?"

"Or stay put. You're getting much more for forgetting what you know than the lady in Paris is getting. She gets a million bucks and an occasional visit. You've got his wedding ring. So think long and hard, Jane. Stay or leave. But whatever you do, stop asking questions."

Her hands were shaking when she closed her telephone. Roscoe wasn't a man given to exaggeration. In all the years she had known him, he had always been factual, unemotional, and precise. And now he seemed to be frightened, not just for her but for himself as well. He was going no further in their investigation into the relationship between Andrews and Selina. He was going to sit in his office, collect his hush money, and try not to attract the attention of anyone connected with Andrews Global Network. He was advising her to do the same. He was a bought man, and he was suggesting that she get used to being a bought woman. She had a better deal than the woman in Paris, he had told her. She had the name, the position, and easy access to the fortune. All Selina had was a monthly check. Stay, if she could live with the secret space in her marriage that held her husband's past. Get out if she couldn't. Those were her choices.

38

Jane walked back to Fifth Avenue and began meandering along the edge of the park. "Not even William Andrews can save you," Roscoe had warned. And that meant there would always be a third party in her marriage. Not just Selina Royce but all the investors that had a stake in Andrews's empire. They would always be watching to see if she was content with her role as the loyal, unquestioning wife. They would always be ready to deal with her if she should ever step out of line. Being married to Bill meant becoming a silent member of the "team" and, like Roscoe, taking care not to attract attention.

It would be like being married to a gangster, pretending not to notice the body in the trunk of the car. Or to a government official, living on the bribes that came stuffed into envelopes. The piano player in a brothel took his tips and smiled politely, feigning ignorance of what was going on in the rooms upstairs. She would be Mrs. William Andrews, accepting the honors and accolades and ignoring the headless body of his first wife.

She should run! But where? Back to her job at one of Bill's newspapers, to sit alongside an equally compromised Roscoe Taylor? Or to a new life? Was there any place she could go where Andrews Global Network wouldn't be waiting for her? They could find her and watch her no matter where she went. They would never let her uncover the truth about Kay Parker's murder. She would be no safer in another country than she was in Bill's apartment, and no more independent than she was in his arms.

How had she let this happen? Obviously, she hadn't been thinking clearly when she let herself be flattered into a relationship with him. But she had known about his first wife from the very beginning, and she had learned about Selina long before they were married. There were clues everywhere. There had been countless warnings. Why hadn't she heeded any of them?

But maybe there had been no chance of escape. From the moment he glanced at the desk in her apartment and saw that she was digging into Kay's death, he had known that she was a danger to him. Perhaps that was the need he had for her. From that moment, he knew that he could never let her get away.

She dined alone, again by the window. The cook had prepared a delicious rack of lamb with a mint sauce and fresh vegetables. Mrs. McCarty had gone to the wine cellar and brought back a Bordeaux that was old enough to need decanting. As she looked out over the skyline, there was no doubt that she was at the top of the world. Everything she tasted, all that she saw, advised her to join Bill's conspiracy of silence. But still, it was hard to put aside the sound of the shotgun blast that had obliterated Kay Parker's face. Hard, too, to ignore the voices that kept asking questions about her husband's role in Parker's death.

In the morning she threw a few essentials into an oversize handbag. "Out for the day," she told Mrs. McCarty cheerfully. She walked downtown to the station and boarded a train for Southport. She took a cab to her apartment, then drove to the house where her first husband rented a room. He was fresh out of bed, still scratching and stretching, when he opened the door.

"Everything all right?" Art asked.

"Fine," she lied. "Just back from Paris."

Art seemed glum. "Sure as hell beats Southport." He staggered off to get dressed.

They drove to a diner for coffee and muffins. He ate hungrily, but the food didn't improve his mood. "How's the play coming?" she asked, and then listened to the problems of getting answers from his producers.

"They're never in, never return phone calls. And when you do get ahold of them, they're still waiting for information. I figured I'd be in the theater in six months. Now I'm beginning to think more like six years."

Jane sympathized, but then brought up the reason for her visit. "I need cover, Art. I need people to think I'm at home here in Southport while I'm upstate doing a bit of research." His interest was piqued instantly. "The thing is," Jane went on, "I think I'm being watched. When I don't go back to the city tonight, I think people are going to come looking for me."

He was mildly amused. "Jealous husband?"

"More than that," she said, and his expression became serious. She took him through the events in Paris, her experience in the sauna and the bogus nurse in her room. She didn't mention Andrews's liaison with his mistress or her suspicions about the woman who had tried to inject her. There was no reason to get into her husband's tarnished love life. But she · clearly conveyed the message that her marriage to William Andrews was proving to be dangerous.

"You know those ghost movies," she said, "where they hear chains rattling and voices telling them to get out? But the idiots stay in the house anyway? That's about where I am. I'm getting a lot of warnings, and I think it's time for me to get out. But there are a couple of things I have to investigate first. If I'm walking out on the marriage of the century, I want to be sure."

"What's left to investigate?" he said. He reminded her of her research into the murder of Kay Parker and the pages on Selina Royce that she had caught him reading. "He's lying to you. They all are. When you smell something fishy, it's probably because there is a fish."

"I want to go up to the place where it all happened. There was a meeting at an inn near the chalet. I need to know who was at that meeting. And then I want to talk to the one-man police force that started the investigation. Someone inside the William Andrews corporation killed Kay Parker, and everyone has been covering it up. I need to know . . ." she trailed off, unable to finish the thought.

"You need to know if it was William Andrews?" Art said, supplying the unspoken name.

Jane nodded. "That's why I need your help."

She explained that she needed to switch cars with him so she could leave hers in front of her apartment. She needed activity in the apartment at night. Maybe he could stay there and turn the lights on and off. And she needed a cover if someone should come knocking on her door. He had to say that she had been in and out all day. That she had met up with a friend. Anything that would make it sound as if she were spending a routine day. Art nodded and tossed her the keys to his car.

"Okay," he said. "But I liked your first idea better. Just get out!"

Jane phoned Roscoe Taylor. She wanted him to give her the same cover. She had been in the office and was out, probably working on an assignment.

"I don't like this," Roscoe told her. "You really should let it go. If you nearly got killed just for raising questions, what do you think will happen if they catch you investigating the crime scene?"

"I love the man, Roscoe," she admitted. "And I think he loves me. That's why I have to know. I need to know how the rest of my life is going to turn out."

Jane drove to a strip mall near her office and went to a public telephone kiosk. Mrs. McCarty answered on the first ring.

"It's me," Jane said. "Is Mr. Andrews home?"

"He's at the office," the housekeeper said, amazed that anyone would expect William Andrews to be home.

"Well, I know I'll never get him there. So, will you tell him that I'm working late and that I'll probably stay at my apartment. Or maybe I'll stay with one of my friends. I'll phone him when I decide."

"Where can he reach you?"

"He can call my cell phone," Jane said, and then hung up quickly. She had established that her plans weren't yet firm and had left a caller ID number that would put her near her office if anyone checked. Then she started north into Massachusetts, where she took the turnpike to Albany. With a little luck, she would be at the inn in the Adirondacks in time for dinner.

39

William Andrews looked away from the faces around the conference table, checked his watch inconspicuously, and scribbled a brief note, which he passed to his secretary. "Call my wife. Leave word that I'll be late." Then his attention went back to the issue at hand—advertisers who had cut their spending. Kim Annuzio had a boggling array of figures and charts. Most of the cuts, she was demonstrating, were cyclical and were offset by other increases. The hard-core declines seemed to come from just two cable systems.

"Anyone know why?" Andrews asked.

His secretary slipped back into the room and leaned close to him, whispering that his wife was away for the evening. He immediately lost interest in the revenue shortfall.

"Where?" he whispered.

"She didn't say. Just that you could call her cell phone."

"Well, call," he ordered, and then turned back to the meeting.

The woman returned, this time with a note that she left next to him. "Her phone is turned off. I left a message for her to call you." He folded the paper into his pocket and switched his attention back to the meeting.

It was another hour before they broke up. As they were filing out, Robert Leavitt suggested that Andrews pay a visit to the offending cable systems. Andrews nodded curtly. "Someone should," he said. But his mind was elsewhere. "Any calls?" he asked as he passed his secretary. There were none.

He phoned the apartment and got Mrs. McCarty, who could tell him only that Jane had called. "Did she have an overnight bag?" he demanded, and she assured him that his wife didn't. "Just a shoulder bag," Mrs. McCarty reported. He tried the cell phone and got her mailbox. He was puzzled but not really alarmed. Jane was bright and independent, clearly able to decide to spend the night with friends. He knew he had been busy, hardly home at all—and distracted when he was. It made sense that she'd welcome an opportunity for a bit of conversation.

But she wasn't generally careless. It was unlike her to turn her phone off, particularly when she had asked him to call her. He packed the report they had just discussed into his briefcase and had his secretary alert his driver.

At home, he took a sandwich into his office but found he was too distracted to get into the numbers and charts. He called Mrs. McCarty and asked her to repeat the message Jane had left. Then he went down to the main telephone set and scrolled down to check for the number she had called from. He recognized the Connecticut area code. No problem! He dialed her office, and her secretary said she had been in. He was switched to Roscoe Taylor, who greeted him cordially and said that Jane was probably out on an interview. Andrews called her apartment and got her voice, promising to call back. As the evening wore on, he made two more tries to her cell phone, sure that she would notice it was off and would turn it back on. He was angry. If her phone had run down or broken, she could have found another phone and called.

Jane was on the Northway, passing Lake George in the Adirondack foothills. Fatigue was setting in, but she had to admit that she welcomed the distraction. Since France, she had thought of nothing but the sauna and the woman in the hospital—the same woman her husband had visited. She had churned up all the possibilities, running one scenario after another. It was relaxing to concentrate on something else, even if it was only the boring task of driving.

But now, as she got closer to the answers she had to find, Jane went back to rerunning the possibilities one more time. The woman near the opera house was certainly Selina Royce. She lived openly and, given the ease with which Roscoe had located her, made no effort to hide her identity. It was also certain that she had a relationship with her husband. The detective's report left no doubts that they had been lovers. And he was still paying her bills. Why? There were two possibilities she could think of. Either he was ensuring her silence, in which case he might not still love her, or he was ensuring her lifestyle, in which case he probably did still love her. Or, at least, felt responsible for her.

Those were facts. William Andrews had a lover, and Kay Parker knew about it. Maybe Kay had confronted him, laughed when he asked for his freedom, and told him he would be her prisoner forever. Or maybe Kay had given him a hint at just how much a divorce was going to cost him. Either way, both her husband and his mistress had motives for murder.

But that was where things became iffy. It was pure speculation to suggest that William and Selina had planned Kay's death. Maybe Kay had decided to do away with her rival. Or perhaps it was Bill alone who planned to get rid of Kay. These were the questions that had to be answered.

Those answers would shed light on the present issues. Why, if he loved Selina, would he have married her? Roscoe had suggested that it was to "keep her on the sidelines," but that sounded much too manipulative. Through it all, Jane felt that Andrews really loved her. Maybe it was her ego, or perhaps just a case of wishful thinking, but she couldn't believe that all their intimate moments had been part of a ruse. But if he loved her, why would he be keeping Selina? If it was only because he needed her to keep his secret, then why wouldn't he tell Jane about her?

The more she thought about it, the more important it seemed to find out who had visited the house in the Adirondacks, and in what order they had arrived. She needed to know whether Selina was actually at the house or at the Bass Inn business meeting, which would have put her in the neighborhood. It was also important to know whether Andrews had brought his wife with him to the chalet or whether she had gone up on her own. The first would imply that Selina was the unexpected intruder. The other would imply that Kay had decided to catch them in each other's arms. And if, indeed, Selina wasn't at the meeting or at the house, then Andrews would have acted alone in killing his wife.

She remembered that her husband had also been wounded, proof that he had been behind his wife when the fatal shot was fired. But that was Robert Leavitt's spin on the events. Could it be that Kay had fired first, only wounding her target, and that Bill had then taken the gun away from her? Or could his wounds have been faked? Leavitt would have no problem testifying that his boss had been wounded, and Andrews had more than enough clout to create a fake medical record.

How could she get the information she needed? Bob Leavitt would know who had attended the meeting, but that wasn't information he would be likely to share. Nor would any of the other top executives talk to her about a subject they had kept secret for so long. Would the airline that the company used still have records of who had been aboard flights to the Adirondack meeting? Would they have kept them all these years? She would have to find the rules and regulations for passenger lists. Another question: How did Selina get away from the crime scene? According to Leavitt's statement, all the attendees had left for New York. So if Selina had been at the chalet when the murder occurred, she would have needed special arrangements for her escape—a private flight, a car rental, a taxi to a train. Would any of that have been recorded? But Jane realized that she couldn't be sure the crime had actually been committed that morning. It might have been the previous evening, which would have allowed Selina to leave with the other executives. It could have been at any time! There was no postmortem examination of the body, and no medical examiner had been involved.

In fact, the available lines of inquiry were few. The police records of the investigation probably held much more information than she had been able to access online. They might give her leads, or names of people whom the police had contacted. The records of the inn would be crucial, if a small, cozy inn bothered to keep records. Then there were Kay's computer files, which might list her plans for that day. For Kay's computer records, she would need to go back to the apartment. She could do that innocently enough if she went back now, without a lengthy and suspicious absence. For the other answers, she would need to spend a few days near the crime scene or find someone to go there for her.

Jane turned on the cell phone and dialed the apartment. Mrs. McCarty answered and put her through to her husband without even being asked to. "He wants to talk to you," she said, and he picked up instantly.

"Hi, I've missed you," he said casually.

She rattled off a quick story about a friend coming into town and then explained that she had left her cell phone off. "I feel like an idiot," she apologized. "I hope you weren't worried."

"No, but now I can call the CIA and tell them to call off the search. When will you be home?"

"Tomorrow," she answered, and then asked, "Are you going to be in town?" He said that he was but would probably be late. Jane promised to hold dinner for him.

It had sounded natural enough. She didn't detect any hint of suspicion, although she knew she would have to come up with a name or two to explain her overnight stay. She drove north past Lake George and on to the Olympic Village at Lake Placid. Then she headed west, climbing higher into the Adirondacks, toward Lake Saranac.

The time of the murder and the timing of the business meeting were looming as important pieces of information. According to Leavitt's testimony, the meeting had adjourned the night before. Apparently Leavitt had arranged transportation to a local airport for the attendees, or had them ferried out by helicopter. He had stayed behind with the limo he used to drive up the mountain road to Andrews's rescue. Why? If Kay and Bill were planning to stay behind for a day of skiing, wouldn't Leavitt have been more valuable back at the office? Quite clearly, Andrews didn't need him there just to provide transportation. His helicopter or his jet would have come back for him. So why did Leavitt stay on in the inn?

But suppose Kay had been killed the previous night. Then anyone who was at the meeting could have been involved. Perhaps one of the executives. Most likely Selina, who would be faced with losing her position and her lover. In one case,

Kay Parker was alone with William Andrews. In the other, Kay would have been alone in the house while her husband was conducting a business meeting down at the inn. Anyone could have left the meeting and driven up the mountain to kill her.

But then Jane corrected herself. No, in the scenario Leavitt testified to, he was the only one with a car. How would one of the others have gotten to the chalet? And how would Bill have been wounded?

Of course! It had to be Selina. If she killed Kay, then Bill certainly could have engineered a cover story. But that still left open the question of how Selina would have gotten to her victim.

Jane reached Saranac and passed the small executive airport where the corporate jet might have landed. It was clearly possible that on learning of his wife's murder, Andrews sent all his people—including Selina Royce—away to protect them from suspicion. But then why stay himself? And why would—

Wait a minute! There was another question. How would both Kay and Selina have gotten up to Mountain Ridge? After reading her detective's reports, would the great Kay Parker have consented to her husband's mistress tagging along on the flight? Was it likely that Kay would stay put in the chalet, knowing that Selina was at a meeting with her husband just down the road? So if Kay was there, wasn't it more likely that Selina wasn't even close to the chalet? Bill probably wouldn't have allowed her to go to the meeting. And if she wasn't there, then she couldn't be the killer. In fact, she couldn't even have been a witness to the killing, which made her being a blackmailer that much more improbable. The more questions she asked herself, the closer Jane was coming to her most dreaded conclusion. Bill had to have killed his wife. And Selina had remained all these years his lover.

Mountain Ridge turned out to be a simple crossroads with a few buildings, functioning as an occasional convenience store for the vacation lodges and camps. She passed a police station, probably the one that had responded to Robert Leavitt's call. A mile farther south was the Bass Inn where, according to Leavitt's testimony, the business meeting was held. That's where Leavitt had spent the night and taken William Andrews's panicky call from his mountain retreat.

She pulled into the inn, found the lobby empty, and waited until a manager appeared behind the desk.

"I don't have a reservation," she began, but he cut her off with a laugh.

"In bass season, you need a reservation. But after the foliage, all you need is a credit card." He explained that most of the inn was closed. "We open weekends during the ski season, but other than that, we don't even keep help on. Just me and the wife take care of what needs taking care of."

Her credit card said "J. J. Warren," so that was the name she used to check in. "I was here seven or eight years ago," she said casually as she filled out the reservation form.

"Is that so? You don't look like a bass fisherman!" They both laughed.

"I was here for a business meeting. A few of us flew in one day and flew out that night. About this time of year! I suppose management didn't want us to have any distractions."

"We don't get a lot of business meetings," he said. "Unless it's a bunch of big shots who say they're going away on business but are really interested in the fishing. I suppose they can have a meeting around the fire and talk a little business so they can write the trip off. But this time of year they're probably holding their business meetings in Las Vegas. Or maybe Hawaii."

"No, this really was business," Jane countered. "I was with Andrews Global Network. We all traveled so much that we had to go to strange places just to get together."

"Oh yeah," he said. "Andrews is that rich young fellow lives up on the mountain. His wife was killed up here, wasn't she?"

Jane nodded. "Tragic! She was a society woman. Very attractive."

"So I've heard." He came around the desk and picked up

Jane's small bag. "He comes up in a helicopter from time to time. At least, that's what I was told when I asked around about the helicopter. Never met him, but I've heard about him."

She tried not to make it sound like an interrogation. "He doesn't stay here? I thought this was his landing site."

"No. He lands up at his house and flies from there. Brings his kids every once in a while."

"I think his wife was killed the weekend we were here for the meeting. Is that possible?"

"Not likely," the manager said. "I remember the state police were in and out when that happened. They sort of took over the place. I don't remember that we had any guests, except the reporters who came pouring in from all over the state."

She tried to hand him a tip, but he pulled back. "No, showing you to your room is the least I can do. There isn't much else we can offer."

Jane put the money back in her pocket. "Bet if you check your records, you'll find that I was here the weekend that murder took place. That was before I got married. My maiden name was Selina Royce."

40

She let out a heavy sigh as soon as the door closed. It seemed as if she had pulled it off and that he had accepted her story. If he had guest registrations from that far back, she had no doubt he would look for her name on the day that Kay Parker had died. If he found it, she would ask him over dinner who else had been there that night. Robert Leavitt, for sure, but maybe other players in the sham they had worked on the local police.

Dinner was at one of the dining-room tables, lit with a candle while the other tables remained dark. There were just three of them: the innkeeper, his wife, and Jane. Over dinner, Jane explained that she was scouting a group house for the ski season. "Is the Andrews place for rent?" she asked casually.

"Doubt it," the proprietor's wife answered. "It's never been on the market. But I could recommend a few places. How many in your group?"

Then the manager got serious. "Did you say you were up here for a business meeting?"

Jane nodded while she sipped at her soup.

"Same weekend as that woman was killed?"

"I think so," she answered. "I know it was about the same time."

"Well, we've got records back to then, but no business meeting. The place was pretty much shut down, just like now."

"But one of our people must have been here. Wasn't one of your guests named Robert Leavitt?"

His eyes widened in recognition. "Yeah, that was the name. He was the only one registered that weekend. And he stayed on for another few days while the police and reporters were here."

She decided to stick her neck out. "Were Mr. Andrews and his wife ever registered here?"

"Not that I know of! I don't think I ever saw either of them."

She was beginning to fill in the scenario. The business meeting had just been a cover to explain why Andrews had gone up to his chalet. Bob Leavitt was doing nothing more than covering his boss's tracks. Jane hurried through the meal so she could get back to her room and absorb everything she had just learned.

It wasn't Bill and Kay who were enjoying a romantic getaway in the mountains. It was Bill and Selina. They must have realized they were being watched and devised this ruse so they could have a weekend together. Leavitt was in on the deception. But then how did Kay Parker get there? Obviously she wouldn't have been invited. Jane remembered the Mountain Ridge police chief's comment. He had mentioned a car parked in front of the house, supporting his contention that an intruder would not have thought he was breaking in to an unoccupied house. That made sense if the car parked in front of the chalet had been Kay Parker's. That would mean Kay had come up on her own, caught the two lovers together, and run for the shotgun. Apparently Selina got to it first and blew Kay's head off. A nice theory. The only question was whether any part of it was true.

In the morning Jane was up and out early. When she reached the parking area, she was amazed to see a light snow sticking to the trees and lawns. Her car windows were already covered. She drove carefully away from the inn and headed back toward the town. Only one store in Mountain Ridge showed signs of life. A truck was making a delivery. Past the truck, the lights were on in the police station. Jane parked, stepped inside, and found herself in a waiting area with one long wooden bench. She went to a door marked PRIVATE and knocked on the opaque glass. No one answered, so she went back to the bench to wait. Almost immediately, a weary-looking man in a heavy plaid shirt pushed through the front door, carrying a brown paper bag. His wire-rimmed glasses steamed up immediately.

"Saw you pull in, so I brought you some coffee," he said. He opened the door to the private office. "C'mon in! The name is Pete. I'm the police sergeant. Whole darn police department when you get right down to it!" He enjoyed the humor of his standard introduction and held out his hand. The palm was callused and the grip firm. Outdoor living had kept his body younger than the mid-sixties lines on his face. Pete lifted folders and circulars from the crowded desk to clear space for the two paper cups. "Take a seat. I hope you like it black."

"The only way to drink it," she answered, and rolled up a wooden swivel chair to her side of the desk. She rubbed her hands together and then wrapped them around the hot cup. "I'm not dressed for the weather. When I left New York yesterday, the last thing I thought about was snow."

"It'll warm up in a minute. The furnace takes a little time to get started. And this snow won't last. Probably be up in the forties once the sun gets going." He sipped from his cup, winced at the scalding heat, and then forced down another sip. "So, how can I help you?"

"I'm a reporter," she said. She took out her wallet and presented her press card as she spoke. "I'm doing a piece on an unsolved crime that happened here. . . ."

"Here? Someone take home a few bass without a fishing license?" He laughed at the thought.

"No, it was a murder that happened eight years ago. A woman was attacked and killed in her home by an intruder."

The friendly expression vanished. "Reporter?" he asked suspiciously. He glanced down at her press pass. "Yeah, I remember that one. That television fella, wasn't it?"

"Andrews," she agreed. "William Andrews."

He pushed the press credentials back toward her. "I'm afraid there's not much I can tell you about that one. State police took over the investigation. They're the ones you'll have to interview."

"I've seen the police reports—at least, the public records—and I've read most of the press coverage. But it's all pretty sketchy. I was hoping you might be able to fill in the gaps."

"That was—what?—seven or eight years ago. There's not much I remember."

"Maybe you could check your records," Jane pressed.

Pete pursed his lips. "I don't have any. The state boys boxed up everything."

"But you must remember something. I think it was the *New York Post* that interviewed you. They said you were the only one with real evidence. . . ."

He smirked. "That's probably true. I was the only one looking for real evidence. The state boys were just going through the motions. They kept searching the woods for someone who wasn't there."

"You said that there was a car parked outside the house, so an intruder would have known people were home. Do you remember that?"

"Sure," Pete said. "There were plenty of empty houses around if someone was looking to break in."

"Whose car was it?"

"A rental car."

"Do you remember who rented it?"

He gave her a thin smile. "Now, that's just the kind of question the state people didn't want answered."

Jane sensed an opening. "Why was that?"

"Why? Politics! Hell, you're a reporter. You must know how these things work. This Andrews was an important man. The politicians needed his television stations and his newspapers. Nobody wanted to get on the wrong side of him."

He crumpled his paper cup with a quick, violent squeeze. "Politicians," he groused, and tossed the cup into the wastebasket.

"Why wouldn't Andrews want the police to find his wife's killer?"

"Lady, if you can't figure that out, you ought to try a different profession."

"Are you saying he was the one who—"

"I'm not saying anything. The state took over the case, so if you want someone to tell you something, you'd have to go see the troopers. Far as I'm concerned, it's all over and done with. So, unless you want a fishing license or something . . ."

He stood slowly, indicating that the interview was over. But Jane stayed seated.

"Has someone threatened you?" she asked.

Pete turned his head away and laughed derisively. "Boy, are you a babe in the woods."

"Then why won't you talk to me?" she persisted.

"Because I like it here. It's a nice, comfortable job, the pay is okay, and the pension I'll start getting next year is damn near my full salary. So the last thing I need is politicians from Albany wondering why I'm talking about one of their old, forgotten botched cases."

"Even if someone gets away with murder?"

"Important people get away with murder every day," he assured her.

Jane nodded, got up, and held out her hand. "Thanks, anyway, Sergeant. I'll take your advice and try the state troopers."

Pete shook her hand, but he didn't let go. "Take one more piece of advice. Get yourself another story. Mr. Andrews still has a lot of clout up here. You keep asking questions and you're going to find out just how much clout."

"Reporters have to ask questions," Jane reminded him.

He patted her hand affectionately. "Watch your back, Miss . . ."

"Warren," she said with a smile. "J. J. Warren."

She stepped back out into the waiting room and paused to pull her jacket around her and button it up to the collar. She had pushed Pete about as far as she could. And although he wouldn't confirm anything, his insinuations had been chilling. The intruder had been a ruse, and the local police chief knew it. He had come to the conclusion that Kay Parker's murder was an inside job. And the reason her husband wouldn't have wanted the police to find the killer was that he already knew what they would find. That he, or someone very close to him, had fired the shot.

Pete had clearly been warned off further investigation and told to keep his ideas to himself. The warning had been graphic enough to frighten him. He seemed paranoid over the Andrews spies that he imagined were still watching him. He was probably afraid that his office was bugged or that she was wearing a recorder. She opened the door, braced herself against the cold wind that was still driving a mist of snow, and started out to her car.

"Can I give you a lift?" The voice came from a car parked just in front of hers, its source unseen but its tone decidedly familiar. Robert Leavitt stepped out to meet her.

41

Jane froze in her tracks, hovering between her car and the door she had just closed behind her. A second ago, the police sergeant's warnings had seemed fantastic. Now Bill's number-one agent was looking up at her, a thin smile suggesting that he had just caught her with her hand in the cookie jar. She leaned back toward the police station. Pete would certainly protect her. But from what? Her husband's best friend, who was offering her a ride in a snowstorm? Once he learned who she really was, Pete would wash his hands of her. If he wasn't going to tell her anything, he certainly wouldn't take on William Andrews face-to-face over her suspicions that she was suddenly in danger.

"Hello, Bob." Jane let him open the door, and she slipped into the passenger seat of his car. "I don't suppose your being here is just a happy coincidence."

"No, but it's not a total surprise, either. I knew you weren't going to let yourself be put off easily. I knew you'd keep digging. You're a damn good reporter."

"How did you find out I was up here?"

"Reliable sources," he said, indicating that he didn't want to compromise his undercover agent.

"Roscoe Taylor," Jane said, supplying the name. "What did you offer him now? A bigger expense account?"

"It wasn't Taylor. Roscoe is too big a man to do anything like that. It's little people that your husband intimidates."

"Like you," Jane sneered, hoping Leavitt was offended.

"Like me," he agreed. "And like your ex-husband."

"Art?" Jane had never credited Art with enough nerve to become a spy.

Leavitt nodded. "Who do you think is the angel backing his play?"

She was stunned. "Bill was paying my ex-husband to spy on me. He compromised that harmless fool."

"He decided to back a play. Art did whatever he thought would make William Andrews happy. Your husband does what he has to do to protect his interests. But he was wrong about you. He was sure you wouldn't be a problem. I warned him that you weren't going to be put off easily, but he was in love with you. He wasn't thinking straight."

"Then why . . ." She was going to ask, Why, if he loved her so much, did he still have a mistress in Paris, but she saw them pass by the Bass Inn. "Where are we going?"

"Up to the chalet. There's more privacy there."

She looked fondly back at the inn. Right then, she didn't want privacy. Roscoe Taylor's remark sprang to mind. "Even William Andrews won't be able to save you." She recalled his warning that she should stop asking questions. She had, indeed, been looking into matters that could get her husband convicted of murder. Andrews's backers simply couldn't allow that. There were fortunes riding on the conglomerate that only he could hold together. She began to wonder who would be waiting for her at the chalet.

He turned off on a road that appeared suddenly through the trees. The car lost traction for a moment and started into a skid. Leavitt turned with the slide and then straightened out when the tires got a grip. Immediately, they were climbing to a higher level.

"Is this the road you took that morning when Bill phoned you?"

Leavitt nodded. "Yes. It was a morning just like this. Snow beginning to build up everywhere."

"And when you got there?"

"When I got there, Kay was dead. Bill was sitting on the steps, the shotgun in his lap, his wife's body at his feet. Isn't that pretty much the way you figured it?"

"What about Selina?"

"She was just coming out of a crying fit. She could hardly talk."

They were driving on switchbacks, turning back and forth

as they climbed the side of a mountain. Leavitt was moving slowly in a low gear, straining the engine to keep from spinning the wheels. The road was narrow, barely wide enough for two cars to pass, and the drop over the edge was nearly vertical. Through the snow and haze, Jane thought she could make out a lake a hundred feet below. They turned another switchback and kept climbing. Her plight seemed to grow more desperate as they moved higher up the mountain.

"Who's going to be meeting us?" she asked, half afraid of the answer.

"Your husband," he said calmly.

"Bill is here at the house?"

"He's on his way, although with this weather, I'm sure he'll be delayed."

"When did you tell him that I was up here?"

Leavitt shook his head. "I didn't. Art called me and I started up here right away. I left Bill a message that he got this morning. But it was snowing here, so he couldn't take off. As soon as our weather clears, he'll be on his way."

"What are his instructions?" Jane asked, dreading the answer.

"Just to keep you entertained. He'll take care of everything when he gets here."

"Meaning that he'll take care of me, like he did his first wife. And then you'll run around and clean up the mess, just like you did eight years ago."

He shifted his eyes from the road to her for just an instant. "Why in hell did you have to keep asking questions? I didn't want anything like this to happen."

They labored up another few hundred feet, listening to the swish of the wipers. Even though the defroster was blasting out hot air, Jane felt chilled to the bone. She knew it was fear more than the temperature. They turned onto an inconspicuous path and brushed through overhanging trees. Then the chalet appeared, just as in the news pictures, with snow on the roof and frost at the corners of the windows. There were traces of tire tracks. Someone had come up to the house this morning, probably about the time she was leaving for the police station. He went around to open Jane's door, but she was already out into the snow. He took her arm as they climbed the few steps to the doorway; he pushed a key into the lock and stepped back from the open door.

Jane compared the layout with the crime scene she had imagined. There was a wing leading off to the left with the guest bedrooms. The open kitchen was to her right. Straight ahead was the great room with a dining area and then the living room with the enormous fireplace. Behind the living room, open steps led up to the second floor, where the master bed and bath commanded a view out over the Adirondacks.

Kay's body had been at the foot of the stairs, supporting the fiction that she had come down the steps and confronted an intruder. Probably she had gone to the bedroom as soon as she arrived, not knowing that her husband was out for a walk. Maybe she found an empty bed, or maybe Selina was still asleep. She probably heard Bill return and started down the stairs to confront him. And that's when he would have reached for the shotgun.

Jane could feel the blasts of hot air coming from the vents. Leavitt had turned on the heating system, probably when he was up there earlier. He lit the gas log in the fireplace and then went to the bar that bordered the kitchen. He was obviously at home with the liquor cabinet. He selected the door that housed the good scotch, poured two snifters, and brought one to Jane. "This will help," he promised.

"Help how? To deaden the pain when Bill blows my head off? What are you going to do? Tie me to a stake and offer me a blindfold?"

He tasted his drink. "Don't talk that way. I don't want to see you hurt."

"Were you here when Kay was killed? Did you watch while she was blown away?"

"No, of course not," he insisted. "I didn't come up here until he called. I was down at the inn."

"Of course," she agreed sarcastically. "Running a business meeting that never took place. So what will you say this time? That you stepped out for a cigarette?"

He started to answer, thought better of it, and went back to sipping his drink. The conversation was over. The next words, she guessed, would come from her husband. Jane knew she didn't want to wait to hear what he would decide.

She got up and started across the living room. Leavitt followed her with his eyes, at first suspiciously but then curiously when she made no move to the front door. He turned back to his drink as she started up the stairs. She closed the bedroom door behind her and quietly turned the lock. Then she checked her watch. She still had several hours of daylight to work with if she could get out of the house.

Her escape was more a hope than a plan. She had seen Leavitt put the car keys into his jacket pocket and then hang the jacket by the door. If she could just get to the keys! Maybe Leavitt would doze off. He must have been up all night, traveling from the city. He might well let his guard down. It wasn't likely that she could escape on foot down the frozen mountainside. All she had to do was get the keys and then beat him to the car. Once she was locked inside, she was free. He had no way to follow her, and she could be down the road and off the mountain before he could summon reinforcements. She would drive straight to town and switch to Art's car. She could leave that at Saranac and use a rental car for her escape.

But her escape was a long shot. If Leavitt saw her take the keys, he could catch up to her before she made it to the car. If she went near the door, he might realize that the keys were in his jacket and retrieve them himself.

The snow was another problem. It was still falling and showing no signs of letting up. She didn't think anything would happen to her until Bill got to the lodge, and the snow was delaying his arrival. But it might also hinder her escape. Could she make it down the mountain and back into town on uncleared roads? What if she got stuck in a drift? The police sergeant had assured her that the weather would clear, but at the moment there was no sign of letup. It made sense for her to wait. Give Leavitt time to get distracted or numb from his drinking. Give the weather a chance to break. But how long could she afford to wait?

She listened at the door. There was no hint of Leavitt moving about. Jane could envision him slumped in the same sofa between the stairs and the front door. She peered out the window. The sky seemed to be a bit lighter and the snow wasn't falling as heavily. It looked as if the sun was trying to break through. Jane sat on the edge of the bed, waiting patiently. Over the next hour, the snow turned briefly to rain and then to a light mist. She pressed against the window and was able to see patches of blue breaking through the heavy overcast. Finally there was sunlight, strong enough to cast shadows into her room. It was now or never.

She turned the lock slowly. When it clicked, she winced as if it were the sound of a rifle shot. She pressed her ear to the door. Nothing! Leavitt still wasn't moving about. She eased the door open and peeked through the crack. He wasn't on the sofa or in any of the soft chairs. Cautiously, she stepped out into the hall and started down the wooden steps. Halfway down, she could see into the kitchen. He wasn't there, either.

She crossed the living room slowly, nonchalantly, trying to appear innocent in case he suddenly appeared. She guessed he might have gone into one of the bathrooms. His coat was still hanging next to hers, so he hadn't gone outside. Through the window she could see the car, its snowy covering beginning to melt into rivulets running down the windshield. The ground was still covered, now glistening in the sunlight. It looked as if it would turn to slush in a matter of minutes. She slipped her hand into the pocket of his jacket. Her fingers brushed against metal.

The key. She could have screamed with relief. But the trickiest part of her plan was just beginning. Jane lifted her jacket off the peg and turned the front doorknob as if she were defusing a bomb. With a glance back to the empty hallway leading to the guest rooms, she slipped through the opening.

There were two keys on the key ring. She fitted the bigger one into the door and smiled when it turned. Then she slid in, pulled the door behind her, and locked it. Now, the key into the ignition. The same key slipped in easily. She twisted it and heard the satisfying sound of the starter grinding over.

At almost the same instant, Leavitt appeared in the doorway. He started out, then suddenly stopped and went back inside. She knew he couldn't get to her. Jane had the key and had locked herself in. All he could do was flail at the car as she drove away.

The starter was still grinding. She switched it off for a moment, stomped at the gas pedal, and then turned the key again. More grinding. The damn engine wouldn't catch. Jane remembered that she had to be careful not to flood it. Again she turned the key off and started to count to ten before trying again. She was at eight when Leavitt reappeared. Jane stopped counting and twisted the key hard. Once again, the starter cranked the engine, but still it wouldn't start. And Leavitt was walking toward her. She clicked the key off once more, gave it a moment, and then turned it again. More grinding, but the engine wouldn't fire into life.

She looked up at him, standing directly in front of her. He held out a thick black wire that had connectors at both ends, and then shrugged. Jane got his message. He had disabled the car. She wasn't going anywhere without the wire harness he had in his hand. She hammered the wheel in frustration. Then tears of rage filled her eyes.

42

Jane surrendered meekly, simply pushing the door open and sagging against the steering wheel. Leavitt was gentle as he helped her out and led her back to the chalet. He even helped her off with her jacket. "I don't like doing this," he mumbled. "If it were up to me . . ."

"It is up to you," Jane said, fighting through her fear. "You're the one who's writing my death sentence. Maybe you were too late to save Kay, but it's not too late to save me."

"You can talk to him," Leavitt tried. "He cares for you. . . ."

"He cared for Kay, but that didn't stop him from killing her. He was madly in love with Selina, but he still got rid of her. What makes me so special?"

He waved away her words. "Let's just wait until he gets here." He turned and began to pace back and forth across the living room. "Look, I'm not just going to stand by and let him hurt you. I'll talk to him. I'll tell him that I'm not going to be part of another eight-year cover-up."

She saw a crack beginning to work its jagged way across the bland façade of indifference. Leavitt seemed to be questioning his lockstep loyalty to William Andrews. She tried to exploit the opening. "Bob, for God's sake, you know that once he gets here, we're both lost. Let's get out of here. Then we can decide what we have to do."

"I know what I have to do," he snapped back. "I've been thinking about it all day. I'm not afraid to stand up to him."

"Of course you're not," she agreed, supporting his fantasy. "But not here! Not in his house on his mountain. We can get help from the police. You saw me at the station house. The police sergeant would love to put the great William Andrews into handcuffs."

He smiled as the idea had a moment of appeal. But then he shook his head. "I'd be in the cell with him. I helped him cover up the murder." He took up his pacing again. "We can't bring in the authorities. We've got to solve this on our own."

She knew his bravado would crumble once Andrews appeared. Leavitt's whole adult life had been given in service to his master. Even if Leavitt found the strength to speak his mind, William Andrews would be able to silence him with a glance. Her only hope was to escape before Bill arrived, which could be at any minute now that the skies were clear. If she could just get Leavitt to take her to a public place—the inn, the store down in Mountain Ridge—anywhere there would be witnesses. Here in the chalet, her husband could do anything he wanted.

"Bob, let's just buy ourselves more time. Maybe we can't go to the police. Maybe the place to tell the truth is in his office, in front of the others. Or in the boardroom. But not here. If he catches us here, then I'm dead and maybe you are, too!"

Leavitt paused and looked up to consider the idea. "He's not crazy, you know. He doesn't go around killing people."

"No, he's not crazy," she agreed. "But he's not going to let anyone threaten his dynasty. You said he's coming up here so we can talk things over. If that's what he wanted, he could have waited until I got back to the city."

"I won't let him hurt you," Leavitt promised. "Enough people have been hurt. The lying . . . the hiding . . . it all has to stop!"

"Then get us out of here! We can find a safer place to confront him. Please, we're running out of time. In a minute, all the decisions will be in his hands."

He listened, nodded, and then moved quickly to the door. Leavitt retrieved the distributor wire he had removed from the car and stepped outside. He worked furiously, brushing the snow off the hood, raising it, and leaning underneath to make his repair. Then he was around to the driver's door, where he leaned in and turned the ignition. The engine caught and roared.

"Okay," he announced when he came back to the house. "We're ready. Get anything you need and let's get going."

It was too late. Even as he was talking, she heard a faint

growl coming over the mountaintops. Then the first popping sounds of an approaching helicopter. How much time did they have? Just a few minutes. Not nearly enough to get the car turned around and headed back down the treacherous road.

"We can make a run for it," Jane shouted, trying to run past him.

"No! The road's dangerous. We'd have to drive slowly. He'd be waiting for us at the bottom of the hill."

"Dammit!" She thought of pushing past him and taking her chances with the slippery road. But then the helicopter broke out above the next peak and its roar grew ominously.

Leavitt pushed her back inside the house. "We've got to hide you," he said with more determination than he had ever shown her before. They both looked around furiously. "In here," he decided. He pulled open a door on the wall near the kitchen. "I'll tell him I let you go. He'll be furious, but he won't do anything to me. Just don't come up, no matter what you hear."

There was a short flight of steps down to a cinder-block basement. Light was flooding in from a back window, and she could hear the sound of the heating blowers. Outside, the roar of the helicopter's turbine was becoming deafening.

"Wait!" He dashed into the kitchen, opened a cabinet, and reached far into the back. He took out a revolver, snapped open the chamber to check that it was loaded, and rushed back to her. "Take this! If he comes down the stairs, use it. Don't warn him and don't let him get close to you." He closed the door in her face.

Leavitt then ran to the front door and stepped out into the swirling snowstorm that the helicopter was kicking up. He waited until the skids touched down, then ducked low to get under the rotors. The door opened and William Andrews stepped out, looking grim and determined. He wore a windbreaker over his business shirt and tie. The men hurried to the house and paused while the machine lifted, hovered, and peeled away to the south. Then they stepped into the house.

Jane had listened to the helicopter's rumbling idle and recognized the turbine scream when it took off. It was too loud for her to hear footsteps or conversation, but she was sure that Bill was already in the house. His first question would be "Where is she?" She wondered what Leavitt would answer. She didn't believe that he could stand up to her husband. He wouldn't admit to letting her go. Most likely, he would say that she had escaped and fabricate a story of how she had slipped out and disappeared into the forest. Probably he would try to coax Bill into following her, which would get him out of the way and give her time to escape in the car. That was it! Leavitt had started it and left it running. He wanted her to take the car.

She looked down at the heavy weapon she was holding in both hands. She knew exactly how to use it. Aim at the widest part of her attacker and squeeze the trigger. But she knew she never would. Maybe she could wave it as a threat and hope it frightened her assailant as much as it frightened her. But fire it at another person—at a man she knew and maybe even loved?

She heard footsteps overhead, one person walking from the front of the house toward the kitchen. Then the door latch at the top of the stairs clicked. Jane knew she should do exactly what Robert Leavitt had told her to. Focus on the stairs. Wait for Andrews to appear. Fire to protect her life. Instead, she turned away from the stairs, opened the back door, and slipped out into the snow.

She ran at an angle, away from the house and out of the sight line of the back door. Despite the sunlight, the cold hit her instantly, carried on a stiff northerly breeze. She tugged her jacket around her and kept her head down to protect her face. In just a few seconds she crossed the clearing and plunged into the woods surrounding the house.

The evergreens closed behind her, giving her a momentary feeling of safety. But she knew she couldn't stop. She had left a fresh track from the back door to where she entered the forest. She had to keep moving, hoping that she would be harder to follow in the darkened woods.

"Jane!" It was Bill calling after her. "Jane, where are you going?"

His voice was getting louder. He was already out of the

house and coming after her. "What's going on? What are you running from?"

She trudged ahead, farther into the woods, now aware of the snow coming in over the tops of her shoes. Her feet were cold and wet. In another few minutes they would be freezing. She had to step carefully over the uneven roots and avoid branches that could snap in her face.

"Jane, for God's sake, you'll freeze!" He didn't sound as if he had gotten any closer. He was having trouble following. All she had to do was keep going. She tried to pick up her pace.

Her ankle turned and her knee buckled. Before she knew what was happening, she was falling face-first into the snow. She got a hand up just in time to break her fall but still landed hard across a tree root. The gun skittered a few yards away from her.

43

Jane? Answer me, please!"

Now he sounded closer. He had come into the woods and was doing his best to track her. Jane got up slowly, stretched out, and picked up the gun. She started to walk but felt herself toppling again. Her right shoe had broken, the heel snapping away cleanly. Each step she took threw her off balance, but she had to keep going.

"It's getting dark in here," Bill's voice called from a distance. "You'll get lost."

He hadn't gained any ground. Maybe he was afraid to go too deep into the forest. Or maybe he had lost her trail and was simply wandering.

She fell again, this time against the trunk of a tree. The damn shoe. She should take them both off and get back her balance. But the ground under the snow was hard and rocky. Her feet would be cut to pieces. Besides, they were already cold and wet. How far could she go barefoot?

Jane hobbled ahead, holding the pistol in one hand and using the other to ease branches aside. The snow from the branches was dropping down on top of her. Her hair was wet and she could feel ice under the collar of her jacket. In another minute, the cold would overcome her. Then it wouldn't take long for her to freeze to death. She had to change her direction and get back to the house, where the car was waiting.

She stopped and listened. There was nothing. The woods seemed deathly still, with just an occasional rustle of wind in the treetops. But she knew he was there, and not very far away. She turned to her right, at a sharp angle from the direction she had been moving. She planned to make a wide turn, away from her pursuer and around to the front of the chalet. Then she would rush out of the woods to the car. Once again, if she could get inside with the keys, and now with the gun, her chances of escape were better than even. There would still be the road with its snow-covered surface and its sheer drop down to the lake below. She would have to move carefully. But Bill would be on foot, unarmed, and without his helicopter to come to his rescue.

"Jaynnee!" he called at the top of his voice, stretching her name into a long cry. He had lost her, she guessed. He was calling desperately, not knowing which direction she had traveled or how far she had gotten. And even with his scream, he sounded farther away. She was going to make it! If she could just fight the cold for another few minutes, she would be safe in the car.

She saw the house through the trees, sitting up in front of her on cleared ground. How far? It was hard to tell through the branches. Maybe a hundred yards. Maybe less.

Something snapped somewhere behind her. Bill's voice cursed, probably at the whiplike sting of a branch. He was close. In turning back toward the house, she had moved closer to him. Jane stood still and held her breath, knowing that any noise she made would give her away.

"Dammit, Jane, why are you doing this?" he shouted nearby. "There's no place to go. You can't keep running."

She pressed flat against a tree, hoping to make herself invisible. She heard his footsteps crunching in the snow, and then the sound of his heavy breathing. Snow fell nearby. Bill swore. Then he appeared, a shadow moving in the spaces between the branches no more than fifty feet away. She was caught. She knew she couldn't make it to the car.

She remembered the pistol, completely forgotten even though it was clutched in her hand. "Don't let him close," she remembered Leavitt telling her. She put the other hand on the gun, raised it in front of her chest, and aimed in the direction of the approaching figure. She caught a glimpse of his face. A branch pushed aside. He stopped abruptly when he saw her.

"Don't come near me," Jane said, her tone more hopeful than determined. "I have a gun."

"Jane, what in hell . . ." He took one more step toward her. She turned her eyes away and pulled the trigger. The sharp crack of the gunshot rang in her ears and echoed in sequence off the distant peaks. She smelled the gunpowder, almost like holiday fireworks. Slowly she turned her eyes back to her husband, afraid of what she might have done.

He was on his knees, looking up at her, his eyes wide with surprise. His lips contorted as he tried to say something through his pain. He glanced down at the red droplets that were already staining the snow. Then he toppled forward onto his face.

Jane watched for a second, the gun still pointed as if she expected him to get up and attack her. She heard him groan. "Bill?" she said, asking him if he was still there. He didn't answer. She let the pistol drop from her fingers, then turned and ran.

She stumbled coming out of the woods and sprawled out on her chest. Snow clung to her hands and face. The damaged shoe had come off and was buried somewhere behind her. But she didn't stop to look or to brush at the snow that was in her mouth and eyes. She pushed up to her knees, crawled a few yards as she scampered to her feet, and raced for the car. Halfway there, she threw a glance back over her shoulder. No one was following.

She tore open the car door and threw herself into the seat. As she was closing the door, she realized the engine wasn't running. She reached down to the ignition. There was no key. Where was it? She did a panicky search of the seat next to her, felt under the seats, and lifted the floor mat. Where had he left it? It was only then that Jane realized he hadn't left it. Sometime after he had pushed her into hiding, Robert Leavitt had gone out, turned off the engine, and taken the key.

She stepped back into the snow and nearly fell. Her feet had no feeling, and she couldn't find her balance. She staggered the short distance to the house and fell against the front door. "Bob," she screamed in desperation, then turned the handle and stepped inside. "I killed him," she said. "He was reaching for me. I shot him."

"Of course you did," a voice answered. It was a woman's voice.

Jane blinked to clear her eyes. Leavitt was standing next to the sofa, showing a thin smile in answer to her obvious confusion. Seated next to him was a face she had seen before. On the street, in a bank, and then faintly in the dim light of her Paris hospital room. "Selina?"

The woman laughed and flashed a smile. Jane recognized her from the pictures. The grainy newspaper photos where the face was formed by a pattern of black dots. The fuzzy reproduction of old magazine photos she had pulled up on the Internet. She knew her. But something didn't fit. This wasn't the woman she had glimpsed only once in a picture of an eight-year-old awards banquet. This face had been in ball gowns at opening nights at the symphony. It had peered out of a tent, flanked by two lovely children. It had been on the dresser of the flowered boudoir that Bill had never redecorated. It wasn't Selina Royce.

"Kay Parker," Jane said. She blinked hard and tried to sharpen her focus. The woman turned her face slightly and glanced upward in a classic pose. "Jesus," Jane said, "you can't be. You're—"

"Alive," Kay said.

44

Jane felt her knees buckling, but she braced herself with a hand against the open door.

"Come in," Robert said. Then he offered, "Stand by the fire and get warm."

Jane had forgotten she was wet and cold. Forgotten, at least for an instant, that she had just shot her husband. She stood where she was, blinking incongruously, trying to make sense of the people she was facing—Bill's dead wife and the business partner who had covered up her murder.

It wasn't Selina Royce she had seen in Paris. It was Kay. William Andrews had gone to see the wife he had buried eight years ago. And maybe Leavitt hadn't been lying when he said he had never heard of Selina.

"But then who . . ." Jane tried to ask. "Who . . ."

"Who was murdered here?" Kay asked, putting into words the question Jane couldn't manage to ask.

"Selina Royce," Jane mumbled, beginning to work her way through the puzzle. Then she found another answer. "You killed her."

Kay smiled as if she had been complimented. "She was stealing my husband," she explained. "I couldn't allow that."

Jane still wasn't able to make complete sense of the images that were flashing through her mind. "Then all these years, you were in hiding. Using her name . . ."

"Where's the gun?" Robert Leavitt interrupted.

Jane heard the question, but it didn't register.

"You buried Selina in your place . . ." Jane went on.

"And I took her place," Kay Parker said. "It wasn't much, but it was better than going to prison."

Leavitt was agitated by the small talk. "Where's the gun?" he repeated. "What did you do with the pistol?"

Jane tried to remember, but the question seemed unimportant. "I dropped it," she said. "Outside in the snow."

"Dammit!" Leavitt hissed. He reminded Kay, "We need that gun. It has to be the same gun." He pushed past Jane and rushed outside, where he followed her footprints back toward the forest.

"Your whole life . . . in hiding . . ." Jane shook her head sadly.

"Oh, not my whole life," Kay corrected. "Not anymore. Those days are over. Now I'm the wife of the new chairman of the board. Everyone knows that Robert is the heir apparent."

"But you can't . . . just . . . come back to life." It still wasn't making any sense to Jane.

"No," Kay told her. "But Selina Royce can come out of hiding. A touch of plastic surgery. Colored contacts. After all these years, no one would recognize me anyway. Then the only person who will know is Bob. And he's in love with me."

"Then Bill wasn't lying to me," Jane said with a sense of relief. "He wasn't going to get rid of me."

"No," Kay answered from her comfortable seat on the sofa. "No, that's something we'll have to do right now."

She was Robert's lover. So then, it was Bob Leavitt who wanted to get rid of Jane. But why? He was Bill's friend. Why would she be a threat to him? The answer was there in a flash, so obviously simple that she should have seen it from the beginning. Leavitt's whole career was as William Andrews's alter ego. His authority derived from his closeness to the seat of power. His wealth was Bill's gift. But then Andrews had turned to her. Jane became the center of his world, and Bill was hoping to move her to a throne next to his own. Her presence was a threat to everything Leavitt had and wanted.

"Why did you want me to kill him?" Jane asked.

Kay nodded to acknowledge the question. "Just before you killed yourself. The dramatic ending of a woman betrayed. You went to Paris, saw him with his mistress, then came home and killed him in a jealous rage. Then, with nothing left to live for . . ."

Jane understood the script. She could reason her way through Leavitt's motivation. But why was Kay involved?

What did she expect to get from Bob that William Andrews wasn't already giving her? Bill was paying for lavish life in Paris. Why would she want him dead?

Her thoughts were shattered by the sound of a gunshot—a crack that rattled the windowpanes and then carried through the mountains. Kay jumped, her color instantly draining. It took Jane a second to realize what she had just heard. Robert had found the gun and then fired at something. What? Had he found Bill alive? Had that been the coup de grâce? She rushed to the window. She could see her own tracks and then the second set of footprints where Leavitt had walked in his search for the pistol. But he was nowhere in sight. He had gone into the woods.

Jane heard a metallic click behind her, a sound she didn't recognize. She wheeled. Kay had gone to the fireplace and taken down the shotgun. She had snapped it open and was in the process of loading shells into the double-barrel. She looked up from her grim work, made eye contact with Jane, and closed the gun. Slowly, she raised the barrel into Jane's face.

Jesus, it's going to happen again. She was going to be the headless wife, killed in a massacre just like the one that had killed Selina Royce.

45

Leavitt had followed Jane's tracks to the edge of the woods, searching the snow for the lost pistol. He cursed quietly under his breath when he couldn't find it and realized that he would have to follow her footsteps into the trees. The light was failing as the shortening day faded. What visibility was left was broken up by the branches. He pushed a branch aside and peered into the forest. The footprints were blurred and indistinct, but he thought he could follow them, at least for a short distance. And he needed the gun. That was the pistol Jane would have to turn on herself.

They had never figured that Jane would run out into the mountains rather than shoot the man who had come to kill her. The plan was simple. Kay had flown over from Paris, leaving a well-documented trail of ticket stubs and credit slips in the name of Selina Royce. It would appear that she had come back to be with her lover, ample motivation for Jane to take action. The wronged woman had killed her husband and then shot herself. It was all to happen in the house, with the same gun. But Jane had run, spreading the crime scene out over the countryside. And then she had lost the gun they needed to kill her with if the murder-suicide charade was to be credible.

Now Leavitt worried that the pistol might be lost. Jane might have tossed it away as she fled, in which case it wouldn't be lying in her footsteps. He wouldn't be able to find it in the dimming light. There would have to be a change in plan. Maybe just take her back into the woods and ram her head into a tree trunk to knock her unconscious. She was half frozen when she came back to the house. She would never survive a few hours lying in the snow.

He pulled up abruptly. Something was moving just ahead of him, snapping twigs and crunching snow. He backed up a step. Finding the gun was suddenly less important than his fear of confronting a bear or a wildcat. Branches moved and there was William Andrews, staggering toward him, supporting himself against the tree trunks, his shirt red and his jacket stained black. Leavitt backed away, looked about hurriedly, and spotted a broken branch on the ground. He rushed for it, pulled it out of the snow, and wielded it like an axe as he turned back to Andrews. Only then did he see the gun rising in Bill's hand. He didn't hear the shot, but noise exploded in his ears as he fell backwards into the snow.

Kay circled the room, keeping the shotgun pointed at Jane. "Get away from the window," she ordered.

Jane moved away slowly and Kay came closer so that she could see who came out of the woods and crossed the clearing to the front door. She was no longer cool and calculating, but plainly rattled by the sudden turn of events. If Robert had to use a second shot to finish off Andrews, they might still be all right. It was plausible that Jane would have used two shots to kill her husband. But if William had lived and found the gun, then everything was wrong. Then her partner would be dead, and what choices would be left to her? Kill the two of them and run for her life? That would leave behind a scene of senseless slaughter. The same trail she had left to suggest a woman returning to claim her lover would now point to a jilted woman bent on revenge.

"Are you going to kill everyone?" Jane asked directly. "And then what? You can't get out of here."

"Shut up!" She stole a glance at Jane, but her attention was on the edge of the woods.

"You'll have to shoot at the police when they come to investigate," Jane taunted. "And then what?"

"I said shut up," Her eyes widened. William Andrews came out into the open ground, clutching the pistol across his chest. He was hunched over, clearly in pain, but was walking steadily along the footsteps that led to the front door.

Kay gasped. "Oh God, no!" escaped from her lips. Then louder, "Robert . . ."

Jane saw Bill cross in front of the window, making no effort to conceal himself nor taking any precaution against
what might be awaiting him inside. Then she watched Kay
move away from the window, set herself at the entry, and aim
the shotgun at the front door. When Bill opened the door, he
would step directly into the line of fire. Jane screamed and
raced across the living room.

46

The gun quickly swung toward her. Then the door burst open. The gun started back, wavering uncertainly.

"Kay!" Bill screamed. He tried to spin back out of the doorway.

The gun decided on his direction just as Jane grabbed for the barrel. The blast was more a roar than a sharp crack. The door exploded into splinters. The doorframe to the right of the opening tore away, and the narrow window next to it simply vanished. Jane sprawled on top of Kay as the two women slammed to the floor. The shotgun bounced against the wall.

"Kay! Don't!" It was Bill's voice screaming outside the door. A second later he turned in through the battered opening, braced himself for a second to catch his balance, and dropped the pistol he had been cradling. He saw the women rolling over each other as they both tried to reach for the shotgun. Bill pushed the shotgun away with his foot. He held out a hand to Jane, and she jumped up to take it.

"Get the gun," Bill told her, pointing to the revolver he had let fall by the door. Jane took just an instant to make sure he was steady on his feet. Then she scooped up the gun she had fired at him only minutes earlier. She didn't aim it at the woman who had now gotten to her feet.

Bill pushed away from the wall and made his way to a chair, where he let himself collapse. At the sight of his effort, Jane no longer cared about Kay Parker. At that moment, Bill was all that was important to her. She picked up the telephone, taking glimpses up from the dial pad to keep track of Kay Parker. Kay was standing in the entrance foyer, glaring back at her. The discarded shotgun was a good two paces away from her.

"I need an ambulance—my husband has been shot," Jane snapped into the telephone. A brief pause, and then she gave

her name and the address of the chalet. "And call the police.
The person who shot him is still here." Another pause. "Don't
tell me about the roads. It's a critical wound. Life or death.
Hurry!" She listened and then hung up the phone.

Her husband needed her full attention, but she was afraid
to take her eyes off Kay Parker. "Get a towel from the
kitchen," she ordered.

Kay laughed scornfully. "Get it yourself!"

Jane raised the pistol in both hands. "I'll fire this before I
have to put it down."

The smirk disappeared from Kay's face. Would Jane really fire? She saw her take careful aim, pointing the gun at
her knees. "I'll get it," she said, already starting toward the
kitchen. The pistol panned to follow her movements.

Jane glanced down at Bill. His face was white and his jaw
set with pain. She approached cautiously and unzipped the
windbreaker. She tried not to react to the bloodstain that was
spread across his left shoulder, down across his chest and into
his sleeve. She could see the entry wound, just under his
shoulder.

She pulled back quickly when Kay approached with a stack
of dishtowels. "Put them in his lap," she ordered. Then she
gestured with the gun. "Stand over there by the door. Away
from that shotgun." Her tone was all business. Kay obeyed
quietly. Jane went to one knee next to her husband, folded a
towel, and pressed it against the wound. He winced, but then
forced a smile. Jane didn't know the extent of the damage, but
she knew she had to stop the bleeding. Gently, she titled him
forward. There was more blood on the back of his shirt, surrounding a broad tear. The bullet had done more damage coming out than it had going in. She folded another towel, again
stealing glances at the woman by the door. It was difficult to
hold the gun while she worked to cover the wounds, but she
was afraid to put it down. The muzzle waved randomly.

Jane settled him so that the back of the chair held the
packing against the exit wound. She raised Bill's right hand
across his chest. "What do I do now?" she asked him.
"Whiskey . . . painkiller?"

"I'm okay," he managed. "It hurts like a bitch, but I'm still strong . . . still thinking." He didn't look strong, and she wasn't sure he was thinking.

"I'll get you a drink, I think. That's right, isn't it?"

He smiled. "As long as the sun is over the yardarm."

She aimed again, assuring Kay that she hadn't forgotten about her. Then she leaned into the dining room to get the liquor bottle. At that moment Kay Parker leaped out through the open doorway.

"Jesus!" Jane raced after her. Before she reached the splintered door, she heard the car door slam. When she turned through the doorway, the engine growled and started. The car went into reverse and backed away, its rear wheels spinning as they buzzed across the snow. Jane stopped and set herself in firing position.

Kay was totally vulnerable. She was leaning forward, trying to see out the windowshield, which her breath was quickly fogging. When she shifted into drive, the rear end began to fishtail. She was plowing forward slowly; slow enough for Jane to have gotten off three or four clear shots through the windshield and side window. But she couldn't force herself to squeeze the trigger.

"Let her go!" It was Bill, who had gotten as far as the front steps, his hand still up to his chest. "Just let her go." This time it wasn't an order but rather a plea.

Jane kept the gun raised. "I'm just trying to make sure she doesn't change her mind. She can go all the way to hell as far as I'm concerned."

He went down the steps, reached around, and took the gun out of her hand. He tried to turn her and lead her back into the house, but Jane kept glaring until the back of the car disappeared around the turnoff and onto the main road.

47

Kay Parker was locked in fear. Her lover was dead. She had just fired a shotgun at her husband. The police were on the way, and the eight-year cover-up of Selina Royce's murder was about to be lifted. She was running for her freedom.

There was no way she was going to prison. She had already served more than enough time for killing Selina. She had been in exile for eight years, hiding in her apartment and using the dead woman's name. For all that time she had been afraid to contact any of the old friends who had once worshipped at her feet, afraid to take even a small step back into society, afraid to make a friend who might learn too much about her. Robert Leavitt had been her only solace—really, her only reason for living. And now he was gone. Her hopes of moving back into the world, even with Selina's identity, were completely dashed.

"Go ahead, kill me, you bitch" was what she had hissed when Jane stood in the driveway and aimed her gun. "Pull the damn trigger." But the car had found a bit of traction and snaked its way out of the driveway. Now she was on the road, which was still dangerous but nevertheless manageable at a decent speed. She was in low gear, steering carefully and trying to keep her foot off the brake.

She had no idea where she was going. Certainly not back to Paris for another appearance in the role of Selina. Or to New York, where there were still important people who might recognize her before she had a chance to alter her appearance. It seemed that there was no life left for her, just as it had been when she caught Selina coming down from the bedroom and fired both barrels. At that instant the life she had known was over. A trial . . . prison . . . disgrace. It had looked completely hopeless until Robert had shown her an escape. He had come up with the idea to switch identities and bury the headless corpse in her place. He had arranged for her life in Paris. She had fled the murder scene and disappeared out of the country on Selina's passport. Now she needed another plan. Where could she go? How would she hide? She needed Robert with her now!

It was Robert who had made her exile bearable. "I'll take care of you," he had promised. "I've always loved you. I'll keep on loving you." He had been true to his word, but now he was gone. There was no one to save her, to love her, and keep her alive. This time she was on her own.

The car began to skid, its rear end sliding toward the mountain and then, when she corrected, out toward the void that lay beyond the road's edge. She steered frantically, trying to get the car back on track, knowing that she would lose all control if she touched the brakes. It straightened out in the center of the road. With her foot off the gas, the car began to slow. When she touched the accelerator, she was back in control and able to take the breath that seized in her throat.

Bill slumped into the sofa and let Jane lift his feet onto the coffee table. The pain had become dull rather than intense. As far as he could tell, the bleeding had stopped. But he was having trouble focusing on the details of the room and even on the features of Jane's face. When he tried to speak, the best he could manage were half sentences. Jane tried to be upbeat. "Your color is coming back. It's just a shoulder wound, nothing life-threatening." Every few seconds she would repeat, "The medics will be here any minute." But, in truth, she was afraid that she was losing him. He was less and less responsive. His clothes were blood-soaked, and the folded towels were showing a stain. She could only guess how much blood he had lost outside in the woods.

She was saying "medics" to imply a skilled medical emergency team. But she remembered the few peeling buildings and the two-room police station in Mountain Ridge. Was there even a doctor? How far away was the best excuse for a hospital? How long would it take to stabilize him from shock and get the lost blood back into his system? How long to get a surgeon to start repairing his shoulder?

She had no recollection of pulling the trigger. He had appeared out of the trees so suddenly, she had acted on impulse. But the image of his toppling forward was there in terrible detail. The crack of the gunshot. The smell of the burned gunpowder. The shocked expression that flickered for an instant in her husband's eyes. The blood on the snow. How could she have thought he would ever hurt her? Why did she try to run from him? How could she have tried to kill him?

Jane heard his breathing, suddenly more labored. "Jesus, where are you?" she screamed at the police. They weren't going to make it in time.

The police Jeep was halfway up the road, its roof lights blinking even though the chief hardly expected to encounter traffic. He was doing the best he could, in a four-wheel drive with the engine laboring. Most of the snow had melted off, but there were still long white patches that were slick and dangerous. Rush to the rescue and he might never get there at all! Besides, he wasn't counting on finding someone to arrest or someone to save. The drive was eerily similar to the one he had taken years ago, when the victim was shattered beyond recognition and the killer had vanished. The woman said that she was Mrs. Andrews and that her husband had been shot. If William Andrews had been killed, he wouldn't be doing any investigating. The state boys would be all over the place within an hour, taking their orders from the media tycoon's next-in-command.

The emergency medical specialist was in the pickup truck that was following the Jeep. The driver, who owned the general store and had taken medical training as part of his volunteer fireman commitment, kept pulling close, hoping that he could encourage Pete to drive faster. In his two years of medical service he had never had a case where a life hung in the balance. The bloodiest thing he had ever seen was a fisherman's foot that had caught in his outboard motor. In his most

serious case, the patient was already dead, his body fished out
of a lake hours after his boat capsized. But still, he wanted to
hurry. He remembered from his courses at the firehouse that
in emergency medicine, time is the killer. A wound that was
superficial when incurred could be beyond repair only a few
hours later. Oxygen never seemed to revive people who had
already died.

Kay saw the blinking police lights appear on the switchback
below. "Don't panic!" she admonished herself. She had to
stay calm and in charge. There was no room for her to turn
around. She could never get away by backing up. Nor could
she even consider surrendering. She couldn't survive an arrest. The grim photographs of her entering and leaving police
stations in handcuffs. The prison cell. The mousy attorneys
trying to line their pockets and get their faces in front of the
cameras. And the trial, with the daily headlines of her jealous
murder, her years in hiding, her adultery with her husband's
best friend. Not the kind of ending the fabulous Kay Parker
could allow. Not as flattering as the global sympathy that had
followed the announcement of her murder at the hands of an
intruder.

She began to see the shape of the car beneath the blinking
lights. It had pulled to the center of the road and stopped. A
man stepped out of the driver's side and began waving a
flashlight. His hand was raised, an unmistakable signal for
her to stop. The police weren't going to let her pass.

Kay stepped down on the accelerator. She thought of turning to the mountain side of the road and passing the police car
on her right. But there was another car right behind, parked in
the inside lane. She had no choice. Still adding speed, she
aimed at the officer who was trying to flag her down.

For a moment he held his ground, waving at her furiously.
But as she bore down on him, he dove across the headlights
of his own car, leaving an escape path between the police car
and the road's edge. Kay eased over until the side of her car
was dinging against the guardrail. She flashed past the road-

block and steered back toward the center of her lane, her face now giddy at her triumph. There was no way that Kay Parker would let herself be stopped by an ordinary policeman.

The rear end began to slip. She had used too much speed and turned back too abruptly. She turned into the skid and hurtled across the road toward the face of the mountain. A quick correction brought the front of the car around just as the rear tires found traction. The car raced to the edge. The cable of the primitive guardrail snapped like a piano string, scarcely altering the car's momentum. A second later it was gone, over the edge.

It fell a hundred feet before striking the sheer side of the mountain, where it sent up a small fireball. Then it cartwheeled back out into space, burning at its edges and leaving a smoky trail. After another hundred feet it hit the lake, nose first, so the splash was minimal. It dove through the surface and disappeared in an instant.

"Jesus!" Pete couldn't believe what he had seen. He was still laboring back to his feet when the car had crashed through the guardrail and gone over the side. He ran to the shattered cables. Halfway down there was a small fire oozing into the crevices of the rocks. Below that he saw the lake, with a few concentric rings moving out from a rough patch of water. The car had vanished.

"We have to get down there," he told the medic, who had come up beside him.

"Down there?" the man asked incredulously.

Pete started back to his car. "There might be someone still alive down there."

"Not as likely as someone being still alive up there." The medic pointed up to the top of the mountain.

Pete thought for an instant, and nodded in agreement. He got back into the Jeep and continued up the road. No one could have survived that fall, he reasoned. And it wasn't likely the car would ever be found. He'd round up a couple of the local divers to take a look. But the lake filled a canyon between two sheer rock faces. No one had ever found the bottom.

The volunteer fireman rushed directly to Bill and began working with urgency. When he snapped open his aluminum medical kit, his hands moved knowingly to the instruments and medicines he needed. "Blood plasma," he said, lifting a plastic bag. "Hold it as high as you can." Jane obeyed.

He shone a light into Bill's eyes. "Okay," he announced.

"What? What's okay?"

"He's okay. Not in shock. Still a decent pulse. We'll get him stable and airlift him out to Lake Placid. They have a pretty decent trauma unit." He called to the policeman, who was examining what little was left of the front door. "Call the medevac for me, will you, Sergeant, I have them standing by."

Pete went to the phone and made the call. "Fifteen minutes," he told the medic, who nodded in response. He was busy spreading antiseptic over Bill's wounds.

"J. J. Warren, isn't it?" Pete said to Jane as he took the plasma bag from her. "Didn't I tell you to find another story?"

"I can explain all that," she answered.

"I'm sure you can. And while you're at it, maybe you can explain that car that went over the cliff back down the road a ways?"

"The cliff? She went over the cliff?" Jane was stunned. She looked down at her husband, who was suddenly alert.

"She? Can you give me a name, because I don't think we're ever going to find her. The car went into the lake."

She kept her eyes on Bill, but his expression told her nothing. It was up to her to decide. "Her name is Selina Royce. She came here to kill my husband. She was in love with him and couldn't give him up."

Jane knew she was joining a conspiracy of lies. But there was no way to explain that Kay Parker, her husband's first wife, had once again died a violent death.

48

Just let him know who's in charge," Bill advised.

"He already knows," Jane answered. "He doesn't respect me. He's just tolerating me."

They were riding side by side, the horses slouching along in an easy walk. Jane was rigid in the saddle, staring down at her mount and looking for any sign of displeasure. Bill was encouraging her to ride more aggressively, but she was afraid to do anything that might anger the animal.

Bill was relaxed, fitting easily into his horse's movements, keeping control with the reins in one hand. He was determined to get Jane back into riding, a sport she had sworn off on her first visit to the farm. "That's better," he told her. "Now you're getting it."

"Couldn't we get a pair of motorcycles?" she offered.

He shook his head. "We own a horse farm, not a speedway. Besides, I like it when you put your hand on my ass and push me up into the saddle." He had no trouble riding, but without the use of his left arm, he wasn't able to swing up onto the horse's back. He was too proud to use a step stool. His shoulder had healed, but it would never be as good as new. The bullet had hit bone and torn away ligaments. He'd never be able to raise his arm over his head.

His business career, too, was permanently damaged. The fact that his most highly trusted executive had tried to murder him showed a certain lack of judgment. The fact that he had been subsidizing the man's mistress for several years reflected badly on his character. The board praised him lavishly, gave him a handsome retainer as a consultant, and used his health as an excuse to put him on leave. Kim Annuzio became president, began consolidating instead of acquiring, and set the renamed Global Networks Corporation on a more modest course.

Andrews took his demotion gracefully and then embraced his new life gratefully. He and Jane moved out to the horse farm in New Jersey and moved the children into local schools. He finally had the time to become a father to his children, and uninterrupted hours to lavish on his beautiful new wife. Jane welcomed the change. She had seemed destined to have only the pieces of her husband's life that fitted between his business commitments. Now she had all of him. It was the business that had to be satisfied with whatever moments he could spare.

Both knew that the true story of what happened would have to remain a secret between them. There could be no going back to the first murder at the chalet without exposing Bill's role in the cover-up. Nor was there any point in explaining how and why Jane had shot her husband. That was best attributed to the jealous rage of Bill's former mistress and the duplicity of his best friend. The fabulous Kay Parker, who had been mourned eight years ago, was best left dead. And Selina Royce could finally be laid to rest. The lake had frozen over her, and even when spring came, officials found little reason to search for the probably decomposed body.

Their version of events put all the blame on the two people who had plotted the crime and had it explode in their faces. It left Jane and Bill as sympathetic victims, which, in a sense, they actually were.

But Bill explained the true events to Jane. His marriage to Kay Parker, while an ongoing public celebration, had been a private hell. Kay, who had expected to be adored, couldn't play second fiddle to Andrews Global Network. And Bill, headstrong in his own right, wouldn't play prince consort to the reigning queen. Kay had retaliated with polo players, leading men, and even a few pretenders to royalty, hiding her affairs from the public but making certain that her husband knew every juicy detail. Andrews had found consolation with a woman more modest in her demands—Selina Royce. Kay, who enjoyed being the betrayer, couldn't stand to be betrayed.

She had gone to the chalet, taken the shotgun down from the wall, and fired both barrels into Selina's face as she came down the stairs from the bedroom. She didn't regret that part of the blast hit her husband.

As soon as the smoke cleared, Robert Leavitt, who had always loved and admired Kay, began directing the cover-up. His purpose was to save the dazzling socialite from arrest and prosecution, and save Andrews Global Network from disgrace. Andrews went along with him for the sake of his children and his empire. But over time, Leavitt's motivation turned sinister. The woman of his dreams had become his prisoner. Because Kay was hiding under a false identity, she had no one to turn to but Leavitt. He realized, too, that he had gained leverage in his relationship with Andrews. He was the keeper of a secret that could put Andrews in jail.

The conspiracy worked until Jane came along and Bill fell in love with her. The day Jane had seen him at Kay's Paris apartment, he had gone there to make his final payment. He couldn't go on lying to Jane, who was getting closer and closer to the truth. He had to cut his first wife off. Whether it was because Kay couldn't stand the thought of her husband finding happiness without her or because she couldn't imagine living without his lavish financial support, she had decided to strike back. Together with Robert, who imagined himself taking Andrews's place at the head of a global communications empire, she had constructed the plot that carried both of them to their death.

Jane had found answers to some of her other questions. Cassie and Craig, who were beginning to like the idea of a home with two parents, had sheepishly admitted to putting the burr under her saddle. "We didn't mean to hurt you," Cassie had apologized. "We just wanted to show our father that you were no horsewoman."

Leavitt was the most obvious explanation for the person who had terrorized her in the apartment and then closed the swimming pool cover over her head. He had full run of the apartment and could easily have rigged the circuit breaker in the foyer. And Leavitt had been at the wedding, with an ample opportunity to drug Jane's coffee.

He was also the angel who had backed Art's play, in ex-

change for Art's keeping him fully informed about Jane's
plans and whereabouts. Art's access to her apartment gave
Leavitt a minute-by-minute account of Jane's investigation
into Kay's death. Art had seen nothing reprehensible in his
role. "The guy had a legitimate reason to protect his company," Art reasoned. "He said William Andrews always in-
vestigated people who got close to him. And I owed him a
favor. I mean, he really liked my play."

The two attacks in France were Kay's work. Leavitt had
shown her pictures of Andrews's new wife, and she recognized Jane the instant she saw her at the bank. She had no
trouble slipping into the spa and locking the door of the
sauna. And when that failed, she had dressed down to play
the role of the night nurse.

At last, the questions were answered and the doubts resolved. Jane had a husband who loved her, and William Andrews had found the life that he had lost long ago. As he told
his wife whenever she asked him if he missed his global empire, "Empires are overrated."

But there was still one issue that nagged at her. "Can I ask
you something?" Jane said, reining in her horse.

"About the horse? Sure!"

"Not about the horse. About us."

He thought for a moment. "No," he decided. "If it's about
something I'm doing wrong, I don't want to hear about it. If
it's something you're doing wrong, I don't want to know
about it."

"Who said anyone was doing anything wrong?"

He eyed her suspiciously. "You have that worried look you
get when you're wondering how to bring up an embarrassing
subject."

She pouted. "I was just going to ask you about something
you never told me."

"There must be a good reason why I never told you."

Jane nudged the horse back into its easy stride. "Okay,"
she conceded.

He caught up with her. "Now you've got me guessing.
What is it that I never told you about?"

She reined in again. "I was thinking that suppose I wasn't a reporter. Suppose I had been a lawyer or a stockbroker."

"You mean if you were richer than I am?"

She smiled. "No. What I mean is, suppose I hadn't been such a snoop. Suppose I hadn't been digging into the shooting and trying to find the woman in Paris. I would have been just . . . your adoring wife. Running the household, entertaining your friends, trying to keep your kids out of jail. I mean, for most women, that wouldn't be such a bad deal. Married to one of richest men on earth. Great clothes, fabulous food, private jets, penthouses, even pretty good sex."

"Pretty good?"

"Don't push it. All I'm saying is that most women would be very satisfied with the whole arrangement."

He shrugged, and then agreed. "It sounds good to me."

"So, suppose I'd just said to myself, 'Hey, stupid, this isn't bad. Don't rock the boat.' Would we just have gone on living as if I were the only one? Would you have ever told me, 'Oh, by the way, I have another wife living in Paris. A very sexy lady with great style, wonderful taste, and dukes and earls snapping at her heels.' Or would you just have kept me in the dark?"

He pushed his hat back and looked around thoughtfully for a few seconds. Then he said, "The question doesn't make any sense."

"Why not?" Jane demanded.

"Because if you weren't such a nosy bitch, I wouldn't have fallen in love with you."

"Time!" Charlene Hendricks announced, clicking the button on her stopwatch.

"Another minute," Steven Armstrong gasped. His breathing was labored as he pedaled furiously on the stationary bicycle. "I can go for another minute!"

"That's enough!" she insisted. "Let's not overdo it. You strain something and you're back to square one. Just stay with the program."

Steven stopped pedaling and slumped forward over the handlebars. Charlene draped a fresh towel over his shoulders and offered him an open bottle of water. He took a drink, then wiped his face with the towel. "You know I can do a lot more than you're letting me," he said.

"You're doing more than enough. I don't want you trying to break the world record for knee surgery. It takes time, and patience."

Steven managed to laugh even as he was gasping for breath. "I don't have a lot of time, and I've never been big on patience. Believe me, Charlie, the knee is fine. I'm just trying to work off the paunch I got from all that time in bed."

She looked at him skeptically. "What paunch? You're in great shape."

"Nah! I used to ride twice as long without even breaking a sweat."

"Sure," she agreed, "when you were in your thirties and forties. But for a man in his sixties, you're way above the curve. You know the rule in personal training: Act your age."

She took her warm-up jacket out of her backpack and put it on over her tank top. "Tomorrow at one o'clock, Mr. Armstrong?"

"Steve!" he snapped angrily. "I keep telling you to call me Steve."

"Okay, Steve, I'll see you tomorrow, same time, same place." She started toward the open door that connected the gym with the rest of the house.

"Charlie! Do I really look like I'm in my sixties?" When she looked back, he seemed desperate.

"No, Mr. Armstrong, you look twenty years younger. And now that you're shaving your head, you look like a stud!"

He smiled and ran his hand over the dark haze that had been a crown of wild hair surrounding a bald pate. "You like this?"

"It's a turn-on," she smiled. "I can hardly keep my hands off you."

She was out the door when he called to her again. "Charlie!"

She poked her head back into the room.

"I'm going to swim some laps. Why don't you stick around so you can tell me what I'm doing wrong?"

She raised her hands in a gesture of helplessness. "I have to pick up my kid. You can hold off on the laps until tomorrow. We'll do them as soon as you finish stretching." She pulled back through the doorway. Steven was still looking at the space she had vacated when he heard the front door snap shut. A few seconds later he heard the telltale rattle of her antique Toyota. She had just left, but already he missed her.

Charlene Hendricks had come into his life along with a steel and epoxy hinge that had been substituted for his fatally damaged knee. Steven had resisted the knee replacement for over a year, managing to get by on a combination of painkillers and grit. Hell, he didn't build his hardware empire by pandering to every ache and pain. Thirty-three years on the job and he had missed only three days of work—one when each of his children was born. Even after he'd taken the company public and retired to his role of disgruntled share owner, he still kept himself busy. He had designed his new home on the Fort Lauderdale waterway, and then become his own construction contractor. Every cement block, every plumbing fixture, every truss and tile had passed his scrutiny.

Why not? He had spent his life in hardware. Nobody was going to put anything over on him!

Then the boat! He had bought a seventy-five-foot motor yacht with a planing hull and twin diesels, and then supervised every step of its construction from laying the resin to installing the running lights. He had been climbing the ladder from the after deck to the flying bridge when his knee buckled under him.

The doctors prescribed a new knee, a prosthesis that would replace the worn joint he had overworked. Steven had absolutely refused. There was nothing wrong with his knee that a little time wouldn't heal. He would simply suck it up the way he had always done when ailments threatened to slow his pace. The doctors shrugged. "When it hurts enough, you'll come back," they assured him. He had struggled for ten months, laboring to move around his house during the day, and sitting with his knee iced at night. Eventually, he had decided that the doctors were right and signed up for the knee replacement.

Charlene had visited him in the hospital right after the operation and introduced herself as his therapist. She had helped him out of bed and supported him as he took his first faltering steps on his new knee. Then she went home with him to help him in the arduous task of rehabilitation.

At first, Steven had wondered why he needed her. He could stretch his own muscles, do his own leg lifts, and climb aboard the stationary bicycle. Why did he need her to twist his legs and stretch his back, or count his repetitions? But slowly he had learned to value her advice and to welcome her company during the grueling hours that he would have been spending alone. Then, halfway through his recovery, he had begun to notice her not as a professional trainer but as a woman. A very attractive woman, totally different from his deceased wife, the mother of his children.

He noticed the rivulets of sweat that trickled down from her headband when she ran beside him, and the stains that spread down the sides of her tank top. He took in the sculptured muscles in her legs, the firmness of her thighs, and the tight buns that pressed into her leotards. Her waist, which frequently flashed as her shirt rose, was slim and flat. The breasts that showed when she bent toward him were firm and erect. Charlene, he had decided, was a new kind of woman, not soft, nor gentle, nor modestly ashamed of her femininity. She was spare, strong, and confident, invariably upbeat and annoyingly capable. As he had worked with her, he had realized that whatever other admirable characteristics she had, she could probably run him into the ground.

Steven found himself competing with her. He'd be damned if a woman young enough to be his daughter was going to be quicker, stronger, or more durable than he was. If she could demonstrate leg lifts with twenty pounds of weight, then he would do thirty pounds. If she could raise the treadmill to fifteen degrees, then he would turn it to twenty. He enjoyed her concern that he was pushing himself too much, and basked in the admiration she had for his determination. In the six weeks of his rehabilitation, Charlene had become his physical and emotional partner. So Steven was not surprised when he realized that he was falling in love with her.

But he *was* embarrassed. He had seen many men his age decide that they were still physically desirable to younger women, and then make asses of themselves as they pursued a ridiculous romance. Some had spent fortunes showering presents and trust funds on bon bons half their age. *No fool like an old fool*, he had thought, shaking his head in despair. Was that what he was becoming? An old fool! Charlie was in her thirties, the same age range as all three of his children. He was old enough to be her father. Hell, he could be her grandfather! What was her first rule of rehabilitation? Act your age!

It's not the same thing, he tried to reason with himself. *Charlie and I are already partners*. Weren't they working together day after day? Weren't they matching each other pound for pound and stride for stride? Hadn't she told him time after time that he was way ahead of his age group in his physical strength and endurance? What was it she had called him—a stud! She didn't talk to him as if he was old enough to be her father. Maybe that wasn't the way she thought about him.

But then he laughed at himself. *Act your age!* What in God's name could he possibly offer a woman like Charlie? More than likely she had her pick of any number of guys her own age. Virile guys with six-pack abs and rock-hard buns, and erections that could lift a woman off her feet. Why would she be interested in an old man with bad knees?

On the other hand, there were things he could offer that most younger men couldn't match. He *was* worth $200 million, so he could provide her with a sense of security that she had never known and wasn't likely to ever know. That had to count for something! There was his house, a modern design on the inland waterway just north of Fort Lauderdale, that had made the cover of *Architectural Digest*. It had to be twice as luxurious as the nicest dream house she had ever imagined. There was the yacht, with its implied promises of faraway places. And the simple comfort of knowing she could have anything she wanted.

But Charlie wasn't mercenary. The most important thing in her life was her daughter, a thirteen-year-old whom she loved without reservation, and whose future was infinitely more important to her than her own. Steven knew that he could change the young girl's life. She could be in private school instead of in one of those left-behind public schools. She could be tutored in art, music, horsemanship, whatever might interest her. Her college education would be assured. Not many young studs could handle all that!

Was he trying to buy her? Perish the thought! Buying was when you wanted something and you paid the price it cost. All he was doing was tallying up the joys he could bring to her life. He was a man of means with global clout who would love, honor, and protect her. It was up to her to decide whether all that was more valuable than great buns.

If he decided to ask her, how would he do it? The easy way would be to simply keep her on as his personal trainer, three hours a day, six days a week. He could pay her lavishly so that she could afford to spend more time with him, perhaps bring her daughter to the house or out on the boat for trips to the Bahamas and the Keys. Foster the relationship until the next step was inevitable.

Or, he could do what he had always done with a difficult decision. Bite the bullet and put it to her squarely. *I love you. I can't bear the thought of you leaving. Please marry me so that you and your daughter can be my new family.* That's what he should do the next day as soon as she showed up at his door. Except she might break out laughing before she knew that he was serious. That would be the most crushing defeat of his entire life. Or, she might explain patiently that lots of men thought they were in love with their personal trainers. It was a hazard of the occupation, and she certainly wouldn't hold it against him. A patronizing evasion would be much more painful than an outright refusal.

What should he do? Steven vacillated during his dinner and his evening walk along the beach. He tossed and turned the entire night. The one thing that he was certain of was that he couldn't live without Charlie nearby. The one thing he feared was that he was just another old fool.

Charlie tapped the steering wheel to the beat of rock music playing through the tinny speakers of her car radio. She needed to get a new radio. One with a big bass speaker hidden behind the back seat, and a couple of tweeters buried in the doors. Heck, what she really needed was a new car. This one had been on its last legs when she bought it, and she had paid through the nose just to keep it running. New brakes, a new water pump, and a new head gasket, not to mention tires and windshield wipers. Worse, the air-conditioning had a mind of its own, deciding on the hottest days in South Florida to shut down and take a rest. She needed to figure a better car . . . maybe even something with a bit of pizzazz . . . into her budget.

The problem was that she had already figured a condo she couldn't afford into her budget. Two bedrooms and two baths in a landscaped enclave of town houses that had its own community clubhouse and swimming pool. She had saved two years for the down payment, and was carrying a mortgage that ate up half of her income. But it was a necessary expense. She had to move her daughter into a neighborhood where drug dealers were unwelcome, and into a school district that was as good as she could hope for in a state where the average taxpayer had no children. She needed a home where Tara could have the privacy of her own bedroom, and a living room nice enough to invite guests home to. The pool was a plus. Tara had one or two girlfriends over each Saturday for splash parties which kept her under Charlie's eagle eye and grew her daughter's circle of friends. The investment in the house seemed to be paying off. The girl seemed happy, easily adjusted, and reasonably popular . . . all values that a new car couldn't possibly deliver.

She watched the explosion of fledgling adolescents that burst out of the school's main doors. As in the big bang theory of the universe, the sudden expansion of energy quickly broke up into numerous constellations, each headed off into its own orbit. Tara was in a group of girls that seemed to be exchanging humorous banter with a nearby constellation of boys. But then she broke away, and with her backpack over her arm, sauntered toward the parked car. She opened the door and threw the backpack over the passenger seat. "Gross," she announced as she reached for the radio dial and tuned in an even more cacophonous rock group. "These guys are really bad!" Charlie smiled. She was adult enough to enjoy being a bit out of touch.

At home, Charlie went straight to the kitchen, took two rock-hard hamburgers out of the freezer, and popped them into the microwave to defrost. Then she began to cut up some yellow squash. "Tara," she called in the general direction of her daughter's bedroom, "can you do the salad?" Tara sulked into the kitchen, certainly less cheerful than she had been in the car, and got out the wooden salad bowl. She ripped lettuce and chopped celery without her usual enthusiasm for working beside her mother.

"Something wrong, hon?" The girl shook her head. "Anything you want to talk about?"

"No . . ."

Charlie dropped the squash into a saucepan, and took the meat patties out of the microwave. "Do you want to grill these?" Her answer was a barely perceptible nod accompanied by a soft "Okay." *No point in pushing it*, she thought. Tara usually found a way to bring up subjects that were troubling her.

There had been the battle of the bare midriff. Tara was beginning to develop a figure and had the perfectly understandable urge to show it off. Low-cut jeans and shirts that stopped below the ribs had become many ninth-graders announcement of adulthood. Tara had pooled her allowances to buy an outfit and then moped for days trying to get up the courage to show it to her mother. She had taken the plunge and worn it to breakfast on a Saturday. Charlie had hidden her shock and controlled her instinct to launch into a lecture. "Hey, that's cute!" she announced and watched Tara blush. "No, I mean it. It's casual, sporty, and it really emphasizes your slim waist. I like it!" Tara's eyes had looked up in relief, a smile beginning to play at the corners of her mouth. "Of course," Charlie had forged on, "it's a little *too* bare for school."

"Mom!" Her voice was heavy with frustration and despair. She began whining about what the other girls were wearing.

It had been on the tip of her tongue to announce that she didn't give a damn what anyone else was wearing, but she had caught herself in the nick of time. "Okay, but you have to break me into this slowly. We'll shop for a top that reaches to your jeans. If it bounces up every once in a while to show some skin, I suppose that would be all right. And maybe after I get used to it, I'll take you out for something just a speck shorter."

The whining had stopped. An understanding had been forged. Tara had agreed reluctantly even though she was secretly relieved. She would have been embarrassed to show up at school with a bare midriff.

There hadn't always been compromises. On coloring the

tips of her dark hair blonde, Charlie had given in completely. She colored her own hair, and couldn't think of a defensible argument why her daughter shouldn't do the same. After all, the kid wasn't asking for spikes of purple and chartreuse. Nor was there a compromise on navel piercing. That discussion had ended in an unequivocal, "No!"

What now? Charlie thought. *Was Tara thinking of a tattoo?*

"Are you at the gym tonight?" Tara asked, while tossing the salad in nearly slow motion.

"Of course," Charlie answered. She ran a senior aerobics class three nights a week at a local health club, which was why they were eating early. "Is that a problem?"

Another head shake for a response. But then the girl added, "I'm sorry."

"Sorry? Is there something happening here tonight that I'm going to miss?"

Tara turned her back and carried the bowl to the table. "Just sorry that you have to work so much. I guess it's my fault. . . ."

"What's your fault, Tara?"

"That you're stuck with me."

"Stuck? What makes you think that I'm *stuck*? I love you. I love being with you."

Tara shrugged, studiously studying the table so that she was keeping her back to her mother. "If you weren't tied down with me, you wouldn't have to work so hard. You could do things for yourself."

"Like what? Go out dancing every night? How many times do I have to tell you that I'm doing exactly what I want to do."

The girl wheeled and hurried through the kitchen, picking up the hamburgers on her way out to the grill. "Like you could get the new car radio you want," she said in passing.

What's this all about? Charlie followed her through the sliders and out to the small patio, scarcely large enough for the grill and a small table. "I'm going to get a radio," she said. "And I'm going to get a new car to go with it."

"No you won't," Tara said gloomily.

"I don't mean a brand-new car. Probably something a few years old. But with low mileage so that I won't have to keep getting it fixed. Something jazzy with a sports shifter and leather seats." Her decision was spontaneous, not that she hadn't been thinking of a new car. But this was the first time she'd realized that her daughter was ashamed of the car they were driving.

"It's not the car," Tara answered, refusing to climb out of her gloom. "It's everything. You could be doing lots of things without me. You could be having lots of fun. . . ." She dropped the burgers on the fire and heard them sizzle. Then she added, "I'm your unlucky penny."

"Unlucky?"

"Well, when you did it, you didn't *want* to have a baby."

"When I did what?"

Tara pushed past her back into the kitchen, looking for an excuse to break the face-to-face confrontation. "You know. People do it and they don't have a baby. You weren't lucky."

Charlie followed at her heels. "You mean when I had sex with a man who wasn't committed to me, I didn't want to have a daughter."

Tara turned to her with the beginning of a tear in her eye. "Well, you didn't, did you? I was a mistake!"

"No!" She grabbed her daughter by the shoulders and held her face-to-face. "The mistake was sleeping with someone who didn't really care about me. That was a terrible mistake. But deciding to have you and become your mother wasn't a mistake. That was the best thing I've ever done. I love you! I love being with you! I can't imagine my life without you!" She drew Tara into an embrace and rocked her as if she were a baby. They were both crying when Charlie suddenly smelled smoke.

"What's burning?"

Tara broke out of the embrace. "My hamburgers!"

They jammed together between the table and the stove as they both rushed to the patio. Tara squeezed into the lead and found a column of flame curling up around the burgers. "Get some water," she yelled.

"Water doesn't work with grease," Charlie said, pushing her daughter away from the inferno. She took the spatula and lifted the flaming meat away from the fire. But she had hardly set the burgers back on the grill with another flame blazed up.

"Do something!" Tara begged.

Charlie lifted the burgers and tossed them over the rail and onto the back lawn. Then she reached close to the grill and turned off the gas. It had no effect. The grill was still on fire, and now there was the beginning of a new fire in the wild grass behind the house. She slammed the lid shut, dousing the high flame, but she could see that the fire was still raging inside.

"Get the hose!" Charlie ordered.

Tara ran off the patio, charged the garden hose, and aimed at the smoldering grass. In just a few seconds she had the yard fire out. Charlie was bent over the edges of the grill, coughing in the billowing smoke. "I think this one is out, too," she reported.

Tara came back to the patio, looked at her mother, and then broke out laughing.

"This isn't funny, Tara. It could have been serious."

The girl laughed all the harder, leaning against the wall for support. She tried to talk, but she fell into a new spasm of laughter, and pointed a finger at her mother.

"What's so funny?" Charlie demanded.

"Your face . . . look at your face!"

Charlie turned into the kitchen, saw herself in the reflection of the hall mirror, cracked a smile, and then began laughing. The smoke had painted her into a comic black face, with white eyelids and bright white teeth. She turned back to her daughter and joined in the hysteria. They fell back into each others' arms, this time howling instead of sobbing. The soot wiped off onto Tara's face, and then the two began painting white circles on each others' cheeks.

"Some pair we are," Charlie was finally able to say.

"You better marry a fireman," Tara teased.

Charlie shook her head. "I wouldn't have to if I cleaned the grill once in a while."

"Let's just have a salad," the girl suggested.

Tara set out the salad while her mother went to the bathroom and washed her face. "It's in my hair," she said when she returned to the table. "I'll take a shower at the spa after my class."

"You look good with dark hair," the girl said, now laughing easily.

Charlie was mystified. Where was the girl tormented with guilt whom she had been embracing only a few minutes before?

She threw herself into her aerobics class with all her energy. They were paying for her instruction, and they deserved her best effort. But she couldn't stop her mind from wondering. What had gotten into her daughter? Tara had never before said that she was her mother's unlucky penny. Not once had she seemed unhappy that she had no father at home, nor had she ever hinted that she felt she was nothing more than a mistake.

Had someone said something in school? Maybe. There was no limit to the cruelties that young girls visited on one another. Had someone told her that she was her mother's mistake? But that wasn't likely. Lots of her friends were from broken families. One of them had a different name from both her mother and father, who also had different names. The family needed three listings in the telephone book.

It might have been something she was studying in class. They were taking a sociology course intended to encourage tolerance for the wide range of ethnic backgrounds and lifestyles. Maybe the teacher had mentioned the problems of single parents in hope of engendering some sympathy. Instead, Tara might have taken it as a personal indictment.

Whatever, Charlie knew that she had to be careful. She would have to use every opportunity to show her daughter just how much she was loved and wanted. She would have to assure Tara that she knew how much Tara loved her. There was no way to protect her from the image of a father who had deserted her even before she was born. But she couldn't allow the girl to think that her mother had been stuck. Charlie remembered all the bad things she had thought about herself and how destructive they had been to her young life. She wouldn't allow her daughter to make the same mistake.